Merryn Allingham was born
spet her childhood moving a
Unsurprisingly it gave her itchy
escaped an unloved secretarial career to work as cabin crew
and see the world. The arrival of marriage, children and cats
meant a more settled life in the south of England, where she's
lived ever since. It also gave her the opportunity to go back to
'school' and eventually teach at university.

Merryn has always loved books that bring the past to life, so
when she began writing herself the novels had to be historical.
She finds the nineteenth and early twentieth centuries
fascinating to research and has written extensively on these
periods in the Daisy's War trilogy and the Summerhayes
novels. She has also written two timeslip/parallel narratives
which move between the modern day and the mid-Victorian
era, *House of Lies* and its companion volume, *House of Glass*.

For more information on Merryn and her books visit http://
www.merrynallingham.com/
You'll find regular news and updates on Merryn's
Facebook page:
https://www.facebook.com/MerrynWrites
and you can keep in touch with her on Twitter
@MerrynWrites

Other Books in this Series

VENETIAN VENDETTA

Merryn Allingham

VENETIAN VENDETTA

First published in Great Britain 2020 by The Verrall Press

Cover art: Berni Stevens Book Cover Design

Chapter One

Nancy bounced from her chair and stood at the front of the gilded box, her hands raised in salute. She had never heard anything so beautiful, so sublime. The soaring strains of Puccini had wrung from her a myriad of emotions and she clapped on, ignoring the tears trickling down her cheeks, longing to share the moment. Leo should be here, not left at the palazzo, wrestling with words. Theirs had been an unconventional wedding, it was true, a rushed ceremony to keep her safe, but they were only days into their honeymoon and a box at the opera had been a special treat.

She had known something was wrong when Leo returned from the conference early. He'd been full of apologies— he wasn't going to make this evening after all. A colleague had handed him new material and he needed to include it in tomorrow's keynote speech. It meant rejigging the whole lecture and he'd be tussling over it for hours. But she was to go, he wouldn't have her miss the opera for the world. Leo's assistant—his bag carrier, Nancy thought sourly—would go with her. She hadn't imagined Archie Jago would have a taste for opera and she'd no more wish than he to spend time together. But here they both were. No wonder Archie wore an even glummer face than usual, standing feet away, arms folded, every contour of his body screaming boredom.

It was as the singers were taking a third curtain call that it happened.

Nancy had been momentarily distracted, looking up at the blue-painted ceiling, when something—somebody?—tumbled from a box on the opposite side of the theatre, a hand loose and helpless scraping the velvet-topped barrier on its downward flight. She started forward, craning her neck to pierce the darkness of the auditorium, unable to believe what she had seen. Surely it could not have been… Bewildered, she looked across at the box opposite. Was that a shadow, the suggestion of a movement?

But then the house lights flashed on, the theatre a flood of red and gold. A scream, thin and terrified, echoed around the open space as the clapping dribbled to a stop. An infinitesimal pause and then the thick green velvet curtains swished across the stage. There was an eerie silence. Someone coughed, a bag fell to the floor. Then a sudden outburst of frantic voices. For a moment Nancy had been paralysed, but certain now of what she'd seen, she sprang into life and made for the door, overturning the chair in her haste.

'I have to go down. Something bad has happened.'

Archie strode past her to the front of the box and leaned over. 'Certainly looks it. We need to leave.'

'I must go down,' she repeated. 'I might be able to help.'

'There won't be any helping,' he said grimly. 'Unless you drive a hearse. The theatre will be calling the police—we need to be away before they get here. There could be problems and Leo won't want you involved.'

'Problems?' His lack of feeling made her voice shake. 'Someone has been badly hurt.' She couldn't bring herself to speak what must be the truth.

Archie remained dogged. 'Once the police come, there *will*

be problems. Come on.'

He attempted to take hold of her arm, but she shrugged him off, tussling with the door handle and throwing the door back with such force, she almost fell into the passage beyond. La Fenice was a maze of corridors but the way to the stalls was well signposted. She ran towards the stairway, down and down and down, her wide organza skirt brushing the marble walls, silver heels soundless on the carpeted steps.

Within seconds, she had reached the scene. Most of the audience had slipped away—taking Archie's advice, she thought angrily—but a small number had gathered around the prone figure. The women patted the jewels at their necks, the men pulled on their satin lapels, no one knowing quite what to say or what to do. Several of the singers, still in their costumes—not the principals, Nancy noted—had emerged from behind the stage curtains and joined the small group. They must have witnessed the terrible fall.

There were whispers among the crowd. Nancy spoke enough Italian to manage a rough translation. *Terrible accident… Or maybe worse…* Someone spoke quietly to their neighbour—*la povera signora… troppo emotiva*, and then the word, *suicidio.*

She sidled forward until she was part of the circle. A woman's body, she could see now. And quite dead. She felt sick to her stomach. It seemed that disaster pursued her wherever she went.

The woman had fallen into the aisle that separated the two banks of red velvet stalls, and so escaped further mutilation. That was something for which to be thankful, though when Nancy looked down at the twisted figure, she was filled with an immense sorrow. A large red stain bloomed from behind the head, hardly noticeable against the brilliant hued carpet unless you were looking hard.

She gave a loud gasp. She knew the woman. She had spoken to her only hours before.

Archie had followed hard on her heels and was at her shoulder. 'We have to go.' His voice was uncompromising, the usual Cornish lilt submerged beneath harsh command.

'I know this lady,' Nancy said softly.

He ignored her and repeated, 'We have to go. Now.'

Her heart went out to the broken figure lying amid a pool of blood. She wanted to gather the woman up, smooth her hair, hold her close. She had spoken to her for less than an hour, yet she'd felt a deep sadness in her, one that was greater than simple loneliness. It had been the oddest thing, Nancy thought, the way she had sensed an immediate bond with this stranger, as though she had met a soulmate.

Archie's insistent tap on her arm made her round on him. 'I should stay. I should speak to the police when they come.'

He looked mystified. 'What good will that do?'

'I told you. I met this lady earlier today. At the *gelateria* on the Zattere.'

'What has that to do with anything?' Puzzlement had turned to annoyance.

'She was involved in a nasty incident there and I should tell the police about it.'

It had been nasty. Nancy remembered how she'd tensed at the loud voices, her hands feeling clammy as the familiar sense of panic threatened to overwhelm her... but somehow she'd managed to contain her fear. *She wasn't in London now. She was in Venice ... safe... with Leo.*

It had happened just as she was finishing the most perfect ice cream—she couldn't remember when she'd enjoyed an ice cream more—but the sound of raised voices had made her lift her head sharply. The now lifeless figure lying at her feet was being harangued by a young man, his voice growing ever louder. He was towering over her in an intimidating manner, his hands gesticulating wildly, his body language threatening, until the woman had had no choice but to back away, one leg limping badly. The waiter who had served Nancy earlier seemed about to intervene when the young man, with one final aggressive gesture, had turned abruptly and strode away, his hands in the pockets of a pair of shabby trousers.

'Whatever you witnessed, keep it to yourself.' Archie's irritation broke through her thoughts. 'I've been told to escort you and that's what I'll do. Are you coming?'

In the few days Nancy had known him, she had been made to feel Archie Jago's resentment, hot and clear. He was implacable now, standing at her shoulder, tight-lipped and glowering. Yet the feeling that she owed something to the woman who'd befriended her, the feeling that the incident at the café was important, persisted still.

'I think I should stay,' she said defiantly. 'The only way I can help the poor woman now is to tell the police what I know. Leo would want me to.'

Archie was unmoved. 'Leo would want you home, not at a police station for hours. And for what exactly?'

Nancy wanted to rebel, to tell him to go away and leave her to do what she thought just, but she knew Archie was right. Leo would not wish her to be involved and, if she persisted, she would risk putting them at odds. Her husband had come to her rescue, and she was grateful, too grateful to upset him so early in their marriage.

Greatly reluctant, she gave in. Within minutes, Archie had steered her through the double doors of the auditorium, past the bar where cigarette stubs filled the ashtrays and half-finished drinks lay uncollected, through the ornate lobby and towards the narrow *calle* that ran along one side of the theatre.

A launch, blue light flashing rhythmically from the forward cabin, pulled up at the side of the small canal, a policeman at its helm. The small boats moored on the opposite side bobbed in its wake.

'Just in time,' Archie said. 'We go this way.' He jerked his head towards the dimly lit *calle*.

'Those people in the theatre—they were suggesting it was suicide, weren't they?'

In the muted light she saw a pained expression cross his face. 'Of course it's suicide. What else could it be? No one falls over a barrier that high by accident.'

'I don't think it can be.' Nancy's voice was firm. 'When I spoke to her, she told me she was looking forward to this evening's performance. Looking forward to the future, too. She made that clear.'

'So she changed her mind.'

Nancy's lips tightened at his flippancy. 'There's something else. Before she joined me in the café, she was talking to a man, arguing with him. He was very angry—I thought he was going to strike her.'

'That's the answer then. She fell out with her boyfriend. She's Italian—wanted to make the grand gesture.'

She was shocked at Archie's callousness and, when he strode forward, remained standing on the spot.

He stopped and walked back, his shoulders rigid. 'I don't know what the hell this is about, but I do know I've been charged by Leo to see you safely home.' His face was hard, his jaw thrust forward. He turned and once more walked ahead.

'There was someone there,' she called after him.

He stopped again. 'What now? Someone where?'

'In her box. In the box opposite. In the tier above ours. I looked across the theatre… when the body… I looked over… I didn't know what was happening. But I saw someone.'

Chapter Two

'Someone? That's usefully vague—who did you see?'

'I don't know. It was only for an instant. It seemed… more like a shadow.'

Archie gave a snort of impatience. 'It was pitch black in there. Whatever you thought you saw will be down to shock.'

Nancy half thought that herself. The event *was* shocking. But still, in that split second, she had been certain there had been movement—at the point where the box curved outwards—something, someone, hovering.

It had begun to drizzle now, a fine damp mist settling over the city. Ahead, Archie had turned up his jacket collar and walked on. Mutely, she followed him: he had decided the death was suicide and it was pointless trying to convince him otherwise. In their haste to get away, her wrap had been left at the theatre and she began to shiver in the thin dress. The season was changing, the last days of summer trailing slowly to a close. The dead woman had warned her only this afternoon that autumn would be with them soon and she must be sure to enjoy these days to the full.

The small, silver-haired woman had taken a seat at the table next to Nancy, even though there were half a dozen others free. 'What flavour did you choose?' she'd asked.

Nancy had been startled. She had deliberately closed her eyes, pushing the angry voices from her mind and sinking into the sun's warmth.

'The flavour?' She gathered her thoughts. 'Chocolate,' she said, and looked down at the empty glass cup, '*cioccolato* and *crema*? Do I have that right?'

'You have made a good choice. Is it your first taste of Italian ice cream?'

'It is and it's very good.'

The woman gave a brief nod as though she would have expected nothing else and sipped the espresso the waiter had brought her. There was little space between the tables and Nancy felt as though she had been joined by an acquaintance, a friend even, someone who'd recognised her from a distance and sat down for a chat. She gave the woman a quick sideways glance, judging her to be around sixty years old, small as a bird, but elegantly and expensively dressed.

'You are English. You make no ice cream?'

'We do, but not like this. And not for many years.'

'Ah, the war. You have the rations.'

It was an awkward moment. The conflict that had consumed the world for six long years was still vivid in the memory and Nancy was uncomfortably conscious that Italy had been on the losing side. Embarrassed, she began to gabble: such an amazing number of different flavours... she could never have imagined how many... next time she might be brave and try pistachio.

'You must try every flavour—if you have the time. How long are you in Venice?'

The woman's English was extremely good and that was far from usual, despite the growing influence of cinema. Nancy had learned her Italian at night school, keen to improve her job prospects within the Fine Art department, but she was finding Venetian Italian, a rich dialect, hard to understand. When Concetta, the maid Leo had hired for their stay, slipped

12

into dialect, she was most often lost and forced to retreat to English.

'We are here for a week,' she answered. 'Maybe more. My husband is attending a conference at the Cini library, but then we hope to have a few days' holiday. It's our honeymoon.' She felt herself flush.

'Then many congratulations. I hope the conference will not take too much of your husband's time. There are far more important things to be doing.'

Nancy felt her face grow hot and thought how absurd it was to be playing the blushing newlywed. 'I'm sure we'll have time together, but the conference is important,' she said quickly. 'I believe experts have come from all over the world. To discuss how best to protect Venice—if the rise in sea level continues.'

Somewhere she had read that the dredging of entrances to the lagoon and the dredging of canals inside the city had seriously increased the flow of tides.

The *signora* gave a long sigh. 'The city is sinking. St Mark's Square has five older pavements beneath the present one, you know. It is industry on the mainland that I blame. Mestre is the most horrible place on earth. What does your husband do at the conference?'

'I think for the most part he is making contacts and collecting information. When we return to London it will help him gather support for a fund he hopes to establish. A rescue fund. He thinks it will be needed. He's a professor of art, you see.'

The woman's eyes widened. 'A professor? I may know him. Who is he?'

Nancy thought it unlikely, but answered willingly enough. 'His name is Leo Tremayne.'

'Ah, Professor Tremayne. I have spoken to him—often.

Such a gentleman. And so very knowledgeable. But I did not know he had married.'

'It was a whirlwind wedding.' Why had she said that? It made it seem as though she'd been swept off her feet by passion.

'How romantic! Often these are the very best marriages. Two people so in love they can do nothing but marry immediately.'

Nancy felt her flush deepen. Fear had driven her particular whirlwind and, though she felt affection for Leo and admired him hugely, passion was sadly absent. Desperate to change the subject, she asked, 'How do you know my husband?'

'I own an antiques business. Moretto. It is the largest of its kind in Venice. We buy and sell paintings among other things, and Professor Tremayne has been a great help in the past. My name is Marta, Marta Moretto.'

'I am Nancy,' she said, a little unsure of the protocol. The woman was a complete stranger, yet oddly it didn't feel that way.

'Well, Nancy, let us hope our experts will soon find a solution. I have seen for myself how much is changing in Venice, and not for the good. I can no longer store anything in my basement. Last year it lay two feet in water.'

She thought of the palazzo Leo had hired and wondered if it, too, might suffer the same fate, but her companion was quick to reassure, as though she had known what was passing in Nancy's mind.

'You must not worry. It will be a few weeks before the high tides come and you will have left Venice by then. But in any case, my house is in Dorsoduro, in *calle dei Morti*, do you know it? And *acqua alta* has been a problem there for as long as I can remember.'

'I suppose you would never think of moving?'

'Moving?' Marta gave a small laugh. 'I was born in that house and have lived there all my life.'

'Then your family is truly Venetian.'

Her companion smiled warmly. It was the first time she had really smiled, Nancy realised. 'Indeed we are. We are a part of the city itself. Over the centuries we have done much for Venice, and now more lies ahead. Our future promises great things. The Moretto name will be honoured everywhere—I am determined.'

It struck Nancy as a strange thing to say, but she didn't like to ask what great things the *signora* had in mind and said instead, 'My husband is taking me to my first opera tonight.'

Signora Moretto sighed again and took another sip of coffee. 'It is Puccini, I think. Always Puccini, but the tourists love him. Venetians do not go to the theatre to hear music. They go to show off their new clothes and be seen by their friends. It is a shame. If they loved the music, we would hear the composers of Venice, but where is Monteverdi? Where is Vivaldi? And the tickets have become so expensive. Soon it will be only tourists who can afford a seat. But I shall go this evening.'

As a tourist herself, Nancy felt unable to comment, and there was silence until the *signora* said, 'You must enjoy, my dear. Enjoy being with your husband. The years go too quickly and you are left wondering how this has happened. How it is that you are alone and struggling.'

Marta's expression was grave, her eyes almost haunted, and Nancy scrabbled around for something cheering to say. Before she could, though, the woman had risen from her chair.

'I am afraid I must go now,' she said, 'but it has been good to meet you, Nancy.' She lifted her hand in a farewell gesture. 'Make sure you enjoy the performance tonight.'

'And you, too,' Nancy said with a smile.

'But certainly—Puccini or not. I will see you at La Fenice, no doubt.'

But Nancy hadn't seen her, at least not alive. That frightening thought entwined itself with the worsening weather and made her shiver more fiercely. Since they'd left the theatre, the mist had thickened, the beginnings of a fog drifting in from the sea or seeping up from the waters on which the city was built. Tendrils of cold damp wrapped themselves around her neck and the drizzle was slowly turning to heavy rain.

She quickened her pace, trying to keep Archie in sight as he weaved his way around corners, down alleys and over bridges. He knew the city well—in his time with Leo he'd often visited—but an umbrella would have been more useful, she thought with irritation, than this hectic pace. She could only hope they would be home very soon.

Then turning a last corner, there was the palazzo. 'You need to experience the true Venice,' Leo had said, 'and you won't get that staying in an anonymous hotel. I'll rent a small palazzo. I'm sure you'll love it.'

Chapter Three

The building was at the end of yet another narrow *calle*, its rear entrance protected by huge wooden doors that opened onto a narrow strip of garden and to one side, a flagged courtyard with an antique well head, its stonework sodden and glistening in the teeming rain. As with so many in the city, the palazzo had seen better days, the garden wild and overgrown, the brickwork crumbling. Nancy imagined this must be the true Venice she was to experience, and couldn't help hanker a little for the anonymous hotel.

Archie pushed open the studded wooden doors and stood back to wave her in. Somehow he made even this harmless gesture seem an affront. Ignoring him, she stood still for a moment, looking up at the stone windows, gossamer in the misty air. A light burned on the first floor—Leo still working on his speech, she guessed. He was passionate about conservation and eager to establish an Art and Archives Rescue Fund, and though Nancy admired his strong commitment to a cause still in its infancy, she had wished very much for his company tonight.

She almost ran to the side door and, once inside, shook out her skirts. A slow drip of water trickled from the organza onto the lobby's uneven tiles, dribbles of water following the old geometric pattern of swirls and waves. She waited for the dripping to stop before she made for the marble staircase, keeping to the middle of each step where hundreds of years of use had hollowed a concave.

At the top of the stairs, she headed directly for the light, crossing an immense open space, its floor thick oak, its walls filled floor to ceiling with books. Then through gleaming double doors to the main salon. Most often Leo took his work to the tiny room he'd commandeered as his office at the back of the palazzo, but tonight he sat at the large oval table beneath two immense Murano glass chandeliers suspended at intervals from the frescoed ceiling.

He jumped up as soon as he saw her, scattering the pile of papers on which he'd been working.

'Nancy—you're back. Thank goodness! I saw the fog coming down and was getting worried.'

'You shouldn't be.' She went up to him and kissed him on the cheek. 'I had the faithful Archie leading the way.' She wondered if he heard the tinge of sarcasm she couldn't quite suppress.

'Where is he?' Leo adjusted his glasses and looked vacantly towards the doorway.

'In his room, I imagine. Changing his clothes.'

'And so must you, my darling. You're wet through. Go and change and I'll ask Concetta to make us hot drinks before she leaves.'

'You haven't asked me about the opera.'

'Later—or you'll catch a chill.'

He hustled her out of the door and up the stairs to the bedroom they shared. It was a large and airy room, overlooking a small canal, and with a magnificent ceiling frescoed in the style of Tiepolo—a woman crowned with a laurel wreath, accepting the tribute of Venetian nobles led by the Doge and the Pope. It rather put the Pope in his place, Nancy thought.

She liked the room, but it was a long climb to get there. The palazzo was a rambling structure, spread over four floors, and seemingly patched up by a succession of plumbers and builders. Already, after only a few days, the stairs had begun to seem unending.

But Leo appeared to think the setting romantic and was working hard to make this a honeymoon. Nancy found it difficult to match him. She had never pretended passion, but hadn't realised just how hard marriage would be.

In a few minutes, she was back in the salon wearing the extravagant silk dressing robe Leo had given her as a wedding present. Concetta was settling their tray on the small *intaglio* table.

'Thank you.' Leo smiled warmly at the maid, eliciting a gentle simper in return. He was a handsome man, Nancy thought, watching the way the light glinted off the strands of silver in his hair. At forty-five he was still able to turn a woman's head.

'So… now tell me about the opera.' He patted the brocade of the sofa and she sat down beside him. 'How was it? Did you love it? Hate it?'

He was almost too effusive and she wished he wouldn't try so hard. 'It was wonderful, certainly. Joyous, sad…'

'Yes…' he nodded for her to go on and when she didn't, he said, 'actually you don't sound too joyous.'

She reached out for his hand. 'Something dreadful happened, Leo. At the end of the performance—a woman fell from one of the top boxes into the auditorium.'

'My God! How did that happen? Was the barrier faulty?'

'I don't know. I don't think so. I saw no wreckage. The police arrived as we left.'

Leo nodded. 'They'll be a post-mortem. I imagine the poor woman didn't survive.'

Nancy shook her head dumbly.

'But my poor darling.' He encased her in his arms and hugged her tight. 'What a thing to happen.'

'I met her,' she said in a muffled tone.

'The woman who died?'

'Yes. I met her earlier today—in the *gelateria* on the Zattere. We talked a while. She was so friendly. And there was something about her that, I don't know, touched me... Her name is Signora Moretto.'

'My God!' he said again.

'She said she knew you.'

'Marta Moretto knows everyone, but then she runs the most prestigious antiques business in Venice. Our acquaintance is very slight.'

'She seemed to know you well.'

Leo spread his hands in a dismissive gesture. 'I've spoken to her several times over the years, but I wouldn't say I knew her well. I was called in a while ago to value a Renaissance portrait. The firm deals mainly in nineteenth-century works— not my period —but in some way or other they'd acquired this painting and there was disagreement over its value. I was asked to set a reserve price.'

Marta had spoken warmly of Leo, but there was no answering warmth in his voice and that surprised Nancy. She wondered if something had happened to disturb their relationship.

'The signora seemed very proud of her business,' she prompted.

'With good reason. Moretto are an excellent firm. And they have a history. They've stayed a family affair. The signora took over when her husband died, and his father and grandfather ran it before him. I believe there's a younger Moretto to follow—Marta's son. Between them all they've built a successful business. Hardly surprising—they're very good at what they do... But what a terrible thing for you to see. I hope Archie took you away immediately.'

'Oh, yes. He did his job.'

This time her tone made him look closely at her. 'I hope he's looking after you.'

'Yes, of course, Leo. Why wouldn't he?'

'He can be chippy at times, I know. And I did rather spring our marriage on him.'

Leo had sprung the marriage on her, too. But in the dreadful situation she'd faced, she had felt only gratitude.

'I suppose all of us are getting used to living differently.' She was trying to sound conciliatory, but she need not have worried. Her husband was only half listening. For the moment, both Archie and Signora Moretto had been forgotten.

'I've some news. Good news. Tomorrow, once this wretched paper is out of the way, I'm a free man—for the afternoon at least. I'm sorry we've had so little time together, but for a few hours I can devote myself entirely to you.'

'Really?'

'Really. Anywhere you want to go, we'll go.'

'I took a walk on the *riva* this morning and I could just see the Lido across the lagoon. I'd rather like to visit.'

He looked disappointed but then arranged his face into a smile. 'We can manage that, I'm sure. There's a drinks reception at lunchtime, at the Cipriani—it's to mark the half-way point of the conference. Spouses are welcome and I'm hoping you'll come and liven things up a little. We can go on to the Lido after that.'

Back in London, she had browsed through the conference programme Leo had left lying on his desk. A number of sessions had interested her and she'd been keen to attend. Working at Abingers, she had developed a much wider interest in art than her college course had allowed. But Leo had said she would find the talks as dry as dust and she'd be better to spend her time discovering Venice.

She'd wondered then if he was ashamed of introducing her to his colleagues. After eight years at the auction house, she had progressed no further than a second assistant in Fine Arts. Not because she lacked the skill or the knowledge, but because the chances of a woman, and a woman without the right background, carving out a successful career was remote. If she moved to Books, it had been said to her quietly, there might be opportunity, but Fine Art was a dead end. It was the preserve of men, of private school, of Oxbridge.

'The Lido it is.' Leo put his arms around her and gave her another hug. 'But we'll have to hope the fog lifts. Otherwise the island will be miserable.'

'It will lift.' She smiled across at him. 'Shall we go up now?'

Going to bed was a delicate business and it was the time of day she had come to dread. She hadn't been ignorant on her wedding day, as so many girls were—though Mrs Nicholson had shied from even the barest mention of what her daughter should expect—and Leo was a considerate lover. But Nancy felt no passion for him, only guilt that her response was so tepid. She had tried to summon more emotion, but it felt wrong, false, as though she were in some way betraying him, which was absurd. He had known from the outset it was only affection she offered; she had told him clearly enough when he'd asked her to marry him.

But it hadn't proved a discouragement and his proposal had come as a shock—it seemed to Nancy they barely knew each other. At the time, she hadn't been sure whether Leo's enthusiasm sprang from thinking marriage the best way to protect her or whether, in fact, he loved her deeply and hoped to inspire the same in her. On their wedding night, though, he had left her in no doubt—it was evident he was deeply in love—and Nancy felt guiltier still. Somehow, though, they had to negotiate this relationship and make the marriage stick. With genuine respect and affection on both sides, it was surely possible.

Tomorrow at the reception she would be by his side, doing her best to play the loving wife and hoping she'd not let him down. But the morning hours would be free. Time in which to ask questions. While Leo talked, her mind had been busy. If she had, in truth, glimpsed a figure in Signora Moretto's box, he or she must be responsible for the woman's death—if only for making no attempt to save her. But when the police came to investigate, they would be told the signora was alone: as far as Nancy knew, no one else in the theatre had seen anything to arouse suspicion.

Where had that figure come from? Who were they? Were they a member of the audience—or even one of the performers? Or were they someone who had slipped into La Fenice unnoticed? If so, it was likely they had chosen the stage entrance, the turnstile at the side of the theatre used by the singers and technical staff.

Nancy felt herself compelled to do something, to keep faith with the woman she had met today. She would make sure, as certainly as she could, that Marta received justice. Tomorrow she would go back to the theatre and speak to the *portinaio*. He would know the singers and the crew by sight; he would even know many of them personally. Last evening, for whatever reason, had he allowed a stranger through?

Chapter Four

When next morning Nancy stepped through the salon windows onto the balcony, she was dazzled. The rain had cleared in the night and the sun was bright on ancient stone, glinting off the waters of the small canal that flowed beside the palazzo. In the distance, over the roof tops, the jagged peaks of the Dolomites were just visible. During the day they would disappear as waves of humidity crept in from the lagoon.

But it was still early—Leo had risen an hour ago to check his speech for the final time —and already the city was humming. She could hear a vaporetto plying its route several canals away. A gondola passed below, making its way to the Grand Canal and the tourists who would pay handsomely for a ride in its black-painted, brass-embellished elegance. A small working boat chugged slowly to its destination, its deck piled high with fruit and vegetables for market, and an expensive *motoscafo,* ornately decorated, cut its engine as it drifted in from the lagoon.

Nancy breathed deeply. She could smell coffee and fresh brioche and cigarettes. She would miss Concetta's breakfast, she decided, and eat outside at one of the small cafés that dotted Castello. Or she'd forget about eating and go straight to La Fenice before the *portinaio* became too entangled with the business of the day.

For that she must walk to the busy vaporetto stop at San Zaccaria—she knew her way there, at least—and then take the number two route to Giglio on the Grand Canal. From that point, it was unlikely she would get lost walking to the theatre.

The vaporetti were frequent and fast and in twenty minutes she was standing outside La Fenice. Avoiding the grand front entrance, she walked around to the side of the building. The *portinaio* was in the small glass-fronted hutch that overlooked the stage entrance, two small espresso cups abandoned on his desk and a third in his hand. Hopefully, it meant he would feel lively enough to talk.

'*Buongiorno*,' she began as confidently as she could, then asked him in her best Italian if there was to be a performance that evening.

'Tonight no,' he said. 'Tomorrow perhaps. You buy a ticket at the box office, signora. At the front of the theatre.'

'Thank you, I will. I have a friend who would like to see the opera,' she improvised. 'I've already seen it myself—I was at last night's performance. The most shocking thing happened. Do you know of it?'

It was obvious he must, but she hoped it would open the conversation. 'The poor Signora Moretto,' he sighed. '*Che tragedia!*'

'Tragic,' she agreed. 'And for it to happen here. I believe she loved this theatre.'

'Always she was coming.' He had switched to a heavily accented English. 'For years a *patronessa*.'

'What happened, do you think?'

He waggled his head. '*Non lo so*. I don't know. An accident? The lady takes medicine for her pain. She has the bad leg. Maybe a mistake and she has too much.'

Nancy nodded in pretend agreement. 'That must be it.

People last night were saying,' —she lowered her voice— 'that it might be deliberate, but I find that difficult to believe.'

'No, no. *Non ci credo!*' He was emphatic. 'The signora was *religiosa, molto devota.*'

'Devoted?'

'*Sì, sì,* a good Catholic. It is not possible. It would be *un peccato mortale,* a sin, a very bad sin.'

'Did you see her last night? I imagine as a patron she was allowed to come this way.' Nancy gestured to the turnstile.

He wagged his finger reprovingly. 'No one is allowed— only singers, workers.'

She smiled at him. 'You must have to watch for anyone trying to come in for free.'

He gave a small smirk. 'No one comes. I told the *Carabinieri* last night. I know all who work here.' He waved his hand backstage. 'I do my job.'

'I'm sure you do. And thank you for taking the time to talk to me.'

The conversation hadn't been easy, but Nancy had understood enough to know that no one who was not supposed to had passed through the turnstile last night.

She walked back into the sunshine, round to the rear of the theatre and into Campo San Fantin, sinking down on the shallow steps of its magnificent church. A column of chattering nuns passed by, their black and white dress a moving pattern against the sun-baked stones. At this time of the morning the square was busy and noise everywhere. Incense and organ music billowed through the curtained entrance of the church. A radio blared from a nearby house, a delivery man yelled for waiters to clear a passage, a small child sobbed loudly from a fall. Think, Nancy, she scolded herself, trying to ignore the hubbub.

If the figure she had seen in the signora's box hadn't passed by the turnstile, he would have walked through the main entrance. He must have had a ticket for the performance — and Nancy was sure it would have been a 'he'. Marta Moretto was tiny, but considerable strength would be required to lift a struggling woman over a barrier that high. He had planned the death carefully, a member of the audience for much of the opera, but then slipping out of his seat—in the interval perhaps—and waiting his chance. Then when the whole theatre was on its feet, the air loud with cheering and the signora out of her chair and clapping each curtain call, he had struck. But why? The *portinaio* had called Marta a pious woman. Leo respected her business acumen. Why would anyone wish to do such a dreadful thing?

Nancy looked blankly into the distance, her mind clutching at stray thoughts in the hope she might solve the puzzle. She didn't notice the young man until he was half way across the square, but then she saw him—the man who'd had the angry confrontation with Signora Moretto on the Zattere. He was dressed in overalls this time and carried a tool bag, evidently on his way to work.

She jumped up and ran across the *campo,* catching up with him as he walked out of the square. '*Scusi,*' she said, her breath coming fast. '*L'ora?*' She tapped her wrist. 'Do you have the time? I have an appointment, but I've forgotten to wear a watch.'

She sounded stupid, but that didn't matter if it meant she could talk to him. He looked down at his own wrist, tanned and leathery. 'Five past eleven,' he answered in English.

'Thank you so much.' When he went to walk away, she said quickly, 'Have you heard about Signora Moretto?'

He turned, looking stunned.

'I saw you talking to her yesterday,' she said in explanation. 'I thought you must be a friend of hers.'

'Friend!' He literally spat the word. 'Marta Moretto was no friend of mine. And yes, I have heard. I am glad she is dead.'

Nancy was aghast, but tried to speak coolly. 'You were at the theatre—you saw her fall?'

'You think I can buy a ticket?' he asked. His tone was bitter and he gestured to his workman's clothes and the bag of tools he'd dropped to the ground. 'If I want to hear the singers, I must stand in this square and listen to them practise. But I wish I had been there—last night. I would like to have seen her fall. The woman was wicked.'

'Surely you must be mistaken.'

'There's no mistake.' His voice grated. 'She has ruined my life.'

'But how?'

'You really want to know, *Signora English*?' He leaned towards her and for an instant his muscular figure blocked out the sun.

Nancy refused to be intimidated. 'I spoke to her myself. Not for long, it's true, but I can't imagine the signora ruining anyone's life.'

'That is the face she shows the world. But what do you say of a woman who locks away her own daughter? A young girl—only seventeen—sent for life to a convent?'

Nancy gave a small gasp. 'You're saying she forced her daughter to enter a convent?'

A different picture of Signora Moretto was emerging and Nancy was confused. The *portinaio* had called her a very good woman, while for this man she was evil incarnate.

He nodded, seeming pleased with the impression he had created. 'For eight years my Angelica has been behind bars. And do you know why? Because I was too poor, too rough, for the Moretto family. That woman has taken years of our lives. Ask her daughter's friends if you don't believe me.

They know what happened. Ask Giulia, ask Luisa Mancini.'

'Angelica is still in the convent?'

'A month, two months ago, she escaped, but only to be prisoner in her own home. Until now. At last now she is free—and we will marry. In a few weeks, she will be Signora Bozzato.'

'Then I wish you well for your wedding, though I imagine there will have to be a post-mortem first. And a funeral?'

'You suggest we wait for that woman's funeral?' His face had reddened and his eyes sparked anger. 'We have waited long enough. I will make sure my angel is far away when her mother lies where she belongs—under two metres of earth.'

He had advanced towards her as he spoke, and she found herself stepping back, fearful of his intent. She had thought him ready to strike Signora Moretto, so why not her?

There was a sudden flurry behind her and Archie Jago appeared at her side. He was looking pointedly at the young man. 'Have you a problem? Can I help you?' They stared at each other for several tense seconds, and then Mario picked up his tools and marched out of the square.

Archie turned to her, a vexed expression on his face. 'What was that all about?'

'His name is Mario Bozzato. He was the man I saw threatening the signora. You can see how angry he gets.'

'Oh yeah, I saw all right. Why were you annoying him?'

'I wasn't annoying him. I wanted to find out why he'd threatened Marta.'

'And did you?'

'I think so.'

'So now you've fingered him for a murderer?'

She flushed since she knew how ridiculous that sounded, yet she was thinking it nonetheless.

'There's very little crime in Venice, Mrs Tremayne.' Why

did he persist in such formality and why speak to her as though he were indulging a small child? 'Regular thievery maybe,' he went on, 'graffiti, badly behaved tourists on occasions. But nothing violent, no big-city crime. Just accept it was suicide.'

He was intent on making her feel foolish and she longed to retaliate. 'Why are you here?' she asked, trying to throw him off balance. 'Have you been following me?' It was unlikely — and unnecessary. It couldn't have been difficult for Archie to guess where she'd be, that she'd return to the theatre at the first opportunity.

He ignored the challenge and answered her first question. 'The reception is starting an hour earlier than scheduled. Leo asked me to find you.'

'Thank you for letting me know.' He shrugged his shoulders. 'And for arriving when you did.' It stuck in her throat to thank him, but she was grateful. Bozzato had felt threatening.

He shrugged again, irritating her even more.

'Why has the reception been put forward?'

An unexpected grin flashed across his face, and for the first time she thought him an attractive man. 'One of the delegates ate a few too many oysters last night and is currently indisposed. His lecture was cancelled — hence an earlier reception and a longer afternoon.'

'All good then, but I can find my own way back to the palazzo.' She was lying. Without retracing her journey on the water bus, she would be lost. The city was a maze of alleys and courtyards, tortuous passages and dead ends. But she felt a desperate need to assert some independence and repeated, 'I'll be fine from here.'

Archie looked bored. 'I'm on my way back anyway — I'm invited, too. Sometimes even the hired help gets treats.'

The familiar edge to his voice was pronounced. Whatever good humour the oyster incident had produced, had already vanished. And she was about to make things worse.

'I'd like to speak to the friend Mario mentioned. A Luisa Mancini. I could ask around. Venice is a small city, someone might know her.'

'You shouldn't do that.' She'd known, of course, that would be Archie's response. 'Leo won't be happy. And why are you even bothering? What is the Moretto woman to you?'

'Nothing... except I know she wanted to live. I heard it in her voice. I saw it in her eyes. And no one else is going to champion her. They will sweep her away—the police, the audience last night, her family, for all I know—she's a tragic accident or a whispered suicide. But she deserves the truth.'

'And you're the one to deliver it?' His tone was sardonic. 'You can't seriously think that man had anything to do with her death. He wasn't even at the theatre last night. I heard him say so.'

'If you heard that, you must have heard him say the signora stole his life from him when she locked up her daughter. He is a very angry man and angry men can do bad things.'

'You think a blighted love affair is worth murdering for?' He twisted his mouth into a grimace.

'I wouldn't expect you to understand, but if love goes wrong, it can do strange things to people.' She knew that better than anyone. 'Disappointment can breed bitterness. And revenge. So yes, I think it's a possible motive. I must try to find this Luisa.'

Archie was walking slightly ahead of her, and there was a pause before he said over his shoulder, 'Don't. You don't want that kind of attention. I'll ask around.' Then added obscurely, 'I know people. Though this Luisa may have left Venice, despite what Bozzato said. A lot of Venetians do.

They move to the mainland for a job, for a house.'

Nancy had no idea who Archie knew in the city, but he was bound to be more successful than she at discovering Luisa Mancini's whereabouts. It was one small step in the right direction. Her pleasure, though, was short-lived. It took a moment only to realise her husband's likely reaction.

'You won't tell Leo I'm looking for her?' she asked, anxiously.

'Why would I?'

'You might feel you have to. He's your friend.'

'Like the squire is friends with his stableman?'

Chippy—Leo's word—was an understatement, she thought. Aloud she said, 'I imagined you would be friends. You come from the same village. You must have known each other as children.'

'No, Mrs Tremayne, we didn't. My family are fisher folk. I went to the only school available—the village school— and left at fourteen to gut fish. Leo was a boarder in Dorset. Shaftesbury School, I believe. That's an expensive education. *He* left at eighteen to go to Cambridge. Slightly different life experiences, wouldn't you say?'

His tone warned her not to pursue the subject and by now they had reached the gates of the palazzo.

'I'll see you at the party, no doubt,' she said brightly, walking ahead to the side door and up the marble staircase.

Chapter Five

Minutes later Nancy was in her bedroom and crossing to the window to look down on the canal. She wished she could slip away on its waters, escape from an event she was sure she would hate. She suspected that Leo's colleagues would talk over her head, and their wives talk behind her back. *A brilliant man like Leo Tremayne,* she could hear them say. *How on earth did he come to marry that little nobody?*

But perhaps she was being unfair and it was her own lack of confidence talking. If so, it was hardly surprising. Her parents had rarely supported her ambitions, had stood in the way of her most cherished dreams, and any pride she'd had in her own judgement had fled when Philip March walked into her life.

She crossed the room again, this time to glance at herself in the wall mirror with its gilded baroque scroll. She found the reflection dispiriting. The floral dress she'd put on that morning was decidedly dowdy and, despite her lack of enthusiasm for this meeting, she knew she would have to do better. The Cipriani, she'd learned from Concetta, was the most prestigious hotel in Venice.

Her wardrobe was modest, but not because she lacked a passion for clothes. She delighted in them: their colour, their line, their texture, part of her pleasure in all things artistic. Rationing had ended six years ago, but she had never had enough money to buy more than one or two special outfits to hang alongside the sober skirts and blouses she wore to work. Leo had wanted to buy her a whole new wardrobe for this holiday, but she had refused. There was a limit to how much generosity she could accept.

And she had only one dress that was good enough for this event, other than the evening gown she'd worn to the opera—a tea dress of eau-de-nil crêpe—bought just before Leo proposed, just before that last terrifying incident.

Colleagues at Abingers had invited her out for the evening, and she had gone to Dickins & Jones and spent far too much money on a dress that until now she had never worn. The dress had proved too smart for *The Grapes of Wrath*—she hadn't known it was a pub the group was planning to visit. But she had wanted so badly to feel for one evening that her life was normal. It wasn't normal, though, and when she returned to her Paddington bedsit, she had found it ransacked.

The crackle of broken china had sounded beneath her feet and when she'd taken a deep breath and switched on the light, she had crumpled. Her newly painted walls were smeared with food, cupboard doors swung off their hinges, each shelf swept clear, and on the floor the remnants of crockery and glass. In the living room every piece of furniture she possessed had been destroyed, the sofa for which she had saved so hard ripped apart, its fabric torn and gaping. Everything that could be broken had been broken. Philip had destroyed it all.

Her bedroom door had been ajar and she'd stood in the open doorway, hardly daring to look. When she opened her eyes fully, though, nothing seemed to have been touched. But then she saw it. A dead crow lying on her bed, its feathers a fading black, its blood seeping into the white linen counterpane.

But she would not think of it this morning. Not any of it. She would enjoy what she could of the day, enjoy being with Leo. She washed quickly, then slipped on the dress and was pleased to see how well it fitted her slim form. A pair of oyster silk wedged shoes, the ones she had worn to the Fitzrovia Chapel, and a matching handbag completed the ensemble. She stood back to look again in the mirror—yes, she would do.

She rarely wore make up, and now that her skin had acquired a golden tint she looked better without. But perhaps she could arrange her hair more stylishly. Instead of tying the unruly chestnut waves into a tight bunch at the nape of her neck, she could sweep them up into a loose coil. She had nice hair, she thought, probably her best feature, though Leo swore it was the dreamy grey of her eyes he'd first fallen for. She hoped he would like the dress; he deserved a wife who took more trouble with her appearance. And it might be good to remind Archie Jago that she was a woman and not an unwanted parcel with which he'd been burdened.

*

Ten minutes later when Nancy glided down the palazzo stairs, both men were waiting in the lobby, Leo having just arrived back from the conference. She saw their eyes widen and their eyebrows rise steeply. In appreciation? Or was that amazement? It was a comical sight and she was forced to stifle a laugh.

Leo strode forward and gallantly offered her his arm. Together they walked down the final flight of stairs and along the narrow passageway that led to the front of the palazzo and the landing stage. For once, the huge wooden door to the canal stood open, its amazing array of locks, chains and antique padlocks, hanging loosely to one side. When she'd laughed at such elaborate security, Leo had told her that Venetians considered it necessary. The city's burglars, it seemed, were skilled at gaining entry to canal-side houses, stealing a handbag or a piece of jewellery, then drifting silently away on the canal.

These days the palazzo's front entrance was used only for deliveries, but this morning a small boat was waiting for them by the moss-covered steps, tied to a huge painted post. The boat gave a sudden lurch to one side and then back again, as the wake of a larger vessel out in the lagoon sent waves rippling up the canals. But Nancy managed to clamber aboard without mishap, taking shelter in the cabin while the men stayed on deck.

The Cipriani was situated at the very tip of the Giudecca, a short ride across the lagoon from San Marco. They threaded their way first towards San Giorgio Maggiore where the Cini library was hosting Leo's conference, then swung right to arrive at the island in a matter of minutes. Nancy could have wished the journey longer. A sharp breeze had sprung up, but the day continued bright and the lagoon sparkled. She felt a new freedom in being on waters that stretched far into the distance, flowing on and on until they reached the Adriatic.

A splendidly uniformed man met them at the hotel's landing stage, helping to steady the boat as they stepped onto the short walkway and into the beautiful old building, then through a marbled lobby and out of double doors into the garden.

For a moment Nancy stood quite still, amazed at its size. When she had first arrived in Venice, she'd thought most houses must be without gardens, but then she'd caught the smell of honeysuckle in the air, and a second blooming of wisteria, and realised there must be an infinite number hidden behind iron gates or ancient brick walls.

This garden, though, was immense. It stretched as far as she could see, planted not just with flowers but, beyond the ornamental beds, with every kind of vegetable. A peacock strode past, squawking with annoyance at the intrusion of so many people, and a mother duck with her babies waddled away, retreating towards the pond that lay to one side of a wide expanse of lawn.

Nancy looked across at her husband. 'How beautiful!'

Leo nodded. 'At one time the Giudecca was the garden of Venice, though when the weather is miserable, the island can be desolate—I've heard people say it feels sinister, a place where nasty things can happen. But on a day like today, it's unbeatable. There are still flower gardens running down to the lagoon. I'd like to show them to you.'

'It doesn't look as though you'll have the chance.'

Nancy gestured ahead to where tables had been set up beneath a row of striped awnings, providing shelter from the sun or perhaps even rain. It was September and the weather this far north could be uncertain. Unlikely today, she thought, feeling the heat of the midday sun on her bare arms. Comfortable chairs, many already occupied by the older guests, had been positioned in groups across the lawn or beside flower beds.

Archie had slipped away as soon as they'd arrived. Nancy saw him now, making his way towards a table that had been set up as a bar and was groaning with every kind of beverage. A waiter swooped on them from behind with a tray of champagne, but before she could take a sip from the offered glass, Leo had hailed a fellow guest, eager to introduce her. The newcomer was well-groomed, a man somewhere in his thirties, and dressed in sleek Italian style.

'Nancy, darling, I'd like you to meet Dino.'

Chapter Six

'Dino Di Maio,' the man said, holding out his hand. She noticed how smooth his skin was, how neatly manicured his nails.

'Dino is the main sponsor of our conference. If it weren't for him, none of us would be here.'

The man made a deprecating gesture. 'The conference has many sponsors, Mrs Tremayne, and it's my pleasure to contribute. This is my city, after all, and it seems we could be facing serious problems. Anything that may help us has to be supported.'

He nodded at Leo and Leo smiled warmly back. 'But, tell me,' he went on, 'how has a beautiful young lady like yourself been spending time while her husband has been hard at work—her new husband?' He smiled archly.

Nancy didn't care for the smile or for the words, but she answered mildly enough. 'I've been discovering Venice, Mr Di Maio—or trying to. Though finding my way around hasn't been easy.'

'The city is complicated,' he agreed, 'even though it's small. Really, it is a collection of villages, each with its own flavour, its own dialect. And finding your way can be most puzzling. The same street names appear in every *sestiere*—no wonder visitors get lost.'

'The postman must have a devil of a job.' Leo gave a

small laugh. He evidently liked this man, and she must try to as well.

'Now that's where you are wrong, my friend. There is a postman for each *sestiere* and within that quarter the buildings on every street start at number one and carry on to the very last house, no matter how many alleys or courtyards or squares are in the way.'

'I remember—' Leo was about to respond, when a large woman, in billowing skirt and tight blouse, bustled up to them, ignoring Nancy but waving a bright pink sunhat at Leo. He looked embarrassed, but nodded at the newcomer.

'Sorry,' he said. 'I think I'm needed, darling. I'll be back in a very few minutes. Dino—I'll see you tomorrow no doubt.'

'So where have you visited, Mrs Tremayne?' Dino asked, once they were alone. She had hoped he might drift away when Leo left, but it seemed he was not to be easily dislodged.

'I've only been in Venice a few days,' she responded, 'so haven't managed a great deal. Let me see—I've queued at San Marco, walked around the Accademia, and taken several vaporetto rides. Oh, and I went to La Fenice last night. The opera was wonderful—*Madama Butterfly*. But...'

At the mention of the theatre, his face had changed.

'Were you there, too?' she asked. It sounded like a challenge, though she hadn't meant it to.

'I was. A dreadful evening. I heard the news late last night. I hope you weren't too upset by the incident.'

'I was extremely upset. I would have been distressed for anyone, but I'd met Signora Moretto earlier in the day and we had talked a while. She seemed a very nice woman.'

'She was. A most respected lady. A patron of the theatre. A patron of Venice, in fact. It is a terrible business.' He gave a sad shake of his head, but she noticed his eyes strayed. He seemed to be contemplating escape.

'You heard the news late last night? So you weren't in the theatre when it happened?'

'No, no. I had to leave early. I'd booked a business call from America. The time difference makes things difficult, you understand, and I had to be home to take it.'

'What kind of business are you in?'

'The luxury business, Mrs Tremayne. These days in Venice, it is the only one to be in.'

She shouldn't be surprised. Everything about this glossy man spoke luxury. But her silence appeared to make him voluble, or was that defensive?

'We Venetians have always traded, you know. In the past, we were a great sea power and traded half way around the world—Arabia, China, India. And defied the Pope to do so. We were happy to do business with Muslims, Jews, anyone who was willing. The Orient began at Venice and even today our buildings are filled with treasures from the East. When you have the time to explore, you will find them everywhere—silks, jewels, mosaics. So you see, we are expert at making money. And we know just how far to squeeze our customer before he says goodbye! We do it charmingly, of course.'

'And what form does your particular squeezing take?'

Dino laughed a little uncertainly. 'I belong to a consortium. We own many palazzi between us and rent them to people like yourself, who want to enjoy the old Venice.' He paused for a moment, his head to one side. 'And I own a beautiful yacht—the *Andiamo* is my particular joy. Occasionally, my friends are allowed to hire her. But perhaps you would like to come aboard? Once the conference is over, I'll have more time to sail. I'd love to take you both for a jaunt—is that the right word?'

'I'm sure you know, Mr Di Maio. Your English is excellent.'

'Dino, please. My English should be excellent. I spent four years at Cambridge. It's where I first met Leo.'

Another part of her husband's life of which Nancy knew nothing. Leo rarely spoke to her of his university days, perhaps out of consideration. A humble art school diploma was the pinnacle of her achievement, and she had gained that only with immense determination and a stubbornness not to be beaten. For her parents, the need for further schooling was incomprehensible, their particular hostility reserved for any form of art education. A typing course was what she should take, with shorthand if possible, followed by a respectable job in an office—just for a few years until she found a husband and had the right number of children.

'So, you will take a ride on my wonderful yacht?' Dino asked.

'Such a kind thought, but really we couldn't trouble you.' She was unsure she wanted to spend any more time with this pampered man.

'It would be no trouble at all and it keeps Salvatore busy— he is my captain. I'd very much like to show you some of the islands. Maybe we can go to Burano. For lunch?'

'Thank you. I'm sure Leo would enjoy it.'

If Dino were her husband's friend, she must be gracious. Although not so gracious that she lost the opportunity to return the conversation to the tragedy that dominated her thoughts. 'Leo was shocked to hear of Signora Moretto's death. He knew her through her business and considered her a very knowledgeable woman.'

Out of the corner of her eye, she caught sight of Archie, glass in hand, talking to a shorter man, dark-haired and compact. Their bodies were hunched, leaning in towards each other; it appeared to be more a confrontation than conversation. Archie, usually so coldly efficient, did not look himself and she wondered how many drinks he had downed.

Dino was nodding gravely. 'Signora Moretto *was* knowledgeable. Her art colleagues in Venice will miss her very much. The Moretto business is most respected in the city. It belonged to the lady's husband—until he had the heart attack, God be with him—and his father and grandfather before him. But now, who knows?'

'I imagine it will continue. I've heard the signora has a son.'

'Yes, Luca. But he could sell, too—eventually.'

'Sell? The family business is to be sold?'

Dino looked around him, as though to check for any likely eavesdroppers. 'I should not be saying this. I can be a little indiscreet.' He smiled as though this image of himself pleased him. 'But I consider you a friend, Nancy, and I will tell you. For some time I have been working for the signora, negotiating for her with buyers from Florence. And we had nearly reached an agreement, but now... as I say, who knows?' He looked suddenly deflated.

The sound of raised voices drifted across the lawn, causing people nearby to turn their heads. Archie, it seemed, was embroiled in an argument that was becoming louder and more threatening by the minute. Nancy wished Leo was around to restrain his assistant, but whatever fracas Archie was involved in, she must ignore it. Questioning Di Maio was too important.

She turned back to him. 'Why on earth would the signora want to sell a business that has been in her family for years? And one that is so successful.'

He spread his hands wide. 'Marta did not confide in me. All I know is that she wished for freedom. She had plans for a different future, I think. She wanted to sell and be free.'

'But she could have been free,' Nancy protested, 'if she'd handed the business to her son.' When he said nothing, she added, 'Do you think Luca Moretto will want to sell?'

'At the moment, no. It seems he wishes to keep the business going, but...?' Dino shrugged his elegant shoulders. 'When I have talked with him more, he may change his mind. He had no part in the negotiations so everything is new to him. Marta was in charge, she was the power, the driving force. A small woman, but that should not mislead.' He smiled as he said this, but Nancy heard the unspoken message. Luca had been unimportant.

'But here is the very man.' Dino half turned—with some relief, she thought—to greet the figure shambling towards them. 'I must introduce you.'

'The signora's son is here?' she asked very quietly. 'The day after his mother's death?' She tried to keep the shock from her voice, but found it difficult.

Dino was quick with an excuse. 'The signora herself should have been here today. I believe Luca felt it right that he represent his mother.'

The burly man had reached them and Dino bounced forward. 'Mrs Tremayne, this is Luca Moretto. Luca, this is Nancy, Leo Tremayne's new wife. She has been busy discovering Venice.'

'How do you do?' Luca's English was laboured, unlike his friend's mellow tones, and he possessed nothing of the other man's polish. 'I hope you enjoy your time with us,' he said slowly.

He wore a heavy suit and was sweating profusely. As they stood there, he passed a handkerchief several times across his forehead. 'Too hot for me.' He grimaced, his awkward figure sagging beneath the wool jacket.

Nancy braced herself to mention Marta's death and offer her condolences. 'I was so very sorry to hear of your loss, Signor Moretto.' She looked directly at him, but his face was an almost complete blank. Dino might be uncomfortably shiny, but this man seemed to lack all life. 'I am so sorry,' she repeated.

He looked even blanker. Then as though a button had been pressed, sprang suddenly into life, his face becoming oddly mobile as if at that instant he had donned a pliable mask. 'Yes, thank you, Mrs…'

'Tremayne,' she helped him.

'Mrs Tremayne. It has been a great shock.'

'And so sad. I spoke to your mother very recently and she seemed bright with plans for the future.'

'Yes, yes. She was.' Luca seemed distracted, appearing not to hear his own words. Then realising he was expected to say more, he added, 'I thought I should be here. Mama would have wanted it.'

Nancy was about to offer an anodyne response when a loud crash brought every conversation to an end. For a moment Luca's small eyes looked hunted, then he straightened his shoulders. 'There is a little problem, I think.'

To Nancy it looked a large problem. A tray of glasses lay shattered on the floor, the pale straw of champagne seeping into the Cipriani's immaculate lawn. And there was Archie walking away, slightly unsteady, but making for the hotel entrance and presumably a boat back to the city. Behind him, a man lay spread-eagled on the grass.

Dino uttered a barely suppressed oath. 'Salvatore,' he said, and hurriedly excused himself.

The next second Luca Moretto had disappeared silently into the crowd and Nancy was left alone. But not for long. Leo was soon by her side and taking her hand. 'Time to go, I think.'

'What has Archie been doing?'

'I've no idea. Except he seems to have taken a dislike

to Dino's captain. But I think we may have outstayed our welcome, don't you? Definitely time to go.'

She thought Leo remarkably unfazed by this sudden turn of events and liked that in him.

Chapter Seven

The view from the Giudecca had to be one of the loveliest in Venice: the basilica of San Marco and the Doge's Palace straight ahead of them, to the left the marble dome of the Santa Maria della Salute rising majestically behind the customs office where for centuries ships from around the Venetian empire had paid their excise duties, then the long stretch of the Zattere with its colourful bars and restaurants and on to the port area at San Basilio and its rows of elegant yachts. No doubt Dino's was among them.

The Cipriani's own vessel took them back across the lagoon to St Mark's Square, where Leo immediately hired a *sàndolo* crewed by a solitary oarsman. 'A small boat will be fine,' he said. 'The Lido looks a distance, but it's not far.'

Nancy spoke little on the short journey, enjoying the sun's warmth on her bare limbs and the stiff breeze tingling her cheeks and teasing her hair. In the distance, silent islands lay all about, their shallows littered with shambling palisades. She could just pick out small figures on the nearest sandbank, knee deep in sludge, and prodding in the mud for shellfish.

The exhilaration of being on water! The village in which she'd been raised, Riversley, was thirty miles from the sea, and her parents had taken her to the coast only once, on a day trip to Bournemouth. They had gone by coach and she had been sick on the way, but she had loved every minute of that day and begged to go again. It was too expensive, her parents had said, and when she'd persisted, her mother had pronounced the town vulgar.

Leo reached across and clasped her hand. 'Enjoying the ride?' He had to raise his voice to be heard over the sounds of water and wind.

For a while, Nancy had forgotten yesterday's horror, forgotten the sense of foreboding she seemed unable to shake off.

'I am,' she said. 'It's wonderful.'

'I hope you like the Lido as much. It should be reasonably quiet today. The *casinò* will still be going great guns, but the film festival chaps will have packed up and gone.'

'Are we going to the *casinò*?'

He laughed. 'Not unless you fancy gambling your lire away. I booked a table at the Hotel des Bains first thing this morning. We're a bit early but I'm sure the hotel will cope. I thought you'd like it—it's reminiscent of the old Lido. A bit stuffy perhaps, but the building is beautiful.'

They were nearing the jetty now and she could see the Hotel des Bains standing proud of a wide beach with its parasols and sunbeds arranged in military fashion. She half stood to get a better view, holding tightly to the side of the boat.

'It's just like a picture I saw—when I was very young—it was in a library book, *Bathing in the Lido* it was called, and I loved it. All the women were in Edwardian bustles and holding frilled sunshades.'

'It's not quite as buzzing these days.'

'Maybe not, but it looks peaceful. More peaceful than the Cipriani, at least.'

She was hoping to prompt him into talking of Archie. His assistant had behaved very badly at the reception, yet Leo had allowed it to pass without comment. Did he know what was behind the enmity between Archie and Salvatore and wasn't saying? There was so much about her husband she didn't know, and it worried her.

The boatman was manoeuvring the vessel alongside the jetty and tossed a rope over one of the mooring posts, pulling it tight until they were both ashore. The smell of the sea hit her anew and the sound of cicadas filled her ears as they walked towards the immense white square of hotel.

It was an idyllic picture, but her mind was still busy with the quarrel they had witnessed. 'Have you any idea why Archie was fighting with that man?'

'None. Salvatore is a friendly enough chap. At least, I've found him so. Dino loaned me his yacht for a few days when I was here two years ago and Salvatore tooled me around the islands.'

'So Archie knows him well?'

'Pretty much. I thought they were drinking buddies. Something must have gone awry.'

If they were drinking buddies, what on earth could Archie have said to provoke the man so badly? Might it have anything to do with the enquiries he'd promised to make? It was strange, too, that Leo appeared so unbothered by his assistant's behaviour, even though from the little Nancy knew of Archie Jago, it was wildly out of character.

'You didn't say anything to Archie before he left.'

'What would you have had me say?' There was a slight coldness to Leo's voice.

'He was embarrassing. He embarrassed you.'

'True, but then he excused us from staying on at the party, and here we are at the Lido.' He waved his hand expansively. 'And just look at that view.'

They had reached the end of the jetty and he'd turned to

face the distant city. She turned, too, and together they gazed across the lagoon at a hazy Venice, its skyline crowded with campaniles and domes and the familiar red rooftops, and here and there a fluttering flag.

'It's wonderful.'

'Quite something, eh?'

He took her hand again and they walked on towards the uniformed man standing rigidly at the hotel's entrance. Hotel des Bains was very different from the Cipriani, which despite its luxury had felt intimate—the modest lobby, the garden, the peacocks even, had made her feel at home. Here the splendour was more intimidating.

'Rather grand, isn't it?' Leo whispered, as the maitre d' showed them to a table nestled between a gigantic potted plant and a pillar of pink marble. 'But worth a visit, I hope. It's a pity we don't have bathing costumes with us.' He gestured to the terrace that ran the length of the dining room and, beyond that, to the beach and the sea. Nancy was quite happy they had left costumes behind—she had never learned to swim.

There followed a lengthy consultation with the waiter over what they should order as an *antipasto*, what for the *primo*, the *secondo*, and which wine should accompany each course. But when, at last, he left them, she found herself returning to Archie. She didn't understand why and, after Leo's small coldness earlier, feared her husband wouldn't either. It seemed almost a compulsion.

'Does Archie often behave like that?'

'Not often.'

'So sometimes?' she persisted.

'Archie is a complicated chap, Nancy. He's efficient, hard-working, generally friendly. And really, best left to his own devices.'

'I thought that as he was an employee—'

Leo's mouth tightened, his expression no longer resigned. 'He is, but he's also a man who fought alongside me.'

'You were in the army together?' That was yet another thing she hadn't known about Leo.

'We joined up the same year and being Cornishmen ended up together in the Duke of Cornwall's Light Infantry. I owe Archie my life—he came to my rescue at Dunkirk.'

She felt slightly ashamed, but it went some way to explaining Leo's predilection for a man she had found rough and ill-mannered.

'You must have been surprised when you joined up and found he was in the same regiment.'

Leo nodded. 'I saw his name on the list and guessed he was a Jago from Port Madron, so I asked for him as my batman. We were from the same village after all.' Though it might as well have been a different planet, Nancy thought, remembering Archie's caustic words.

'We served together for a few years, then both of us were posted—to separate regiments. Archie had made corporal by then, though he was the equal of any officer.'

'You would have known him before the war, I suppose?' Archie had denied it, but she'd found that difficult to believe. 'Port Madron must be quite small.'

Leo didn't immediately answer but began fidgeting with his cutlery, moving a dessert fork and spoon to one side and then moving them back again.

'It is, but I don't think I ever met Archie. Not properly. I may have glimpsed him in the distance—he has any number of strapping brothers and they all look much alike. His mother would come to our house most weeks, to Penleven, with fish to sell, and she'd stay for a cup of tea in the kitchen. I met her there once or twice—Cook was always my favourite and I spent a good deal of time with her—but I didn't see Morwenna Jago very often. Mostly I was at school.'

The first course had arrived and Nancy took up her knife and fork. 'This looks delicious.'

The beef carpaccio and horseradish *was* delicious and for a while she was content to eat. But Archie was an itch that wouldn't go away. He was an irritant—that was the reason— she told herself. Nothing more.

'I'm sure he is a good worker,' she said, 'but what made you employ him? He told me his family were fishermen.'

'Not everyone in a family follows the same path.' Leo's voice was reproving. 'And Archie could never cope with the sea. Every time he went out on the *Morwenna*, that's the Jagos' boat, he was seasick. Becoming a fisherman was never an option for him.'

'Seasick?' She almost choked on a mouthful of beef. It seemed so unlikely. 'He doesn't seem to have a problem travelling around Venice.'

'Catching a vaporetto is very different from going out on a fishing boat in high seas. Archie is seasick all right. And that makes it difficult for a Port Madron man to find work. I met him one day after we'd both left the army. I was down at Penleven to see my family, and walking back from the village when Archie passed me driving a van. He'd got casual work doing a few deliveries here and there, but essentially he was unemployed—a lot of men were after the war. But I was over-employed and needed help. I'd gained some success as an art pundit and my life had exploded.'

More than some success, Nancy knew. Leo was the youngest professor with whom her colleagues had ever worked. But her husband was habitually modest, insisting it was the large number of good men killed in the war that had made room for those who survived.

'Anyway,' Leo went on, 'I was finding the diary appointments, the travel arrangements, that sort of thing, pretty overwhelming. Archie could drive and he'd worked in the adjutant's office so I knew he could manage paperwork. I offered him the chance to come up to London and work for me. The house in Cavendish Street had plenty of room and I gave him the top floor.'

She had been amazed at how spacious a townhouse could be. When Leo had found her, tearstained and terrified, knowing for sure that someone—and it had to be Philip— had access to her flat, he'd taken her back to Cavendish Street. After her parents' cramped bungalow, it had been a revelation. The house was warm and welcoming and above all, safe. She'd known she would have to go back to the torn underwear and *Jezebel* scrawled in red lipstick across the wall, but for that moment she had felt secure.

She shook herself free of the dangerous memories, as the waiter removed their dishes with a practised swoop and served the crab linguine. 'The food is fabulous. And this is a fabulous day.' She gave Leo a brilliant smile.

'I think so, too. Let's forget Archie and his transgressions. I'll see he behaves in the future. After lunch we can walk on the beach—even if we don't swim. You can take off those very smart shoes and feel the sand between your toes.'

*

An hour later Nancy was enjoying the warm silk of sand beneath her feet. When she bent to gather up her shoes, Leo was before her, scooping them into one hand and holding her tight with the other.

'Tell me about your years at Cambridge,' she said, as they began a stroll along the beach. She wanted to know all she could about her husband. And it might help to keep her mind from thinking too much.

'There's not much to tell. I was a model student—of course! And it was a relief, really, to get away from Penleven, to get away from Cornwall. Dad and Perry were businessmen, my brother still is. Art is wholly foreign to them.'

'And business is foreign to you? Mining didn't appeal?'

'Not remotely. Perry is four years older than me and spent his school holidays at Wheal Agnes with Dad. I spent mine with my mother—drawing, painting, sculpting.'

'You've never told me about her.' Nancy had wanted to ask, but hadn't found the right moment. Now seemed a good time.

'I still find it difficult to talk of her, even after all these years. She died when I was sixteen and it broke my heart. I lost a dear friend as well as a mother.'

'And a fellow artist?'

'A brilliant one in my view. Marriage and children meant she never fulfilled her potential. But isn't that the case with so many women? Her watercolours adorn every wall of Penleven.'

'I shall see them when I visit. What about Perry—has he inherited her talent, too?'

Leo laughed aloud. 'He'll tell you he doesn't understand art…'

'But he knows what he likes,' she finished for him.

'Exactly. I think for my father and brother I'm a cuckoo in the nest. I'd always painted and drawn, but when my mother died I decided I'd make art my career. In a way, it was a kind of homage. But it turned out to be right for me. My father was nonplussed. Art was fine as a hobby, he told me, but mining was what mattered. I would never make a living as an artist.'

'But he didn't try to stop you.' She was thinking of her own very different experience.

'I was the younger sibling, and he had Perry eager to take on the business. So I was allowed to go my own way. In the end I chickened out of being a starving artist and took the academic route. I think he was relieved—much safer financially—but he still has no real idea of what I do. I don't think Perry knows much more. They respect what I've achieved—at least I think they do—but I'm an oddity. When I go back to Penleven, there are a few casual enquiries about London and my travels, but then the talk reverts to Wheal Agnes. It's all about the mine.'

Nancy felt a new warmth towards her husband. She, too, had been a cuckoo in the nest. The Nicholson home had provided food and shelter, an attempt at love, she thought, but little understanding. She had never felt she belonged, and shared with Leo the same lack of connection to the family that had reared her.

But today was not one for sadness. Today she walked in a world of warmth, of pleasure, of well-being. A flotilla of little boats puttered by, a rower passed them taking his daily exercise, and in the distance she could see a horse and rider galloping across the sands.

They had been tracing a path beside the water's edge as they walked, and Nancy was tempted. 'Why don't I paddle? The water looks so good.'

'Why don't you?'

'Come and join me.'

'Better not. One drowned guest will be enough for the Hotel des Bains.'

She let go of his hand and hitched up her skirt. 'You'll just have to watch me having fun then.'

And truffling her feet through the wet sand, she skipped and jumped over the small waves that broke on the beach. When she had thoroughly saturated the skirt of her best dress, she walked back to him and took his hand.

'I'll have to dry off before they'll let me into the hotel again.'

'I hope you haven't ruined that beautiful frock.'

'I hope so, too. But today I'm not going to care.'

She felt blissfully light and free—until a sudden fear assailed her. 'I shouldn't be this happy,' she said.

'What nonsense.'

'Maybe, but I have a dark feeling. That poor woman… and then what happened in London.'

'You're to think of neither.' His grip on her hand became painful. 'You can't help Marta Moretto and as for what happened in London, that's over. I'm your husband and I'll protect you.'

'You are a kind man, Leo.'

'More nonsense! I'm not kind, I love you.' He stopped walking and dropped her shoes on to the sand. His arms went round her and his lips found hers. 'I love you very much, Nancy. Rescuing you from that crazy man was by the by.'

She kissed him back as tenderly as she could. She knew he loved her in a way she doubted she'd ever match, but she wanted very much to bring him pleasure. 'Hardly by the by,' she said, trying to lighten the moment. 'You barely knew me at the time.'

'Enough to realise you would make me very happy. And I want to make *you* as happy. It worries me that I won't; it's worried me from the moment I met you. I'm so much older and I never believed you could care for a middle-aged man. It was only your troubles that brought me properly into your life. I suppose I should thank Philip March for something.'

'You're not middle-aged,' she said stoutly. 'And in any case, age is unimportant. You make me happy. You're making me happy right now.'

For that moment, it was true. The sound of bells was

drifting towards them across the lagoon, the swish of the sea was in her ears, the sun on her skin and the smell of oleander in the air. She wished she could stay here for ever.

Chapter Eight

Nancy was out of bed early the next morning to kiss her husband goodbye: two more days and the conference would be over. Their afternoon at the Lido had brought them closer together, and she was looking forward to spending more time with him. Today she felt a new confidence, her worries fading that she had acted precipitately in marrying, had taken advantage of Leo's feelings for her. She had done the right thing. There would always be a small doubt deep within, an unease she would never quite lose, but she was surer than ever that she had chosen sensibly. Stalked by a man intent on hurting her, she had found in Leo a refuge.

Her parents had refused even to speak to her after she had broken the engagement with Philip March, she had disappointed them so completely. She *was* a disappointment, she acknowledged. First her determination to attend art school—they had been so vehemently opposed and only a small legacy from her godmother had enabled her to go — then the gossip she'd provoked among the neighbours when as a young girl she'd left home to live alone in London, and the final ignominy for them, her rejection of a man she should think herself lucky to have won. At twenty-eight she was most definitely on the shelf and Philip was a prize. How could she be so ungrateful?

The day Nancy had taken Philip March home for the first

time was incised in her memory. The effect on her parents had been magical. For so long they had tried, without success, to interest her in whatever unfortunate man they'd managed to inveigle. Whenever she went home to Riversley, someone would appear at the door to escort her to a dinner party—how had her mother engineered those invitations, she wondered? Or to the village fair, or a local show. Her parents had even gone to the extreme—for them—of inviting a young man to stay, a final and doomed throw of the dice.

So when Philip March had stood on their doorstep, a courteous greeting on his lips, they had been rendered silent. Amazed, overjoyed. Here was a man of quality, one they could never have hoped for. A London journalist no less, with a stable job and a good income. And prospects. That word, so important to the Nicholsons, rang loud and clear. Nancy had been relieved at their reaction. More than relieved, she had been delighted, feeling at last that she belonged, that she was the daughter her parents had always wanted. But it had been too good to last, and it hadn't.

*

When she went downstairs for breakfast Concetta was busy in the kitchen, arranging brioche for the oven and setting the coffee to heat.

'I'll eat here, if that's all right with you,' she said to the maid. The dining room was too imposing for a solitary breakfast.

But before she could fetch a plate, Archie appeared in the doorway. He looked pale but otherwise unaffected by yesterday's scuffle. 'If you want to speak to Luisa Mancini, you better come now,' he said brusquely.

Nancy gaped at him. 'You found her? How did you find her?'

He ignored the question. 'She's at the Rialto market and she shops early, so either wait for breakfast or come with me.'

'I'll come,' she said hastily. 'Sorry, Concetta, I have to go. Keep some brioche warm.'

'And the coffee, Mrs Tremayne?'

'Have a cup for me.'

She rushed out of the kitchen and up the small spiral staircase that led to their living quarters, then across the immense book-lined space that functioned as a landing and into the salon to retrieve her handbag.

Archie had gone ahead and she found him waiting for her by the gates. 'We need to be quick or she'll be gone,' he said. 'And it's the only chance you'll get of seeing her. I don't know where she lives and I can't ask.'

'Why not? And how do you know she'll be at the market?'

'It's a long story.'

'Then tell me as we go. And for goodness sake, don't walk so quickly. I can't keep up.' She saw him give a brief glance at her feet. 'And don't criticise—I'm wearing sensible shoes.'

His mouth gave the small twist that seemed to substitute for a smile. 'Okay, but you're the one who's desperate to see this lady.'

'So how did you find her?'

'She's Salvatore's wife.'

Nancy stopped in her tracks, forcing him to stop, too. He looked annoyed at this further delay.

'Salvatore's wife? You didn't know he was married to Luisa?'

'Why would I? We've drunk together several times, but I've only met him in bars. I've never been home with him. And won't be going any time soon.'

Archie turned and marched on and she followed, breathing hard. Slowly, a light began to dawn. 'Is that what you were fighting about yesterday?' she said to his back.

'Not fighting, Mrs Tremayne. A slight disagreement.'

'One in which you knocked him to the floor. I'd say that was more than slight. And stop calling me Mrs Tremayne. It gets on my nerves.'

'Regretting it are you? The Mrs bit?'

She was astonished at his impudence and furious. 'No, I am not regretting my marriage. And how dare you suggest it?' She tried to find a calmer tone. 'My name is Nancy. It's a perfectly good name—use it.'

He shrugged. 'As you wish.'

They walked on in silence, Archie navigating a path towards Santa Maria Formosa—Nancy vaguely recognised the square—then across several bridges, past a bewildering array of dead ends and on through a series of twisting alleys, the houses on either side seeming to close in and almost touch each other. In daylight they gave the impression of warmth and seclusion, the windows open, bedding hung on balconies to air, while a canary in a cage chirped his morning song. But in darkness, with the streets ill-lit and the windows shuttered, these alleys would take on a very different appearance. It would not be somewhere Nancy would choose to walk alone.

They emerged from a particularly narrow corridor to find themselves amid a wall of noise and movement. Crowds of tourists filled the street, idling among shops selling every kind of souvenir—postcards, ornaments, silk scarves—while housewives, intent on their daily business, were forced to push a way through to the other side of the market, to stalls loaded with fruit and vegetables.

Here there were juicy peaches, piled high alongside oranges from Sicily. Onion strings hung from poles, lettuce flopped in untidy heaps and pieces of artichoke floated in buckets. It was a splendid sight, but led Nancy to ask despairingly, 'How on earth are we to find her in all of this?'

'We won't. She won't be here. We need to walk further on to the fish market.' As he spoke, he ducked to avoid a man carrying a huge conical basket on his back, filled to the brim with potatoes.

She grabbed at Archie's arm. 'We're to go to the fish market now? Before we do, I want to know why you argued with Salvatore. If we find his wife, I don't want to be talking to her not knowing what happened between the pair of you.'

Archie frowned, but pulled her to one side, out of the path of hurrying shoppers. 'All I did was ask him if he knew a Luisa Mancini. I figured he was a Venetian, about the right age, and he might know her or have heard of her. It turns out he married her—who would have thought? And he got very Italian about it. Accused me of running after his wife.'

'Why would he think that?'

'Like I said, he's Italian. He put two and two together and made five. He thought I must have known her before they married. So I was an old lover and I'd come back for some repeat action. I tried to tell him I'd no interest in Luisa, that I was asking for someone else, but he'd got this fixed idea in his head and he wouldn't let it go. He'd also been drinking.'

'So had you.'

'True.' His mouth gave another small twist. 'Anyway, I had to land him one to quieten him down.'

Before she realised, Archie was off again, weaving a path through the crowd and she had to rush to catch him up. 'It certainly quietened him down,' she said. 'But how do you know Luisa will be at the fish market?'

'Because Salvatore wants to eat fish tonight.'

'But *how* do you know?' The man was infuriating.

'Simple. He told me.'

Nancy grabbed his arm again and pulled him to a halt.

'You're going to tell me exactly what happened. Why did he tell you where his wife would be, when he was fighting you over her? And when did you speak to him?'

'I went to his favourite bar last night and made him listen. I told him that personally I had no interest in his wife, but my boss's wife did and she was driving me crazy. I told him Mrs Tremayne wanted to speak to Luisa about a man she'd known when she was young. A Mario Bozzato. The name acted like a charm. *Oh him*, Salvatore said. Mario, it seems, is a bit of a loser. The upshot is that I'm allowed to find his wife and then hand her over to you.'

She supposed she should be grateful that Archie had deigned to tell her this much, and she let go of his arm. They walked on, zigzagging a path through the crowds that packed the vegetable market to reach the side of the Grand Canal. She hadn't seen the famous waterway at such close quarters before, and it seemed to her more like a river than a canal. It was as busy as any grand boulevard, hosting a churn of gondolas, water taxis, vaporetti and delivery boats.

They were soon at the fish market, though Nancy had smelt it long before it came into sight. In the dawn hours fleets of barges had brought the day's supplies and now the stalls were filled to brimming with creatures of the lagoon: wriggling eels, fine red mullets, crabs, small flat fish, all lying damp and cool on stalls lined with green fronds.

'Does Luisa know we're looking for her?' she asked.

'She should, and with a bit of luck she'll be looking for us, too.'

Most of the women busily inspecting the fish were middle-aged, a number elderly. Very few were young women, since at this time of the day the market was no place for small children. Presumably Luisa and Salvatore had not yet become parents.

At a stall a little to the left, Nancy saw a tall young woman wearing a sleeveless blouse and full skirt, her bare arms and legs tanned and golden. A bright red lipstick defied tradition and no doubt scandalised her family. But women's lives seemed to be changing, even in Italy. They wanted more, Nancy thought—greater independence, wider opportunity.

Luisa was waiting her turn to be served, but looking around expectantly.

'I bet that's her,' Nancy said.

'Probably. Nice legs. Salvatore has taste.'

'You can go now.' She would have liked to hit him, but settled for sounding severe.

He saluted, making her feel stupid. 'Right away, Mrs Tremayne. Sorry... Nancy. I'll be back at the vegetable market.'

Without another word to him, she walked over to the young woman. 'Luisa?'

The girl smiled brightly back. 'You are Mrs Tremayne?'

'Yes. Nancy.' She held out her hand. 'Can you spare me a minute? After you've done your shopping, of course.'

The man behind the stall clicked his fingers impatiently and Luisa hurried to choose a pair of grey mullets, reaching into her basket for money to pay for them.

'Can I buy you a coffee?' Nancy asked, when the fish were safely stowed. She had noticed a shabby café close by. It was unlikely anyone would take much notice of them there.

Luisa nodded agreement and they were soon ensconced at a small table tucked to one side of the café's frayed awning. From here the noise of the market reached them clearly, but it suited Nancy. She had no wish to be overheard.

'I'm sorry if Mr Jago's enquiry has made things difficult,' she began, 'between you and your husband.'

'*Puff*. Salvatore is *idiota*. But he is a man, what can you

63

expect? And you want to ask me about another man?'

Nancy found she could follow the girl's Italian quite comfortably and was grateful Luisa was willing to go straight to the point. 'Yes. Mario Bozzato—I believe you knew him when you were younger. Were you at school with him? And Angelica Moretto?'

Luisa shook her head. 'I was at school with Angelica but not Mario. He was older. That is why Angelica liked him. At first. She was *lusingata*. He was twenty and she was a schoolgirl still.'

So Angelica had been flattered by Mario's attention. 'How old was she at the time?' Nancy asked.

Luisa put her head on one side while she thought. 'Sixteen, no maybe seventeen.'

'How did she meet Mario if it wasn't at school?' It seemed strange to Nancy that these two could have become friends, and more, if Marta Moretto were such a controlling person.

'At church. Angelica was very religious. She went to mass every day. And then Mario started going. I think he saw her in the street and decided to go to church so he could meet her.'

'And her mother, Signora Moretto? Did she know Mario?'

Luisa waggled her head. 'A little. But he was not important to her.'

This ran contrary to everything Bozzato had said in the square yesterday. 'She didn't mind Angelica being friends with him then?'

Luisa thought again. 'I remember Angelica telling me her mother said he was too old for her.'

'So that's why the signora broke them up?'

Luisa stared and Nancy tried again. 'That's why her mother stopped Angelica seeing him?'

'Signora Moretto did nothing. It was Angelica who said goodbye.'

Nancy's eyes widened. 'She dumped him?' she said in English.

'What is this "dumped"?'

'Sorry.' Nancy reverted to Italian once more. 'She told him to go away?'

'*Certo*. He was always—do this, do that, you wear this, you must come. Angelica was a strong girl. She did not like orders. *And* he made a big fuss. He did not like she went to church so much. It was God or him, I think. And she chose God.'

'Is that why she escaped to a convent? To get rid of him?'

'A little it was to escape, but she wanted to go. I don't understand it, but she said the life was right for her.'

'And her mother. Did Marta want her daughter to become a nun?'

'I think not, but it was Angelica's life, her choice.'

'I heard—somewhere or other—that Angelica left the convent a while ago. I wonder if you've seen her?'

Luisa shook her head.

'Do you think Mario has?'

'Not if Angelica saw him first.' Luisa leant back in her chair, a wide grin on her face.

Nancy was puzzled. 'He seems to think she will marry him in the next few weeks.'

The girl put down her empty coffee cup, her hand shaking from a fit of giggles. 'I must go.' She looked down at her almost empty basket. 'I must shop more.'

'And I'm holding you up.'

'No matter. I have told you what you wanted to know?'

'Oh yes, more than I could have hoped. Thank you so much.'

The girl's large brown eyes glinted. 'That Mario. He is a jerk, no?'

Nancy was taken aback that this lovely girl should use

such an insult, but she couldn't help laughing. 'I think so,' she agreed.

*

She found Archie looking morosely at a pile of aubergines. 'Can't stand them,' he said. 'And they're in everything you eat here.'

'Never mind the aubergines, I must tell you what Luisa said.'

'Do I need to know?'

'Yes, you're helping me.' She said it decidedly. The only way to deal with Archie Jago, she'd decided, was to confront him head on. 'I'll tell you as we walk back.'

This time the walk was more like a saunter and she was grateful for it. 'Apparently Marta Moretto had nothing to do with her daughter going into the convent. She didn't much like Mario, but then no one seems to have liked him very much—but she didn't forbid her daughter to see him. It was Angelica who decided to dump him.'

'Who could blame her? But why a convent?'

'Mario turned out to be controlling. He wanted to organise her life.'

'Becoming a nun seems a pretty drastic solution.'

'Well… she *was* very religious and she must have felt a calling. But I think it was probably a way to escape, too. Sometimes people do the most extreme things if they feel trapped.'

'Like getting married, you mean?'

She kept walking, but froze inside. It was as though he had looked into her soul. But then she gave herself a mental shake and went into battle. 'Why do you say that?'

'I'm not stupid. You meet Leo a couple of times, he brings you back to the house crying fit to bust, and the next thing while I'm away is that you're married. I can put two and two together, but in my case I make four.'

'I doubt it. You know nothing about my marriage and your assumptions are insulting. l love Leo.'

'Yeah, of course you do.'

Their walk to the palazzo gates was completed in silence.

Chapter Nine

Nancy was still furious from the spat with Archie Jago when she went downstairs to find Concetta. The domesticity of the kitchen was comforting. The long wooden table had been scrubbed, the range black-leaded, and the terracotta floor shone with new polish. How one small woman could make this rambling pile sparkle—their living quarters were immaculate—was a miracle.

Archie had disappeared almost immediately on an errand for Leo, and Nancy felt huge relief to be alone except for the maid. Leo had said his assistant was a complicated man and she had to agree. Archie never lost the opportunity to mock the marriage she'd made, yet he had gone out of his way to find Luisa for her and organise a meeting. Had that been to save Leo embarrassment or had Archie genuinely wanted to help? Why would he though? He'd shown her nothing but hostility since he'd returned from Cornwall and found Leo married. Archie was certainly complicated.

'Any chance of a late brioche and coffee?' she asked from the doorway. Concetta was preparing their lunchtime salad and singing quietly to herself. 'You sound happy.' Nancy took a seat at the table. 'Did you get a bargain this morning?'

The maid waged an unending war with the local *fruttivendolo* over his prices, but she still continued to shop in the square. If she couldn't buy what she wanted locally, she didn't buy it.

'The salad too much money.' Concetta dropped the knife she was wielding and waved her hands in the air. 'But fresh this morning—from Sant' Erasmo.' She pointed to the lettuce waiting to be washed. 'And I have olives, a good cheese, tomatoes to cook.'

'I love your roasted tomatoes.'

Concetta nodded. 'Mr Leo, too. Here—some brioche still in the oven.'

She tipped several into a basket and took the coffee pot from the stove. 'But I sing because of good news.' She wiped her hands on her apron and came over to the table with the brioche and coffee, sitting down opposite Nancy. 'This morning I hear from my friend in the *panetteria* when I buy the bread. *She* hears from another friend who has a *cugino*—'

'A cousin?'

'*Sì*, a cousin in the hospital.' Concetta got up to retrieve the knife from the draining board and made a slicing movement. 'Where they do this. To dead people.'

Nancy blenched. 'A post-mortem.'

The maid nodded. 'And it is decided: Signora Moretto has an accident. She takes too much medicine.'

'I see.' But Nancy's mind was already rejecting the verdict. 'Do you know what kind of medicine?'

'Pills. Too many pills for the pain. I have same pain.' And she thrust her hand forward for Nancy to see. The fingers on her right hand had begun to curl inwards, and the knuckles were raised and distorted. Arthritis? That would certainly tally with the bad limp Nancy had noticed when the signora had backed away from a furious Bozzato.

'Do you know the type of pills the signora took? Do you take them, too?'

'No, no.' Concetta shook her head violently and waggled

the knife. 'No pills. But the signora has a new one—something like *zona*? The cousin say it comes from America.' She tutted. 'America is wonderful, but this pill dangerous, I think.'

Nancy finished her brioche and dusted off the crumbs. A second strong cup of coffee was making her head buzz. 'Why dangerous?'

The maid turned her head in circles to demonstrate. '*Confusa.*'

'I understand. You think Signora Moretto took pills that made her dizzy and that's why she fell from the balcony?'

'*Sì*. Too many pills. A mistake. But happy for the family. She was good Catholic and now they bury the poor lady.'

'You were fond of the signora?'

Concetta's face broke into a sad smile. 'I work many years for her. When I am young maid, you understand. I look after little girl when the signora at work. This is very shocking for people, but what can she do? Her husband dead, her children too young. Luca is at school but Angelica only—'and she indicated a height with her hand. 'A lovely *bambina*. Accident is good. Good for family.' She gave a long sigh, closing the conversation.

The post-mortem was over and the death certificate would register an accident. It would mean the police could strike the incident at La Fenice from their list of enquiries. And perhaps it had been accidental, Nancy thought, perhaps she had been making something out of nothing. It was what the *portinaio* at the theatre had suggested yesterday. But deep down, she remained unconvinced. How could a small woman topple over a waist-high barrier, no matter how confused? She must either have jumped or been pushed and from what little she knew of the woman, Marta Moretto would not have jumped.

But who was the assassin? Mario Bozzato had proved a dead end. According to Luisa, Marta had not been responsible for ending her daughter's relationship with him, and he had nothing for which to blame the woman. Yet he *had* blamed her, and angrily. Could he really be such a fantasist that he believed the only thing keeping him from the woman he loved was her mother?

Nancy took her cup and plate to the sink, deep in thought. Without realising, she turned the tap on hard and water gushed forth, drenching her arms. She hardly noticed. Those tablets—the maid had called them dangerous—but then for a woman such as Concetta, modern medicine could well seem dangerous. Could they be that risky?

Nancy had to find out. She needed to be on the move, to be doing something, and if her instincts were wrong and the tablets were indeed to blame, she could put this whole business out of her mind and finally enjoy the rest of her stay.

She must look for a library, but the only one she knew was at the Istituto Superiore, to all intents and purposes the university of Venice. She would go there, take one of Leo's business cards and hope it would smooth her passage to their reference section.

*

Ca' Foscari, the university building, was in Dorsoduro and necessitated another boat ride. According to the map, it was only a few streets away from the vaporetto stop of Ca' Rezzonico but, in the event, Nancy became hopelessly lost. It had all seemed quite simple in her bedroom, but it was many anxious enquiries later and much wading through some impossible dialect, that she finally walked through its main entrance on the widest bend of the Grand Canal. The courtyard of Ca' Foscari was the biggest she had ever seen and it was astonishing to think it had once been a private home. She turned full circle, looking up and around at the magnificent palace, its Gothic arches and carved window heads one immense rhythmic sequence.

Once inside, she headed for the *biblioteca*. The university, she knew, specialised in the arts along with classics and languages, so it was unlikely she would find a medical reference section. But there would be encyclopaedias and, if they were up to date, they might contain information on any new treatments for arthritis.

No one asked her for identification and she tucked Leo's card into her handbag and walked as confidently as she could towards the *biblioteca*. A number of students were at the small desks when she arrived, heads bent, pens in hand, and she chose a seat a little way away from them. The reference section was enormous and general encyclopaedias in English not easily located. It took her a good thirty minutes of wandering up and down the aisles to find the several volumes she wanted.

Her search for 'arthritis' produced long descriptions of the painful condition and several illustrations confirmed that arthritis was indeed Concetta's problem. From the maid's personal knowledge of her former mistress, it must have been Marta's problem, too. But doctors seemed to agree there was little the patient could do to alleviate suffering, other than taking an analgesic.

It was only when she heaved the third and final volume into place that Nancy saw mention of any new treatments. The book had been published earlier in the year and included recent advances in rheumatology, key among them a new wonder substance developed in America. That fitted with what the maid had said, and so did its name—Cortisone was not too far from Concetta's '*zona*'. The writer of the article seemed mesmerised by this miracle treatment. It could turn pain to nothing, transform twisted hands and feet into strong limbs again.

It was only when Nancy read to the end, she saw listed the possible side effects, the dangers Concetta had warned against. Dizziness was right there, just as the maid had suggested. But so, too, were changes in mood and behaviour, and more worryingly, depression and suicidal thoughts. Under the influence of the drug, Marta's death could well have been the accident it was assumed to be, or the suicide of which no one would speak.

*

Sitting on the trim little water bus as it chugged a purposeful path back to San Zaccaria, Nancy was close to giving up. The Moretto death was a mystery unlikely to be solved. But that thread of determination in her—stubbornness according to her parents—was nagging her to continue. Had her discoveries at the university made an essential difference to what she believed? The tablets in excess were dangerous, that much was certain, but how likely was Marta, an intelligent woman, to forget how many she had taken? If someone else had been involved though... had somehow ensured the signora took more than she should? By the time Nancy reached the palazzo gates, her belief in the murder was alive and well. She wouldn't give up just yet.

For the rest of the day, though, she must put it out of her head. This evening, Leo had promised her a special dinner to celebrate the end of the conference. '*There's a group meal at the Venice casinò,*' he'd said, '*but I can't stand another official get-together. We'll go somewhere small and intimate and eat by candlelight.*'

*

She wore the eau-de-nil crêpe again—she had few other

choices—but made sure to pin to its delicate bodice the antique brooch Leo had given her weeks ago. It had belonged to his mother and was precious to him. To her, too, now, and he looked delighted when he saw it.

She was touched he'd gone out of his way to dress in his smartest clothes: charcoal suit, pristine white shirt and a dashing silk tie. When he handed her into the gondola especially ordered for this evening, she was as near to feeling a princess as she'd ever been.

She had seen pictures of gondolas, plenty of them—who had not?—but she had never imagined for a moment that she would one day ride in one. And never realised until now quite how fast or how sturdy they were. On her first evening in Venice she had glimpsed them in the lamplight, riding side by side, and found them vaguely sinister. Lines of shiny black varnish, their ornamental prows glinting steel, they seemed gleaming talismans from a violent and long ago past.

But now, settled on an array of cushions, her feet sinking into thick carpet, she felt nothing but comfort. And complete ease. The gondolier, his toes facing outwards ballet style, was skilful in directing his lopsided craft along the network of small canals, until suddenly they were out in the lagoon. There was no wind tonight and the moonlight lay softly on the waters, a sheet of silver stretching into the distance. Above, a wide sky filled with stars.

'What do you think?' Leo sat facing her, his face pale in the moonlight.

'It's an experience I never thought I'd have.'

'You like it, though?'

'How could I not?'

He had gone to great lengths to make this evening special and part of her wished he hadn't—the feeling that she was an inadequate wife was never far away. Yet she would not have been human if she hadn't loved every minute of the journey and wanted its magic to stay with her. She lay back against the cushions, her fingers catching idly at the water, as they scythed through the lagoon.

In no time at all, though, the gondolier, his body twisted in the opposite direction, had spun the boat to his right and with a swing brought the vessel into the Grand Canal. They began a stately drift along the parade of magnificent palaces that lined both banks. Nancy noticed the way that water lapped constantly at their cellar steps, suggesting the damp and decay that lay beneath the splendour. A metaphor for life in Venice? But the moon's silver was everywhere, softening cracks and fading crumbling stone to an old, all-conquering beauty.

The gondolier was bringing the boat to the landing stage with a flourish, whipping his oars neatly out of the rowlocks to act as brakes and coming alongside in a surge of water. They had arrived at the restaurant.

She couldn't remember afterwards the name of everything she had eaten—she was still adrift on the gondola—but she knew it had tasted good, very good, and it was late when they left for home, Leo insisting on a nightcap after the bottle of wine they had shared.

'We'll walk, shall we? I can't go to bed just yet.'

'Nor me.' She tucked her hand in his. 'I'm happy to walk. As long as you know the way!'

'I'll do my very best, I promise.'

It was a quiet stroll, the tap of her heels loud on the warm stones as they sauntered through narrow streets, past shadowed courtyards and across deserted squares. There were few other people around: here and there a couple slowly making their way home, enjoying what was left of the beautiful evening. But when they reached the canal that fronted the palazzo, Leo stopped.

'Why don't we sit a while?' He pointed to the stairs that led down to a landing stage, where a solitary gondola danced on the coming tide as it waited for morning.

He took out a handkerchief and brushed whatever dust there was from the top step and she slipped down to sit beside him. For a while they were silent, feeling the gentle air on their faces and watching the light of an almost full moon shimmer over the canal and spill across the shuttered houses opposite as they lay sleeping in the day's warmth.

'I'm always sorry to leave Venice,' he said at last, 'and conference or not, it's been a very happy week.'

'It's been wonderful,' she agreed, slipping her arm around his waist and hugging him close. Tonight even the palazzo, cold and damp and inconvenient as it was, felt benign.

'We can come back,' he assured her. 'And next time, I'll make certain I'm not working. There are all kinds of treasures I wanted to show you, but there hasn't been time.'

'There will be, I'm sure. We've years ahead of us.'

There was a pause before he said, 'It's the next week or two I've been thinking about.' He threw a small twig into the canal and watched as it swirled its way under the nearest bridge.

Nancy was surprised, believing their plans already fixed. 'I thought we'd be returning to London. I know you have meetings there.'

'I have, but once they're over, I'd like us to travel down to Cornwall for a few days. I want to show you Penleven. More importantly I want you to meet my family. How would you feel about that?'

Nancy wasn't sure how she felt. She knew she should embrace Leo's home, Leo's family, but neither his father nor his brother had come to their wedding and meeting them for the first time was bound to be awkward.

As if he realised her thoughts, Leo said, 'Perry has written. I had a letter forwarded here a few days' ago. He's looking forward to meeting you.'

'And your father?'

'He has been a little unwell, but he'll be wanting to see us.'

Nancy suspected the illness was an excuse, but said nothing. She had the impression that Leo's father was as stuck in his ways as her own parents. He must have been shocked when his brilliant son announced out of the blue that he was about to acquire a wife, a girl nearly twenty years younger and one without any discernible advantage.

'It's important you get to know the area,' Leo said encouragingly. 'Not that we'll ever live in Port Madron, but it might give you a clue of how I came to be me!'

And that was what was missing, Nancy recognised. That deep sense of really knowing a person. She had come to know the surface Leo, the protective husband, the generous man for whom she felt genuine affection. But there had been moments in the days since they married that she'd glimpsed someone a little different, a Leo who could be cold, one who disliked being questioned, one who expected his wishes acted upon.

When they'd married, her knowledge of him had come entirely from his work—as a Renaissance expert consulted from time to time by Abingers. She had been helping with the hanging of a work that Leo had authenticated when they first met and been struck by the way he spoke to everyone in exactly the same manner—the porters, the chief curator, herself. And that was unusual. There was a strict hierarchy operating in the auction house, as in all others, and porters and a second assistant were rarely addressed directly.

After that they had spoken several times when he was visiting; she'd had the impression he'd come looking for her, but that had seemed outlandish. Until the day he found her in floods of tears over the gossip that was being spread around the firm and had taken immediate action to stop it. It was then she'd discovered she had a friend. But the person behind the professional expertise, behind the decisive action, the kind gesture—Leo's hinterland as it were—was unknown to her. As hers was to him.

As if to underline that point, he said, 'We should visit your parents, too. When you're ready. They ought to know you're married, Nancy. And Riversley sounds a beautiful village.'

It *was* beautiful, she acknowledged, but she had no intention of ever returning. And no intention of telling her parents of her marriage. Their refusal to help when she feared for her life had broken an already flimsy relationship. And crucially, she dare not tell them. They might still be in touch with Philip, and he could easily trace a Leo Tremayne. Trace Leo and he would trace her, and the terror would begin again.

'I'll show you around Riversley one day,' she said, her promise deliberately vague.

Chapter Ten

It was probably Nancy's worry that she would never fit into Penleven or feel part of Leo's family that made her confront Archie the next day. She caught his assistant, briefcase in hand, at the top of the marble staircase as he was about to leave. Leo was conveniently absent, tucked away in his office and writing a review of the conference.

'Could you come into the salon for a moment?' she asked.

Archie said nothing but followed her as far as the doorway.

'I wanted to thank you for finding Luisa Mancini.'

'All part of the service.'

Nancy quailed a little. She had dressed in her most business-like outfit and pulled her long hair into a tight knot, but against Archie's flippancy it was going to be difficult to say what she wanted.

'I'm grateful for your help, but I also want to clear the air with you. I know you're not happy that I've married Leo. I understand it's been a shock. You went home to visit your family and found me in Cavendish Street when you returned. But I'm here and married to Leo, whether you like it or not. So... whatever you think, keep it to yourself. No more remarks, please, casting doubt on my feelings.' She hoped she sounded authoritative.

He leaned against the doorway, his legs crossed at the ankles. 'You know what, Nancy—see, I'm learning—I don't give a tinker's cuss what your feelings are. I found Luisa for you, but that's an end to it. Don't bother me again. I've no intention of being dragged any further into your hare-brained schemes. In which case, we hardly need meet and you won't be bothered by my remarks.'

'It wasn't hare-brained,' she protested, losing something of her dignity. The careless way in which he draped himself against the door felt undermining and made it hard for her to stay in control.

'It was barmy,' he retorted. 'Mario Bozzato as the murderer? *If* there was a murder. Nobody, police included, have considered the possibility for a moment.'

'No one else saw what I saw. I know there was someone in that box.'

'You saw a shadow, that's what you said. How does that become a person?'

'I saw a moving shadow,' she said, stubbornly. 'After Marta… after she fell… I know there was someone there.'

'And have you told this to Leo?'

'No.' The suggestion jangled her nerves. 'Why would I?'

'Possibly because he knew the Moretto woman. Possibly because he's your husband. The question isn't why would you, it's why would you not.' He sounded animated. 'And the answer is simple. Because you're making a wild guess that's just got a lot wilder. What Luisa told you yesterday has thrown your grand theory out of the window.'

Nancy was surprised he spoke with so much energy. Moments ago he'd made it brutally clear she was on her own. But something about her search had caught his interest.

'I don't agree,' she said. 'I know everyone wants to believe it was an accident. It's convenient that Marta took pills for her arthritis. They could have made her dizzy, so she toppled over or, if people secretly think it was suicide, that she deliberately took them to dull the fear of falling. But there is a third possibility. She could have been fed the pills by someone else. They would have made her confused so that when the killer struck, she was unable to save herself.'

Archie's expression was derisive. 'Another load of inspired guesswork, and that's putting it politely. How do you come up with this stuff?' He detached himself from the door jamb and walked up to her, standing only inches away. He was not a tall man, but she felt menaced and took a step back.

'Let me spell it out for you,' he said. 'The old lady didn't like Mario B, but she didn't stop her daughter from seeing him. So what possible motive did he have? He had absolutely no reason to kill her, quite apart from the somewhat crucial fact that he lacked the opportunity.'

Nancy steadied herself. She had thought it through. 'It's not true that Mario lacked the opportunity. He could have got into the theatre in some way. He could have bought a ticket or sneaked past an usher when the man's back was turned. And as for motive, it's enough that he *thought* that Marta was working against him. He has this fantasy in his mind and he can't accept the truth, even now. Luisa laughed when I asked her if Angelica would be interested in him all these years later. She wouldn't be, but that's not what Mario wants to hear, so he tells himself a different story. The truth is too difficult for him. It's easier to accuse the signora of destroying his dream—and then destroy her.'

Archie shook his head pityingly. 'You *are* barmy. You've made him a killer without any evidence, other than a few minutes' angry exchange which you barely overheard, and his remark that he was pleased the woman was dead.'

She lowered her gaze, aware that the case against Bozzato was thin. 'I'm convinced Marta was killed. And Mario is the only possible suspect,' she muttered.

'Is he? I could have news for you. There just might be others in the frame.'

Was he playing with her? If so, it might explain his new-found interest. 'There is no one else and you know that,' she responded angrily.

'What about anyone who benefits from Marta Moretto's death. Does Mario?'

'He thinks he will.'

'His fantasy—yes, I get it. But who will really benefit? I'm talking worldly goods here, not some sick dream.'

She plumped herself down into one of the shabby armchairs that dotted every floor of the palazzo. Whenever she spoke to Archie, it felt like war. And it was exhausting. 'Her children, I imagine.'

'Precisely.' He strolled across to the sofa opposite and sank back into its brocaded depths, completely at ease. 'And who are her children? The girl is a nun or an ex-nun. Is she likely to be interested in running an antiques business? I think not. But the son is a different matter.'

'I met him at the Cipriani. Dino Di Maio introduced us.'

'And?'

'And I didn't greatly care for him.'

'Neither does his wife by all accounts.'

'You're being cryptic again. Tell me what you mean.'

He leaned forward, evidently pleased with what he had to say. 'Francesca Moretto is a very pampered lady, I understand. Wants only the best for her home, for her life. She's a gold-taps-in-the-bathroom kind of woman—oh, and has two sons who have to be sent abroad to very expensive boarding schools. It means that poor old Luca is in debt. And according to my drinking mates last night, badly in debt.'

'Are you saying that Marta's death will help him?'

'It has to, doesn't it? He gets control of the business.'

'He must already have a share. Would you kill your own mother simply for a bigger one?'

'You might if you're so far in debt. But according to my fellow drinkers, he doesn't in fact have a stake in the business. It's common knowledge that his mother kept a very tight reign. Luca was on a salary. He was probably paid extra on occasions, if the firm was doing well. But lately, word is that it wasn't. So... worth thinking about?'

Amazingly, Archie's interest appeared genuine, though it had little to do with her, she thought. But something had sparked his curiosity.

'Luca could have been at the theatre that night,' Nancy said slowly. 'But could he really have flung his mother to her death? I didn't like him, but I can't believe that.'

'Yet you're prepared to believe Bozzato did. Did you know there's talk that Moretto is to be sold?'

She nodded. 'Dino mentioned it.'

'The business may not have been going great guns, but it's still worth money. A lot of money would be my guess. It occupies a prestigious position and the land alone would fetch a fortune. But if it were sold when the old lady was alive, the proceeds would have flowed into Mamma Moretto's coffers. Her son would have had to make do with whatever she was willing to hand over, which by all accounts wouldn't have been very much. So a motive for murder? Much better than Mario, the fantasist.'

'It might be, but for one thing.'

Archie got up, fidgeting with the briefcase he carried. 'What's that?'

'Luca isn't going to sell. He intends to keep trading.'

'You know that for a fact?' Archie frowned, annoyed perhaps that his suspect had been dismissed as quickly as hers. 'Who told you?'

'Dino. He mentioned the negotiations with the buyers from Florence. Dino has been the middle man.' Archie raised a satirical eyebrow. 'Yes, I know, he would be. But he knew what he was talking about. He seemed deflated that the sale might not go through now.'

'And because Luca isn't selling, you're back to your fantasist? It still won't fly. Mario would have to be seriously deranged to murder for a pipe dream.'

'I think he is.' For Archie, it was ridiculous that a man would behave in such a fashion, but it was too near Nancy's own experience for her to dismiss it.

He spread his hands, shrugging off the suggestion, and making for the door. 'I had a Mario in my life,' she said to his retreating form. 'And I thought *him* capable of murder.'

He stopped and walked back to her. 'When was this?'

'Recently.'

'Did Leo know?' His eyes locked with hers, and she was startled once more at how blue they were.

'He knew.'

There was a pause and she could see his mind turning. 'And then he came to your rescue. So that's what this is all about.'

He didn't specify what he meant by 'this', but he didn't need to.

'Leo and I are very happy together,' she said.

He gave a sour smile. 'Who could doubt it?'

*

When he'd gone, she went up to her bedroom feeling bruised, as she so often did after talking to Archie. It seemed that at every turn he must accuse her of marrying for her own ends. In a way she had, but it didn't stop her caring for Leo, a man she admired as much for his good nature as for his professional expertise. Even if they were never to reach the heights of passion, it was surely possible to walk through life together in friendship.

And what, after all, was it to do with Archie Jago? He was her husband's employee, nothing more. So why did she want so desperately for him to believe she loved Leo and had married in good conscience? Deep down, she knew why. If she convinced Archie, she would convince herself—that she hadn't sold out for security, that this marriage would work, that temptation would not come her way. She thought of Archie's blue eyes and his negligent form draped across the doorway.

What on earth was she doing? Swiftly she shut her mind down and walked to the window. The soft splash of oars drifted through the open casement, then, further away, the swish of a light boat moving fast and the ripple of waves against the bulwarks of the canal. The sounds of an old Venice, defying the noise of the modern world. She felt her heartbeat settle.

Gradually she allowed herself to think again of Marta Moretto. Could Luca really be a suspect? If the signora had gone ahead with the sale, her son might not have benefited. Now she was dead, he was set to inherit the business. If he chose, he could continue with the buyers from Florence and easily pay off the debts he'd accumulated. So why was he intent on keeping Moretto going, particularly as the business was failing? Intent enough to kill, to stop the sale going ahead? But to murder his mother! It was unthinkable.

Tomorrow was Sunday and Leo had mentioned at breakfast that Dino di Maio had invited them to spend the day with him on the *Andiamo*, sailing to Burano and being treated to a splendid lunch. '*The weather's set fair,*' Leo had said, '*and I know you'll love the place.*' Nancy was reluctant to spend an entire day with Dino but, after her trip to the Lido, eager to see more of the outlying islands. She'd learned, too, that Signora Moretto's funeral was to be the day after, so a breezy Sunday spent on the water might be welcome.

Leo was going to the funeral. Despite his seeming lack of warmth for Marta, he had felt it right to attend, but had stressed that Nancy should feel no obligation to join him. She hadn't had to think about her response. Marta's strange words that afternoon on the Zattere, her shadowed face, her haunted eyes, and then the terrible image of a body falling, none of these had left Nancy for a moment. She would go to the funeral; it was the least she could do for the poor woman. She had managed so little else.

Chapter Eleven

A *motoscafo* arrived promptly at the palazzo's landing stage at ten the next morning. Dino, true to character, had sent the most luxurious boat plying the Venetian canals to take them to San Basilio. Nancy was the first one downstairs and waited at the landing stage, eager to board. Her husband arrived shortly after, with a last few instructions for Archie who had followed him down: two or three London appointments to confirm, a packet of books to despatch and several letters that needed answers. After Archie's fracas with Salvatore, it was as well, she thought, that he was staying behind.

'See if you can put this Morris chap off, Archie.' Leo frowned and handed over an envelope. 'He's a persistent blighter.'

'I'll try, but he'll almost certainly write again.'

'You can make my response as abrupt as you like. It might do the trick.'

'It might.' Archie looked dubious. 'I'm pretty sure it won't, though.'

'No, damn it. He's like that sergeant we had in the Second Battalion. What was his name?'

'Adamson?'

'Yes, you've got it.' Leo punched his companion lightly on the arm. 'Sergeant Adamson. My God, but wasn't he persistent? Kept coming to me with tales of gambling in the barracks even though he'd not a shred of evidence to back it up.'

Archie's face assumed a bland expression. 'Doesn't mean it wasn't going on, though, boss.'

'Was it?'

'That would be telling tales, wouldn't it?'

Both men laughed and Leo waved a goodbye, following Nancy into the boat's cabin. 'See what you can do anyway,' he called after Archie.

'I will. Have a good day.'

Nancy settled back on the embroidered seat, looking past tasselled curtains to the bustle of a Venice morning. The sun was hot and bright, the sky cloudless, and ahead were several blissful hours on water. The Giudecca Canal, glittering a thousand diamonds, was hectic with activity: water buses, ferries, gondolas, delivery barges, mingling in terrifying fashion but amazingly without mishap. A group of young boys were swimming off the Zattere and she smiled at the games they were playing.

She was getting used to this pampered lifestyle and it worried her. She had worked all her adult life and worked hard, and it felt strange to have hours every day free of necessity, free to do exactly as she pleased. When they returned to London, she could foresee a similar life emerging. Leo had a housekeeper, Mrs Brindley, whom Nancy had found dour and unbending in the short time she'd spent at Cavendish Street. It had been obvious the woman would not willingly relinquish control of the household, especially to a girl who'd appeared in her employer's life apparently out of nowhere.

As for a job, she could not return to Abingers, not married to Leo. He worked independently, but was regularly requested by the auction house to authenticate a painting, or sit on a particular committee, or represent them in the newspapers or on the wireless. For a married woman to work was difficult enough, but if she were to return to Abingers as a humble assistant, it would be embarrassing for him and awkward for her. She had to accept that her life there was over, but it left a void and it was one she needed to fill. Something other to pursue, a new goal to achieve.

In a moment of startling clarity she wondered if that was the real reason she was so intent on discovering the truth of Marta Moretto's death. Was it perhaps not the simple response she'd assumed, of one person to another, of sympathy for a woman who had not deserved such a fate from one who could help bring the perpetrator to justice, but rather a desire to find purpose in her own life?

'We'll be at San Basilio in ten minutes,' Leo said, seeming anxious at her continued silence.

'That's good, but in any case I'm enjoying the journey.' She smiled reassuringly.

*

Dino was waiting to greet them at the port. The sleek Italian suit had gone, but his yachting outfit was only a fraction less smart. A peaked white hat, she thought, that's all he needed to pose as the captain of an ocean-going liner.

'Leo and Nancy!' he exclaimed, as though he was surprised to see them. 'How wonderful. You have come.'

He slapped Leo vigorously on the back and raised Nancy's hand to his lips, a gallantry that made her feel awkward. But he was smiling and gracious, and evidently wished to be a good host.

'Please, come this way. You will find the yacht in excellent condition. I have had Salvatore polishing for the whole of yesterday!'

They followed him across the dock, their shadows dark against the expanse of concrete, and made their way to the commercial quay at the far side where the *Andiamo* was berthed. Nancy caught sight of a sharply cut prow and gleaming white bodywork, the yacht moving lazily on the gentlest of waves. Polished silver rails and glistening glass bore testimony to Salvatore's efforts. He was at the helm and waved to them. Beside him was a young boy—an apprentice, Nancy assumed.

They had reached the short gangway, Dino standing back to usher them on board, when a man bustled towards them from a nearby warehouse.

'Signor Di Maio, *buongiorno*. I have not seen you for so long.' The man spoke in rapid Italian.

'Signor Montisi.' Dino shook the man's hand—with reluctance, Nancy thought. 'These are my friends,' he said in English. 'Mrs Tremayne and Professor Leo Tremayne.' He turned back to them. 'Nancy, Leo, this is Signor Montisi. He is the Port Superintendent.'

'How very good to see you.' The man was a little too hearty and Nancy wondered why. Perhaps Dino was a very important customer and exerted unusual influence at the port.

She glanced sideways at her host, waiting for him to continue a conversation he had evidently hoped to avoid. He was no longer looking at Signor Montisi, but directly behind the man to a figure who had followed the Port Superintendent out of the brick-built warehouse. A younger man, as far as she could judge. She watched more closely. There seemed to be some kind of unspoken conversation going on between them, but then Dino turned to the Superintendent, his face wiped clean of expression.

'We must be going.' His tone was brisk, verging on

nervous. 'I am taking my friends to Burano for lunch and I'd like them to see as much of the island as possible.'

'The island is most beautiful,' Signor Montisi agreed.

'Who is your colleague?' Nancy's question came out of the blue. She hadn't meant to speak, but something about the young man's steady gaze disturbed her. As one, they turned to look at the figure silhouetted in the doorway.

'That is Pietro,' the Superintendent said, with a puzzled half laugh. 'He is my assistant. A very good assistant, too. Since he is in place, my lunch takes three hours!' And he gave another small laugh. 'But please, I am keeping you.'

One more round of handshakes followed before he turned back to his office. Nancy was first to walk up the gangway, but at the top she stopped to look across to where the young man still stood in the doorway watching the yacht. Watching Dino? Dino himself had turned his back, deliberately, or so it seemed, and was busy fussing over a consignment of wine being loaded on board.

It had been an odd incident. Pietro's appearance had certainly disconcerted their host. For once, Dino had lost his smooth polish. He'd seemed flurried, agitated even. But none of it showed when he finally climbed aboard and ushered them into a large cabin. After the glaring light of the quay, Nancy felt as though she had stepped into a black cave and it took a while for her eyes to adjust. Out of the darkness, a figure came towards them. A woman. And dressed in an emerald silk sheath that was the tightest Nancy had ever seen, skimming her body and leaving little to the imagination.

'This is Francesca Moretto.' Dino introduced her. 'She is joining us today. Francesca, let me introduce you to Nancy and Leo Tremayne.'

The woman nodded and extended a limp hand. 'How nice to meet you,' she said in English. Her tone of voice suggested she wasn't at all sure this was the case.

The engines had started up and they began to slide away from the dock. Leo smiled encouragingly at the woman. 'It's a beautiful day for a trip to the islands. We're very lucky.'

'Yes.' The word was almost dragged out of her.

'I take it your husband was unable to come,' he continued. 'Such a shame.'

Francesca gave a vague nod in Leo's direction. She had no intention, it seemed, of taking the conversation further, but continued to stand in the middle of the cabin and look around her, as though she was waiting for the entertainment to begin.

Nancy hardly knew what to make of her. She was amazed that Marta's daughter-in-law had come on a pleasure cruise so soon after the woman's death, but then Luca had attended the Cipriani party on the very next morning. Perhaps that was the way the Moretto family dealt with death. But why was only the wife here? And how would she find anything to say to the woman? She looked around for Leo, hoping for support, but with a murmured excuse he had joined Dino on the top deck.

With a sinking heart, Nancy turned to her fellow guest. 'I met your husband the other day,' she said, grappling for something, anything, to say. 'At the Cipriani.'

'Oh that.' Francesca's bored expression became more pronounced. 'So tedious these conferences, don't you think?'

'I don't know. I've never been to one,' Nancy confessed.

'You didn't attend? But then you wouldn't, I suppose.' She looked Nancy up and down.

She is mentally pigeonholing me, Nancy thought angrily. Fitting me into a box, the one for dimwits and hangers-on. But aloud, she kept her tone neutral.

'Your husband was at the hotel to represent Signora Moretto, I believe.' She wanted to see Francesca's reaction to the mention of her late mother-in law; it might offer a clue to Luca's own relationship with Marta.

'Now I think of it, I remember Luca coming back from the Cipriani. Not a great bash, I believe, but it's always possible to do some business at these things. A little flattering here and there, you know. And Luca is good at that.' Flattery might be her husband's sole attribute, the words implied, but not one Francesca herself chose to emulate.

Nancy felt sorrow for the dead woman. Her family seemed to have no feeling for her. There had been no expression of sadness or regret at her passing; her death had not rated even a mention, her absence at the Cipriani gone unnoticed. The party had simply been an opportunity to do business. And that word 'bash'. Where had that come from?

'You must have lived in England for some time,' she hazarded.

'Years. The most god-awful years of my life. Boarding schools! But I don't suppose you know about those either.'

For a moment, the woman's evident disdain crushed Nancy, but then a surge of indignation had her furiously biting back a retort—as a guest she felt constrained not to quarrel.

'Come on up, the two of you.'

Leo's voice saved her and she turned with the ghost of a smile to make for the staircase that led to the upper deck. This proved smaller than the one below, but a dining table and chairs sat above the bow and to the stern another open space filled with sunbeds and parasols.

Francesca had followed her, tottering dangerously up the stairs in four-inch heels, and looking annoyed.

'Sorry,' Dino was quick to say, as her head appeared at the top of the staircase. He helped her up the last two steps, but when she glanced at him, her eyes were cold. 'A little late, my dear,' she said sourly.

He stroked her arm. Sorry,' he said again, and Nancy saw Francesca's expression soften a little. 'You can pour me an *aperitivo* to make up for it.'

'Right away.'

Dino smiled at her and something in the smile made Nancy suddenly aware that she was in the presence of two lovers. Her first reaction was shock. At home such blatant immorality would have the lovers universally shunned, but she was in Italy and maybe they did things differently here. Venice, though, was a small town and a hotbed of gossip, she'd learned from Concetta. *No secrets*, the maid had said.

Nancy's second thought was for poor Luca, who must suffer greatly from the wagging tongues. She wondered if Leo had realised the situation, or perhaps he already knew. He must, if gossip was as rife as Concetta suggested. She could see why the woman was attracted, of course: Dino was wealthy, clever, stylish, and from what Nancy had seen of Luca, Francesca's husband was anything but. As well as being deeply in debt. A gold-tap kind of woman, Archie had said. He'd summed up Francesca precisely.

Dino waved them into the easy chairs. 'I've asked Salvatore to sail around some of the smaller islands on the way. More time for us to enjoy the sun and the sea.' He gestured towards a drinks trolley parked beneath the awning. 'Nancy—what will you have?'

'A juice, if you have one.'

'A bit tame for a jolly day out.' Francesca's tone was shrivelling. 'You don't drink?'

'Not at eleven in the morning.'

'You should try it some time. It does wonders for one's energy—and for one's skin.' Her eyes lasered in on Nancy's face.

Nancy schooled her expression to blandness, though she could happily have pushed this objectionable woman over the side. 'Thank you for the thought, but I'm sure a *succo d'arancia* will work just as well.' She might be a guest, but she would not be browbeaten.

'And Leo? How about you?' Dino asked.

'A juice for me, too. Much the best choice this early in the day.' There was a flash of anger in her husband's eyes as he spoke.

'So have you been to any more operas, Nancy?' Dino asked genially, in an effort to sidestep the growing hostility.

It was a tasteless question. Spectacularly so. She saw Francesca watching her closely and made an effort to change the subject. 'No, I haven't. I've been busy finding my way around Venice. I visited the Rialto the other day. The markets were amazing.'

'Tourists always find them fascinating.' Francesca laid back in her chair, manoeuvring a footstall into place with her feet.

'Not only tourists,' Nancy retorted. 'I met plenty of Venetians. Crowds of them shopping at every stall.'

'But shoppers of a certain kind, wouldn't you say?'

'The kind who need to buy food?' Leo intervened. 'Where do *you* shop, Francesca?'

She looked scandalised. 'I don't shop. I have a housekeeper for that. Don't you employ one? If not, Leo, you are treating your wife very badly.'

'We have Concetta,' Nancy said mildly, 'and she is excellent. She's made this a true holiday—for me at least.'

'A true honeymoon for both of you!' Dino assumed a false exuberance.

'Venice has been a beautiful city in which to spend our first days of married life,' Leo put in gallantly.

'Dino tells me you live in London. What do you do there, Nancy?' Francesca looked at her over her glass.

'Before I was married, I worked at Abingers. It's an auction house. Do you know it?'

'Should I?'

'I imagine you might. Moretto buy and sell works of art, don't they? Abingers auction them. I would guess there must be an occasional contact between the firms.'

Francesca puffed her lips. 'Perhaps, but I have little interest in the family business. What was your job at this… Abingers?'

'I was an assistant in the Fine Arts department.'

'An assistant?' The woman's tone left no doubt of her opinion.

'The work was varied and enjoyable. I catalogued, booked restorers, helped with auctions. Every day was different.'

'It sounds fascinating.' Francesca's smile barely reached her lips. 'And when you go back to London—I think Dino said you were returning soon—what will you be doing?'

'Yes, we'll be leaving any day now, but I'm not sure exactly what I'll be doing.' She looked across at Leo, who smiled but said nothing.

'I'm sure the auction house will want you back.' Francesca sipped at her *aperitivo*. She was already well into her second glass. 'Assistants must be very precious.'

Nancy had had enough of the blatant offensiveness and laid back in her chair, closing her eyes and allowing the sun to smother her in its warmth. The breeze was in her hair and on her face and she could hear the swishing of the waters as they cut a passage across the lagoon towards Burano. Gradually she fell into a dreamlike state, her mind empty, Francesca dismissed. It was enough.

Chapter Twelve

She came out of the dream when she felt Leo put his hand on her knee. 'We've arrived.'

Nancy opened her eyes and was astonished not to see the lagoon flowing past. They were in a narrow canal and berthed alongside a line of small boats. She walked to the boat's rail and looked across at the houses clustered around the harbour. Her first impression was of colour. Bright, dazzling colour— pink, orange, turquoise, yellow, white—an extraordinary rainbow that stretched as far as her eye could see.

'Is Burano what you expected?' Dino had come up behind her.

'I don't know what I expected. Something like the Lido, probably. But it's stunning. Is there a reason for the colours?'

'There's a legend the fishermen painted their homes the same colour as their boats, so that if they faced disaster at sea, the boat's colour would tell people at which door to knock and relay the sad news. Whatever the reason, the tradition has stayed.'

'It's like a real-life canvas painted by a Fauvist,' she said.

Leo had joined them and laughed. 'Spot on. Shall we go and explore this wonderful painting?'

'We'll leave you to do that together, my friend, if you don't mind. Francesca and I have seen Burano many times,' Dino said. 'But we'll meet you for lunch. I've made a reservation at

Da Romano at one o'clock. It's in the main street. I think you'll like it. The walls are covered in paintings—drawings and messages, too. Some of them from the very famous. Matisse, Miró, you'll see.'

'What a kind thought, Dino.' Leo put a hand on his friend's shoulder, while a silent Francesca remained slumped in her chair.

Nancy could understand—just about—what Francesca gained from this liaison, though it offended the moral principles instilled in her from childhood, but what Dino saw in this sulky, spoilt woman was a mystery.

She gathered up her sunhat and followed Leo down the gangway. Then, hand in hand, they strolled up the main street, taking delight in the brightly hued houses and competing with each other to find as many different colours as they could. Every house appeared to have a balcony filled with flowers as brilliant as the building itself. A woman peered over her flower boxes to look down on them, and in holiday mood they waved up at her.

They passed Da Romano half way along the street and paused for a moment to look through the open door into the trattoria's bright, airy space. 'I can see why artists come to this island,' Nancy said. 'It's a fantasy of colour.'

'It became popular after the First War, but I read somewhere that Leonardo da Vinci discovered Burano centuries before. I'm not sure if I believe that.'

'The island is quite isolated. I can't imagine what it would be like to live here in winter.'

'Tough, I think, and likely to get tougher if the waters continue to rise. Some of the figures presented at the conference were frightening. If the predictions are true, this place, the other islands, Venice itself, will be under threat and not too far into the future.'

It was what Marta had said, though she'd seemed resigned to the yearly flooding of her home. She had laughed at the suggestion that she might move house. Marta would never have moved, Nancy realised, she was part of the fabric of Venice. Only death could have moved her—and it had. Even on a pleasure outing like today's, Nancy's mind was never far from the tragedy, yet Marta's own family appeared to have brushed it from existence.

Trying hard to push the sadness away, she looked again at the beauty that surrounded her. 'I guess it's tourism that earns the island its money.'

'Visitors are certainly important,' Leo said, 'but fishing even more so. The seafood is magnificent—for a fraction of the price in Venice. I imagine Dino has already ordered our meal at Da Romano and it's sure to be fish, fish and more fish!'

'Do we have to go?'

Her husband stopped walking and stared at her.

She touched him lightly on the arm. 'I really don't want to share a meal with that appalling woman.'

'I agree. She is appalling.' Leo took her hand again. 'But we can't avoid it. Dino is a good friend and he's keen to give us a special day.'

Nancy shook her head despairingly. 'What on earth does he see in her? And what about her husband? Why isn't he here?'

'I think that's pretty obvious, but perhaps we shouldn't make judgements. We've no idea what goes on in a marriage.'

Was Leo thinking of his own? Theirs was an unlikely pairing and it was doubtful that anyone would ever guess the truth behind it.

'I still think it's odd that Luca hasn't come,' she said determinedly. 'And that young man at the port. That was odd, too.'

'What young man?' Leo frowned.

'Pietro, that was his name. There was something strange going on between him and Dino.'

'There's something strange going on here.' He ruffled her hair affectionately. 'Let's not worry about Dino—or Francesca. Let's enjoy the day as much as we can.'

Nancy said nothing but she knew she was right. There had been something disturbing about that young man's gaze, as though he knew Dino's secrets, was storing them up, enjoying the sense of power it gave him.

'What about this shop?' As they were passing, Leo's eye had been caught by a window display and he pulled her over to look.

A trio of lace sunshades sat proudly on a pedestal. 'They are beautiful!' she exclaimed. . 'Are they handmade, do you think?'

'Almost certainly. It's what many of the women do in Burano. Their lace is exported all over the world.'

She pressed her face to the window, taking in every curve and stitch of the three sunshades. 'They are exquisite.'

'Let's go in. You might see something else you like.'

Nancy thought it only too possible and all of it far too expensive. She glimpsed the price tag on the simple tablecloth displayed to one side of the sunshades and knew she was right. But she followed Leo inside and wandered along the shelves, admiring everything she saw. Runners and napkins to match the tablecloths, fans and collars, and fabulously worked blouses.

The shopkeeper came forward, a hopeful expression on his face. 'You would like to try?' He unhooked one of the blouses from its rack.

'No, no,' she said in a hurry. 'I'm afraid it's too expensive.'

'It is handmade. Needle lace,' the man said. 'Very difficult work—each woman makes only one stitch that is her own, so the garment must be passed from one to the other. That is why the work is expensive.'

'I can see.' Regret sounded in her voice.

'But we have cheaper,' the man was quick to point out. 'These are made by machine. Much cheaper.' He gestured to a second rack of blouses, but even from where Nancy stood, she could see the work was nowhere as fine.

'Maybe I'll be content with one small thing.'

'You should have the blouse,' Leo whispered in her ear. 'We have the money.'

She tried to smile. She knew he had the money, but she wanted no more spent on her. He had spent enough already, buying expensive presents, paying for a ceremony at the Fitzrovia Chapel, then a wedding breakfast at the Goring Hotel and now this honeymoon in Venice. She'd sometimes had the uneasy sense of being another of Leo's projects, and was determined that a blouse of handmade lace would not be added to the list.

'This is what I'd like.' She had seen a case of lace bookmarks, small and delicate. One of them depicted the Madonna and child and she swooped on it. 'This is quite lovely. And so unusual. I shall keep it with me always.'

Once the shopkeeper had wrapped the small present in coloured tissue and tied it with a satin ribbon, he presented it to her with a solemn handshake. 'If you are interested in Burano lace, signora, there is a School of Lace not far from here. You may visit and watch the women at work.'

'I'd love to see it.' She turned to Leo, her face alight. 'Can we go?'

He looked at his watch. 'I doubt we'll have the time. If you want to see the square and the church—oh, and its leaning bell tower—we won't make Da Romano by one.'

'Da Romano,' the man said, replacing the case of bookmarks. 'That used to be a lace factory many years ago. But then everything changes.'

*

They made it to the restaurant only five minutes late. Two jugs of local wine—a red and a white —were already on the table and it looked as though Francesca and perhaps Dino, too, had managed several glasses while they waited. Francesca tapped the crisp linen tablecloth with polished fingernails. She wore her customary bored expression.

'Have you finished being tourists?' she drawled. 'If so, we can order.'

'We've finished,' Leo said brusquely, 'and very enjoyable it was, too.'

Dino sprang into action, pulling out a chair for Nancy and handing her a menu covered in signatures. 'You see, Nancy, messages from the rich and famous who have enjoyed this restaurant. And an art gallery to browse as you eat.' His hands waved expansively at the walls.

The restaurant was certainly special—a treasure chest of artwork filled every available space—and Nancy tried to feel grateful for his thoughtfulness. But Francesca's presence made it difficult.

'After the *antipasto*, I think a *primo* of fish and asparagus risotto,' Dino was saying 'We've had it here before and it was excellent. What do you think?'

Leo spread his hands wide. 'We're happy to go with whatever you've chosen.'

'Good, good. Then a *secondo* perhaps of branzino al forno with a fresh salad. Dessert? We will have to see if we have the room.'

He beamed. Nancy thought that almost certainly she

would not. She was unsure how she was going to manage the three substantial courses he had already ordered. But by dint of leaving a little on her plate each time, manage them she did.

Conversation over the meal was desultory though Nancy tried, recounting how much she had enjoyed simply walking through the streets, how she'd liked the church with its mosaics and its beautiful old statues. And how astonished she'd been at the leaning tower.

'But souvenirs, Nancy, did you buy any?'

She was encouraged to unwrap the lace bookmark and show her small trophy. Francesca looked bewildered that anyone could have come away with so little.

*

Nancy walked back to the boat feeling very glad she had worn a dress with a forgiving waistline. A narrow sheath such as Francesca's would have given her immense trouble, not that she possessed any such dress or was ever likely to. Francesca herself had hardly eaten a mouthful of the bountiful lunch; it was no wonder she could pour herself into the dress.

Back on board, they took up position in the easy chairs and once Salvatore and his young helper began guiding the boat from its mooring, the regular thrum of the engines, the heat of the sun the sheer feeling of well-being, had Nancy slowly close her eyes and fall into a doze.

When she woke, Francesca had disappeared down the stairs and, though Nancy could feel her arms burning in the hot sun, she covered them with a scarf rather than joining the woman on the lower deck.

Dino had pulled his chair close to Leo's and was talking animatedly. 'You remember I wrote to you last spring?' he asked. 'After my house was burgled? I lost a whole room of paintings and it nearly broke my heart. I gave the police photographs of every missing item—the insurance company had copies on file—and the art fraud people circulated them around Europe. To be honest, I never thought I'd hear anything more. There's a lucrative smuggling racket between here and Albania, you know. I reckoned that's what had happened to my paintings.'

'But it's a closed country, isn't it—under Enver Hoxha?' Leo asked.

'There will always be openings for men who want money, and Albania has an interesting coastline. All that wild landscape, all those small coves where a boat can land unseen. I've heard there's a group of men there willing to move pictures around Europe almost overnight.' He tapped his nose. 'Men not to be tangled with.'

There was a pause, then he went on, 'But a few days ago, I had a call from Rome, from the art fraud chaps there. They think they've recovered two of my paintings.'

'That's good, but how did it happen?' Leo yawned, lying back in his chair, his face to the sun. He seemed to be finding it difficult to drum up the necessary interest.

'The pictures were sold. On the black market, of course. The scoundrel who stole my Chassériau, for instance, had money from some shady dealer, who then took his cut by passing the artwork off as his own property. I don't know how much the villains earned from the paintings, but it will be far less than they're worth. You would think the man who finally bought them would have suspected something. But no, the *stupido* paid up.'

'Maybe he didn't want to know they were stolen.'

'But then he *is* stupid. Because he took them to a dealer in Rome to be valued. The dealer immediately checked his list of stolen items, and *puff*: the man has no paintings.'

'The police are sure they're yours?' Leo asked lazily.

Dino nodded. 'They're fairly certain. And they're pretty good, the fellows who work in art fraud. They have to be, there's so much of it. But they want me to go down to Rome and identify the works. And I have to take with me as much paperwork as I can find.'

'Sounds good.'

'The thing is, Leo, I need an expert to come along—to testify that the paintings are what they appear to be.'

'Can't the dealer do that? The one who was asked to value them.'

'Apparently not. It has to be an independent expert, someone not involved in the theft in any way. And you *were* the chap who discovered the paintings.'

'One of them, Dino. And though I found it for you, I'm not an expert in the period. The nineteenth century is not my forte.'

'True, but you could do it, Leo. Would you consider coming with me?'

Her husband seemed to become aware that Nancy was no longer dozing. 'We'll talk about it later, shall we?'

The conversation moved on to the recent conference, and what might be the next step now that Leo was ready to establish the rescue fund, once he was back in London.

'We'll need to form a suitable committee, and that might be difficult,' he said. 'There are so many calls on people's time, particularly on those who can wield influence. But I'm armed now with the latest facts and figures and I'll do my very best.'

'You are a good chap.' Dino clapped his arm. 'Now what about a drink? Sitting around is thirsty work! Nancy would you care for another juice?'

'A glass of water will be fine,' she said. 'But first I must find the bathroom.'

'Down the stairs to the lower cabin, then walk to the front of the boat and you'll find another smaller staircase. Would you like me to escort you?'

She was quick to shake her head. 'I'm sure I'll have no problem finding it.'

'If you lose your way, Francesca is downstairs. She'll help you.'

Nancy had every intention of slipping past Francesca as silently as possible. When she reached the cabin, she saw the woman was fast asleep on the sofa, her mouth slightly open and breathing heavily. She would have loved to take a photograph, but scolded herself for the mean thought. Then it was down the second staircase, as directed, to what must be the hull of the boat, but at the bottom she hesitated. Right or left? It was something Dino had omitted to say. If she turned to the left, it looked as though she would come to a dead end. She chose the right.

The passage ran a fair way but she walked its length without finding a bathroom. Instead, a large wooden crate blocked her from going any further. It was unmarked and heavily bound with steel straps, though the lid seemed to have been prised off at some point.

She was surprised. It looked like heavy cargo and this was a luxury yacht. Why would a pleasure craft be transporting cargo? She bent down to take a closer look. Where the lid had been removed, it had not been firmly nailed down again, and there was some kind of raffia protruding, wrapping material perhaps. She bent closer and saw a flash of gold, or was that gold leaf? Either way, it looked very much as though it might be a picture frame.

She reached out to touch it through the narrow gap and instantly a large hand slammed heavily down on hers, trapping it painfully against the side of the box. She felt an initial shock, then terror as the old fear returned. A solid figure pressed close up to her, his grip like a vice, pressuring her hand to such an extent that she could feel every grain of the wood.

'You have lost your way, Mrs Tremayne?' The voice was devoid of expression.

It was Salvatore. He must have left his young helper at the wheel and crept up on her. And he had crept; she had not heard a sound. But Salvatore! He was Dino's captain, Luisa's husband, yet she felt menaced by him. She straightened up as best she could, but he continued to pin her tightly to the narrow space.

'I'm sorry.' She could feel her skin, already hot from the sun, burn more fiercely. 'Dino told me how to get to the bathroom, but not which way to turn when I got to the bottom of the stairs.'

'It is the other way.' He glared at her for a moment and she wondered what he would do. Leo was two staircases distant and would not hear her if she cried for help.

But then he said, 'Please—' and thrust out his arm out to steer her away.

She had no option but to retrace her steps along the passageway with Salvatore walking inches behind.

Chapter Thirteen

He touched her on the shoulder, pointing to a small door to the right of the stairs that she'd not noticed earlier. 'Here.'

In a few seconds she was in the bathroom and had locked the door behind her. She took a deep breath. Her pulse was still beating fast and her hand stung from Salvatore's grip. She ran cold water into the basin and slowly bathed her face.

What had that been about? She had stumbled on something she shouldn't have done, that much was obvious. But paintings? A large crate of them? A yacht was hardly the place to store expensive pictures, so they must be en route somewhere, though not to Burano it was clear.

And if it was a puzzle where the paintings were going, it was an equal puzzle where they had come from. Perhaps the boat was being chartered by a dealer in Venice to deliver artwork to one of the islands, but then why had Salvatore been so threatening? His attitude suggested the paintings were in some way illegitimate, and why after all would Dino turn his beautiful yacht into a delivery service?

Bewildered by this latest twist of events, Nancy stood, hands either side of the basin, staring hard into the mirror, trying almost to pierce the glass in an effort to find answers. Whatever was going on, Salvatore was in the thick of it. Then she remembered the young man at the quay, the assistant to the Port Superintendent. And that strange look he and Dino had exchanged. Was he in some way connected to these paintings? Was Dino?

But to suggest that Dino was involved in something bad was ridiculous. He was a wealthy man and well-respected in the city. There was the small fact, too, that he'd invited them on this pleasure trip and been happy for them to wander the boat at will. If there *was* something suspicious going on, he couldn't know about it.

She unlocked the bathroom door and looked down the passageway. There was no one in sight. Slipping quietly out, she began to climb the stairs, hardly noticing where she was going, her mind was in such turmoil. If she hadn't taken the wrong turning, she would be none the wiser, but now she had seen the crate she knew deep down that something was wrong.

When she emerged on the top deck, she saw that Leo had fallen into a doze—the meal and the sun and the rhythm of the boat had cast its spell on him. Dino was reading a magazine and she attempted a brief smile. He adjusted his sunglasses and smiled back. For a moment, she was tempted to ask him about the crate, but something made her decide otherwise, and she settled back in her chair and tried hard to enjoy the rest of the cruise.

*

Another *motoscafo* took them back to their palazzo. The temperature had dropped, as it often did on these September evenings, and she nestled close to Leo, wanting to speak of her discovery but not knowing how to start. Previously, she had dismissed the idea that such a wealthy man as Dino could be involved in anything dubious, but now she had begun to wonder. How likely was it that Salvatore's employer would be ignorant of what was on his own boat? If there was a simple explanation for what she'd found, her husband was the one who might have it. Leo knew their host well. They were friends, close friends, if Dino were to be believed.

'Dino mentioned you met at Cambridge,' she began, for want of a better way to introduce the subject.

'We did. We were students on the same course. History of Art.'

Being on the same course hardly seemed the kind of friendship Dino had suggested at the Cipriani. 'Did you spend much time with him at university?'

'We attended the same lectures when Dino decided to turn up, but I can't say we spent a lot of time together. I've probably seen more of him in Venice than in Cambridge. He had his own circle of friends and I had mine.'

'What kind of friends did he have?'

'Ones who preferred to play rather than work,' Leo said lightly.

'He doesn't sound too committed. Why do you think he went to Cambridge?'

'Dino is a clever man. And I imagine he liked the idea of having a Cambridge degree.'

'But if he didn't study…?'

'He studied some of the time, but was easily distracted. He'd go off to London for days. Brighter lights there.'

'It must have been an expensive lifestyle,' she hazarded. 'But I imagine he comes from a wealthy family.' It would be interesting to know where exactly his money had come from, Nancy thought.

'Dino doesn't have family. Both his parents were killed in a car accident a few years before he came to England. I think his father was reasonably well off—he had an important job at the oil refinery at Porto Marghera. He must have left Dino a fair amount and that probably helped him on his way.'

'Could money have come to him from elsewhere? He *is* very rich.'

Leo moved slightly to one side. She saw him staring at her in surprise. 'What do you mean?'

She was starting to wish she hadn't begun this. 'Nothing really.' Leo continued to stare and she hesitated. 'It's just that… it doesn't sound as though his father left him a huge fortune, yet Dino couldn't have been worried about getting a job after university or he'd have worked harder. So maybe he had money from somewhere else and didn't need to bother.'

'Well, whatever his situation, it didn't do him too much harm. He had a great time and took a Third. I was the boring one—intent on getting the best.'

She laid a hand on his knee. 'I can't imagine you were boring. And your studies paid off, didn't they, so maybe boring was better.'

'I wouldn't swear to that. Dino's the one who's ended up living in a magnificent palazzo and owning a yacht like the *Andiamo*.'

*

She was very tired when the *motoscafo* deposited them at the palazzo's landing stage, as much from the stress of her imaginings as from a day in the sun and fresh air. Leo took her hand and together they climbed the stairs to the first floor. Archie was waiting for them in the salon, a sheaf of papers in his hand.

'Good day?' he asked.

'Very good, thanks, Archie. But what have you got for me?'

'Sorry, boss. Some letters, arrived this morning. And a few others to sign—I'd like to get them off tonight if possible. I've had to change some of the arrangements we'd agreed for

London, but I'll go through it with you later.'

Leo sat down on the sofa and took off his shoes. 'Phew. That's better. They've been pinching me for the last hour. Did you get anything from home in the post? It must be time.'

'Yes,' Archie said in a toneless voice. 'Ma's back in hospital again.'

Leo jumped up sharply and walked over to his assistant. 'My dear chap, why didn't you say?' He put his hands on Archie's shoulders. 'I am so sorry.'

'I only heard this morning. After you'd left.'

'You must go home. Back to Cornwall. Forget the paperwork and just go.'

Archie shook his head. 'There's not much point. I'll leave when you do. I need to keep an eye on you, Leo. The last time I left for home, I found you married when I got back!'

'You can be sure I won't be doing that again!' The joke fell flat. 'But you should go. It's important you see your mother.'

'A few more days won't matter. Ma's condition isn't too serious. Still the same old heart murmur. She went back to work too soon, that's the problem. I told them but they never listen.'

'Your brothers are looking after things?'

'As best they can. They're pretty useless around the house, but Grace, my sister-in-law, goes in regularly. And they think Ma will be home again in a week or two.'

Leo walked back to the sofa and sat down again. When he spoke, he sounded diffident. 'What about losing her income? Bills to pay?'

Archie's lips closed in a fine line. 'It will be okay.'

'Look, Archie,' he said awkwardly. 'You know I'm always here. I mean if things get too difficult.'

'It's okay,' Archie repeated in a voice that made it clear the subject was closed.

Leo shuffled the neatly typed letters in his hands, a guilty look on his face. 'I'm sorry, old chap. These won't be any good. Not now. It's a damn nuisance, but I'm going to have to change arrangements again and that lands you with extra work, I'm afraid. The Moretto funeral is tomorrow, but the day after I'll be travelling to Rome. I should be back well before the end of the week—in fact, I'm hoping I'll be away a day at most. It will be safe to reschedule our London tickets for Friday.'

Archie looked resigned, but took back the papers and walked to the door.

'Oh, and while you're at the station,' Leo called after him, 'buy me a first class return to Rome for Tuesday—with a seat reservation. The early train?'

Archie nodded, his face expressionless. 'Shall I use the Italian account?'

'Yes, that would make—'

'Rome?' Nancy interrupted.

'That's right, darling. I don't know if you heard what Dino said, but the police are holding a couple of his paintings that were stolen when the palazzo was burgled, and he's asked me to authenticate one of them. It's tiresome, I must admit—I was hoping we'd start for home sooner. But it's a painting I helped him find and I feel duty bound to go.'

'And duty bound to leave me?'

Leo looked uncomfortable. 'I wouldn't put it quite like that.'

'I would. But perhaps I can come, too?' Nancy felt herself fizzing with annoyance.

'It's a nice idea, darling, but it's business. I think it best I go alone.' Leo picked up his shoes and began to carry them to the door. 'We'll visit Rome another time, I promise.'

'But I'd like to go with you on Tuesday. It surely won't be

a problem for Archie to buy two tickets.'

She had never before spoken to Leo in so definite a tone. Archie's eyebrows twitched and her husband remained standing awkwardly in the doorway. 'Can you wait a while?' he said to his assistant. 'I'll be back to sign the letters. Nancy, would you come upstairs for a moment?'

She followed him into the bedroom and he closed the door behind them, walking across the room to place the painful pair of shoes beneath one of the easy chairs. Then he turned to face her.

'I'd rather you didn't disagree with me in front of Archie. Or if you must, not quite so emphatically.'

His cool manner did nothing to placate her. 'And I would rather you didn't decide to leave Venice without telling me.'

'You're right. I should have mentioned it and I'm sorry. But I thought we could talk when we arrived home, then Archie was here wanting to get off and it was the obvious thing to ask him to get a ticket for Rome at the same time as he changed our London booking.'

'It might be obvious to you, Leo, but not to me.' She plumped herself down on the bed and looked across at the window. The sky had turned every shade of peach, a beautiful day coming to an end. 'I accept our marriage was unconventional, but however it came about, I am your wife and I deserve consideration.'

'Oh God, Nancy! Of course, you do. Forgive me for barging ahead without consulting you, but I honestly didn't think you'd want to come. I'm going on business and it will fill most of my time. You would be quite alone and I thought you'd hate that—being on your own in a city you don't know. You've never been to Rome, have you?'

'I've never been anywhere, as we both know.' Her voice was sharp. She was angry, but trying hard to keep control.

'I'll make sure we visit. Next spring perhaps? We'll stay at the St Regis and gallop round all the sites together—or nearly all, there's so much to see.' He was soothing her, like a parent with a fractious child.

'I would still prefer to go on Tuesday.'

She was infuriated by Leo's cavalier behaviour. This was their honeymoon. She'd understood the necessity for him to attend the conference. The arrangements had been in place well before there'd been any suggestion of a marriage. But this was different. They could have spent the next few days in this beautiful city together, a delightful interlude before they left for London and another round of Leo's busy schedule. Instead, to placate Dino, her husband was leaving her high and dry, and had decided to go without feeling any need to discuss it with her. She was that unimportant.

'Archie is waiting below,' Leo said, a slight snap in his voice. 'He'll want to get things sorted out this evening. I hope we can agree that it's sensible for you to stay.'

'I don't have much option, do I?'

He walked over to the bed and lifted her chin with one finger. 'We mustn't quarrel, Nancy. I'll be back from Rome before you realise I've even gone.'

'Fine,' she said brusquely. 'I'll do as you wish. I'll stay.'

'For goodness sake, a lot of women would be happy enough to do just that. You're in Venice, Nancy. Venice!' Her anger seemed at last to have pierced his façade of goodwill.

'I *am* in Venice, Leo. And I must thank you for bringing me here. I hope I sound grateful enough.'

He got up and walked to the door. 'I have to see Archie.' His voice had grown a few degrees colder.

She felt her stomach twist. It was the first serious disagreement they'd had, but she remained unrepentant. He paused in the doorway, looking back at her, his face impassive.

'I hardly dare ask, but are you still willing to accompany me to the funeral tomorrow?'

'Naturally. Marta means a lot to me,' she said pointedly.

Chapter Fourteen

She regretted their quarrel for the rest of that evening. Her husband hardly spoke. Instead he sat in the salon, his lap full of papers, seemingly reading his way through every report that had been produced for the conference. Nancy perched on the chair opposite, pretending to be immersed in her book, but in reality reading nothing. The words danced before her eyes and during the next hour she read and re-read the same page over and over. It was a relief when at ten o'clock she could fetch the tea tray that Concetta had left them. She drank a swift cup, then climbed the stairs to the bedroom.

But it was no better here. She had hoped the double bed might ease the situation, but Leo took an inordinate time in the bathroom and when he finally pulled the bedcovers back, it was to turn on his side, plumping the pillow beneath his head and resolutely ignoring her. He had never before treated her in this fashion, and though she was sorry to be at odds with him, his silence did nothing to lessen her anger.

She felt grateful to Leo. That was the wifely role after all—every agony aunt, every advice manual, stressed that wives were in debt to their husbands. Men brought them a much-needed security: they paid the housekeeping, the rates, taxes and insurance, and provided a sheltering roof. Leo had done all that and more. He had given her protection against a man who meant her actual harm.

But no matter how grateful, she couldn't allow her husband to treat her with indifference. Nancy had never pretended this was a love match, but even if it had been, she would have kicked against such high-handedness. He had apologised for not consulting her on the trip to Rome, but the apology had come late and was hardly fulsome. And when she'd refused to soften, he had become cold and unforgiving.

She felt bullied, stripped of the shelter she had purchased at such high personal cost. Tears came into her eyes and she had to scold herself severely. She was used to following a lonely path, and it was foolish of her to think that marriage could transform her life so completely.

For an hour or so she dozed, but always hovering on the brink of wakefulness. Beside her, Leo slept soundly, seemingly unaffected by their quarrel. But Nancy was still deeply upset, and after tossing and turning for minutes on end, abandoned the attempt to sleep and swung her legs to the floor, feeling with her feet for her slippers. Then slipped on her dressing gown and padded down the two flights of stairs to the kitchen.

It was a chilly space at this time of night and the thought of a hot cup of tea was appealing. She had only just lit the gas ring and filled a small saucepan with water when she heard a noise from above. She stopped, holding the saucepan mid-air. Had Leo woken and found her gone? Would he come looking for her?

But they were shoes she heard on the stairs, not the slap of bare feet, and it was Archie who ducked his head through the doorway and pulled up in surprise. For a second or two he looked directly at her. Nancy felt flustered and very conscious of how little she was wearing.

'Can't sleep?' he asked casually.

She nodded, trying to appear unconcerned, and put the water to boil. 'I'm making tea. Do you want a cup?'

'Yeah, thanks.' Archie's eyes rested on her for a moment before he walked quickly over to the long, wooden table, pulling a large envelope from his jacket pocket.

She glanced at the packet he'd thrown down. 'The ticket to Rome, I presume?'

'Amongst others.'

Nancy would have expected him to rejoice at her discomfort but he sounded awkward. She padded over to the refrigerator and peered inside. 'Do you want milk with your tea? There's not much left in the jug.'

'Black is fine. I need something to sober me up. Too many beers.'

She brought the tea over to the table and sat down, making sure she wrapped her dressing gown tightly around her.

Archie took a sip from his cup, and when he spoke he sounded unusually tentative. 'Why did the Rome thing turn into such a drama?'

Nancy paused before she answered. She wasn't entirely sure herself. 'I didn't mean it to. I had something I wanted to talk to Leo about—something important—and then he decided to go off to Rome at a moment's notice without even telling me.'

Archie made no response and for a while they sat drinking their tea without speaking. To Nancy's surprise, she found herself gradually relax. The silence was companionable and Archie seemed different—*she* seemed different. It was as though they'd left behind the daytime people they usually were.

'I'm sorry about your mother,' she said at last. 'I hadn't realised she was unwell.'

'There's no reason you would.'

'I hope you have better news in the next post.' She smiled at him, but his expression stayed serious.

'I doubt I'll hear anything before I get home. My brother isn't the best letter writer in the world.'

They relapsed into silence once more before Nancy suddenly asked, 'Who were you drinking with tonight?'

Archie's mouth gave a small twist. 'The usual suspects.'

'Was Salvatore there?'

'He was. And friendly. I didn't floor him again if that's what you're thinking.'

'It wasn't. But did he seem okay? Not nervous or worried?'

'Why do you ask? What's this about, Nancy?'

She took a deep breath before launching into the story of the crate she had found, the odd appearance of Pietro, and how Salvatore had scared her. When she had finished, she looked across at him hoping for a reaction.

But Archie remained unimpressed. 'The Pietro thing is a red herring. The bloke's job is to oversee shipping in and out of the port, so of course he was looking at Dino and the yacht. And the crate isn't a big deal either. Dino could be using it to store paintings before he gets around to hanging them.'

'Storing them on a yacht?'

'He's rich. He can do anything he likes.'

'Your chip is showing, Archie.'

'What's that supposed to mean?' His voice had regained its old edge and for the moment the spell was broken.

'I don't think you like successful people.'

'I've no problem with success when it's honestly earned, but not when I see people climbing the ladder on the backs of others.'

'Is that how you think of Leo?'

As soon as she spoke, Nancy wished she could unsay the words; the upset with Leo was making her needlessly bitter.

'Leo Tremayne is a good bloke,' Archie said gruffly, 'and I'm glad to work for him. He took me on when not many would. Rescued me from the ranks of the unemployed—or the uselessly employed.'

Something in his voice made Nancy reach out to him and fleetingly lay her hand on his. It was warm beneath her touch. 'I'm sorry. That wasn't fair of me. I know Leo is thoroughly good-hearted and it's hardly his fault he's been granted a charmed life.'

A golden life, and one that made it difficult for her husband to understand the narrow horizons against which others had to fight so hard. Unlike Archie and herself, Leo had never had to fight.

'The boss has made the most of the cards he was dealt, don't forget,' Archie said. 'Not everyone does. But Salvatore—you're sure he was threatening?'

'I know when I'm being threatened. And that crate—I reckon Dino must know something about those paintings.'

'He will do if he bought them!'

She shook her head. 'That makes no sense. If he'd bought them, Dino wouldn't store them in a crate at the bottom of his yacht. Think of the danger if the boat hit rough seas. He takes enormous care of his art collection, loves it with a passion. He was talking to Leo about the paintings he lost last spring and he said the burglary broke his heart. That's what the trip to Rome is about—for Leo to identify one of the paintings that was stolen.'

'What happened to the rest of the haul? The stuff that was stolen last spring?'

'The paintings ended up in Albania, or so Dino thinks. He mentioned a smuggling ring for stolen artwork. They sell the paintings to shady dealers around Europe who then sell them on to innocent buyers.'

Archie appeared to be thinking deeply. 'So… Dino learns about this smuggling ring when his own pictures are stolen. His captain will know about it, too. What if Salvatore decides to go into business himself? Maybe the crate you saw is destined for Albania.'

'You're suggesting that Salvatore is a thief? Or in league with thieves? But surely he couldn't use the boat to store stolen paintings without Dino knowing?'

'Perhaps Dino does know. They could be in the scam together. Dino is the contact, the fence, and Salvatore sails the stolen goods off to Albania.'

Nancy gave a small laugh. 'It's a great theory, but quite mad. Why on earth would Dino suddenly become a smuggler? Why become any kind of criminal when you're as wealthy as he is? Unless…' she broke off. A sudden thought had come to mind. 'Unless he's like Luca, and not as wealthy as everyone assumes… perhaps even in debt. Maybe having his pictures stolen tipped him over a financial edge—but gave him the idea.'

She spoke with suppressed excitement, but in her heart Nancy knew they were building a case out of nothing. All she had seen was a crate with—possibly—a stack of paintings inside.

'The crate could mean anything or nothing,' she said gloomily.

Archie put down his cup and stretched his arms above his head. 'It's a pretty stupid idea,' he agreed. 'Whatever Dino might get from fencing paintings, it would be a fraction of their true value. And the risk is enormous. If he needs money, why not set himself up as a legit dealer? He'd earn a lot more.'

'He wouldn't like it though, would he? He wouldn't like to be seen to need money.'

When Archie raised an eyebrow, she said, 'You know Dino

well enough. He would hate people to suspect his finances were shaky. Think how certain he is of his position, how at ease. And if he were ever suspected of money problems, his backers could withdraw their support. At the Cipriani he mentioned a consortium.'

Archie tapped his spoon on the table while he thought about it. 'The blokes he's involved with will be as wealthy as he is, I guess. You don't get that wealthy by being kind. And you're right, if he were in trouble, he couldn't let on or they'd pull their money out and that would finish him.'

Nancy picked up the empty cups and took them to the sink to wash. 'So maybe the possibility that someone is dealing in illegal goods isn't so ridiculous after all,' she said over her shoulder.

'It would be an extraordinary way for Dino to get money, but then the rich are extraordinary. And before you say anything, that's not my chip showing. They definitely don't play by the rules.'

'And you do?' Her smile took any sting from the words.

'Most of the time. But whatever's going on, you can't do anything about it. And why would you want to?'

'Marta,' she said slowly, realising for the first time what had been at the back of her mind all along.

'Not Marta Moretto again. What's she to do with it?'

'Selling stolen goods is a wild speculation, I know, but what if it were true and somehow Marta had found out?'

Nancy felt her heart beat a little quicker. Was Dino involved in a crime far greater than theft? She tried to calm herself, slowly drying her hands and then walking over to Archie, where he hovered in the doorway.

'Marta was the *doyenne* of Venice dealers and would have an ear to the ground for anything illegal going on in the art world here. What if she threatened to expose Dino? Wouldn't that be a motive for murder? He would be ruined, his whole life destroyed. And *he* was at the theatre that night. I only have his word he left for home before the signora fell.'

'I thought I was crazy suggesting Dino might be a fence, but you've just lost it completely. Go to bed, Nancy, and get some sleep. You look all-in.'

Chapter Fifteen

Nancy woke the next morning with a start. A shaft of sunlight had pierced the closed shutters and danced a path across the room to hit her squarely in the eyes. She scrabbled to the other side of the bed and realised she was alone. Grabbing her bedside clock, she brought the dial close to her eyes. Seven o'clock — she had not slept late as she feared.

Last night, she thought... it seemed almost a dream. Had she really sat talking to Archie, dressed in little more than a nightgown? She smiled to herself as she thought back to their conversation. They had come up with some improbable ideas, but it hadn't mattered. She had been desperate to tell someone of her suspicions, and it had felt good to talk. It should have been Leo, though, on the other side of the kitchen table.

Her husband was waiting for her in the dining room and it was immediately clear the chilliness between them was to continue. After Leo's curt *good morning,* silence descended. The two of them sat marooned at either end of the table — Archie had chosen to eat with Concetta.

Nancy cast a surreptitious glance at the figure sitting stiff and unbending at the head of the table. Leo wore a newly ironed white shirt with dark suit and tie, perfect attire for a funeral. It made the coming day even more of a trial — she'd had immense problems herself in finding anything suitable in her meagre wardrobe. In the end, she had chosen a dark grey and very unflattering skirt, along with a jacket of indeterminate colour. The clothes matched her mood which, as she'd dressed, had become steadily more downbeat. Now, sitting here, she felt drained of all energy, the bright spirits of recent days vanished. Even her tan seemed to have faded.

She took a brioche from the basket and pulled it into small pieces, but made no attempt to eat. Her appetite had fled along with her spirits and she was finding the continuing silence unnerving. From beneath lowered eyelashes, she studied her husband again, wondering how they could have descended into this miserable state so very quickly. As she did so, he looked up from his plate, and fixed her with his gaze. His soft brown eyes, usually so alert and lively, were filled with sadness and she suddenly felt incredibly guilty.

She jumped up from her seat and walked around the table, reaching out for his hand and clasping it in hers. In response, he got to his feet and put his arms around her waist, pulling her close to him and kissing the top of her head. Neither spoke for a long while.

'I'm sorry, Nancy,' he said at length. 'So very sorry. I didn't mean you to feel ignored. The last thing I would do is disregard you, after all you've been through.'

She felt tears rise to her eyes and hugged him tighter. It felt immensely good to be safe in his arms. 'I'm sorry, too,' she said. 'For getting angry. It was a stupid argument over nothing.'

'It was,' he agreed, letting his grip slacken and smoothing her hair back from her face. 'I've no appetite for going to Rome, and if I have to, I would love to take you with me. But that would be selfish. You'd have no company for most of the day and I doubt you'd find sightseeing much fun on your own. But I should have discussed it with you last night, on our way home. I've learnt my lesson—in future, we'll make decisions together.'

She gave his hand a last squeeze and went back to her seat, feeling able now to start on the brioche and coffee. She took a sip before she said, 'If you're still offering that spring trip to Rome, I'd like to go.'

'I'll make sure we visit for at least a week.' He laid his napkin to one side. 'But this business with Dino—I'm hoping I'll manage Rome and back in a day. All I'm required to do is confirm the picture they've impounded is the one he bought a year or so ago.'

The mention of Dino and his picture made Nancy uneasy, but she was reconciled with her husband and that was what was important. And she wasn't sorry after all not to be going to Rome. Since her midnight conversation with Archie, she'd had a growing sense that her place right now was in Venice. It was instinct only, but instinct was most often right.

Leo looked at his watch and pushed back his chair. 'We should be leaving soon. The funeral is at eleven and there's no *motoscafo* for us this morning. We're travelling peasant class, I'm afraid.'

'Don't worry, I love the vaporetti. They're much more fun, particularly when the water is choppy and they're ploughing through the lagoon. They're such... such rollicking little ships.'

'Rollicking and much less expensive! I'll rally the troops. Concetta will want to fetch her hat and veil, the full mourning, and Archie... I haven't seen him today, but I guess he's around. I need him to get on with changing those appointments yet again.'

Leo's assistant was waiting for him in the lobby. Archie was at his most businesslike, wishing Nancy a brief good morning and betraying no hint of their night-time meeting. It took him a matter of minutes to go through Leo's diary with him and decide how best to rearrange the various meetings he had in London.

It took a good deal longer for Concetta to finish her kitchen chores, find her coat and handbag, and then be satisfied that her headgear was pinned firmly enough to weather a journey across the lagoon. Eventually, they emerged from the palazzo, the maid still fussing with her veil and Leo looking anxiously at his watch as they set out for the walk to San Zaccaria.

It was a Monday morning, a normal working day, and they had supposed the water bus would keep to its regular timetable, but though one boat after another arrived at the vaporetto stop, none of them was a number four that would take them to the island of San Michele and the cemetery. Concetta began muttering to herself in thick dialect, clearly agitated they might be late for the service or even miss it entirely.

When, for one moment, she stopped muttering and started forward, they took notice. Not a vaporetto, though, but a funeral cortège, emerging from the Grand Canal and forging its way through the lagoon immediately past them. In the lead, a black-painted boat carrying a flower-laden wooden casket on its open deck, with a little flotilla of mourning gondolas following. The undertakers' men stood alongside the coffin, while the mourners, Nancy presumed, had taken shelter in the curtained cabin. Who would be behind those curtains? If this were Marta's cortège, Luca, for sure, together with his unpleasant wife. And the sister, no doubt. Angelica, of whom no one talked and no one had seen. But were there other relatives?

The passing of the cortège seemed to heighten Concetta's worries that she would be late, and once it had disappeared across the lagoon, she began to mutter even more frantically. Nancy's nerves were so thoroughly on edge that by the time a number four finally hove into view, she felt she had been given a very special present.

It was a bright morning but the wind was whipping across the open waters, ruffling its surface to an unusual degree. The vaporetto wallowed deeply, the helmsman in his little glass cabin intent on steering his course, while spray surged wildly around them. One stop followed another—Arsenale, Giardini, Sant' Elena—and Concetta had begun to twist the handle of the large raffia bag she carried, her lips again on the move, this time soundlessly. Leo frowned but said nothing, and the vaporetto ploughed on.

More delay faced them when they arrived at the San Michele landing stage. A huddle of small boats was rapidly becoming entangled as each craft backed and drifted in an attempt to moor. Nancy tried to make herself heard above the noise, bending low to speak to Concetta.

'Can all these people be for Signora Moretto?' She gestured to the confusion of mourners gathered on the landing stage.

The maid shook her head.

'Several funerals are often booked for around the same time.' Leo had overheard her question. 'The cemetery serves the whole of Venice—has done since Napoleon's time. We may have to battle our way through.'

He turned to help Concetta from the pitching vaporetto while Nancy made an undignified scramble onto dry land. A procession of mourners was making its stately progress through the cemetery and on towards the church, and the three of them followed, walking abreast along a wide path that flowed through large gardens studded with cypress trees.

The cemetery was filled with hundreds of graves, some exceptionally lavish with extravagant domes and avenging angels to guard their doorways. Every so often they passed a tomb containing portraits of the departed on its inner walls, as though the family had decided to meet together and discuss what had happened to one of their number.

They walked through this avenue of death in silence, feeling no need to speak, the solemnity of the day laying its touch on them. It came as a shock when they were hailed by a loud, cheerful voice.

'Leo, Nancy! How are you on this unhappy morning?'

It was Dino Di Maio in carefully chosen funeral garb. 'The sun has deserted us, I think.'

The sky had clouded over from its early morning brightness and was now settled into a dull grey, while the wind was dropping and the air becoming uncomfortably humid.

'It hasn't deterred these annoying creatures, though.' Dino swiped at his face. 'Mosquitoes, Nancy. They're a plague on San Michele at this time of the year. Do take care.'

She was glad she had worn long sleeves and stockings. Only her face was vulnerable and the wide brimmed black straw she had found in one of the palazzo's wardrobes should be ample protection.

'It's a busy morning, sun or not.' Leo pointed ahead towards the long straggle of people making their way to the corner of the island and the church of San Moisè.

But Dino had not stopped them for casual conversation and was quick to introduce his most pressing concern. 'You will be meeting me in Rome tomorrow, Leo?'

Her husband looked anxiously across at her and moved closer, nestling her hand in his. Leo gave his questioner a brief nod. 'I promised, didn't I, and I will. I understand we are to meet the police at the premises of the dealer who reported your paintings stolen.'

'Yes. I found that odd, but they wanted all of us to be present, including the man who did the reporting, and apparently he can't leave his shop. The appointment is at twelve. I hope that won't be too early for you.'

'Don't worry. I'll be there.'

'I would travel with you, old chap, but I've urgent business in Venice before I leave. It means hiring a helicopter to get to Rome on time. A bit of a bore and damn expensive.'

Nancy wondered what the urgent business might be. Was it something to do with the infamous crate, as she had begun to think of it? And why couldn't Leo have travelled in the same helicopter since he was doing Dino a favour?

'I'll make it up to you,' Dino said. 'I promise. Let's aim to get the business done in an hour or two. Then I'll take you out for the best lunch you've ever had.' He slapped Leo on the back. 'The meeting should go smoothly enough, and we can travel back on the train together. It's a red-letter day for me, Leo. A painting I love will soon be hanging in my home again.'

He gave them a careless wave and peeled off to greet effusively a couple walking a few paces behind. Nancy was glad when he had gone. She hadn't much liked Dino from the moment they'd met, but now her mind was filled with suspicion and she found it difficult to meet him with any semblance of cordiality.

Another few minutes along the wide path and they were walking into the church. Inside it was cool and austerely beautiful—white walls, white marble pillars, several arches of pale pink and grey, and only a chequered nave to add warmth. Leo ushered them into seats towards the rear of the church and Nancy allowed her gaze to wander over the wooden pews immediately in front of her and to one side. They were almost full. It was evident that Signora Moretto had been a popular or, at least, a greatly respected figure in Venice.

Her gaze travelled on to the pews at the very front of the church. These were reserved for the family of the deceased. She immediately made out Luca's shambling figure sitting to one side of the aisle and beside him a woman she took to be his wife, a jaunty piece of black lace on her head. It was what she would have expected Francesca to wear. But there was a looming space beside her, so where were the other members of Marta's family?

Nancy looked across the aisle from where husband and wife sat. Another figure knelt in prayer, a lone woman, her head and shoulders covered in a black veil. She had to be Angelica. The daughter, at last! But why had she chosen to sit apart from what was left of her small family? There was no time to ponder. The coffin was being carried down the aisle, and by men from the undertakers, or so Nancy assumed, since they were dressed in matching black suits and each wore a white rose in their lapel. The pall bearers, it seemed, were not friends or family, as Concetta had told her was the case for Italian funerals, but anonymous employees.

Nancy had not attended a church service for many years. Escape to London had meant escape from the rigid Sunday ritual her parents, strict Methodists, had observed. And since fleeing her Riversley home, she had never felt the need to return to church, not even in her lowest moments when she'd been frightened and despairing.

This was a Catholic service, too, so that once the priest began on the Latin funeral mass, she had to exert huge effort to understand even the bare outline of what was being said and done. It was fortunate the service was over quickly, but even so she felt a lingering unhappiness at its brevity. She had thought that someone, a family member perhaps, or a close friend, would have stood at the lectern to say a few well-chosen words in praise of Marta. But except for the priest, there had been only silence.

A final blessing and the large congregation waited in their pews to allow the family to leave first. Luca and his wife walked alone down the aisle, looking neither to right nor left. Angelica, though, made no attempt to accompany them. Instead, she waited in her pew until the church had mostly emptied of mourners before she rose slowly from her knees. Nancy had deliberately loitered, ignoring Leo's gentle nudge. She was desperate to see this mysterious woman and had her reward when Angelica, making her way towards the entrance, passed within a hair's breadth. She was tall and stately and, from the small glimpse the veil afforded, beautiful, too. A mystery indeed.

Chapter Sixteen

'We should join the rest of the mourners,' Leo urged. Concetta was already at the church door and Nancy picked up her bag and followed in the maid's footsteps.

Outside, a stream of people headed towards a newly dug grave at some distance from the church. It was a peaceful spot, away from the main path and overlooking the lagoon. Nancy stood beside her companions and listened to the priest deliver the final rites. She watched as one or two people detached themselves from the gathering and walked up to the open grave to throw a fistful of dirt or drop a flower onto the casket. Concetta, crying quietly, burrowed in her raffia bag and brought out the flower she had been carrying, then shuffled forward and threw it into the grave.

When the maid returned to stand beside them, Nancy reached out for her hand—it was evident Concetta had loved her former mistress greatly—but the attempt at comfort only made the woman cry harder. The maid's tears were difficult to bear. Nancy, herself, felt deeply saddened and she was relieved when, after a few minutes, Concetta began another shuffle through her bag and this time brought out a large, white handkerchief with which she wiped her face. It seemed to bring her a measure of calm, even when the air filled with the sounds of earth falling, shovel by shovel, onto the wooden coffin.

Nancy turned away, not wishing to witness this last act, and surreptitiously observed the people around her. She saw Luca and Francesca, with Dino a few yards away, but apart from them, she recognised no one. Though... was that Salvatore at the very edge of the group? And there, almost opposite him, was Angelica, not by the graveside with her brother and sister-in-law, but as far away as the situation would allow. Something very bad must have happened within the Moretto family to cause such a rupture.

After the incident on the *Andiamo* and her doubts about Dino, Nancy's suspicions that Luca might be involved in his mother's death had faded. But did Angelica suspect her brother of something bad? Was that the reason for their estrangement?

People had begun to move away from the graveside and Francesca disappeared into the distance—Nancy saw the small piece of black lace bobbing amongst the crowd. She imagined the woman would be making for Dino. Luca had stayed, though, and walked directly over to Salvatore. Their two heads were bent in earnest conversation. Why had Salvatore come? Did he know Signora Moretto or was he here at Dino's request? As far as Nancy could make out, he'd made no attempt to speak to his employer. She inched a little nearer but their voices were too low for her to catch anything other than the odd word.

Salvatore was engaged in something illegal—of that she was certain. And maybe Dino, too. But Luca? Were the trio involved in whatever wicked thing was going on, and had Marta found them out? Antiques, paintings, were her world, and if there was something dubious that involved her own son, wasn't it likely she would have discovered it? That would be motive enough for getting rid of her.

'A penny for them,' Leo said.

His voice startled her, she had been so deep in thought. Inexpertly, she batted away a buzzing mosquito and tried to excuse herself.

'Sorry. The day has been a bit overwhelming.'

'I know, but it's over—at least this part of it is—and I'm sure the signora would be happy for us to enjoy a good lunch. After that, I'm afraid I'll have to pack for Rome. As well as my professional judgement, Dino needs evidence to prove the painting's provenance and he's hoping I can help. I'm not sure I have anything in Venice that he can use. There may be the odd letter that would do the trick, but it's not something I expected to have to unearth. Hopefully Archie will bring his magic to bear.'

The three of them walked back to the landing stage along the winding path, passing a never-ending flow of visitors sauntering between graves and among flower beds. As they arrived at the vaporetto stop, a boat came steaming towards them on its way from Murano. Nancy was relieved that this time there would be no long wait; she would be glad to get off this island.

The water bus had drawn almost level with the landing stage, when a scuffle broke out behind them. She turned to look. It was Dino and a young man she had never seen before. He wore a pair of creased and slightly dirty linen trousers with a ragged shirt hanging loose. His bare feet were in sandals, the leather straps fraying badly.

As Nancy looked, he tugged at Dino's jacket sleeve and spoke in a low, angry voice. Equally angry, Dino threw off the detaining hand and tried to walk away. But the young man was persistent, following his quarry to the private *motoscafo* Dino had hired, clutching at his arm all the while, his voice rising in volume. Francesca, she saw, had already settled herself in the boat.

The vaporetto docked at that moment and Nancy had no option but to climb aboard. She made sure, though, to keep the *motoscafo* in sight. When Dino finally shook himself free of the boy's grasp, he almost ran to the boat, jumping across the gap to the deck and leaving his assailant, shoulders slumped, watching as the craft pulled away.

'My goodness, who was that?'

Leo shrugged. 'I've no idea but Dino is a wealthy man. I imagine he gets all kinds of cranks importuning him.'

He walked into the cabin and she went to follow, but then thought otherwise. 'Do you know who that was?' she asked Concetta quietly.

'The boy? He is painter.'

'Of houses?'

'No, no.' Concetta wagged her finger. 'You trick me. He is painter.' And she drew the shape of a canvas in the air. 'Renzo 'Astings. I know his mother.'

·'Hastings? But that's an English name.'

Concetta wagged her finger again. 'Not English. American.'

'The boy we saw is American?'

'*Sì*, but his mother born here. I know Sophia at school. Come—we sit down.'

'Before we do, tell me—why is he in Venice? And where are his parents?'

Concetta sighed quietly and leant her thin frame against a steel pillar. 'His father back in America, I think. His mother, who knows?'

'So he is on his own? I suppose that would explain his clothes.'

The maid nodded. 'No money,' she said succinctly. And before she could be detained any further, stepped into the cabin and found herself a seat.

Nancy said no more, but Concetta's words had sent her

mind whirring. The connection between that young man and Dino had to be paintings—what other could there be between a penniless artist and a wealthy collector? The crate she had found on the *Andiamo* had been filled with paintings, so was Renzo Hastings involved in whatever scam was being practised? And if so, how precisely?

He had come to San Michele when he looked as though he could barely afford the vaporetto fare. It had to be to find Dino. He must be desperate. He would know about the funeral—the whole of Venice must know—and the cemetery would be the one place this morning he could be certain of finding the man he sought. The one place, too, where he could actually get to him. There was no office door to act as barrier, no palazzo gates to hinder.

'That young man is a painter. He looked desperate,' she said aloud to Leo.

'He probably is—for work. Maybe in a weak moment Dino promised him a commission, but hasn't made good on it.' He took hold of her hand and smoothed it with his fingers. 'Don't be too concerned. There are a dozen young men in Venice like him, eking out some kind of living.'

She looked down at her hand lying in Leo's and knew she must tell him her suspicions. Renzo's appearance on the scene had convinced her, but even before that she had begun to think that Leo should know. It was her husband and not Archie to whom she should turn. It was Leo who loved her.

She shrank from the trial ahead but it was crucial she speak before Leo set off for Rome. He would be authenticating a picture he had helped Dino Di Maio buy and Nancy was concerned that his professional standing might be placed in jeopardy—if Dino were ever found to be involved in illegal dealings.

*

The search for the papers Leo needed was as prolonged as he'd feared, but by the time Concetta served the evening meal, his briefcase and a small overnight bag for emergencies were packed and waiting in the lobby. The two of them took their time over dinner—a bake of chicken and pasta and a shared bottle of Soave. Archie had disappeared to his own room on the fourth floor and a relaxing evening should have lain ahead. But once Concetta had cleared away and they had moved across the huge landing to the salon, Nancy took a deep breath and began on a speech she had been rehearsing for hours.

'Leo, there's something I need to talk to you about, before you leave for Rome.'

'I was hoping there wouldn't be too much talking this evening. After a sad day, kisses might be more in order.'

'Yes, those, too,' she said swiftly. 'But there is something worrying me and I need to tell you before you go.'

'That sounds ominous.' But he was smiling as he spoke. 'Come and sit down.' He pulled her onto the old sofa and for a second they rolled together. 'These springs don't get any better, do they?' He gave a small laugh. 'Now what is it? I can't have you worried—not any more.'

'It's Dino. I think he may be embroiled in something bad. And if he isn't, then Salvatore is. You seem quite involved with Dino's business and I think you may need to be careful.'

Leo's smile grew indulgent. 'Bad? In what way, apart from the Francesca affair? I can't imagine you want me to do anything about that little liaison.'

'No, of course not. I think it's shocking—they are so blatant—but it has nothing to do with us. It's a private matter. But this isn't.'

He looked at her expectantly and she steeled herself. 'Yesterday, when we were on Dino's yacht, I went to the bathroom on the bottom deck, but I walked the wrong way. In the gloom I nearly tripped against a wooden crate. I thought it strange that it was stored there, at the end of a passage that went nowhere. It was bound with steel hoops and quite plain with no indication of its contents. The lid must have been removed at some point, and then nailed back again, but not very securely. There was raffia, straw maybe, escaping from the gap that had been left.'

'Forgive me, darling, but is this going anywhere?'

'It is,' she said firmly. 'I bent down to look through the gap and I saw gold.'

'Real gold?' He looked bewildered, the indulgence gone from his face.

'Not real gold. Gold leaf, I think. The frame of a painting, that's what it looked like. I think the crate contained paintings.'

'It's possible. Dino is an avid collector. But you know that.'

'But if they were paintings he'd bought, why were they stuffed in a wooden box on his boat?'

'I've no idea. Perhaps he purchased them elsewhere—a place he'd visited on the yacht—and hadn't had time to unpack them. Does it matter?'

'It seemed to matter to Salvatore. He appeared out of nowhere and threatened me.'

'You must be mistaken. Why on earth would he do that?'

'That's the point. He wanted to deter me from exploring further. And I *am* quite sure he threatened me. I should know what that feels like by now.'

'It could simply be that Salvatore was protecting his employer. He obviously didn't like the sight of you poking around in his boss's possessions. And really, he was right.'

'But what if those possessions were stolen goods?' Last night's conversation with Archie loomed large in her thoughts.

Leo laughed out loud. 'Dino hoarding stolen paintings! My dear, he could probably buy the Accademia. I exaggerate, but no, he has no need to engage in criminal activity.'

'He might if he's not as wealthy as people think. Luca Moretto isn't, is he?'

'I've no detailed knowledge of Moretto's financial state, but if you mean that most of Venice knows his business hasn't been doing well, then his lack of funds is fairly common knowledge. But if people know that, they also know that Dino is very successful. And why would he be dealing in stolen pictures? It's a ridiculous suggestion.'

'There may be reasons,' she said stubbornly. Perhaps because of Leo's condescension, the theory she'd dismissed last night as foolish began to take on more solid form.

He laughed again. 'Do you think Dino put on a mask and climbed through windows with his swag bag? That would be a sight to see.'

'What I think is that someone did, or something like it. Maybe even Salvatore. And now the *Andiamo* is being used to transport the goods to Albania. Remember, Dino mentioned the traffic in illegal art to you?'

'Correct me if I'm wrong, but when he mentioned Albania, wasn't it because the paintings stolen from his own house had been shipped there, or so he believed?'

Leo's tone was no longer light-hearted and she drew slightly apart, a tight little knot in her stomach. 'It was. But it's possible, isn't it, that it gave him the notion—to use his yacht to transport stolen artwork to thieves in Albania?'

'You've been reading too many novels, Nancy! It's an absolutely crazy idea.' Leo jumped up from the sofa and poured himself coffee from the pot Concetta had left for them.

'You can mock,' she said, 'but there's a stack of paintings at the bottom of his yacht that can't be explained—and an employee who uses brute force to stop anyone investigating.'

Her husband made no response and maintained a cold silence. But Nancy would not give up. 'I think you need to be careful,' she repeated. 'That's all I'm saying. You're going to Rome to authenticate a painting that was stolen and possibly ended up in Albania. Isn't that so?'

'If the painting is the one I'm expecting to see, yes, I'll confirm it belongs to Dino,' he said heavily. 'I'm not sure where that leaves your fantastical claim.'

'In the same place as it was before. An unexplained crate. Who do those paintings belong to? Have there been any thefts of artwork recently? I think we should at least consider going to the police. They could search the yacht—maybe give it a clean bill of health—but if not, you won't be linked to it in any way.'

Leo had remained standing. 'It just gets crazier. I don't know whether to laugh or cry. But you can be sure I've no intention of going anywhere near the police with a story like that. What can you be thinking?'

Nancy had waded deep and now was not the time to stop. She would tell him the full extent of her suspicions and wait for the likely explosion. Archie had told her she was mad, but the more she thought about it, the more likely it seemed she had hit on a motive for Marta's murder.

She looked up at him from the sofa. 'What I'm thinking, Leo, is that stolen paintings may be the reason for Signora Moretto's death. If she discovered a scam and threatened to expose Dino, he might have taken drastic action to make sure she never spoke to the police.'

'Enough of this.' He sounded furious. 'It's not only mad, it's deeply insulting to Dino and I'll hear no more. Don't mention it again, and certainly don't repeat what you've just said beyond these four walls. I trust you haven't?'

'Not yet. But—'

'No buts, Nancy. There is widespread corruption in Italy, everyone knows that. And I don't doubt Dino has his fingers in all kinds of unsavoury pies, but your suggestion is frankly bonkers. As for my visit to Rome, I'm going there for a specific purpose—to authenticate one particular canvas. Once I've done that, I'll come straight back with no harm done. Then we'll make tracks for home, and by the sound of it that won't be a minute too soon.'

She could feel her mouth tighten and her teeth bite into her lips. She had no real evidence of Dino's wrongdoing and she knew her suspicions must sound wild, but she was disappointed that her husband had dismissed them without a second thought.

After a few tense minutes when neither of them spoke, he seemed to relent slightly. 'I appreciate your concern for me, my dear, but I'm in no danger and you can forget any fears you have.'

She wouldn't forget, she vowed to herself. And she wouldn't forget Leo's indifference, even disdain. She bristled at the way her husband had made no attempt to hide it. He believed he had reason, of course. He considered her mind blown to pieces by the trauma she had suffered and it was easy for him to dismiss her suspicions as an aberration to be ignored.

She could have carried on arguing. There was more she could have added—what, for instance, had been behind the agitated conversation between Luca and Salvatore at San Michele? But to continue would only alienate Leo further and it was not worth the risk.

Her silence made him put down his cup and walk over to the sofa. He pulled her to her feet and put his arms around her, holding her close. 'We must forget this conversation,' he said into her ear. 'And forget whatever you mistakenly think you've found. We leave Italy in a few days and we have a bright future ahead of us. We can't let this nonsense spoil it, Nancy. You do understand, don't you? Now how about that kiss?'

'I understand,' she said, and gave him the kiss he asked for. But understanding wouldn't stop her from digging deeper. Marta, newly laid to rest, was depending on her. Now more than ever.

Chapter Seventeen

L eo was awake very early, intent on catching one of the first trains out of Santa Lucia, and Nancy tumbled out of bed soon afterwards. Neither of them wanted more than strong coffee at this hour of the morning and in a very short while Leo was at the studded wooden door that led down to the courtyard, his bags by his side, waiting to say goodbye.

He had not mentioned Dino again since his insistence Nancy say no more of her suspicions, and she was glad. It would have led to a new coolness between them and would, in any case, have been futile: it was clear Leo would dismiss her fears as something to be expected from a woman who, for months, had lived in terror.

And it was true that she still found herself looking over her shoulder or hesitating as she rounded a corner, not so often here in Venice—it was unfamiliar territory—but certainly in London.

The night she had found her room destroyed, the walls smeared with ruined food, her china and chairs smashed—everything broken that could be broken—and the final horror, her bed despoiled, she had stumbled blindly from the wreckage, her legs no more substantial than a rag doll's. Then Leo had appeared. He'd called at the house, concerned for her safety, and found her shaking on the small landing. He'd been calm and reassuring, guiding her down the stairs and into the waiting cab. Back to Cavendish Street.

But even there, within the safety of his home, she had continued to see shadows. Every slam of a door, every squeak of a window hinge had her body stiffen and her soul freeze. Leo had been kindness itself, talking to her gently, comforting her, making tea in the middle of the night when she couldn't sleep for dark dreams. It was no wonder he assumed her concerns over Dino were fantasy, another token of the deep trouble she was battling.

There was something else, though, that made her hesitate to say more: a discomfort with Leo's association with Dino and with the Morettos. A small discomfort, it was true, but it felt to Nancy as though something were being hidden, though what that was and how important it might be, she had no idea.

'I've something for you,' Leo announced, as she arrived beside him in the lobby. 'Yesterday's local paper.' He handed her a copy of *Il Gazzetino*. 'Old news but good practice for your Italian. I'll test you when I get back!'

Good for her Italian and also a way of keeping her busy, she thought. Keeping her mind from the madness in which she'd indulged.

She gave him a small smile. 'I'll try to make sense of it, but I'm not promising.'

'Do your best—but make sure you get out, too, and enjoy the sun while it's shining. There's a storm on the horizon but this morning the weather's beautiful. Why don't you take a walk along the Riva to the Arsenale? You could visit the Giardini at the same time.'

She remembered the vaporetto to San Michele had stopped there and she had thought then that the gardens looked interesting.

'It's where the Biennale Art Exhibitions are held.' Leo was

warming to his theme. 'There must be around thirty pavilions now from different countries, some of them designed by big names in architecture. Even if you don't do the sightseeing stuff, the gardens are delightful, and there's a café, too. You could get lunch there—a *tramezzino* perhaps.'

It was a lovely suggestion despite being an obvious way of keeping her occupied. A prosciutto and mozzarella toast would make the perfect snack and maybe a glass of fresh orange or even a sparkling wine. And once beyond the confines of the palazzo, the walk would give her the space she needed. Space and time to think what her next move should be.

'You forgot these, boss.' It was Archie with Leo's reading glasses. Archie kept his employer's office in strict order but Leo's personal possessions were another matter. Nancy had soon learned that her husband was utterly unable to keep hold of pens, keys, glasses, all of which went missing on a regular basis.

'Thank you. I'd be stymied without those.' Leo tucked the glasses into the pocket of his linen jacket, then picked up his bags. 'I'd better be off or I'll be cutting it too fine. It's a scenic trip up the Grand Canal, but it will take me a good forty minutes to reach Santa Lucia and I need to be on that train.'

She had expected Archie to accompany his employer to the busy station, but apparently there had been an agreement between them that her husband was to go alone. Nancy wondered if that was because he'd asked his assistant to keep a close watch on her.

'Don't forget.' Leo gave him a clap on the back. 'If you get bad news today, Archie, you're to buy a ticket for home immediately.'

He turned to say goodbye to her. 'Enjoy your day, Nancy. With any luck, I'll be home for dinner.'

A swift kiss and he was out of the door, down the steps, and walking to the palazzo gates. She had hoped for more, an embrace, a kiss that said *I love you*, but he seemed wary, a little distant. Her heart felt dull when she turned to climb the stairs to the salon. She had been stupid last night to voice her suspicions.

Archie was already half way up the staircase and continued on his way to the fourth floor. With both of them gone, Nancy felt curiously listless. Idly, she drifted into the salon. If Archie had been detailed to keep an eye on her, she had the chance now to escape. But she was unsure of where to go or what to do, so instead she sank into one of the stubby armchairs and spread out the newspaper Leo had given her. She would try her hand at translating yesterday's *Il Gazzettino*.

It proved hard, more than hard, and she felt her mind wander and her eyelids close, unsurprisingly since she had slept badly. The crackle of the newspaper, as it slipped from her lap and brushed against her bare legs, had her start awake. She must find something to read in it that would grab her attention.

She flicked through the pages, searching for this precious nugget, and then she saw it. A small paragraph at the bottom of page six. It began with a brief mention of Marta Moretto's funeral, but it was the lines that followed that riveted Nancy. Marta's lawyer had registered her will with the authorities—by English standards that was early—and its details seemed already to have leaked out. She wasn't surprised that rumours had spread. This was Italy, and in particular Venice, where everyone knew everything about their neighbour. It was only a rumour at the moment, and the reporter had been careful to frame his article as speculation rather than fact, but it was unlikely such an extraordinary story was false. Who would have thought of making it up?

Marta Moretto had left her entire estate—business, money, the house in *calle dei Morti*—to the convent of Madonna del Carmine. Was that what Marta had meant when she'd said she intended to do great things in the future? If so, she must already have known what those great things were when she'd spoken to Nancy. She must have discussed with the convent exactly how she wished the money spent. And there would be a considerable amount to spend once the Moretto business and palazzo were sold and the bank account emptied. Was it perhaps her daughter's convent she had decided to endow in this way? That would make sense.

'I'm going out for an hour. I have to send telegrams.' Archie had appeared in the salon doorway. She had been so intent on the newspaper article, she hadn't heard him come downstairs.

She twisted round to face him. 'That's fine. I'll be okay here.'

He nodded but said nothing. When he began to walk away, though, she called out to him. 'Archie, there's something in the paper you might find interesting.'

He reappeared in the doorway. 'I doubt it, if it's Italian. Their footballers are the only thing worth reading about.'

'It's not about football. It's about the Moretto will. Take a look.'

He took a few steps into the room. 'I don't read Italian.'

'Don't be difficult. You know the language as well as I do. I've heard you speak.'

He walked over to her and reluctantly took the paper she handed him. 'There.' She half rose to tap the paragraph she'd been reading.

'So Marta has left her money to a convent,' he said, after he'd read a few lines.

'The writer of the article says the will is likely to cause shock waves. Does that sound right?'

His brow furrowed. 'Probably. She's disinherited her children. I would imagine that's a no-no in Italy.'

'I know you can do it in England, but here?'

Archie slumped down onto the sofa opposite, and tipped to one side as the springs readjusted. His eyes were blank and it was evident his mind was miles away.

'There was an Italian chap in the war,' he said at last. 'One of the prisoners we took at Monte Cassino, and I got talking to him. He spoke good English—he'd been a school teacher. We were talking about how we'd both ended up where we were and I remember what he said. His father had gone a bit *doolally* towards the end of his life, started going on pilgrimages to holy sites, giving money to neighbours when they asked, that sort of thing. Anyway this chap owned a house and several shops in Florence, so he had a bob or two, but when he died, he left everything to the woman who lived next door. The prisoner, Luigi was his name, was so pissed off he joined up there and then, and then wished he hadn't. He didn't want to fight, he hated the army.'

'So where does that get us?' Luigi's story seemed to have only minimal connection to Marta's.

'The point is while Luigi was away he heard from one of his sisters—he had a host of them—and they told him they were going to court. There's a law in Italy that says you can't leave your money how you like. Or not all of it. You have to leave a certain portion to your spouse, and your children.'

'So you think Marta's will is likely to be contested?'

'Almost certainly. We're not talking a small portion here. If I'm remembering rightly, Luigi said it was two-thirds of the estate that had to be divided equally between him and his sisters. Two-thirds of the Moretto estate is big money.'

'You're saying that Marta would legally have had to leave two-thirds of her estate to her son and daughter, and only then could she decide who else would benefit.'

'Exactly.' Archie stretched his legs and locked his hands behind his head.

'So she acted illegally?'

'Which is why, no doubt, Luca's lawyer will be on the case.'

'The article makes no mention of that, but I'm sure you're right.'

Archie jumped up and stretched again. 'I'd be very surprised if the bloke isn't working on filing some kind of claw-back action right now.'

Nancy rescued the newspaper from the sofa where Archie had abandoned it. She trawled down the article again. 'I think they actually mention that possibility—it's called an *azione di riduzione*. Marta must have known that would happen. Why did she do it?'

'To send a message? To tie Luca up in a legal morass for years? The Italian system works very, very slowly.'

'Meanwhile, he's likely to go out of business. It's almost like a punishment. But what was she punishing him for?'

'Unless you can bring her back from the dead, you'll probably never know.' He started towards the door.

It was probable, Nancy thought, she would never know, but someone else might. Angelica, for instance. And what of Luca himself—what had he known?

'There's definitely something odd about Luca,' Nancy said slowly, following her train of thought. 'At the funeral yesterday, he was engaged in this strange conversation with Salvatore. They were in a kind of secret huddle and talking almost frantically.'

Archie stopped in the doorway and swivelled round. 'So Luca is your villain again? What happened to Dino? Or even Mario?'

'I still have them in mind,' she said firmly. 'But there

was something else going on yesterday. Angelica was at the funeral, yet she didn't sit with her brother and his wife. She refused even to stand near them when everyone gathered at the graveside.'

His smile was laconic. 'Families have feuds all the time. You should come to Cornwall—we can show you a few.'

'I think Angelica's refusal to speak to her brother, even to acknowledge his existence, might be because she suspects he is involved in something bad. She left the convent weeks ago and has been living all this while in *calle dei Morti*. She could have heard rumours.' There was a small pause before she continued decidedly, 'You're right, though. I mustn't forget those other names, particularly Dino.'

Archie gave a groan, but she took no notice. 'Just as we were getting on the vaporetto to leave San Michele, Dino was making for the *motoscafo* he'd hired, but he was accosted by a young man. Concetta said the boy's name was Renzo Hastings.'

'The American dropout you mean?'

'He is American, but I wouldn't say he was a dropout. Concetta called him a painter.'

'She can call him what she likes, but in my book he's a dropout.'

Archie was never going to overflow with the spirit of goodwill, but she tried not to let it deflect her. 'He wanted something from Dino.'

'Money, that's what he would've wanted.'

'Leo said it might be work he was after, a commission.'

'Sounds right. Why don't you listen to your husband?'

Nancy felt a burst of anger. *Listen to the man in your life. Defer to his decisions. He knows best.* They were horribly familiar phrases.

'I would listen if I believed that all Renzo was after was

a commission,' she said irately. 'But if it had been only that, Dino would have shrugged the boy off and done it gently. He's a polished enough character and he had Francesca Moretto waiting for him. He'd want to disentangle himself as smoothly as possible. But he didn't. He became really agitated and almost flung the boy to one side. Renzo is obviously very poor and he would not have gone all the way to San Michele if he hadn't had a very good reason. I'd like to know what that reason was.'

Archie turned to leave once more, a determined look on his face. 'I have to go. I've work to do. But a word of advice... drop this, Nancy. It's getting out of hand. Find something to do while Leo is away. Or just enjoy the sun.'

She couldn't blame him for the advice. He was right, the whole thing was getting bigger and bigger. And it frightened her. But she'd had enough of being frightened. She hadn't fought back in London, but it would be different here. She would confront head-on whatever wrongdoing there had been. Keep digging until Marta's killer revealed himself.

Out of the blue, she was struck by a sickening thought. If Marta had died because she knew too much, what of her daughter? Vague suspicions, servants' gossip, were unlikely to have kept Angelica from her brother—not on a day when they were burying their mother. So did the girl know for sure that Luca was involved in wrongdoing? Had Marta told her daughter what she knew... showed her proof even... and was Angelica now in danger, too?

Chapter Seventeen

She must find Angelica. She would go to the street Marta had mentioned—*calle dei Morti*, the street of the dead—and look for the Moretto house. It was in Dorsoduro but shouldn't be too difficult to find. People were bound to know it, particularly after Marta's well-publicised death. And while Archie was absent sending telegrams, it was easy enough to slip away from the palazzo.

Once outside, Nancy wound her way through the streets towards San Zaccaria. She could make the journey there almost blindfolded now. A boat was pulling into the landing stage as she arrived and she was quick to buy a ticket. The route would take her to the Giudecca first, a little out of her way, but from the island to the Zattere was only minutes across the canal. In just a few days, her confidence in navigating Venice had grown immeasurably.

A quarter of an hour later, she disembarked and began the walk along the Zattere, the promenade that edged the lagoon. There was a bridge to cross, spanning a wide canal— the San Trovaso, the sign told her—and a boatyard below. A gondola yard, in fact. She was tempted to stop a while and watch the boat makers at work, intrigued by how intricate the construction. A hundred different pieces and seven types of wood for each gondola, Concetta had told her.

But she was on a mission this morning and she walked on.

It was a fair distance to *calle dei Morti* and when she got there it seemed to Nancy an odd street. On the left, large impressive houses marched solidly into the distance, but on the opposite side of the *calle* was a terrace of small and largely unkempt buildings.

A house that had stood on the corner had disappeared altogether, leaving a yawning gap. Makeshift fencing had been erected around it and Nancy walked over to look. It seemed as though the earth had subsided and taken the house with it. She leant over the fence and peered down into a deep pit of fallen masonry, but quickly took a step back. The left-hand side of the *calle* felt a great deal safer. A few houses along, she found the Moretto building. It was easily identified, a very old and very imposing palazzo, with the family name clearly written on the gate pull.

She hesitated, her mind working hard to order the story she had to tell. She must warn Angelica though she had no firm evidence to offer. And it was difficult to know who best to warn her against—Mario, Dino, her own brother? All she could do, Nancy decided, was to alert the woman to a possible threat and do it as credibly as she could. It would have to be believable. From her brief glimpse of Angelica, she was fairly certain the woman would be quick to spot pretence. At the funeral, Nancy had sensed Angelica's quiet strength, a conviction that she was beholden to no one and judged the world on her own terms. She had judged her brother, it seemed, and found him lacking.

But it was not Angelica who answered Nancy's ring, but a *portinaio*.

'*Sì?*' She was taken aback by his abruptness. It hardly made for a good beginning.

'I would like to see Signorina Moretto,' she said in her best Italian.

'The signorina is in mourning. She sees no one.'

'I understand. I was at Signora Moretto's funeral yesterday and saw the signorina there. I have something I wish very much to speak to her about.'

'No, signora. It is not possible.'

'Can you take a message for me then?'

He looked blank. 'A message?'

'Can you tell your mistress that I wish to speak to her about Mario Bozzato?' Nancy hoped the mention of Mario's name might provoke a reaction. And it did.

'I am Angelica Moretto.' The tall, statuesque woman of yesterday appeared at the *portinaio*'s shoulder. 'What do you want with me?'

'I will take only a few minutes of your time, signorina. I am worried for you and wish to tell you something that may be important.'

For several seconds Nancy felt herself appraised before Angelica reluctantly nodded and murmured a few words into the *portinaio*'s ear. He stepped aside, suspicion still writ large on his face, but allowed Nancy to walk through the door into the white and black marble of a magnificent hall.

'Come.'

Angelica motioned her visitor to follow her, up a flight of red carpeted stairs and into a large square-shaped room, its walls filled with paintings of every shape and size—water colours, oils, pastel landscapes, pencil sketches. The display was stunning and at the same time bewildering. A circle of soft-cushioned chairs filled the centre of the room, surrounded by several small tables, each covered with an array of porcelain bowls and figurines, and overshadowed by a huge sculpture that stood to one side. It was a copy of a figure Nancy knew well, Antonio Bregno's *Virgin Annunciate*, and one she had never greatly admired. From its commanding position, it seemed to suck light and air from the room.

Angelica motioned her to one of the chairs, but instead of sitting, Nancy walked to the long windows that overlooked a large square. It was an instinctive gesture, a desire to shake off the sheer weight of so many objects and rid herself of the statue's oppressive presence.

'You have a very attractive view,' she said. The square below possessed a mellow beauty.

'That is Campo Sant'Agnese. Have you visited its church?'

Nancy was relieved the woman spoke in English. This wasn't going to be an easy conversation in any language. She looked across the square at the red brick building at its far end, badly out of harmony with its surroundings.

'No. Perhaps I should,' she said diplomatically.

'It has a very plain façade, but inside it is wonderful. It was almost destroyed by Napoleon, all its beautiful art stolen. Such desecration! But God is merciful, God is good. His bounty has allowed the friars to restore a hallowed place to its former glory.'

Angelica's religious fervour was obvious and her decision to become a nun easy to understand. But it made her sudden departure from the convent much less explicable.

'Please sit.'

The sharp tone cut through Nancy's thoughts and this time she did sit, sinking down into a sumptuous velvet seat, and thinking how nice it would be if their own palazzo possessed a chair half as comfortable.

'You would like coffee?'

Feeling extremely nervous, she would rather not have to drink in this woman's presence, but it was politic to accept and she nodded. Angelica walked to the doorway and called down to an unseen pair of hands.

'Now what is it you want with me?'

It was clear there was to be no polite small talk. Nancy wasn't sorry. 'I met your mother the day she died,' she began. It was better, she judged, to come straight to the point. This woman would not want to hear protestations of sorrow. 'We were sitting at adjoining tables at a café on the Zattere.'

'At Nico's? I know it.'

'Before your mother joined me, she was stopped by a young man whom I later learned was Mario Bozzato. He was very angry about something, haranguing Signora Moretto violently. Then quite by chance, I saw him the next day—I think he must have been on his way to work—and I mentioned the tragedy at La Fenice. His response was not pleasant.' Mario's actual words were not something Nancy would repeat.

'He boasted to me that now your mother had passed away, he would marry you within weeks. He felt threatening and it worried me. I imagined you must live alone except for servants, and I was concerned. I know you have a brother, but it might be difficult for him to help you, if you were ever in trouble. I thought I should warn you of Mario's intentions.'

A maid had brought in coffee and a plate of small, inedible biscuits while Nancy was talking. She had hoped her comment might elicit a hint, at least, of any fear Angelica had—of Mario, of her brother—but her companion simply stared at her, then picked up a silver spoon and slowly stirred her coffee.

She took a while before she spoke. 'Thank you for coming, Signora…?'

'Tremayne.'

'Signora Tremayne. But you need not worry. I have no fear. Neither have I the intention of marrying—Mario, or anyone else.'

'He seemed to think you were promised to him,' Nancy

ventured. 'He seemed almost crazed in his belief.'

Angelica gave a short laugh that grated on Nancy's ears. 'Once, many years ago, I wanted to marry him, but now he is simply a nuisance. I was a different person then. A girl, a child. My years as a nun have changed me forever.'

'Naturally, I can see they would.'

Nancy wanted very much to ask this woman about her life in the convent. She needed to hear from her that she had suffered no false imprisonment as Mario claimed, that Signora Moretto was completely innocent of such a dreadful deed. But the question seemed too personal. Nevertheless she ventured it.

'And you were happy in the convent?'

'I could not have been happier. A daily routine of work and prayer in tranquil surroundings. What more could I ask?'

'So you were not forced to enter the convent?'

'Forced?' The woman gave another short laugh, broken before it began. 'Who can force a woman to enter a convent? We are no longer living in the Middle Ages. No doubt it is Mario's nonsense you speak.'

'I didn't believe him,' Nancy said quickly. 'I was sure Signora Moretto would never have acted in such a fashion.'

Angelica unbent a little. 'My mother did not wish to lose me. What mother would? And I was her only daughter. But she knew I had a vocation and would not go against God's will.'

'It must be a sadness then for you to have left the convent.'

'Duty takes many different forms and this was mine.' Angelica gathered the folds of her gown across her knees. 'My mother's health was poor and she needed me. She had become very frail in recent months.'

That did not accord with Nancy's impression of Marta. But perhaps she had been frailer than she looked. She had been taking serious medicine after all.

'Do you think she was ill the night... the night she had the accident?' Nancy held her breath, wondering if this might prove a question too far, but Angelica answered calmly.

'Without a doubt. She had been taking strong pills for severe pain and it blurred her mind.' The woman passed her hand over her face. 'I am sorry. This is extremely painful for me.'

Nancy felt instant guilt at having intruded so badly, and what in fact had she found out? Only that Luisa Mancini had been right.

'I'm sorry to have mentioned such a painful subject,' she said, putting her cup back on the tray. 'But happy that I can dismiss Mario from my mind.'

'I dismissed him from mine years ago,' the woman said, rising regally from her chair and walking towards the salon door. 'The *portinaio* will see you out, Signora Tremayne.'

At the door, Nancy turned to shake hands and, as she did so, caught sight of a small, gold statuette. It appeared to be the image of a female saint and sat high on a pedestal tucked into a corner of the room. It was exquisite and Nancy moved towards it without realising she was doing so, drawn by its elemental power. The figure glistened, smooth and glowing, every small detail—the folds of the woman's clothing, her hair, her halo—had been crafted by a master goldsmith.

'That is one of the most beautiful pieces I have ever seen,' she said. And meant it.

'You appreciate art?'

'Very much. Who does it depict and who made it?'

'It is an image of Santa Susanna. She is the patron saint of people forced into exile.' Angelica gave the phrase a curious emphasis. 'She was born in Rome at the beginning of Diocletian's reign and made a vow of virginity. When she refused to marry, she was accused of being a Christian and suffered a martyr's death. She is close to all our hearts at Madonna del Carmine. As for who made her? That is lost in time.'

It was the longest speech Angelica had made and a revealing one, if Nancy could only fathom its meaning. The most obvious fact to emerge was that the convent named in Marta's will was indeed that of her daughter's.

She gave a last, lingering glance at the statuette. 'Your mother had excellent taste.'

'It is not my mother's.' The tone of voice surprised Nancy. It was forceful, confrontational. 'It belongs to the convent alone.'

'And you…'

'And I am to supervise its cleaning and then return it to its rightful place.'

Nancy gave a smile or tried to. She found this woman stern and uncompromising. At the door, the *portinaio* was waiting to make sure she left the premises. He need not have worried—she was delighted to breathe fresh air, to feel the sun on her face once more. The Moretto palazzo had been strangely intimidating and not at all the kind of home she would have expected Marta to inhabit.

Chapter Nineteen

The visit had not been a success. Nancy had learned little more than she already knew. Her mention of Luca had been brief, but she'd hoped it might have loosened Angelica's tongue. Instead, she had been met by silence and a stare that made her stomach lurch. It seemed to confirm, at least, that the siblings were at daggers drawn and if Angelica were at risk from anyone, it was from her brother and not Mario, whom she clearly despised. Nancy's warning had fallen on deaf ears, but she'd come away feeling that Angelica would be a match for any threat her brother might pose.

Nancy had not previously penetrated further into Dorsoduro than the Accademia on the eastern edge of the district and the quarter was largely unknown to her, but when she began a slow walk westwards, she thought it delightful. The crowds that gathered in St Mark's Square and the streets surrounding the Piazza were absent—instead there were picturesque *calli*, empty squares and ancient churches.

At one of the many bars serving cheap *cicchetti*, Nancy stopped to eat a small snack and, though she had not thought herself hungry, managed to devour a large plate of crostini topped with salt cod and pistachio cream, washing it down with a glass of red wine from the house cellar. It was one of the best lunches she had eaten in Venice and cost very little.

Emboldened, she began walking further west, making

for San Sebastiano, the parish church of Veronese, that Leo had mentioned was worth a visit. Sauntering through a series of narrow, paved streets, across one beautiful square after another, she stopped occasionally to glance into a shop window. At a florist's, she paused for longer. Its glass was hazed with humidity, but inside tubs of yellow roses and clouds of pale jasmine created a burst of colour.

The small shops of Dorsoduro were enchanting, a remnant of an older age. Those around St Mark's were beginning to change—a pharmacy closing down; what was once a *fruttivendolo,* according to the old sign, being refurbished as a boutique. And nearer to home in Castello, Concetta complained bitterly that the cobbler who mended her boots had disappeared and, much to her disgust, a shop selling souvenirs had sprung up in his place. It was a foreshadowing of the future, Nancy thought, useful shops gradually replaced by tourist trivia.

Concetta had told her it was possible to walk from one end of Venice to the other in less than an hour and a half, but Nancy doubted it; the journey to San Sebastiano was proving longer than she had anticipated. The sky had clouded over and an ominous grey was gathering ahead. Crossing a square, she was aware its trees had begun to rustle loudly, flipping in a wind that was increasing all the time. Leo had spoken of a coming storm and she sensed this was it. She should turn back now.

The boatyard she'd passed on the way to the Moretto house should be easy to find. She had walked directly from the vaporetto stop, past the San Trovaso bridge and on to *calle dei Morti,* but later she had stopped at a bar to eat and drifted westwards to the tip of Dorsoduro. Still, she was more confident now at finding her way and she was sure it would not be difficult.

She turned back across the square and plunged down the *calle* she thought had led her there, but fifty yards on she was met by a dead end. A palazzo's locked wooden gates barred her way. She walked back towards the square and tried another turning—it was surely the only other street she could have taken. This time she found a canal at its end, and no bridge to take her over. She stood for a moment trying to orientate herself and wishing she had brought a map. Why had she thought she could manage without it? She should know by now that alleyways were unpredictable, sometimes ending abruptly in dark, deep canals or plunging into arcades or even emerging, without warning, into a breathtaking view.

She retraced her steps a short way and saw on her left a *calle* she hadn't noticed before. Should she take this or keep returning to the square? It was narrower and darker than the others, but it seemed to be going in the right direction—east towards San Trovaso—and as far as she could make out, stretched into the distance without a dead end or a canal in sight. She picked up her pace, feeling more cheerful, the small dread she constantly carried with her of being alone and pursued—by a man who looked very much like Philip March—was for the moment dismissed.

Halfway along the *calle*, she had to stop. A small stone from one of the lanes—its surface had been roughly finished—had become wedged in her left shoe, and she had to bend down to shake it free. As she did so, she thought she heard footsteps that stopped abruptly. She stood stock still, listening, but there was only silence. It was her imagination. It had to be. It was the small dread that never quite left her..

The rattle of a shutter further down the alleyway sounded loudly. Venice was a closeted city and the houses on either side of her were shuttered tight. She looked behind her, but the *calle* was empty. Ahead, an archway spanned the lane. In a sudden burst of light, the sun broke through the lowering cloud, and the shadow cast by the arch's corbelling looked for all the world like three figures lying in wait. She could feel her heart racing, but told herself not to be foolish. She must not allow her fears to get the better of her.

She walked on, her ears now sharp and attuned. A few seconds later, the echo of a heavy tread on the rough ground came clearly to her. She quickened her pace, but the echo quickened, too. She was desperate to get to the end of this interminable *calle*, looking either side of her for possible escape: a door ajar, a window open, someone, anyone, she could ask for help. But the street remained shuttered and silent.

By now she was almost running and whoever was behind her was running, too. She would turn and confront the man, she thought. Then realised how stupid that would be. Her breath was coming fast and she had no idea how long she could keep up this pace. Her legs were beginning to tremble violently in the way they had so often in the past. Frantically, she broke into a full run, her breath now coming in sobs.

And then, praise be, there was the boatyard. She must have walked or ran exactly parallel to the lagoon and arrived a little further up the San Trovaso canal. There were men still in the yard, men who would come to her rescue if necessary. She slowed her pace and tried to breathe normally. Passing the workers on her way to the bridge, she managed a cheerful wave, though it took an heroic effort.

At the vaporetto stop, she continued to look around her, fearful that at any moment her would-be attacker might burst from one of the narrow alleyways running off the Zattere. Her eyes darted back and forth, but there was only the odd workman going about his business, a woman with a pushchair making her way along the Fondamente and an older lady clutching a shopping basket. In a few minutes, shaken and weak, she had climbed aboard a number two vaporetto. Now all she had to do was to get home.

*

The small craft bulldozed a path through choppy waters while Nancy sat staring through the window at the grey world beyond. Ordinarily she would have delighted in the toss and swell of the boat, but she felt no pleasure in the ride. Her limbs had gradually quietened, but her pulse was still tumbling. It was stupid, stupid. It had been only footsteps and once she had reached the boatyard, the footsteps had stopped. It was the reminder of past terror that haunted her. She had thought herself safe in Venice from the constant fear, but it still burned bright. And the unfamiliar city and unknown assailant had given it greater strength.

Alighting from the vaporetto, she was met by a torrential downpour. The storm had well and truly broken. She should run for shelter, but it was as much as she could do to force her legs to walk forward into the thick curtain of water. The teeming rain gathered in deep puddles on the hollows of flagstones, stirring the mud at the bottom of the canals, and streaming off the marble statues as she passed. Pigeons clustered dejectedly in whatever crannies they could find. A dank and desolate landscape that she hardly noticed.

It was only a short distance to the palazzo, but she arrived at its gates with cheeks burning, yet her body cold and sodden. A sick flush had taken the place of breathless fear and her legs were once again trembling. She barely had the strength to push open the wooden gates and almost fell into the courtyard beyond.

Archie was in the garden, sheltering beneath an umbrella. It was a strange sight, but to her confused mind, a part of the nightmare through which she was moving. He followed her when she stumbled towards the palazzo door.

'Mrs Tremayne, Nancy. Are you all right?'

She didn't answer but twisted the handle uselessly. Why wouldn't it open?

'Here, let me.'

Archie brushed past her and opened the door, stepping back to allow her to escape from the rain. He threw the umbrella into a corner of the lobby, then turned to her, a deep crease in his forehead. 'What's happened to you?' He must have seen the shaking she still couldn't control. 'Apart from coming home like a drenched scarecrow, I mean.'

'I've had a fright, that's all,' she managed to say, trying to keep her voice steady, but failing. 'I'll be fine in a short while.'

'Hmm,' he muttered, and waited for her to climb the stairs.

Desperate to keep some dignity, she made it to the first step, but she had spent her last ounce of strength and could go no further. Archie came up behind her and, without a word, linked his arm through hers and helped her tread a faltering path up the stairs and into the salon. None too gently he pushed her into one of the armchairs.

Then he went back to the staircase and called down to Concetta. The urgency in his voice had the maid bustle up from the kitchen, wiping her hands on her apron as she did. One look at what awaited her in the salon had her rush to Nancy's side, clucking reprovingly.

'Can you help Mrs Tremayne to her bedroom, Concetta, and see she has a warm bath and dry clothes?' Archie asked.

Still clucking, the maid guided Nancy out of the salon and climbed with her up the stairs.

Chapter Twenty

Nancy had only just shuffled into the silk dressing gown when there was a knock on the door. Archie stood outside, a tray in his hands.

'This is what you need,' he said decidedly, and without waiting for an invitation, walked into the room and put the tray down on to the marble console table: two mugs, a pot of steaming coffee and in the centre, a tall, thin bottle.

He poured the coffee, then a small amount from the bottle into each mug. '*Caffé corretto,*' he said. 'Try it.'

She hesitated. The bath had stopped her shaking, but despite the hot water and a fierce towelling, her body remained intensely cold. Archie was probably right. She took a sip from the mug he handed her, and her face puckered.

'I'm sorry, I can't drink this. Whatever it is, it's too strong.'

'It's meant to be strong. It's grappa. But keep going—it will be worth it.'

Nancy resigned herself to trying again and took another small mouthful. The second sip tasted marginally better and very slowly she was able to finish the mug. Archie went to pour her another coffee, but she held up her hand. 'No more, thank you. I'm fine.'

That was a trifle optimistic, but she was warm now, feeling the liquid coursing through her veins, hot and fiery. She caught a glimpse of her face in the mirror and saw her cheeks were looking a more normal colour. Archie must have seen it, too. He put his mug down and fixed her with a stare.

'Now, what the hell has been going on?'

She took a while before she replied. 'I went to see Angelica Moretto and on the way back I was followed.'

'That's it?'

It sounded so tame when she said the words, but how frightened she'd been. 'I thought I was trapped.' She struggled to explain. 'I don't know Dorsoduro—I'd never ventured that far into the district before, and when I turned to go home, I got lost. It was the maze of alleyways—I couldn't find my way out. Then the footsteps started. Someone was following me. I began to run and whoever was behind me ran, too.'

'Were they trying to catch you up?' he asked prosaically. 'You may have dropped something.'

'It wasn't like that. And if you're going to patronise, I'm saying no more.'

'I was just stating the obvious.'

'It wasn't obvious—not to me. When I stopped, the footsteps stopped. Someone was definitely following me.'

'A purse snatcher perhaps? But you evidently got away.'

'The *calle* I was running down suddenly opened out and I found I'd reached the canal by the gondola yard. There were men working there and whoever was chasing me must have seen them and turned away.'

'So no harm done.'

'No.' She spoke quietly, but was keenly aware of the harm that no one could see.

There was a long silence and then Archie said thoughtfully, 'I wouldn't say you were a woman to be frightened by a few footsteps. What else is there?'

'It reminded me of something.' Nancy faltered. She didn't want to talk about it; she never wanted to talk about it. But the grappa had eased the tension she always felt, and instead of closing down the conversation, she said, 'It was too reminiscent of what happened to me before... when I was in real danger.'

'This was the man you spoke of, the man who was your Mario?'

Archie was acute, she had to hand it to him. 'Yes, my Mario. I was engaged to him and when I decided I no longer wanted to be, he didn't like it.'

'So what did he do?'

'He started following me. He'd appear at odd moments when I least expected it. I never knew when, and I was always looking over my shoulder or round corners. I got scared of even leaving the house.'

Archie stirred his coffee and spoke without looking at her. 'Did he hurt you—I mean, physically?'

'He never actually got to that point, but he was working his way up the scale.'

And he would have got there in the end—she was convinced—but she wouldn't say that. Archie seemed determined to play down her recent fright, and she must, too.

'In what way?' Archie asked bluntly.

'He started with the stalking. Then there were anonymous calls in the middle of the night—they nearly got me evicted. And when I refused to be intimidated, he spread a rumour around Abingers—that's where I worked—a rumour that I was...' She hesitated, finding it difficult to continue. 'That I was no better than I should be, if you understand me. He picked the girl who was the biggest gossip in the building and told her a vile story. I'd introduced him to some of the staff at the Christmas lunch, so Brenda Layton was happy to believe him, and happy to spread the untruth. It wasn't long before all of Abingers was whispering. Until Leo put a stop to it.'

Archie appeared to be thinking hard. After a long pause, he said, 'Is that why you were crying, that time in the street? When Leo got me to drive him to Paddington?'

Nancy shook her head. 'That was something else, though Brenda Layton certainly made me cry that day. I'd been buying lunch at the cafeteria and I remember that when I heard what was being said, I dropped my tray on the table and ran. Leo found me tucked away in a dark corner and went to the Managing Director. Leo had influence at Abingers—he was always being called in to value a painting or sit on a committee, that sort of thing. He told the MD what had been going on and then spoke to Brenda Layton himself. Very severely, I imagine, because the gossip stopped immediately.'

Archie poured himself another mug and laced it with a generous splash of grappa. 'Are you sure?' He pointed to the bottle.

'I don't think so. My head already feels as though it's not my own.'

'That's grappa for you. Seventy per cent proof—does the trick beautifully. So when I drove Leo to find you, what was that about?'

Nancy took a deep breath. This was the most difficult part and she knew she had not yet coped with the terror Philip had unleashed. 'That was later, after the stalking and the calls and the gossip mongering. My life just disintegrated then.'

'Jesus. What kind of man was this fiancé?'

'On the surface, very pleasant. He had a good job, he worked as a journalist on a national newspaper. And he wasn't what you might expect of a newspaper man. He had an old-fashioned courtesy about him. I met him on Coronation Day. We were both in the crowd outside Westminster Abbey and he accidentally bumped into me and knocked some art magazines I was carrying out of my hands. There were lots of apologies and then he asked me about my connection with art. It turned out he'd published an article on auction houses, Abingers included, a few months previously. He was very easy to talk to.'

'He sounds a paragon,' Archie said drily.

'He was, until I wore his engagement ring. Then he changed.'

It was difficult to remember back, to those words, deeds, interventions, that had gradually altered their relationship. Small and unimportant at first, but over the weeks increasing in number and strength.

'He wanted to control who I met. Who my friends were,' Nancy continued. 'Told me what clothes I should wear. He even started buying them for me. Then he planned our wedding and my parents went along with it. I wasn't allowed to choose my own flowers, not even my own dress.'

Now she had started talking, she couldn't seem to stop. 'The crunch came when I found him reading a letter a friend had sent me. When I asked him about it, he said I shouldn't mind if I had nothing to be ashamed of, and that once we were married, nothing would be private. It was then I knew I had to break it off. He couldn't believe I was serious and when he realised I was, he was angry. Very angry. He told me he'd rescued me from spinsterhood and I should be grateful. Then he started following me.'

'And after that? You said he was moving up the scale.'

'He started breaking into my bedsit. At first, it was just things being moved around the room—shoes where I hadn't left them, a sugar bowl missing. I thought I was getting forgetful, perhaps the stress of his not leaving me alone. But then I came home one day and my favourite dress had been cut up and my underwear ripped to pieces.' She couldn't bring herself to mention the scrawled *Jezebel*. 'I knew it was

172

him and that he'd been getting into my room for weeks. That's when I phoned Leo and you drove him to Paddington.'

Archie leaned forward, his hands in his lap, but his expression intent. 'Did you report the break-ins to the police?'

She bowed her head. 'Leo said I should. But the police couldn't put a watch on me twenty-four hours a day. I thought if I reported Philip it would make matters worse—if I could just weather the threats, he might get tired and go away. After he ruined my clothes, I promised Leo I'd get the locks changed the following day, but I never had the chance. There was a big exhibition I was helping to set up and I was busy the whole time. When I got back that evening, all my belongings had been smashed—china, ornaments, furniture. The door to my room even. And there was a dead crow bleeding on my bed.'

'Jesus,' Archie said again.

'I was trying to run when Leo arrived. He was worried after what had happened the previous day and decided to check on me. He had a cab waiting and I went back with him to Cavendish Street... you know the rest.'

As she told her sorry tale, she had begun once more to shake, unable to control her juddering limbs. She hoped Archie hadn't seen.

'Here,' he said, and reached out for her hand, giving it a tight clasp. His fingers were smooth and that surprised her. When her eyes met his, he let go.

'So what did Angelica Moretto have to say?' he said quickly, leaning back and drinking his second mug of coffee.

'I didn't learn much,' Nancy confessed. 'Except that Luisa was spot on when she said Angelica had no interest in Mario Bozzato and would never marry him. In fact, she's unlikely to marry anyone. I'm fairly sure she'll go back to the convent soon, if they permit it. And I imagine they will, particularly as the Madonna del Carmine has inherited the Moretto fortune.'

'She didn't mention it?'

'She wouldn't. She is one very composed woman. Tight-lipped and quite formidable. Not someone who gives information away lightly. It was evident she didn't want to talk about her brother—I've learned nothing new. From what I saw at the funeral, I'd already guessed she was estranged from him.'

Nancy got up from her chair and began a slow walk back and forth to the long windows that overlooked the canal, despondent at the way the day had turned out. 'I had hopes for this visit,' she said dolefully. 'That Angelica would tell me something, anything, to help me find out how or why her mother died. But it's been a miserable failure.'

'Maybe not. Not entirely.'

She stopped walking and looked at him in surprise.

'The fact that you were followed proves someone is worried. Can you remember when you first heard the footsteps?'

'It was when I turned to come home. I'd been hoping to get to San Sebastiano, but it was much further than I'd anticipated and the weather had started to change, so I turned back. That's when I first heard someone.'

'Is it possible you were followed from the time you left the Moretto house?'

'I suppose it is. I was on fairly wide roads until I turned to walk back to the vaporetto stop, and I might not have noticed anyone following. It was only when I found myself in that labyrinth of alleyways, I realised I had company.'

Archie seemed deep in thought again and she sat down, waiting for him to speak. 'Whoever followed you, couldn't have known you would call at the Moretto place today. So it has to be someone who was already watching the house and saw you go in and come out.'

'Something bad *is* going on and I'm convinced Marta knew. If only I could find some proof, I could take it to the police. Then at least they would investigate her death. At the moment, I've nothing. They would put me down as an hysterical woman.'

Archie gave a slight shrug. It was clear that hysteria wasn't far from his mind either, but at least he had the grace not to say it. And he was making an effort to understand.

'Tell me why this Marta is so important to you.'

'I know it seems bizarre. I don't understand it either. I talked to Marta for such a short time, yet I felt she was a friend. I could sense the sadness in her and I think she wanted me to. It was as though she'd chosen me.'

Archie's eyebrows rose astronomically.

'I know it sounds ridiculous. But she singled me out to sit next to, to talk to. She spoke about the great things she was planning to do, the way she would ensure the Moretto family would be remembered, but all the time I felt there was pain behind her words, that the great things were, I don't know, some kind of atonement. She would have said more, I think, but she had to leave. I expected to see her that night at La Fenice, but I never got the chance.'

'You're right about the police dismissing your story. It's all hunches, and feelings. How are you going to convince anyone it's true?'

'I'm sure it has something to do with the paintings on Dino's yacht. If only I could have opened that crate.'

'The crate could be long gone—if it really did contain paintings, and Dino and his sidekick have been selling them fraudulently.' Archie was right. Whatever proof there might have been, was probably no more. 'But... ' he tapped his fingers on the console top, 'there might just be others.'

'Where?' she asked eagerly, her face suddenly alight.

'Di Maio rents a boathouse for his yacht when he's not sailing. It stays there most of the winter or when it needs repair or repainting, but in the summer it's virtually always in the harbour and the boathouse is empty. I played poker there once—it's Salvatore's little hideout. It's just possible that if the pair of them are up to something, they might be holding stuff there.'

'Can you take me?'

'No. Definitely not.'

She jumped up and rushed across to him, grabbing his arm. 'Please. Or tell me how to find it.'

He pushed her away. 'Listen to me, Nancy. You have two choices. Either you ignore what you think has happened and go back to England and forget it—which is much the wisest move—or you keep digging, and if you're right about the criminality involved, land yourself in serious trouble.'

'There is no choice,' she said dully. 'I can't abandon Marta. Now will you tell me how to get to this boathouse?'

'*You're* not getting anywhere. If you insist on knowing, I'll be the one to go. But not until tonight. I can't go poking around on private property in broad daylight.'

'Thank you, Archie. Thank you. You're a decent man.'

'Well, isn't that a surprise,' he said sardonically.

'I mean it, but I want to come with you. I have to. Maybe Leo will be back late from Rome and won't know.'

'That's what I came to tell you. It's why I was in the garden. Leo phoned and wanted to speak to you, but you'd disappeared. You weren't anywhere in the house and I thought you might be lurking out there, though God knows why in that downpour.'

She ignored this and asked urgently, 'What did Leo say? Is he unwell?'

'He's fine, just a bit cheesed off. It's the other bloke who's unwell. The shopkeeper. The fraud team is insisting this chap is present at the meeting—no idea why—but it's been postponed until tomorrow. It means Leo has to stay over.'

'In Rome?

'No, Timbuktu. I've booked him into a hotel for the night and he should be back tomorrow evening.'

'So tonight there's a chance I could—'

'A chance *I* could.'

'That both of us could. Please, Archie.'

'If you hadn't been followed, I wouldn't be doing this at all,' he warned.

'You didn't believe me until I was threatened? Is that what you're saying?'

He grinned. 'Would you have believed you?'

'But now?'

'I still don't buy this Marta thing, but if you're worth following simply because you paid a call at the Moretto house, it has to mean something's amiss.'

He got up, collecting the tray as he did. 'Eight o'clock this evening,' he said tersely. 'And wear dark clothes.'

Chapter Twenty-One

They met in the lobby. As she'd been instructed, Nancy had dressed in grey slacks and high-necked sweater while Archie had found dark trousers and a zipped jacket that looked as though it had done several trips on the *Morwenna*. She guessed it belonged to one of his brothers.

'You'll need another layer,' he greeted her brusquely. 'The rain may have stopped but the fog hasn't. And it's thick.'

She climbed back up the stairs to her bedroom and hauled out a cardigan she hadn't worn since leaving London. It wasn't as dark-coloured as Archie had suggested, but it would have to do. When she arrived back to the lobby, he was already in the garden below, pacing up and down the gravel path. He seemed unusually on edge, and Nancy shared his misgivings. She had a hollow feeling that this evening would prove a wild goose chase, and even worse, might lead to serious trouble for them both.

Once they were through the tall wooden gates and out into the street, she saw better what Archie had meant. The fog was a dense blanket. She could hear the canal rather than see it, hear the sad slapping of water on a tethered boat, as the slightest movement in the lagoon rustled up the narrow waterway.

It was too far to walk to San Basilio—they hadn't the time, Archie decided—so they headed for the vaporetto. Nancy had walked this way a dozen times before, but tonight the journey felt very different. The path they trod was ghostly, buildings on either side rising spectrally through the haze and every street deserted, mist-laden statues their only companions.

An unexpected setback awaited them at San Zaccaria. The vaporetti operating along the Giudecca Canal had been cancelled for the night and their only option was to take a boat to Ca' Rezzonico, the same journey Nancy had made to the university. From there, the walk to San Basilio should be little more than ten minutes or so. But even this most popular of routes had suffered disruption, the boats appearing randomly through clouds of fog, their schedules abandoned, their radar screens spinning.

The ferry, when it arrived, was almost empty and Archie took a seat several rows away. Keeping a low profile perhaps? Or was it a wish to maintain a distance between them? She could understand if it was. Their midnight meeting, her confession of what had happened to her in London, had gone a long way to dissolving the barriers between them, and she hoped they might become friends. It would certainly help Leo if they could establish some kind of rapport. Her husband had said little, yet he must be aware of the tensions his marriage had caused. But it would always be a friendship with limits—she felt that, and she knew Archie must, too.

She wondered what Leo was doing now. Out to dinner, she supposed, no doubt with Dino as his companion. He would be shocked if he knew what she was engaged on. More than shocked—angry. He had made it plain that she was not to interest herself any further in the Moretto affair, and here she was going directly against his wishes. Her comfort lay in the fact that he need never know. Certainly Archie would say nothing. It was more than his job was worth to have taken his employer's wife on a burglary.

And that's what it was, she realised, swallowing hard. She was about to become a criminal, and turn Archie Jago into one, too.

'Time to go.'

Archie had stood up and was gesturing to the landing stage ahead. She peered through the window at the damp whiteness beyond, trying to decipher the name of the stop. It took her a while to make it out, but he was right, it was Ca' Rezzonico, and she got up to join him, holding tightly to the back of the seat. But instead of the usual smooth glide, the boat slammed heavily into the dock, rocking the empty landing stage and causing Nancy to lose her balance. She fell awkwardly against Archie and for a moment felt the warmth of his body, but in a trice, he had set her primly back on her feet.

The streets on this side of the Grand Canal were no busier than those of Castello, deserted except for stray cats sheltering where they could. Nancy's ears seemed more than usually alert, compensating, she imagined, for her restricted vision. In the distance the clanging of a fog bell cut a path through the muffled silence and she could hear the tinkling of buoys out in the lagoon. Then the trumpeting of tugs in the Giudecca Canal and the deep boom of a ship's siren out at sea.

They walked along the side of a narrow canal, several streets inland from the Zattere. This was the district she had walked this very afternoon. Was that only a few hours ago? It hardly seemed possible, though the memory stayed vivid — of footsteps pursuing her, of feeling alone and hunted. Suddenly, to her right a shape emerged from the mist, ghostly in the half light, and she felt her breath catch. But it was merely a solitary gondolier. He gave them a casual wave as he crouched low on his vessel to pass beneath the squat, dark bridge.

Archie turned to her. 'Are you all right?'

He must have heard her sharp intake of breath. Nancy nodded, though she couldn't truly say she was, but the search of Dino's boathouse was something on which she was determined. Thank goodness, though, it would be over soon and they could return to the safety of the palazzo, the cold sprawl of a house that she had once disliked but now began to feel a haven.

They had turned left and were walking towards the lagoon. Even through the fog, she could feel the air fresher. In several minutes, they had emerged onto the Fondamente that bordered the water and would take them directly to San Basilio. Several more minutes more and they had reached the harbour itself.

'The boathouse is on the other side of these warehouses,' Archie said, his voice so low she could hardly hear him.

A vast concrete space lay before them and she recognised the place immediately. It was where the *motoscafo* had dropped Leo and herself on that difficult trip to Burano, but instead of walking beside the lagoon to where the *Andiamo* would be moored for the night, Archie walked away from the water, following the line of warehouses until they reached a single gauge railway track. A line of trucks sat empty, waiting for their morning cargo. They crossed the track and turned a sharp left, bending round and back to the water again.

She couldn't fathom how they had reached the lagoon once more, but the boathouses were there in front of her, a line of red tiled roofs just visible, their wooden jetties jutting out into the water. As they drew nearer, a row of doors gleamed through the white curtain of fog. The boathouses seemed to have been freshly painted. Beside the nearest building, a boat had been tied to an iron stanchion, but otherwise the moorings were empty.

Archie came to a halt. 'What is it?' she asked nervously.

'I'm trying to remember which was Di Maio's. All these boathouses look the same. It had a blue door, I think.'

'They've been repainted,' she pointed out.

'So they have.' He didn't seem unduly fazed by it. 'If my memory serves me right, Di Maio's had a small weather vane on top. It would, of course. The man always needs to go one better.'

She looked ahead, her eyes travelling down the line, trying to pick out the weather vane.

'C'mon, we need to get closer. And walk quietly,' he warned, 'there are security guards who work shifts through the night.'

That was something he hadn't mentioned before and her nervousness increased.

'There, there it is.' They had walked past several of the boathouses, but without hesitation Archie stopped outside a blue painted door.

'Blue is obviously a DiMaio favourite,' he said, 'but the door might be a problem.'

The boathouse was built of brick and slatted wood, its double doors constructed of thick planks. It would take a power saw to break through them, she thought. In addition, a huge padlock sat squarely between the two doors, and a double chain ran across the entire frontage. How had she imagined it would be any different? The boathouse was bound to be locked and double locked if it contained material it should not. And they had brought no tools. But then what could they have brought that would open those impregnable doors?

'How—' she began.

'There'll be another way in. Let's find it.'

Archie led the way down one side of the boathouse, then

round to the rear. On the third side there was a small window, high up in the wall. 'And here it is.'

She raised her head. 'You're expecting me to climb up there?'

'You'll have to if you want to look inside. Or you'll have to trust me to do the searching.'

She was silent, thinking it over.

'I thought you wanted to be in at the kill,' Archie prompted.

It was an unfortunate expression, but it reminded Nancy why she was here and what she had to do. Feeling a new burst of energy, she studied the wall hard, looking for a way in which she might climb to the window. But when she turned round, Archie had vanished and she found herself surrounded by an empty whiteness. Her heart gave an unpleasant jolt. Was she now alone? Was it some kind of trap? Had Archie brought her to this deserted place only to abandon her? But she was being neurotic. Of course, he hadn't, and before she could lose her nerve completely, he had returned carrying a small ladder.

'Where did you discover that?' It seemed an improbable find.

'Careless of people, isn't it? Leaving ladders around to help you through windows. One of the painters left it, I guess. But it will do us a treat.'

And before she could say anything, he'd produced a sharp knife from his jacket pocket and bounded up the ladder. At the top, he slid the knife down one side of the window frame and after a few seconds was rewarded with a definite click.

'Here we go.' He pulled the window open and hauled himself on to the ledge, then swung his legs over and disappeared. Nancy heard him land on the floor below.

'There's quite a drop,' he called quietly to her. 'You'll need to be careful. And' — there was a flash of light from inside the room — 'you might not want to bother. There doesn't seem to be anything worth looking at.'

The beam of light continued to trace an arc through the darkness. 'What's that you've got? Did you bring a torch?' she asked.

'Flashlight. Old army days—comes in useful. It sends Morse code, too, though there might not be much call for that tonight.' He switched off the light and the boathouse sank back into darkness. 'Are you coming or shall I call it a day?'

'I'm coming,' she said determinedly.

The ladder was the easy bit, but pulling herself up to the window required a great deal more effort. Within minutes, though, she was sitting astride the ledge and swinging first one leg and then the other across the sill and into the boathouse.

'Here.' Archie put up his arms to catch her. He'd taken off his jacket, she saw, and now stood in shirt sleeves. It felt a little too intimate, and she hesitated, but this was no time to be shy. She dropped down and felt two strong arms encircle her, and then her feet met the floor with a very definite thud.

Archie switched on the flashlight again. 'As far as I can see, there's nothing here.' The light roved around the space, into each corner, across the earthen floor, over the ceiling joists. There was nothing. The boathouse was completely empty.

'Sorry,' he said and sounded it. He must have seen the dismay written on her face.

It was desperately disappointing. They had risked much in coming here: Archie, his job, and she, her marriage. If Leo ever knew… she dared not think of it. Not to mention the possibility of arrest if they were found by the security guards. And all for nothing.

'Can I borrow that?' She pointed to the flashlight.

'Be my guest. But you can't manufacture what isn't here.'

'I'll take a walk around the perimeter, just to make sure.'

She had reached the third side of the boathouse when she bent to pick a piece of litter from the floor. Litter was hardly helpful, but when she turned it to face the light, she saw it was a scrap of canvas.

'Canvas,' she said excitedly. Archie came over to her. 'At least it proves that paintings have been here.' She looked again at the scrap. Grass was visible, the tip of a bare toe.

'I wonder... could this be from one of the paintings, the ones on the yacht?'

'Dino acts as a fence for stolen paintings and then tears one of them into shreds?'

Archie's derisive tone was familiar, but she ignored it. 'Why torn?' she wondered aloud, and then caught sight of marks on the piece of canvas she held. 'There's a name.'

She peered closely. 'It's the artist's signature. Di Cosimo. Piero di Cosimo?'

'What does that mean?'

'It means that if this fragment is di Cosimo's work, the painting it comes from is worth a lot of money. He was a Renaissance artist—from Florence. Not as well known as others perhaps. He painted mythological subjects but with realistic figures. I'm not sure how many of his paintings have survived, but any one of them would fetch thousands at auction.'

'So you take a pair of scissors to a painting you could sell for an immense sum of money? Or you're so careless, you don't worry if it's badly damaged? I don't think so.'

'I don't either.'

Nancy peered down again at the scrap, bringing it up to her eyes as closely as she could. 'Look at the brush work,' she said slowly. 'It's quite rough—and the colour of the grass. It's a green that doesn't feel true for the Renaissance. What do you think?'

'Why ask me? I'm the peasant, remember.'

She found his churlishness irritating. But then he surprised her—when she looked across at him, he was grinning. 'As it happens, I agree with you.'

'So you do know what you're looking at?'

'I've been with Leo a long time. When you leave school at fourteen, you've a lot to catch up on, but you're bound to learn something. Even me.'

'So if it's not a di Cosimo—'

Archie held a finger up in warning and she was immediately silent. They stood listening intently—a soft shuffling just outside the locked doors? Archie had snapped off the light as she stopped speaking, and now glided towards the window.

'We need to be careful,' he whispered. 'I'll go first and look around. I'll give you the nod if the coast is clear.'

'But how am I to reach the window from this side?' she hissed, but he had already jumped and was swinging his body over the window sill. All she could do was wait for him to return.

For a few seconds she heard nothing. Then what she thought was a scuffling, followed by a definite thwack, then a splash. Then silence. Until in the distance she caught the sound of soft-soled footsteps running. She tried to remember what shoes Archie had been wearing and couldn't. What if the footsteps weren't his?

Galvanised, Nancy picked up the flashlight and stuffed it back into the large pocket of Archie's jacket, then quickly donned the jacket herself. It drowned her slender figure, but to leave it here would incriminate Archie. She hoped it wouldn't impede an escape that was already looking horribly difficult. There was nothing in the boathouse to help her up to that window. She would have to jump for the sill as Archie had done, but without his size and strength.

She backed herself against the opposite side of the building and made a run, desperately pedalling her feet up the wall and reaching with her arms for some kind of purchase, but it was useless and she fell back. It took three attempts before she managed to get her right hand on the sill and, frantic not to slide to the ground again, she forced her left arm upwards to make a grab at the window ledge. For a while she hung there, her arm muscles torn in two, or so it seemed, but then slowly began to pull herself up, at the same time using her feet to climb the wall.

As soon as she reached the sill, she flung her legs over, and dropped on to the top step of the ladder. Then down and around the side of the boathouse with such speed that she almost fell into the lagoon, lapping peacefully at the landing stage.

She stripped off the jacket, it was too heavy to wear for long, then fumbled in the pocket for the flashlight. Not caring now who saw it, she brandished its beam from side to side and out over the water. A head, a face — was that a face? Could it really be? My God, it was! She tried to hold the light steady but her hand was shaking. Then for an instant, the flash focussed on a single spot of water. It was Archie! Archie's face! And there was something streaking his forehead.

As Nancy peered into the darkness, his body seemed to sway to the ebb and flow of the water, knocking gently against a mooring stake. She flashed the torch again. Yes, his shirt was caught against one of the wooden posts that dotted the lagoon; it appeared to be the only thing keeping him afloat. But surely he could swim? He had spent his entire childhood by the sea. So why wasn't he swimming to land?

She ran forward to call to him and tripped over a piece of wood. Swinging the light downwards, she saw it was a bat of some kind, a wooden handle with a large square head — a rounders bat? Did Italians play rounders? It really didn't matter. That was the noise she'd heard. The thwack of wood on an unprotected head, and Archie was out there in the lagoon, unconscious.

Nancy couldn't swim. She could wade towards Archie, but how deep was the water at this point? Pretty deep if a boat was able to sail up to the boathouse doors. She ran on to the landing stage and a small mercy, a boat hook had been left lying to one side. She would have to use it, there was nothing else. Lean out and try to get the hook into Archie's clothing. That way she could keep his face above water. She was terrified that at any moment, the movement of the tide would detach him from the wooden stake, the one thing that was keeping him safe.

The boat hook was a good six feet long and awkward to control. Abandoning the flashlight, Nancy scrambled down onto the decking and lay flat on her stomach, stretching her body to reach as far out as she could. Water might be wonderful when she was safe in a boat, she reflected, but hanging a few inches from its surface was truly terrifying for a woman who couldn't swim.

The murk was still thick and she could barely see the floating body. It took a long agonising minute before she caught the hook in the collar of Archie's shirt and with a superhuman effort pulled him upwards, just in time to stop him slipping beneath the surface of the lagoon. By now her own arms and chest were submerged in water and she was finding it painfully hard to keep the boat hook high enough. She needed to be standing, but if she were to try to get to her feet, she might dislodge the hook that was keeping Archie alive.

Wake up, she pleaded silently, fearing they would soon both drown if he stayed unconscious. She would never relinquish her hold—she couldn't do that, it would be abandoning him—even though her strength was almost gone and the weight of the boat hook was dragging her closer and closer to the water. There was only one thing she could do. It was a last desperate effort and could go very wrong. But she must try; there was nothing else. Slowly, achingly, she began to pull the boathook in towards her, towing the dead weight of Archie inch by inch towards the landing stage.

It was a slow and arduous business with long pauses between each pull, and she was constantly fearful she would lose her hold on him. It seemed to take forever, but finally Archie was within reaching distance. Nancy leaned even further out, expecting to feel the cold slap of water closing over her at any moment, but in a swift grab she managed to hold on to a wodge of shirt. Abandoning the boat hook, she reached out with her other hand and grabbed a waterlogged sleeve. Cautiously, she moved her hands down the sleeve to the wrists beneath, trying desperately to keep his head above water. *Wake up, wake up*, she repeated to herself.

Aloud, she said, 'Archie, please try to help. I'm not strong enough to pull you out.'

Whether it was her voice, or the warmth of her hands, or more prosaically the movement of his body through the water as it nudged up against the side of the ironwork, Archie opened one eye and then the other. After a dazed moment, he seemed to understand the danger he was in, and with one hand made a grab for the wooden jetty. She held fast to his other arm and somehow he managed to get a knee onto the landing stage, then the other knee, and coughing and spluttering, crawled out of the water. He fell on his back, arms and legs splayed, the red gash on his forehead livid.

He lay there for only a second. The next moment, he turned on his side and rid himself of the mass of water he'd swallowed. Nancy watched him anxiously, but when he laid back gasping, she fell back, too, and laid beside him. Every one of her limbs felt shredded and every breath had been punched from her body.

They lay in silence for long minutes. Then Archie said, 'The bastard!'

Chapter Twenty-Two

'That bastard, Salvatore.' Archie jerked himself upright, water dribbling from his shirt. 'I'm going to get him. Now.'

Nancy sat up, too, alarmed by the ferocity in his voice. 'You can't.'

'What do you mean, I can't? The man springs out at me from the dark, tries to knock me out and then when he fails, hits me with some weapon he's hiding.'

'It was that. Over there. Some kind of bat.' Nancy waved a vague hand in the direction of the piece of wood she'd stumbled over earlier.

'Whatever it was, I have a lump on my head the size of a fist. And not content with that, he proceeds to try and drown me.'

'Salvatore pushed you into the lagoon?' She couldn't prevent disbelief colouring her voice. It was unimaginable that the man had deliberately tried to kill Archie.

'He didn't need to push,' her companion retorted, shaking his head like a dog who had just emerged from swimming, and sending droplets of water spraying wide. 'His swipe with the bat sent me flying.'

'So it was an accident?'

'What do you mean, an accident?' His question was angry. 'It wasn't an accident. Feel that.' She imagined rather than saw him point to his head, but made no move to comply. 'There's no doubt in my mind—the man tried to kill me.' Archie staggered to his feet. 'I can't waste more time. I'm on my way.'

'But how do you know it was Salvatore? I can barely see my hand in front of me. You could be mistaken.'

'I've fought him before, remember. It was him all right. And why all these excuses?'

'I'm not making excuses. I'm simply trying to inject a little calm into the situation. I didn't rescue you so that you could go bolting off and get into more trouble.'

'Okay. And sorry—I didn't thank you for that.'

'Why would you?' she said tartly. 'It's hardly your style.'

'I'm not hanging around arguing the toss.' Archie was back to his customary abrasiveness. 'Are you coming or not? We need to get a move on. I suppose you don't have the flashlight, do you?'

She scrambled to her feet and, bent double, felt along the landing stage for Archie's jacket. It was there by the water's edge, slightly damp but undamaged. Burrowing into its largest pocket, she drew out the torch and walked back to him.

'Your flashlight, sir,' she said, switching it on. 'And your jacket, in case you'd forgotten it.'

'I had. Thanks for that, too.' His gratitude didn't sound quite so grudging this time, and she decided to make peace.

'Can we use the light now, do you think?'

'There will still be guards patrolling the area, but I'm beyond caring. I need to catch up with Salvatore and that means moving as fast as this fog allows.'

Archie had already turned and was walking briskly away, lighting a narrow path in front of him. As usual, she had to run to catch up. 'I thought you didn't know where Salvatore lived,' she said breathlessly.

'I don't but I'll bet my boots he isn't going home—at least not yet—which is why we need to be quick.'

'Where then?'

'To his employer, of course. To Dino. He'll be anxious to report a break-in at the boathouse. Anxious to warn his paymaster that whatever game they're playing has been rumbled.'

'Not quite rumbled. All we discovered was a piece of canvas. And he won't find Dino. He's in Rome. Salvatore will hardly be travelling there this evening.'

'What's the betting that Dino is back in Venice right now? He hired a helicopter to get to Rome, didn't he, so why not keep it on? That way he can get back pronto to see his girlfriend. And even if he has stayed in Rome, there's still Luca. You say Salvatore is thick with him, so in the absence of Dino, that's who the swine will go to.'

'And you know where Luca lives?'

'I don't have to. He'll be at the *casinò*. That's where he and Dino spend every evening. Dino is a professional gambler as well as orchestrating all the other little ventures he has up his sleeve.'

'You sound pretty sure of that.' She was still finding it hard to keep up and her words came out jerkily.

He tapped the side of his nose with one finger. 'You'd be surprised at how little notice people take of the menials who serve them. It's amazing how much you can learn by simply standing around and listening.'

'Anyway, you can't go to the *casinò* like that. They'd never let you through the door.'

Archie looked down at his trousers shedding water and the shoes squelching beneath his feet and gave a harsh laugh. 'Okay, a quick return to the palazzo to change, and then I'm off.'

'Even if you're right about the *casinò*, by the time we get there, Salvatore will have been and gone. The palazzo is a long walk from here.'

'Except we aren't walking, if we can possibly help it. We'll go to the landing stage at San Basilio. There won't be a vaporetto, but water taxis wait there. Even in this weather, there should be one or two for hire.'

'I don't have money with me.'

'But I do.' Archie patted his jacket. 'You're a clever girl— you saved my wallet!'

They were lucky when they arrived at San Basilio. A solitary water taxi was parked to one side, seemingly without much hope of a fare that evening. The fog was still thick and the streets still deserted. The boatman brightened considerably when he saw them approach and was eager to get them swiftly back to the palazzo, helped by the fact that tonight there was little water traffic even on the narrower canals. It seemed that most of Venice was sleeping, and ten minutes later they were scrambling out of the taxi and onto the palazzo landing stage.

Archie gave the boatman a handsome tip and asked him to wait. Then took the stairs to his bedroom two at a time.

'I'm coming with you,' Nancy called up to him. 'To the *casinò*.'

'No,' he shouted back.

'Yes, I am. You owe me.'

She had to go with Archie. She had a vague idea that if she did, she might prevent him doing something stupid. The thought of Leo, and what he would say if his assistant were involved in a catastrophic brawl, was always in her mind. It would be her fault if it happened. She had persuaded Archie that something was amiss and he'd gone along with it.

Nancy was unsure he'd truly believed her, but even if he

hadn't, he had been willing to embark on this small adventure. She thought she understood why. He was a soldier doing a clerk's job, a menial he'd called himself. An adventure, small or otherwise, offered a welcome break.

Until, that is, Salvatore had attacked him. Then things had changed. The man had hurt Archie badly and left him to drown. Even if she were generous and told herself that Salvatore couldn't have realised Archie had lost consciousness, it was still a wicked thing to do, to leave a man you'd clubbed on the head to fend for himself. And as for Archie, the small adventure had become personal, a matter for revenge. Precisely what she feared.

'I'm coming,' she shouted again, following him quickly up the stairs.

'Suit yourself. If it goes pear-shaped, it's your problem.'

Upstairs, she tore off the wet cardigan and jumper and her soaking underwear—they smelt of lagoon—and in a few minutes had thrown on another set of clothes and snatched up the bottle of grappa Archie had left earlier.

Nancy met him on the wide landing, about to leap down the stairs. 'Do you fancy some grappa? It's good for shock, I believe.' She waved the bottle at him.

'So I'm told.' He grinned. 'But no. I need to be alert. I have a few shocks of my own to administer.'

It was bidding to be a very difficult evening, and she could have done with the grappa herself. Barely recovered from the terror of rescuing Archie, she was facing another severe trial.

Archie was half way down the stairs when he turned, his eyebrows raised. 'Well?'

'I'm coming', she said, hastily discarding the bottle on a nearby table.

*

They were at the *casinò* in minutes, the boatman expertly guiding his craft from one small canal to another. The fog had lifted slightly, but still blanketed the ill-lit alleyways and dark corners on either side of them. The buildings they passed slipped in and out of sight, as though they themselves were moving, visible one moment and the next swallowed up by the dense haze that filled the narrow streets and lay over the dank waters.

Here and there a narrow boat had been moored for the night and to an apprehensive Nancy they seemed almost like coffins, patiently awaiting their occupants. Even the few people scurrying along the canal side were spirit-like, transformed into phantoms of shimmering grey.

When, finally, they emerged into the Grand Canal, she was relieved to see signs of life at last. Lights from the old palaces that lined the great waterway were blazing bravely, relieving the monochrome of a fog-bound city and dappling the surface of the canal with small pools of illumination.

The *casinò* was located on the Grand Canal itself and housed in a former palace of solid white stone. It was an impressive building. Three tiers of delicately traced window arches towered over them as they pulled up at the red-canopied landing stage. Archie paid off the boatman. A considerable sum, Nancy guessed. He must want to settle the score with Salvatore very badly.

A man in a dark tailcoat and top hat was at the entrance and his white-gloved hand barred their way. 'You are members?' he asked.

It seemed for a moment he was about to refuse them entry and Nancy could understand why. They were no longer dripping water, but were hardly dressed in style.

'No, but we are friends of Mr Di Maio,' she was quick to say.

The man inclined his head in a dignified gesture and

waved his hand towards the open doorway. 'If Mr Di Maio is here, you will find him on the lower floor, signora.'

'Thank you.' She slipped past him, hoping he didn't expect a tip.

'It's the gaming rooms that are on the lower floor,' Archie told her.

She nodded and made for the thickly carpeted staircase, with Archie following close behind. 'We'll go for the roulette table,' he said. 'I reckon we'll find Salvatore there, or at least Dino. I'll make him tell me where to find the bloke.'

Nancy was certain Dino would still be in Rome and, if for any reason he were not, he was hardly going to oblige Archie, but she said nothing and took her time to look around the enormous room they'd entered. A thick pall of smoke hung in the air, so that for a moment she was unable to see clearly. But as the cloud shifted, she noticed the plush velvet sofas lining each side of the room: a luxurious retreat for punters taking a break from the play while observing their fellow gamblers.

Now several card games came into view—blackjack? poker?—and that was a baccarat table, she was sure. Archie pointed ahead: the roulette wheel was where he was headed.

A circle of well-dressed men and women ringed the roulette table, which took up the centre of the room. Nancy stood with Archie behind the seated players, trying to look inconspicuous. She had never been in a casino before and its louche atmosphere made her uncomfortable.

There was a reverent silence as chips were put down across the felt board, stacked one on top of the other, and the croupier gave the wheel a sharp turn. The ball ricocheted around the bowl, the noise loud in the silence, all eyes riveted on the whirl of metal and colour as it slowed and slowed and finally came to a halt. The croupier's rake was swift and snake-like. In one movement, he swept the losers' chips towards him and nudged a few to the winner. Then a repeat of the same motions—the flurry, the spin, the fixed eyes nailed to the spinning ball.

Nancy's eyes roved around the punters. She was looking for Salvatore, but he was not among them. But then he wouldn't be. Common sense told her that a working man could never compete with these compulsive gamblers.

Halfway round the circle of people, she spotted Francesca, dressed in yet another silk sheath, this time one of midnight blue. Nancy's eyes slid leftwards and there was Dino right beside the woman. Not in Rome as he should have been, but here, just as Archie had foretold. Had he left Leo waiting uselessly in Rome?

Archie waited for three complete throws of the roulette ball, watching Dino all the time, but when the man moved away from the table, he followed him.

Dino had just raised a glass of wine to his lips when Archie pounced. Nancy remained standing feet away from the little group. She saw the look of surprise on Dino's face and the distaste on Francesca's.

'Archie!' There was a forced heartiness in Dino's voice. His eyes, Nancy noticed, told a different story. They were hard, wintry. 'How are you? Come to try your luck? And you've brought...' He peered over Archie's shoulder. 'Mrs Tremayne. Nancy! Well, well.'

Archie dispensed with any courtesies to swoop immediately on his goal. 'I'm looking for Salvatore. I thought I'd find him here.'

'You would have, old chap. A little earlier. I'm afraid he left for home a few minutes ago. Back to his lovely Luisa.'

'Can you tell me where home is? I have a particular reason for seeing him.'

'Have you?' The eyes bored further into Archie's face.

'And does that go for Mrs Tremayne, too?'

Archie ignored the comment. 'Well?' he demanded.

'Come on, Archie, you must know I can't divulge my employee's whereabouts.' The tone had reverted to hearty and sounded even more false this time. 'That would be abusing his privacy, wouldn't it? But perhaps *I* can help?'

'Perhaps you can.' Archie's chin jutted and Nancy saw his fists begin to curl. She stepped in front of him.

'How nice to see you again, Dino,' she said. 'And you, too, Francesca. Such a wonderful trip you gave Leo and myself to Burano. It was such a pity that Mr Moretto missed it, but I've been thinking that perhaps we could organise another small journey before Leo and I leave Venice. We are here for a few more days.'

Francesca looked decidedly unexcited by the prospect and Dino merely took another sip from his glass. '*Is* Mr Moretto here tonight?' Nancy went on. 'If he is, perhaps we could arrange it this very evening.'

She was being unbearably pushy, but she needed to give Archie time to calm himself. And it was important to know if Luca were indeed here. If he had been with his wife and Dino at the *casinò* all evening, he could not have been the attacker, and Archie must be right about Salvatore.

'Luca has gone out for a breath of fresh air, but he'll be back very shortly,' Dino said smoothly. 'It can get very stuffy in here. But it's a wonderful idea, Nancy. We should plan something stupendous, shouldn't we, Francesca? A leaving party for you both.'

And that was all they were going to get. Salvatore had been here earlier and, though Dino would undoubtedly know what had happened at the boathouse this evening, he was giving nothing away. He was as impervious as a chunk of agate, and to stage any kind of showdown here, in a gathering of the rich and fashionable, would be stupid. She hoped dearly that Archie would see the uselessness of it and come away quietly. If he really must settle his score with Salvatore, he would need to find the man elsewhere.

She nudged Archie's sleeve and he took her hint. He wasn't going to make a scene and she breathed relief. They said their goodbyes, Nancy falsely eulogising over the trip that would never be, and was nearly at the door when out of the corner of her eye, she glimpsed a familiar figure.

Leo! It couldn't be. Leo was in Rome, wasn't he? He had phoned Archie and told him to book a hotel for the night. But then Dino was supposed to be in Rome, too, and here he was, three hundred miles away. What was going on?

It was evidently something that Leo wanted to know, too. He put down the drink he was carrying and strode across the room to them.

'What on earth are you doing here, Nancy? And Archie?'

She thought his tone unfriendly and didn't answer. Instead she bounced his question back. 'What are *you* doing here? You're supposed to be in Rome.'

'I came back with Dino. He kept on the helicopter from this morning and gave me a lift. I thought I'd have a drink with him to celebrate a successful day, then be on my way home to surprise you.'

'But I thought you weren't able to complete the business today.'

Leo's hunched shoulders relaxed a little. 'The police relented in the end. The dealer was still unwell and likely to be for several days, so rather than keep us kicking our heels in Rome, they decided that our testimony alone would be sufficient.'

Dino had wandered up to them while they were talking and overheard this last remark. 'They did indeed. And the paintings will be with me tomorrow. Isn't that splendid?' His smile this time was genuine. 'But why don't you all stay? We can make those arrangements we talked of, Nancy. And you may be lucky at the tables. Luckier than I've been.'

'Or me.' Francesca had joined them now. 'But Nancy might feel uncomfortable, we mustn't press her to stay. Unless of course she'd like to go home to change…' The woman gave a small moue in Nancy's direction.

'I don't think so,' Leo said firmly. 'We have to be getting home.' He looked down at Nancy and his eyes held the coldness she had come to dread.

'Another time then?'

'Yes, indeed,' Leo said insincerely, picking up his briefcase and putting out his arm to shepherd Nancy ahead. Archie was already through the door and walking up the stairs towards the *casinò* entrance.

Leo caught up with him there and swooped. 'What the hell's going on, Archie? Why are you here, and why is my wife with you?'

'I came to find Salvatore.'

'Salvatore? Why would you want to see him? He was here, but left a while ago.'

'So I understand. He'll keep.'

Archie made a move towards the arched entrance doors, but Leo stopped him with an outstretched hand. 'What I don't understand is why you brought Nancy on a fool's errand and in dreadful weather.'

'He didn't,' Nancy intervened quickly. 'Archie didn't bring me.' Archie looked as grateful as he would ever look. 'I brought myself. I wanted to see a casino, that's all. I'd never been to one before and I was becoming bored at the palazzo.'

She tried to inject a degree of *ennui* into her voice, though in reality her mind and body were in a state of tension.

She didn't understand why Leo had not returned home immediately. He'd made the journey from the Lido airfield, so why not ask to be dropped off at the palazzo? And the story of the art fraud police, previously so rigid in their demands but suddenly wonderfully amenable? Was any of it true? Had Leo actually been to Rome?

Her husband gave her another hard look. 'We'll talk of this later. We need to get back in case the fog gets any thicker.'

The fog hadn't stopped him visiting the *casinò*, Nancy reflected. The bad weather should have made his return home more pressing, but he'd come here instead. And if she hadn't accompanied Archie, she would never have known. Leo wouldn't have told her, she was pretty sure.

Despite her best efforts, suspicion was growing. Why hadn't her husband phoned to say he wasn't staying in Rome after all and would be back this evening? There had been time to tell her he'd changed his plans. A surprise, he'd said, but somehow that didn't fit. In the short time Nancy had known him, surprises had been noticeably absent. Would Leo have returned home tonight, if she hadn't seen him here?

And how much did he know of this evening's events? He'd seen Salvatore, he said, but had he heard what the man had to say to Dino? Salvatore would have reported the break-in at the boathouse as Archie predicted, and if Archie had recognised Salvatore in the dark then the opposite must be true. Salvatore would have recognised Archie and relayed his suspicions to his employer.

If Leo *had* heard … he would know his assistant was guilty of breaking and entering, and suspect that his wife was just as guilty. But he had said nothing of it. Was that because he had things to hide himself? Did she have to add Leo to the three she'd already found guilty in her mind? And where was Luca in all of this? It had been a long breath of fresh air he'd taken.

The questions kept churning as she passed out of the lobby and into the fog once more. Apparently they were to walk home. The weather had improved slightly, but the alleyway leading from the *casinò* was still very dark, a solitary street light burning only dimly. Archie was slightly ahead of them while she walked beside Leo, but her husband made no attempt to offer his arm.

Suddenly Archie stopped and raised his hand. Then he bent down and seemed to roll something over.

'What is it?' Leo's voice was sharp, slicing through the stillness.

'Who is it I think is the question.'

'Let me see.' Leo pushed ahead and bent down beside Archie.

'It's too dark, boss. We need a light.'

A man came running up behind them at that moment from the direction of the *casinò*. 'Professor Tremayne,' he shouted. 'Your holdall, sir—you left it in the cloakroom.'

'Damn the holdall, man, do you have a light? If so, bring it over here.'

The urgency in Leo's voice had the uniformed man fumble in his coat pocket for a torch. 'Here.' Archie pointed his foot at whatever was barring their way. Nancy had begun to shiver. She knew it must be a body and that was bad enough. Two dead bodies in as many weeks. But she had a horrible premonition of whose body it would be.

And she was right. The torchlight flashed downwards and there he was. Luca Moretto. His staring eyes looked glassily up at them, a thin trickle of crimson bisecting his throat. But even worse, his mouth was wide open, and stuffed with crumpled banknotes.

Nancy ran to the side of the canal and was violently sick.

Chapter Twenty-Three

It was the small hours before they arrived back at the palazzo and, by then, Nancy was asleep on her feet. The *casinò* had called the police once the news of Luca's death became known, and the officers who attended the scene had insisted their small party go to the *Questura* to give signed statements. But it hadn't finished there. Interviews had followed. A detective plodded through what seemed hours of questions with each of them individually, and it was only when he seemed satisfied that none of them were involved in Luca Moretto's untimely death that they were allowed to leave.

It was clear from the detective's questions that the police were hoping to pin the man's death on a particularly violent mugging. His wallet apparently was missing and a gold watch had been taken from his wrist. But the lire notes stuffed in his mouth were a challenge to the theory. They suggested bitterness, some kind of personal message to Luca, rather than a random killing. Unless, the detective had mused, they were dealing with a mugger who nursed a particular hatred of the wealthy along with a desire to rob them.

It was unlikely, Nancy thought, but not inconceivable. What was inconceivable was a second member of the Moretto family meeting a violent death within weeks of each other. This new tragedy, coming so close on the heels of the last, had Nancy scrabbling to adjust. She could no longer think of Luca as a potential killer; like Marta, he had become a victim himself. But why had he died, if not in a random attack?

Was it for the same reason that Marta had died? Perhaps the signora had enjoyed a closer relationship with her son than first appeared and confided her fears to him. He was, after all, helping to run the Moretto business, and if she were concerned for the reputation of the Venice art world, he must be, too. If so, he had followed his mother in paying the price for that knowledge.

Nancy slept badly during what was left of the night. The image of that poor, mutilated body haunted her as soon as she closed her eyes, but made her more determined than ever to get to the bottom of this deadly mystery. She had little confidence in the police investigation. The detective who'd questioned them had seemed disinclined to stretch his imagination further than a mugging, but she knew if she were to be believed, she would need to bring him hard evidence that Luca had been deliberately targeted by a determined and ruthless adversary.

*

Her eagerness to keep probing received a severe check the next morning, however. Leo had risen early and skipped breakfast to bury himself in his office. Nancy had no idea what he was doing—she would have expected any issues from the conference to have been settled by now. It added to the unease she'd felt last night, the awkward questions concerning Leo's movements. She'd tried hard to quash the worries but it was difficult, and made no easier by the fact that her husband had barely said a word since their return home.

It seemed important to smooth things over between them and she asked Concetta to make a tray of coffee that she could take to the office herself.

Leo must have sensed her standing in the doorway, and looked up. 'Nancy! I'm glad you're here. I was coming to find you. I have to go out later this morning. The police telephoned an hour ago and they want me back at the *Questura* at one.'

'But why?' She set the tray down on the desk. 'You gave a statement last night. We all did. What more can they want?'

'They're interested in how much I knew of Luca's business dealings.' He laid back in his chair, twirling a pen through his fingers.

'But you know nothing about them, do you?'

'No. I tried to tell them that, but they were adamant they needed to see me.'

She handed him a coffee and sat down on a heavily carved upright chair. 'Perhaps you won't be too long. We could walk out together when you get back. See some of the places you haven't had a chance to show me yet.'

He frowned and dropped the pen onto the desk. 'I doubt there'll be enough time. And to be honest, I'm not in the mood for sightseeing.'

'I know,' she sighed. 'That poor man.'

'I'm exceedingly sorry about Luca, naturally, but it's you that's causing me more concern.'

Startled, she put her cup down too quickly and spilled coffee into the saucer. 'Me?'

He took up his spoon and stirred slowly. 'After last night, why do you sound so surprised? What were you thinking, going out with Archie, who happens to be my assistant, on such a filthy night and to the *casinò* of all places?'

'I told you.' She tried to speak calmly, but felt a ripple of annoyance. 'I was interested to see the place. And I hadn't expected you back. You never phoned. You could have, of course, and then I wouldn't have gone.' Nancy hoped that was pointed enough.

'There was no chance to telephone,' he said curtly. 'And *my* movements are not in question here.'

'And neither are mine, Leo. Unless of course you see me as some kind of bondswoman, destined to go only where you choose.'

'That's ridiculous. I see you as my wife. And I think you'll agree that as such you must be careful to behave in a way that doesn't encourage talk. How do you think I felt, seeing my wife accompanying my assistant to a place such as the *casinò*, and dressed like a... a...'

'Ragamuffin?'

'Not a ragamuffin, of course. But out of kilter certainly. It made you look an oddity—Francesca noticed it.'

'Francesca is the worst kind of woman. How dare you cite her judgement as something I should care about!'

'I accept that, but if she thought it, so did others. As I say, how do you think I felt seeing my wife in such a place when she should be safely home?'

'The same, I imagine, as I felt seeing my husband in such a place when he should have returned to the palazzo the moment he was back in Venice.'

'The case is not the same.'

'It's exactly the same.' Her tone was fiery. 'Or are you saying that a wife is not equal? I'd no idea you were so Victorian, Leo.'

'I'm saying no such thing, and you know it. But it does my professional reputation no good, Nancy—and yours neither for that matter—for my wife to behave in the fashion you did last night. I hope you'll forget such nonsense in the future.'

'You can be sure I will check with you every time I wish to leave the house.' She got up sharply, thumping her cup down on the tray. 'Now may I go? Is that servile enough for you?'

Leo jumped up, too, and took hold of her hands. 'You are an independent woman. I recognise that. I don't see marriage as binding you to me in the way you suggest. It would be preposterous to think so. But what I see is that we should be together in the way we do things. We should be making this marriage work as a couple. Not, as so often it seems, being at odds with one another.'

She lowered her head, feeling the justice of his words, and was about to say so when he continued, 'You worry me, Nancy. You've developed some strange ideas since we've been in Venice. I know, I realise, that much of it goes back to your troubles in London but I can't stand by and let you cause problems for yourself—and for me. Not to mention Archie. Have you thought of the gossip you must have provoked last night?'

'Gossip in Venice? Surely not,' she mocked. 'But then we're leaving soon and can kiss Venice and gossip goodbye, unless you were planning another trip to Rome.' Or wherever it was you went yesterday, she added silently to herself.

'We'll be leaving in two days,' he said abruptly. 'Archie has gone to Santa Lucia to confirm our reservations. But in the meantime, can't we be kind to each other?'

Nancy looked at him and tried to feel kindness, but his words had stung. Leo might deny he was trying to curb her, but that's how it felt. She knew she should not have gone to the *casinò* and even more that she should not have been at the boathouse last night. But she had no need of a husband to tell her so.

Leo held out his hand to her and she willed herself to be loving. His behaviour this morning, though, was too reminiscent of what she'd endured before, and she hesitated. Was her experience of Philip March making her unduly sensitive? Perhaps so. And she needed this marriage to go well—her future happiness depended on it. Both their future happiness.

She reached out and took her husband's hand. 'I'm sorry I upset you, Leo. My going to the *casinò* was a silly whim. Archie certainly didn't want me with him, but I insisted. It was as I said: I was bored, stuck at home in the fog, and thought it would fill an evening. But I agree, it was a foolish thing to do.'

'Friends again?' His eyes held the warmth she'd come to know, a far cry from the ice of last night.

'Friends.' She smiled at him. 'But I'm so sorry you have to return to the police station.'

'It's tedious, but I shouldn't be long. Try not to get bored again while I'm gone.' He flicked a finger against her cheek. 'That's a joke, by the way.'

'I know. But come back soon.'

It was only as Nancy made her way up to her bedroom to find a book she'd been reading that she realised Leo had said nothing of the boathouse. He could not, after all, have overheard Salvatore's account. She said a little thank you to the gods for that small charity.

*

She ate an early lunch in the kitchen, with Concetta humming in the background, and was half way through a plate of chicken and salad when Archie appeared by her side and helped himself from the bowl of washed lettuce, sprinkling it liberally with olive oil.

Concetta waved to him from the sink where she was busy washing up.

'So,' he said quietly in Nancy's ear, 'was it a mugging?'

'Luca Moretto?' She spoke quietly, too. Concetta seemed not yet to know that another member of the family she loved had met with death and Nancy needed to break the news gently.

'No, I don't think so. Do you?'

He shook his head and plunged his fork into the salad. 'But if it isn't, who did it and why?'

'If we knew that, we'd know who killed Marta.'

She felt him glance sideways at her. 'You're sure it's the same person?'

'It has to be. If you discount a random attacker—and what random attacker would stuff money into a victim's mouth?'— she felt sick again at the thought of it. 'It's too much of a coincidence.'

'So who's still left on your grand list of the guilty?'

'I haven't yet discounted Mario. As for the others, Francesca? But she was in the *casinò*, expecting her husband back.'

'So she says.' Archie reached for a slice of roast chicken.

'You really think she planned her husband's death last night?'

'It would suit her by all accounts, but my guess is that it's more likely his erstwhile business chum who did the deed. A falling out among thieves, perhaps. The stuffed notes might carry a message—you died because you wanted too much money, so here it is.'

'But Dino was in the casinò, too. So he has to be out of the picture—for Luca's murder at least.'

'Not Dino in person. Far too fastidious to cut throats. Salvatore though…'

'You're prejudiced.' Nancy put her empty plate to one side.

'Being drowned by someone tends to have that effect. But think about it—Salvatore goes to the casinò to tell his tale to Dino. He leaves before we get there, and when we leave by the same exit and walk along the same path half an hour later, what do we find? —a dead Luca.'

'What is that?' Concetta had come over to the table while they were deep in conversation. 'Signor Luca dead?' Her mouth was open and her expression bewildered.

Nancy jumped up and put her hands on the maid's shoulders. They were already beginning to shake. 'Concetta, dear, sit down for a moment. Archie, do something useful, make a cup of tea.'

'With grappa?' he asked, pretending innocence.

'This is no time for joking,' Nancy said.

'No joke,' Concetta ground out. 'Give me grappa. Then tell me.'

*

It was some considerable time before Nancy could leave the kitchen. She had sat and listened for nearly an hour to Concetta's muffled voice telling stories of Luca as a baby, Luca as a small boy, how wonderfully he had grown to manhood, what a beautiful house he had and a beautiful wife, this latter said less enthusiastically, every story followed by an outburst of weeping. The Moretto deaths were exerting a heavy emotional toll on them all, Nancy reflected, making her way upstairs to the salon and flopping exhausted onto the battered sofa.

'Is she okay?' She hadn't noticed Archie sitting in the shadow thrown by blinds that had been drawn against the midday sun.

'Just about, but it's hard for her. She must be one of the few people in Venice who truly loved those two.'

He nodded and took up the newspaper he'd been reading, but saw her looking across at him. 'Don't fret. I'll finish this article and then be gone.'

She shook her head. 'It's not that... Archie,' she began,

'I don't understand why Leo was at the casinò last night. Do you?'

Archie looked puzzled. 'He told you why.'

Leo had, but she hadn't believed him. She admitted that to herself now. It felt dreadful to do so, but she'd begun to feel sure her husband, in some way or another, was connected to the disreputable crew that seemed to run a large part of Venice. Her protector, if not a wrongdoer himself, was perhaps an accomplice of wrongdoers. It seemed she had escaped the terror of London to be plunged into another frightening situation.

Archie was looking strangely at her. 'What's the matter with you? Your face is the colour of Concetta's mixing bowl. Don't upset yourself over Moretto. He wasn't exactly a valuable contributor to society.'

'It's not Luca, though his death was horrible. It's Leo. I'm not sure… I'm not sure I can believe what he said.' Her voice faltered. She couldn't believe either that she was saying this to Archie.

'Why ever not?'

'Something feels wrong. I don't know what it is, but Leo's involvement with Dino feels wrong.'

'You honestly think the boss is connected to whatever scam Di Maio is running? C'mon, be sensible.'

'I don't know what to think, but there are too many questions and none of them has an answer. It's driving me crazy.'

'Crazier than usual?' Archie got up from his chair in leisurely fashion and threw the newspaper onto the seat. 'There's one question we could settle. Do you still have that scrap of canvas we found?'

'The one from the boathouse? Yes. It's in my slacks' pocket.'

'Then go and fetch it. There's an answer there.' He folded his arms and waited.

'How is that? It's just a small piece of a picture, a dead end.'

'Not that dead. Didn't you say the painting was signed by a bloke called di Cosimo, but that it didn't look right?'

'Yes… and?'

'If it doesn't look right, then it must be a forgery.'

'Yes…'

'And if it's a forgery, someone is forging. Now, who do we know who's a painter, desperate for work, desperate for money?'

'Renzo Hastings,' she said slowly, light beginning to dawn.

'Renzo Hastings, indeed. Why don't we pay a visit to Mr Hastings? It's past midday. He might have got out of bed by now.'

'But Leo—'

'Leo has just left for the *Questura* and if I know anything about Italian police, he'll be there a very long time.'

'Are you willing to risk it? I mean… I'm sorry I caused you trouble last night.' She had wanted to apologise but hadn't known how best to do it. 'I don't want to land you in any more.'

'Leo bawled me out but at least there were no awkward questions.'

There might be a very good reason for Leo's forbearance, but she wouldn't voice the thought. Instead she apologised again. 'It couldn't have been pleasant for you.'

Archie shrugged. 'Leo is the commanding officer. He lays down the rules.'

She wasn't sure how much Archie believed that. His chippiness never quite left him; it bubbled always beneath the surface. The odd word, the fleeting expression, the occasional flash in his eyes. It was always there, and why wouldn't it be?

His family, like many others, relied on houses like Penleven to make a living, to put a roof over their heads and food on the table. The inclining of heads, the doffing of caps, was something they did in order to survive. The fact that Archie liked Leo as a man, that he'd been shown kindness and to a large extent been taken into Leo's world, didn't change the gross inequality. An inequality that was reinforced every single day.

'Well?' Archie was looking enquiringly at her.

Did she dare go against her husband again? But would it really be going against him? Why shouldn't she visit a poor painter and maybe offer him work?

'Do you know where Renzo lives?' she said.

'No, but I know someone who does. And so do you.'

'Concetta!'

'Exactly.'

Chapter Twenty-Four

Renzo Hastings lived on the Giudecca, though his home, it turned out, was a far cry from the luxury of the Cipriani. Concetta had naturally wanted to know why they were interested in the boy and Nancy, sensing she might well need the maid's help in the future, had been at pains to invent an imaginary offer of work for Renzo, prompted by seeing him in such a pitiful state at San Michele.

She was on her way down from her bedroom when she met Archie on the landing. He put out a hand as though to stop her going further. 'You don't have to do this, you know. I can question the boy on my own.'

'I thought you were keen that I come. Why the change of heart?'

He pursed his lips, appearing to deliberate. 'Second thoughts, perhaps. It feels to me there's some kind of web here, and you've broken into it. And what do we know about webs? That it's their job to trap.'

She tilted her head to one side. 'A bit dramatic, don't you think?'

'Okay, but the nearer the centre you've got, the more dangerous it's become. You've been followed, I've been hit over the head and left to drown. So what's next on the list?'

'You think calling on Renzo could be dangerous?'

'Who knows? I didn't think I'd nearly die breaking into a

boathouse.'

'Whatever happens, I'm going to come,' she said determinedly. 'It may be dangerous, but I've had enough of being scared of my own shadow.'

'That bloke in London—he really got to you, didn't he?'

'Yes, he did,' she agreed, then slipped past him and ran down the stairs. Archie spread his hands in a gesture of resignation, but followed her out of the palazzo.

He didn't speak again until he'd closed the gates behind them. 'That man—what was his name?'

'Philip March.' Her voice was dull. She hated speaking about Philip, though she was warmed by Archie's concern.

'So where were your parents when this March character was tormenting you? That's if they're still alive.'

'They are alive. And they were nowhere in sight,' she answered briefly.

'Why not?'

'They were angry. They liked Philip, they were in awe of his job, and delighted I was finally getting married. I was the unwed daughter, you see, and they were ashamed of that.'

Archie said nothing but strode ahead, as always setting a rapid pace. The most direct route to the Giudecca was by vaporetto from Murano and as they approached the landing stage, they struck lucky. A number four was pulling in and they settled themselves into adjoining seats.

'So...' Archie was not going to let the subject go. 'You must have told your parents what was happening.'

Nancy sighed. 'I tried to explain, but they didn't understand. Or maybe they pretended not to. They thought I was being unjust, abusing an honourable man. I was the one harming him. They didn't believe me when I told them some of the things he'd done. I couldn't tell them the worst of it.'

There was silence for a moment and then, unexpectedly,

Archie reached out for her hand. 'So no support there,' he said.

She shook her head. 'None. I shouldn't have been surprised. My home life was never particularly easy. But even so, it felt very bad.' She let go of his hand. It had been a little too comforting.

'And now? Do they know you're married?'

'No, and they won't. I'm no longer in contact with them. If I told them I'd married, they might pass the news on to Philip and he could trace me.' Nancy's body sagged at the thought. 'I know that he will eventually,' she said unhappily, then mustered a bright voice. 'But I've fought my own battles for a long time, and if Philip March reappears, it will be another one I'll have to fight.'

'You'll have Leo.'

It was a familiar sentiment and she stiffened. But this time, she realised, it had been meant kindly.

The journey was swift though chilly. Last night's rain and fog had gone, but the sun had not yet recovered its strength and Nancy was glad that at the last moment she had taken a jumper.

The Giudecca, too, seemed nowhere near as inviting as it had on the day of the reception. As the boat approached the landing stage, she saw the Redentore for the first time, the immense church built to thank God for delivering the city from a great outbreak of the plague. It dominated the skyline, looking placid enough in the pearly light, but when the skies darkened and the waters of the lagoon turned grey, she imagined it forbidding. It was altogether too white and too cold.

Once on land, Archie took the lead. 'I looked up the map and according to Concetta the layabout lives in the warren of streets across the Ponte Piccolo. First the Ponte Lungo, though. We go this way.'

'I hope you're not thinking of calling him a layabout to his face. It's unlikely to get us much information.'

'Don't worry, I'll let you do the talking. You're good at that.'

Archie might have softened but he could never resist a taunt. She didn't attempt to answer, but walked with him in silence until they'd crossed the two bridges that bisected the island. On the other side of the Ponte Piccolo, as Archie had said, there was a veritable warren of small alleys, narrow enough to rival anything in the city proper. The stink of sewers filled the air.

'This way.' He pointed to a street that looked poorer even than the rest. 'It's down here, I think.'

She wondered what they would find. The danger Archie feared? Certainly misery. Renzo Hastings might be a layabout, though she disputed that, but if he was idling, it certainly wasn't in luxury. The street smelt of poverty, the air raw and fetid.

Arriving in Venice, Nancy had seen for herself how Italy still struggled to absorb the experience of war and occupation. She had glimpsed pockets of severe deprivation and been shocked. The long journey to an affluence that might transform people's lives was slow and seemingly only just beginning.

Renzo's front door, when they reached it, was splintered and faded, looking as though a strong kick would demolish it entirely. Archie raised a fist and knocked. There was an eerie silence and he knocked again, this time more loudly. Another silence, then the sound of shuffling feet, hardly the gait of a young man. Nancy supposed they had come to the wrong house. Archie's Italian was better than hers but by no means fluent, and he must have misunderstood Concetta's directions.

The sound of bolts being pulled back had her straighten herself imperceptibly. It was Renzo at the door, white-faced and shivering, an ill-smelling blanket around his shoulders. Beads of sweat dotted his forehead. 'I'm unwell,' he muttered, his voice barely audible. He spoke in English with the slightest American accent.

'Looks like it,' Archie said cheerfully. 'If it's not infectious, can we come in?'

Renzo didn't answer but turned to walk back along a narrow corridor, kicking aside a roll of flannel that had been placed beneath the front door.

Nancy grabbed hold of her companion's sleeve to stop him following. 'Should we go in? If he's got something catching… we're leaving Venice in two days.'

'Don't fret, it's nothing catching.'

'But—' she began.

'The DTs almost certainly.' He saw Nancy frown and added, 'Delirium tremens. Our friend, Renzo, has been drinking cheap brandy or maybe meths.'

'Oh, my God!'

'C'mon. In the state he's in, he should talk.'

Archie's brutality stung, as it always did, but she followed him down the dim corridor, then along another dank passageway into a small, dark kitchen. In the middle was a very old kerosene heater hardly alight and an equally old armchair, layered with moth-eaten blankets that seeped a stale odour.

She skirted the armchair, Archie too, both of them choosing to sit on rough, upright chairs instead. Renzo was still standing, but bent almost double.

'Can I offer you something?' He waved a hand at a battered saucepan sitting beside the cement sink, and laughed harshly. The laugh started a bout of coughing that he couldn't stop and Nancy jumped up and poured cold water from the one tap into a chipped glass that lay abandoned on the draining board.

Renzo took it without thanking her, but she didn't notice. She felt such sympathy for the boy that she thrust her hand in her bag and brought out a wad of money. 'Please take this. You must eat properly or you'll struggle to recover.' She looked across at the fly that was buzzing aimlessly over an open packet of salami.

Archie put out a restraining arm, stopping her from handing over the banknotes. 'Before you spend your surprise windfall on more gut rot,' he said to the boy, 'we want some information from you.'

Renzo had reached out eagerly for the money, but now he fell back into the armchair, hiding his hands in the torn sleeves of a dirty white shirt. 'What information?' He sounded recalcitrant and hardly a willing source.

'We've come to talk to you about this.' Archie fished from his pocket the piece of torn canvas. 'Is this your handiwork?'

Renzo peered at the scrap and once he had managed to gain focus, his eyes registered alarm, then quite deliberately he scrubbed his face clean of all expression. 'It looks like it's from a di Cosimo,' he said haughtily. 'But I wouldn't expect *you* to recognise it.'

There was something desperately sad about his boyish arrogance; it was all that was left for him amid this pit of squalor.

'No, you're right. I wouldn't,' Archie responded evenly, 'but my friend here would. She works in art and can tell a fake a mile off.'

Renzo's arrogance fled, his face crumbling. 'It's not a fake. It's a di Cosimo,' he said forlornly, but without hope of being believed.

'And that's why a painting worth hundreds of thousands, maybe even millions, has been torn into pieces, is it?' Archie asked conversationally.

'Stupid, eh?' Renzo gave a nervous giggle.

'Stupid to leave a trail of evidence behind. Evidence of wrongdoing that leads to you. You painted this.' Archie leaned forward, waving the scrap of canvas in Renzo's face.

'No, no. I didn't.' The boy's voice broke.

'Yes, you did. Don't keep denying it, son. You did it for money.'

'I have to eat.' His face had grown sullen. He'd given up any pretence now that the painting was authentic.

'Indeed you do and who would blame you for using the only talent you have in order to live? They might, however, blame the man who commissioned you to paint it: Dino Di Maio.'

Renzo gave a gulp. 'How do you know that?'

It was not stolen pictures then that Dino was involved in, Nancy thought, but forgery. She looked at Renzo, slumped and shivering, and said gently, 'How many of these paintings did you do for Dino?'

'Lots,' the boy said miserably.

'Twenty?' Archie put in.

'Fifty,' the boy mumbled. 'But he didn't pay me—not for the last batch at least.'

'And that's why you were at the San Michele cemetery. To confront him?' Nancy asked.

'You saw?'

'I did. I was at Signora Moretto's funeral.'

'It was the only thing I could do. I couldn't get near the man at his house or on his boat or at the *casinò*. I wheedled my way onto the vaporetto—I didn't have a single lira to make the journey—but it wasn't any good. He wouldn't even speak to me,' Renzo finished despondently.

'And you're sure you've never been paid for those last paintings?'

The boy shook his head, his chin sunk onto his bony chest. His shivering seemed to be getting worse. But then he suddenly lifted his head, his eyes alight with a rush of anger. 'And look what he's done to my work. He's a philistine.'

'There we can agree,' Archie said. 'Tell me, did you deal directly with Dino?'

'No. His captain, or whatever he is. Salvatore. He came here with a list of paintings his master wanted and colour plates for me to copy. Then he came back to collect the paintings when they were finished.'

'Did anyone else come?' Nancy asked.

The boy looked blank. 'Why would they?'

'I'm not sure,' she went on. 'Salvatore may have been busy or away sailing the yacht. Perhaps Dino sent a friend, someone like Luca Moretto?'

The boy looked bewildered. 'I don't know him.'

'And did you know Marta Moretto? It was her funeral you gatecrashed.'

'No. I've heard of her though. She's some big noise in Venice. Or was... she was the woman whose funeral you were at?' His poor, battered brain was struggling to remember. Methylated spirits or whatever he was drinking hadn't yet destroyed his mind completely, but Nancy knew she must rescue him and urgently. He was little more than a child.

Archie was made of sterner stuff. 'So,' he continued, 'you were given precise instructions as to which painting to copy?'

Renzo nodded. 'And it wasn't always easy. I have my own style, you know.' He rallied for an instant in defence of his artistry. 'I had to keep adapting it. It's me you can see there,' and he pointed to the grass that had struck the false note with Nancy.

'Were they mainly Renaissance artists you were asked to copy?' she asked.

'No, and that's another thing.' His voice had got stronger as he contemplated the ills he'd suffered. 'They were works from every period and just when you think you've cracked the Renaissance stuff, you have to do a French Romantic or a Russian impressionist.'

'None of them seem to be the very biggest names in art,' Nancy mused.

'No. The second division, I guess. But Dino must have sold them.'

'Oh, he did,' Archie answered him. 'He crated them up and sailed them to Albania where, I imagine, some crooked middle man bought them from him and in turn sold them on to a network of equally crooked distributors, who then resold them to unsuspecting and largely ignorant punters.'

'Everyone making money.' Renzo looked down at his grubby toes and frayed sandals. 'And I didn't get a tenth of their value, I bet.'

'Less than a tenth,' Archie said cheerily. 'You're not a good businessman, Renzo. But you are a criminal.'

'You're going to report me?' That seemed to electrify him. He jumped up from the foul-smelling chair and cast wildly around for a weapon, his eye coming to rest on a rusty kitchen knife lying unwashed by the sink.

But Archie was before him, grabbing his wrist and twisting it until the boy cried out in pain. 'I wouldn't do that, son. I really wouldn't. It can only make matters worse.'

The boy sank onto the floor, seeming to fold in on himself. He began rocking backwards and forwards in a worrying fashion. Nancy bent down to him and tried to take the hands that were tightly swathed in the ragged sleeves of his shirt.

'Renzo, how old are you?'

There was a pause before the boy said, 'Seventeen.' His voice wavered.

'Do you know where your parents are?'

He looked up with the smallest hint of hope in his face and sounded stronger. 'Dad's in the Caribbean. Some island. He sent me a postcard at Christmas.'

Nancy waited and after a while the boy scrambled to his feet and went over to the only shelf the kitchen possessed, nailed unevenly to a wall criss-crossed by mouldy patches. Renzo rescued the card which seemed to have pride of place and screwed up his eyes to read. 'Malfuego. That was it. Looks great, eh?'

'And your mother?'

He shrugged his shoulders. 'She went off with some guy two years ago and I haven't seen her since.'

'What would you say to joining your father on Malfuego?'

'You've gotta be joking. It costs thousands of lire to get there.'

'If you were able to get there, do you think your father would welcome you?'

Renzo thought for a moment. 'He did kinda suggest I might want to make the trip.'

'So…' Nancy sounded briskly practical. 'If you had a ticket to sail, you could go.'

'I s'pose. *If* I had one. But what would I do when I got there?'

'Forge paintings?' Archie suggested.

'Shh.' Nancy hushed him. 'You need to be with your father, Renzo. You need someone to take care of you, until you're properly well.' She looked down at the postcard the boy had handed her. 'There's a phone number here. I'm guessing your father meant you to call him. It's probably not that easy, but did you try?'

'How could I? I've no money.'

Nancy pulled out another wad of notes from her purse and placed it on the scratched wooden table beside the first pile. 'This is for food and this,' she pointed to the new money, 'is for the phone call. You can book a call to your father this afternoon. Tell him you're in trouble and need to come to Malfuego for a while. Ask him to send you a boat ticket—a ticket, mind, not money. He's a businessman, I believe. He should have the funds to do that.'

'He's got enough,' Renzo said truculently. 'But I'm stuck here. I can't get out of this hovel.' His shoulders bent over and he began the disturbing rocking again.

Nancy took hold of him and gave him a sharp shake. 'You can and you will. You will phone your father, get a ticket sent here and I'll make sure you have the money to get you to whichever port the ship sails from.' His eyes brightened at the thought of another pile of lire notes. 'But not,' she said severely, 'until you have the ticket.'

Archie's eyes were signalling that she was making a promise she couldn't keep. They were leaving for London in two days' time and Hastings senior was unlikely to have sent a ticket by then. But she had Concetta in mind. Concetta had known Renzo's family and she was a good woman. She would help, Nancy knew. And she would also keep the boy to the agreement. Nancy could see that would be very necessary; a crafty look had come into Renzo's eyes.

'And what if I don't spend the money like you say?'

'More meths or low-grade brandy?' Archie asked briskly. 'Then you'll be dead before the police find you. And they will find you because we'll have turned you in.'

'You can't do that.' It was a futile protest.

'We can and we will. Now before we go, a list of those

paintings you forged—the ones you can remember.'

'I don't have any paper,' he said sulkily.

'That's where you're lucky.' Archie pulled a sheet of paper and a fountain pen from an inside pocket. He took the cap off the pen and handed both to Renzo.

Nancy's eyebrows arched in surprise. She should have thought of listing the paintings Renzo had forged, but she hadn't.

Archie saw her expression. 'Once a Boy Scout,' he said, with a wry smile.

Chapter Twenty-Five

Nancy felt vindicated—her suspicions of Dino Di Maio had proved correct—and on their way back to the vaporetto stop, she was eager to remind a silent Archie that she had got it right.

'I knew that crate on the *Andiamo* was contraband of some kind,' she said triumphantly. 'Forgery rather than stolen pictures, but still criminal.'

'How you're going to prove it is another matter.'

Archie's tone was dour, but she remained unabashed. 'I *can* prove it, or rather the police can, now we have a list of forged paintings. Surely that will prod them into taking action.'

'A list that does nothing to tie Dino to it—or Renzo Hastings for that matter. I wanted the boy to sign the paper but he'd have refused, and I didn't want to risk him tearing it up.'

'Well, I'm glad you didn't press him. But even though we can't connect the forgeries directly to Dino, once the police start investigating they should be able to.'

She glanced hopefully at him, but Archie remained morose. 'How do you propose getting them to start an investigation? Have you thought of that? Are you going take the list to the *Questura* yourself and spill out your suspicions?'

She couldn't do that. It would mean Leo knowing she had continued to dig after he had expressly asked her not to. Had more or less banned her from considering Dino as any kind of wrongdoer. After their difficult conversation this morning, they had reached a kind of truce, but it was fragile and Nancy knew that if any more of her doings came to light, the marriage would be in serious trouble.

She was haunted, too, by the lurking doubt that Leo might know more about those forgeries than he'd said. After all, he had valued a number of Dino's paintings. What if Dino had involved him in false valuations? The fact that her husband had been so adamant his friend was not involved in criminal activity, and so keen to paint her claim as outlandish, only increased her uneasiness. But she could say none of this to Archie.

'Perhaps,' she suggested hesitatingly, 'we can pass the list to the fraud team with an anonymous note.' That would ensure the Tremayne name was not involved.

When Archie made no response, she redoubled her efforts to convince him. 'The police would be duty bound to take some action, and if they find any of those paintings—and they must, I think —then the trail will lead them to Di Maio.'

'And to Renzo.'

'You think they would find him?'

'Why not? If they find Dino, they'll find our prolific painter.'

'Still,' she brightened, 'that's some way ahead. By the time Renzo's name appears in the police files, he should be in the Caribbean. Hopefully there's no extradition treaty between Italy and Malfuego.'

'Even if there were, it would probably be too much bother to extricate a minion like Renzo Hastings. Di Maio is the big fish and they'll enjoy frying him if they ever get hold of him.'

They had reached the Redentore landing stage in record time. Nancy glanced to her left, hoping to see a ferry on the horizon, but the lagoon was calm and on this side of the Giudecca Canal, largely empty. She had begun to fret she'd not be home before Leo returned from the *Questura* and would be forced to concoct an elaborate lie as to where she had been. In his present mood, he was unlikely to believe her.

'If they get Dino, they'll get Salvatore, too.' Archie broke the silence and was thinking aloud. 'That would be extremely satisfying.'

Nancy hadn't given Salvatore a thought this morning. Or his wife. 'Poor Luisa,' she said. 'How awful! She is such a nice woman.'

'Don't waste your sympathy. Salvatore is in it up to his neck and his wife must know that. In any case, from what I hear there are plenty of others who think she's a nice woman. The men will be buzzing around if her husband goes to prison. Luisa is a quite a girl by all accounts.'

Nancy looked startled.

'What?' he said. 'Nice girls don't... Why do you think Salvatore was at my throat the minute I asked about his wife?'

She was saved from answering by the sight of a number four chugging towards them. As it pulled in, she could see it was nearly empty and once on board, she made her way to a seat near an open window. Archie sat across the aisle from her, relapsing into a familiar silence as the boat's engines began their churn.

They had been travelling several minutes before she said, 'The police may eventually get Dino for forgery—I hope they do—but they won't accuse him of murder. No one will make the connection between the forged paintings and Marta's death.'

'If there is a connection.' Archie stretched his legs full length and lay back in his seat. 'Are you still sure of that? The boy didn't know her. He'd never met her or Luca Moretto.'

'That means nothing. I doubt Marta would have gone to the Giudecca looking for Renzo. Something else must have alerted her to what was going on or made her suspicious. Then she confronted Dino with it.'

'Why would she though? That's what I don't get. The woman owns the most prestigious antiques business in Venice. She's wealthy, she's nearing retirement…'

'Why is that a problem?' Nancy wrinkled her brow.

'It's a problem because I can't imagine why she would challenge a man like Dino, a man who belongs to the same wealthy elite. Why would she accuse him of being a common criminal, even if she suspected it?'

'Because she believed, or she knew for sure, that he was besmirching the honour of a city she loved.'

'Wow. That's certainly something.' Archie's expression was hard to read. He was either going to laugh uproariously or say something very scathing.

Nancy rushed to defend her words. 'I know it sounds desperately old-fashioned, but I believe it. It was something Marta said—it felt odd at the time, but it's stayed with me. She was determined to make the Moretto name great again, determined to do wonderful things for Venice. She loved her city and if she was intent on ensuring a splendid future, the last thing she would have wanted was someone like Dino working against her. A man with ties to her family, a close friend of her son's. Dino could bring her whole project into disrepute.'

'So why didn't she go directly to the police?'

'She knew Dino well. Like you say, they moved in the same circles and he was close to her family. She must have known him since he was a small boy. She gave him the chance to defend himself and if he couldn't, to stop doing what he was doing and clean up his business. But he carried on regardless and *then* she threatened to go to the police. That was what sealed her fate.'

Archie leaned towards her. 'More extravagant guesses?'

'Not that extravagant, but guessing, I agree. It does sound plausible, though, doesn't it?'

He thought for a moment. 'Minimally perhaps. What doesn't sound plausible is that she told all this to Luca.'

'Why not?'

The boat bumped up against the San Zaccaria landing stage. Nancy had been so absorbed in arguing her case, she hadn't realised they were nearing their destination and had to scramble to follow Archie down the gangway.

'Why doesn't it sound plausible that Marta would tell her son what she feared?' she asked again after they'd been walking for several minutes.

'Because she didn't involve him in the business in any meaningful way, if you're to believe the gossip. She wasn't close to Luca, treated him as an employee and not much else, it seems.'

'Maybe, but I don't see that would stop her telling him.' Nancy was trying to keep an open mind, but it was hard. She was so certain that Marta had died because of what she knew.

'And there's another problem with it,' Archie said. He sounded a trifle smug. 'If Marta *had* told her son what she'd discovered, wouldn't she have let Dino know? Made it clear to him that she'd passed on information to Luca? She'd be piling on the pressure *and* ensuring that Dino was aware someone else knew what was going on. It would be a way of protecting herself. But it means that Di Maio would have to kill them both.'

'They *were* both killed.'

'But Luca didn't die until ten days later. If we're saying that Dino killed him because of what he knew, why didn't he kill him on the same day that he supposedly killed Marta? Or very shortly afterwards. And that's going some. I guess you have to plan a murder, maybe even pace it to avoid suspicion, but ten days? Any time during that period Luca could have gone to the police.'

Nancy walked on in silence. Archie's argument seemed unassailable… but not quite. 'Luca died after Marta's will was read, didn't he? Perhaps Marta left papers with the will, a letter maybe, and Luca learnt of Dino's crime only after his mother's death.

'He may have gone to Dino with the letter. He'd be apologetic for even raising the subject. We mustn't forget he's a close friend. He'd say he didn't really believe his mother's accusations, but he needed to put the matter to rest. Of course, Dino would have the perfect answer. "Your mother was old, on strong medicine," he'd say. "Look what happened at La Fenice—and her letter is rambling, clearly the work of someone who's unwell. We've been friends for years, can you really imagine me doing something like that?" He'd suggest they destroy the letter and if Luca demurred, seemed uncertain… maybe demanded money to destroy it—he's in financial trouble after all—that would be it. Dino won't pay and the next day he kills Luca.'

Archie looked at her admiringly. 'You're a wasted talent. Forget art, you should be writing a novel.'

He could mock, but she was more and more certain something like that must have happened. 'Whoever killed Luca Moretto had some kind of business connection with him. Remember the money in his mouth?'

The ghastly image floated into her vision. For the last few hours she had managed to forget, but now she felt her stomach twist and heave.

'A mouth stuffed with money is pretty graphic,' Archie

admitted. 'But murder is a desperate game. Why would Dino risk such a thing? If the police questioned him about possible forgery, he could just brazen it out. And without sufficient evidence, they'd have to believe him. But murder someone! There's no death penalty here, but he'd be banged up for a very long time, whereas forgery carries a far lighter sentence. Would he risk killing for it?'

They'd reached the palazzo and once in the lobby, Nancy stood and listened. The house was wonderfully quiet—she had made it back in time.

'It wouldn't just mean a prison sentence, though, would it?' She turned to Archie before climbing the stairs. 'If Dino were found guilty, he'd be a disgraced man. No one would want to do business with him. He might even lose his own. And even if he were never convicted, the gossip would be as dangerous. His reputation would be shot to pieces and I doubt he could afford that. I don't think he's as well off as he makes out.'

'You know what I think?' she asked, as she was half way up the staircase.

'No, but I'm sure you're going to tell me.' Archie was close behind.

'Dino has been speculating—we know he's a gambler— and has had his fingers burned. But unlike Luca he's managed to keep the poor state of his finances quiet and still passes in the world for a wealthy man. That would make sense.'

'So would a lot of scenarios. You're going to have to leave it, Nancy. Forget Marta Moretto. And hope Dino is eventually nailed for forgery and your protégé escapes prosecution. Which reminds me—' Archie had turned towards the staircase leading to his room, but now walked back towards her. 'How are you going to check Renzo actually makes it onto a ship?'

'That's simple. Concetta. I know she'll help, be my stand-in as it were. I'll leave her enough money to make certain the boy gets to his father. And a little extra—so that she can buy herself something special.'

They were standing facing each other in the large, open space outside the salon, and Archie was looking hard at her.

'It's my money, not Leo's,' she said defensively. 'I saved it while I was working. For my wedding, if you want to hear a joke.'

Before she realised what he was doing, Archie had put his hands on her shoulders and was holding her in a firm grasp. 'You're a kind woman, Nancy,' he said.

His hands were warm and strong and she felt her body tingle—a powerful sensation she had not felt for months. In fact, had never truly felt. A kind of recognition. Exciting but very dangerous. Desperate to make light of the moment, she laughed off his comment. 'You're not such a grump yourself.'

His eyes met hers and for an instant she held her breath. Then quickly he dropped his hold. 'Though definitely not a Boy Scout,' he said lightly.

Chapter Twenty-Six

Ten minutes after Nancy had walked through the palazzo door, Leo returned from the *Questura*. She felt a rush of relief as she heard him bounding up the stairs. The tingle was still there and disturbing, and she wanted to forget it. She wanted to lose herself in Leo. He was her husband and he loved her dearly. Archie Jago was nothing to her. Indeed, since the moment they'd first encountered each other, he'd been a constant irritant.

She met Leo at the top of the stairs and hugged him tight, then linked her arm in his and walked him into the salon.

'So what happened at the *Questura*? You've been an age.'

'Why don't I tell you over lunch? I'm ravenous.'

He seemed younger and happier, as though a weight had been lifted, and though she tried not to, she found herself wondering why. Then scolded herself for doing it.

'That's a marvellous idea,' she agreed. 'Shall we eat out? Where shall we go?'

'The sun came out on my way back and I thought we'd take a walk. Towards the Giardini, then maybe on to the Arsenale? Did you ever get to the gardens?'

'No,' she confessed. 'I meant to the day you went to Rome, but it was too hot to venture far.' She hoped the excuse sounded credible.

'It's not too hot today, and we can pick up some lunch on

the way.'

Emerging from the tangle of narrow streets a short while later, they began to saunter along the Riva towards the Arsenale.

'So what did the police want with you?' Nancy asked.

'As I thought, questions about my relationship with Luca Moretto. Did I know him personally? Had I had dealings with him? How much did I know about them? Did he have any enemies, and so forth? I really wasn't too helpful. I had to tell them that on the few occasions I've dealt with the Moretto business, it has always been the signora I spoke to. And socially, I know Luca only through Dino Di Maio. I've probably met him twice, three times at most.'

'It took a time for you to tell them that.'

On one level, she was glad of it. She had travelled to the Giudecca and back while Leo was out, but three hours was a long while to answer a few questions. Again, there was the niggling worry that he was keeping something from her.

'That's the Italian police for you, but I think I probably escaped lightly. They kept me waiting an age before they even spoke to me. Then I had to repeat everything I'd said to one detective, to several more from different offices. After that, I had to wait for my statement to be typed up—in triplicate— and finally I had to read it through—they were watching to make sure I read every word—and sign each copy. It's a wonder it didn't take longer. Shall we walk through the gardens?'

'Yes, let's. I'd like to see them.' They turned in through green iron gates and sauntered down the gravel pathway.

Nancy looked around her. 'The grass is looking a trifle brown, but not for much longer, I imagine.'

'No. The rains will come very soon I'm sure, and the dreaded *acqua alta* with them.'

The phrase made Nancy think of Marta and the basement the signora was unable to use in the winter months. If only she could have secured justice for the poor woman. Instead, Dino might never be caught and, if he were, would spend just a few years in prison and then be free. True, he might have lost the trappings of a life of luxury, but he would have a life. Marta would not. Nor her son. And perhaps not her daughter either. Increasingly Nancy was concerned for Angelica, but she could see no way of helping her.

'The café is closed.' Leo sounded disappointed. 'I was thinking we could eat there.' They had turned a corner in the path and a small red-roofed building stood to one side, its shutters down and a general air of desertion surrounding it. 'We'll have to walk further, on to the Arsenale.'

Nancy slipped her hand in his. 'That's fine. It's good to be outside. Perhaps we can find a café with a garden.'

They walked out on to the Riva and within a few minutes came across a small trattoria situated on one of the narrow streets running down to the lagoon, its tables spilling across the pavement.

Leo stopped. 'No garden, but why don't we eat here?'

Bright chequered tablecloths fluttered in the breeze and a window of salami and round cheeses looked inviting. Leo took up the wine list and pronounced it good, then led the way to an empty table in the shaded alleyway.

The food was excellent, but Nancy couldn't shake herself free of the morning's events and ate sparingly. Despite her best efforts, Renzo's woebegone face and Archie's firm touch, continued to trouble her.

To mask her lack of appetite, she encouraged Leo to talk. 'You must be very happy to be going home. To Cornwall, I mean.'

He smiled across at her. 'I'm hoping you're a little

happy, too.'

'Of course, I am. I'm looking forward to seeing the house and meeting your father and brother. Perry is an unusual name—is it short for Peregrine?' It seemed suitably aristocratic.

'He's Perran, in fact. True Cornish, which is as it should be. Perry *is* a true Cornishman.'

'And runs a true Cornish business?' She laughed.

'He does. Now that Dad is frailer, he's certainly the boss. My father never really got to grips with the mine, to be honest, so it's good to see it being run by an expert. Dad was like his own father. Neither of them saw the need to know much about tin mining. They employed managers and appeared at intervals to give the miners a wave and a pat on the back. But Perry is different. He's made it his business to know the ins and outs of the process. He has a manager, but they work together.'

'I was surprised when you said the mine was still working. I thought tin was exhausted back in the last century.'

'Wheal Agnes is one of the few mines left. And that's thanks in large part to Perry. He went to Camborne, to the School of Mines there, and studied the best extraction methods. It made him very safety conscious, too, and the men are grateful for that. They trust him and they work well for him. The mine doesn't produce anywhere near as much tin as it did in its heyday, of course, but enough to pay the men and fund Penleven.'

'Penleven is a large house?' She could hear the note of anxiety in her voice but hoped Leo hadn't.

'Fairly large. And beautifully old, with wonderful gardens, but it takes a good deal of money to keep it pristine. Which is why the mine is so important to us.'

A different world, she thought. Leo is from a different

world. How would she ever cope? But she was going to have to. Two more days in this beautiful city—that was all—a few more back in London, and then she would find herself in Leo country. And Archie country, too. Something else not to think of.

'We still have a little time here.' She tried to sound cheerful. 'What do you think we might do?'

She saw Leo's face fall slightly and he took a sip of wine before he answered. 'I hate to tell you this, darling, but I have a business meeting the day before we leave. I'm afraid it's unavoidable. I had to rearrange my schedule, or Archie had to, because of that damn trip to Rome. I should have met the chap in London, but he's travelling back to Italy today and breaking his journey in Venice. But... we do have tomorrow still. Have you any ideas?'

'The other evening you mentioned a whole list of places we haven't had time to visit. How about one of them? There was the bell tower at San Giorgio Maggiore, I remember, and the oldest building in Venice.'

'The Scuola Grande?'

'Yes, that, and there was a bookshop you talked about. The eccentric one. I'd love to see it.'

'The Libreria Acqua Alta? Yes, why not. It's in Castello, very close, just north of the palazzo.'

He reached across the table and squeezed her hand. 'You know, I think that's a great idea. I want to get a present for Archie's mother. A kind of get well, welcome home gift. And I thought I'd take her a book—I mentioned the title to Archie, but he hasn't been able to run it to ground. We might be luckier at the Acqua Alta.'

Nancy hoped that didn't mean sharing the day with Archie and cast around for ways to wriggle free. She was being foolish, she knew. All the man had done was hold her by the shoulders, for goodness sake, and she was behaving like a Victorian miss. But in that instant, she had felt her breath stutter, had felt driven by anticipation, by an excitement she could never acknowledge. Even worse, Archie had felt it, too. He had been exceptionally quick to disengage himself.

'Morwenna is a keen botanist,' Leo was saying, 'and this book, I saw it reviewed a year ago, is a complete guide to wild flowers. There are plenty of similar books out there, but what makes this one so special is the art work. The drawings were exquisite.'

'I wonder how Mrs Jago is?' Nancy asked, in a vain attempt to push the book to one side.

'As far as I know, Archie has heard nothing more. But no news is good news. We'll get the night train from Paris and as soon as we hit Dover, I'll make sure he is on his way back to Cornwall. I can make do without him for the few days we'll be in London.'

*

That night Nancy engineered an early bedtime, determined to make their marriage more of a reality. She'd had a warning today that if she were not wholehearted in her commitment to being a wife, she was courting trouble. Trouble that would fall as heavily on Leo as on herself. And he didn't deserve that. She turned her head on the pillow and watched him earnestly reading. He must have sensed her gaze because he took off his glasses, folded them carefully, and laid them down on the bedside table.

'Tired?' he asked

'Not too tired.' She put her arms around him and drew him close.

His face betrayed a small frisson of surprise—most usually he was the one who persuaded her into lovemaking. But he seemed touched and delighted, and with one hand gently caressed her face, and with the other looped her curls around his finger.

'You have enjoyed our honeymoon, Nancy?' he asked quietly.

'I've loved it,' she said. 'And I love you.'

It was the first time she had said that to him. He gathered her up in his arms and kissed her deeply. Their lovemaking that night was long and passionate and when Leo finally let her go, she felt happy. She had managed at last to lose herself in the moment, though the image of Archie's blue eyes had never left her.

Chapter Twenty-Seven

Nancy's hope that she would spend the day alone with her husband disappeared early the next morning. Archie would be with them, it seemed, at least until lunchtime. He was needed at the bookshop. Over breakfast she tentatively suggested they look for a book once they were back in London where the choice might be greater, but apparently there would not be sufficient time and, in any case, Leo wanted Archie alongside. The Acqua Alta might not have the title he sought, but it would have others and he was eager to buy a book that was new to Morwenna Jago, one she would treasure.

'Mrs Jago has a shelf groaning with plant books,' he said, 'and it's difficult to find something original. That's a fact, isn't it, Archie?'

His assistant had arrived in the dining room carrying the day's mail, which he left on the table beside Leo. 'You're sure to find something, boss,' he said, with the ghost of a smile.

'The shop is only a short walk from here, Nancy,' Leo went on. 'Once I've made the purchase, we'll have the day to ourselves.' He jumped up and walked round to her chair, then bent to kiss the top of her head.

Out of the corner of her eye she saw Archie's ironic smile before he disappeared to the top floor.

*

Half an hour later, the three of them were winding their way through Campo Santa Maria Formosa on the way to the bookshop. Nancy made sure she linked arms with her husband and walked ahead with him.

'It's a strange name for a shop. How did it come about?' She was genuinely interested.

'*Acqua alta* is their nemesis. The building gets completely flooded. The shop's fire escape is a door leading to the canal — the sign pointing the way shows a figure swimming! They've certainly a sense of humour, but they've come up with a novel solution.'

'What's that?'

'You'll see,' Leo teased.

Nancy had to be content, but he was right about the short walk. In ten minutes they had reached the small passageway leading to the bookshop, itself piled high on either side with books stacked on wooden pallets.

Once inside, Nancy looked around, intrigued by the shop's oddities. It was chaotic: a series of over-stuffed rooms stacked wall-to-wall with books, magazines, maps and goodness knows what else. A mixture of a serious library and a flea market. She saw immediately the solution to which Leo had referred: the books were piled into bathtubs, waterproof bins, rowing boats and, in one room, a full-size gondola. When the shop flooded, the books would simply float. It was a bizarre but quite brilliant idea.

'What do you think?' Leo smiled across at her.

'It's the strangest bookshop I've ever visited. All these boats. I can't believe how many.'

'Whimsical but wonderful, don't you think?'

'*Buongiorno signore.*' The proprietor had come forward and was pumping Leo's hand enthusiastically, but when her husband handed him a slip of paper and he read the title Leo sought, he gave a sad shake of his head.

'No, sorry. Not this one. But I have many other books that will interest you. Please, come with me and take a look.'

He shepherded Leo through an archway to yet another room, with Archie following. Nancy stayed where she was. Botany held little interest for her, and she felt restless and unsettled. She had since the moment she'd woken. In part it was Archie's presence this morning, but not that alone. There was something else, something more serious bothering her. Ever since she'd known of the forgeries, she had been worried for Angelica's safety. The fear had always been there in the shadows, but now it was darker and more urgent.

Last night after Leo had fallen into a deep sleep, she had lain awake for hours, going over in her head what Dino might do. He would know of the break-in at the boathouse, and know that Archie was the intruder—Salvatore would have been definite on that—but since that night there had been no repercussions. Perhaps Archie's exploit had seemed a foolish joke to Dino. Perhaps he presumed there was no evidence to condemn him and felt safe from discovery. He wouldn't know that a scrap of canvas had been left behind and that someone with a knowledge of art had seen it. Nor that it had led to Renzo and exposure.

But at the very least, he must be puzzled. A foolish joke maybe, but why had Archie broken in? And what was Nancy Tremayne doing by Archie's side at the *casinò*? If Dino were asking himself these questions, it was possible he might sense the net closing in. That would make him more dangerous; he would be looking for anyone who could possibly unmask him. Marta was no longer a threat, nor Luca. But Angelica?

It had always worried Nancy that Angelica might face trouble. At first she had thought the danger might come from Mario or Luca—it was why she had braved the Moretto palazzo days ago, trying and failing to warn the woman. But now Dino was the cause of her anxiety. How much did Angelica actually know? Was Dino or his henchman watching the Moretto house? Perhaps it was one of them who had followed Nancy on the visit she'd made there.

'No luck.' Leo ducked his head as he came back into the room. 'Some lovely books but none of them quite what I'm looking for. However—I hope you don't mind, Nancy—the owner has suggested another bookshop. In Dorsoduro, just beyond Ca'Rezzonico. It specialises in life sciences, particularly plant science. I thought perhaps we could call in?'

Her husband must have seen the disappointment on her face because he said quickly, 'I promise that if we're not successful there, we'll call it a day. What do you think?'

Another hour or more with Archie in tow was the last thing Nancy wanted. He'd been careful to keep his distance—all morning she'd felt him deliberately ignoring her. It was an actual physical feeling that in some way made things worse. It was clear he'd recognised the danger they had courted and stepped back sharply, but it made a normally casual relationship almost impossible. There was little, though, she could say against Leo's plan, and she resigned herself to going along with it.

They walked through the back lanes to the Grand Canal and took a *traghetto*, a gondola ferry, to the other side. It was as they disembarked that the idea came to her. They were in Dorsoduro and not a million miles from the Moretto house. Would it be possible to slip away? It was a crazy plan, but crazed was how she felt. While she was still in Venice, she couldn't rest as long as there was something she could do to prevent another tragedy. She must speak to Angelica again—this time really speak to her—tell her honestly of her suspicions.

The second bookshop was far more traditional, but in Nancy's view more promising. There was more shaking of heads, however, when Leo mentioned the title he was seeking. The shop's owner, who must have been eighty if he was a day, laid a hand on Leo's arm to detain him, then darted behind the counter and brought out two large volumes which he hefted onto a battered desk.

Leo stopped and walked back, picking up the first book the proprietor had offered, and beginning a quick flick through. 'I think we might be lucky with this,' he said to nobody in particular.

Nancy started to wander slowly around the shelves, only vaguely listening to the men's conversation. 'You see how very skilled the drawings,' the old man was saying. 'The volume was only published this month. It will be very popular with our customers, I know.'

'The drawings are beautiful,' Leo replied. The sound of turning pages came to her. 'But the book doesn't appear to be as comprehensive as I had hoped.'

'This one then?' The proprietor pointed to the second volume. 'This book covers the wild flowers of the world, but the illustrations are…'

'Prosaic? What do you think, Archie?' Leo turned to his assistant and Archie dutifully took up the book for a closer look.

Suddenly, Nancy had to get out of the shop. She could not bear to wander in this aimless fashion another minute. She had to take action. If she turned right out of the bookshop, she would reach the Zattere. And along the Zattere was the *calle dei Morti*. Hardly realising what she was doing, she broke into a run. She had no idea what she would find at the Moretto palazzo; all she knew was that she had to get there. She had to try to see Angelica.

Last night she had wondered if someone might be watching the house, but why would Dino set a watch? If Angelica had information on him and wanted to use it, she could as easily telephone the police from home and he would be none the wiser. Yet there were still those footsteps to account for, that frightening chase Nancy had endured. If not Dino or one of his minions, who had that been?

Halfway along the Zattere she had to drop the run for a swift walk. There was a stitch in her side and her breathing was shallow, but she reached the *calle dei Morti* quicker than she'd believed possible. She had no clear plan in mind, only that she must warn Angelica. If the woman knew nothing of Dino's activities, had not even suspected, she would think Nancy unhinged. But what did that matter?

Hopefully the encounter would take only minutes and she could return to the bookshop before her absence was noticed. If Leo finished his purchase more quickly than expected, she would claim she'd found the shop too stuffy and gone for a stroll beside the lagoon. He would think it odd behaviour, but she was sure she could carry it off.

Nancy slowed her steps as she approached the house and stood for a few seconds at the front gate trying to gather her skittering mind. Then she raised her hand to the bell pull. But as she did so, another hand—a large, male hand—came crashing down on hers and twisted her arm behind her back. Her yell of pain was cut short when a second hand clasped her mouth so hard she was barely able to breathe.

A voice she did not recognise growled in her ear. It was guttural, unnatural. 'Why are you here?' The hand across her mouth did not move and it was evident her attacker expected no answer. The voice ground on. 'You spy, and you must be stopped. For good.'

Nancy struggled against the iron grip, but the hands only

tightened further. 'Move!' the voice commanded. 'Now!'

The old fears rose in all their fury and her mind fractured. She was overwhelmed with terror, its tentacles spreading through every part of her body and paralysing her. Who was this man threatening her? Could it be... no, surely not? Not Philip March. He could not have traced her here from London.

A knee was thrust into her back and she swayed forward, almost falling to her knees. Her captor jerked her upright and pushed hard again. This time she stumbled a few paces and found herself on the other side of the street, close to where the remains of the shattered house lay buried. The fencing was still there—she could just see it if she raised her head a little—but part of it had been trampled down and the deep pit now lay open and perilous. With fearful certainty she realised what this man intended. He would push her over the edge and she would plunge to her death. But at whose hands? She would not even know her murderer.

Then, in an instant, his hold slackened. Nancy heard a sharp crack, as though a head had been thrust hard against stone. The hands that had imprisoned her disappeared and she tumbled to the ground. When she had recovered sufficiently to look, she twisted her head and saw Archie. He had pinned the arms of her attacker behind the man's back and forced him to his knees.

Nancy got slowly to her feet and walked towards them. Then trying for a calm she didn't feel, she peered into the man's lowered face. Mario Bozzato!

'You,' she said. 'What are you doing here? And why attack me so brutally?' She rubbed her sore arms attempting to get the blood to flow again.

'You are a spy,' the man spat out. She noticed the guttural voice had gone.

'And you are mad. I'm no spy. What would I be spying on?'

'Save your breath,' Archie advised. 'The man's a complete nutter.'

'You tell Angelica lies. You turn her against me,' Mario gasped, as Archie twisted his arms into an even more painful position.

'That is ludicrous. I've seen Signorina Moretto once and we spoke only of her mother.'

'I told you, the bloke's a nutter. You won't get any sense out of him.' Archie had Bozzato in a fearsome lock from which there was no escape. Mario was a man daily engaged in physical work, but Archie was an ex-soldier and it was no contest.

'Did you follow Mrs Tremayne a few days ago?' Archie asked, giving his victim a kick to help his memory.

'She is a spy,' Mario gasped out.

'Did you follow her?' Archie repeated, administering another swift kick.

'Yes,' came the surly reply.

Nancy looked down at her attacker, bewildered and angry. 'You followed me and scared me half to death?'

'You are a wicked woman.' Bozzato had got his breath back now and raised his head defiantly. 'Angelica left the convent for me. She chose *me*, not the church. We were to marry—until you came. Then she turned against me.'

'Angelica left the convent for her mother's sake,' Nancy said. 'The signora was unwell.'

'It is because of you that Angelica does not speak to me,' he continued doggedly.

'It has nothing to do with me,' Nancy retorted, doubting that anyone could influence that young woman against her wishes. 'And if you had the smallest grain of sense, you would know that. You have to accept that if the signorina won't speak to you, Mario, it is because she has decided you are no longer part of her life.'

'And why would you be?' Archie put in. 'Get off your knees and apologise to this lady for the coward you are. For the threats you've made and for hurting her.'

When Mario made no move to respond, Archie tightened his grip. 'Do it!'

Bozzato staggered to his feet and mumbled an apology through clenched teeth. 'Get going now,' Archie instructed, 'but keep away from Mrs Tremayne—and this house. Or you'll fare even worse.'

He pushed Mario to one side and gestured to Nancy to walk back along the *calle*. 'What the hell were you thinking?' he muttered, once they had reached the Zattere. 'Sloping off like that.'

'He was going to push me into that pit,' she gulped. The realisation of how narrowly she'd escaped had begun to bite.

'He's mad. You know that. You should keep away from him.'

Nancy looked incredulous. 'Are you saying it was my fault?'

'I'm saying we need to hurry. So forget the pit and let's get moving.'

'Why should I?' She couldn't stop herself sounding petulant. She was angry that Archie seemed happy to dismiss the danger she'd faced as insignificant.

He looked exasperated. 'I would have thought that was obvious—you disappeared from the shop without a word. Once Leo had bought his damn book, he went to find you. We waited around like a couple of lost lemons, hoping you'd turn up. Then he started getting agitated, thinking you were having a funny turn.'

'A funny turn?' she echoed.

'He's worried you're still affected by what happened in London. He thinks you going off half-cock is part of it.'

'Where is Leo now?' she asked abruptly, hating that her husband had shared such personal worries.

'As far as I know, still pacing up and down outside the bookshop. You need to hurry or he'll be calling in divers to search every canal in the city.'

Nancy picked up her pace accordingly, though she still felt wobbly from Bozzato's attack. And frustrated, too. She hadn't accomplished what she'd set out to, but had managed to ruin for Leo one of their last days together in Venice. He would not be pleased.

'How did you find me?' she blurted out. She hadn't thought of it before, but now Archie's appearance when she most needed help appeared nothing short of a miracle.

'It wasn't too difficult. You've got the Morettos on the brain. And you've been particularly twitchy this morning.' How did he know that, she wondered? He'd been steadfast in ignoring her. 'And the Moretto house is only a short distance from the bookshop.'

'Will you mention it—that you found me outside the house?'

'Not unless you do.'

They were barely in sight of the bookshop again when Leo came into view, fairly dancing along the street towards them.

'Nancy! Thank God! Where did you find her, Archie?'

'I was taking a walk by the lagoon,' she managed to say before Archie was forced to answer. 'The weather is so beautiful and I wanted to enjoy it before we go back to grey skies.'

'But why didn't you tell me you were going for a walk?'

'You were busy, Leo, choosing the right book. And I didn't

want to disturb you.'

'But to wander off like that,' he murmured, 'and for all this time. My darling, are you truly all right?'

Before she could answer, he had decided for himself. 'We have a busy few days ahead once we're back in London, so we should make tomorrow as quiet as possible—a gentle walk, or a drive in the country perhaps? Right now, though, we should go home. You need a rest.'

'I'd love to drive out tomorrow and see something of the countryside.' She said it with enthusiasm, hoping to mollify him.

'And I'd love to take you.' A guilty expression suffused his face. 'I know I suggested it, Nancy, but I can't be with you. I have this meeting with Signor Trevi.'

She had forgotten that Leo had a business engagement the next day and tried to row back. She had an uncomfortable premonition where this conversation might lead.

'Never mind,' she said brightly, 'I'll take a chair out into the palazzo garden. There's plenty of shade and the fresh air will do me good. *And* it will be as restful as you could wish.'

'No. No, we can do better than that.' The idea of an excursion seemed to have lodged itself in Leo's brain. 'I'll hire a car—I'll ring when we get back—and Archie can drive you. All right with you, Archie?'

Archie nodded, a blank expression on his face.

'You don't need to be gone for long,' Leo continued, 'but a few hours in the countryside will be perfect. The Veneto looks particularly beautiful at this time of the year. I only wish I could come.'

So did Nancy, since now she would be spending another morning in Archie's company, this time locked in close proximity.

'That's a wonderful idea,' she tried to enthuse. 'How kind of you to arrange it, Leo.'

A few paces away she sensed Archie glowering.

Chapter Twenty-Eight

Halfway through the afternoon Leo put his head around the bedroom door. 'How are you feeling now?'

Nancy laid aside the exhibition catalogue she'd been reading and put on her best smile.

'Fine. Absolutely fine.' She'd spent several hours taking the rest that Leo had prescribed, trying hard to distract a mind that was busier than ever.

'You had me worried, you know.' He walked over to her and sat down on the bed.

'I'm sorry, Leo. You're not to worry. There's really no need.'

'But to go walking off like that…'

'It's as I said, I was enticed by the sun and the water—and lost track of time. I didn't realise how far I'd walked.'

He nodded, seeming this time to accept the explanation, and laid down beside her.

'You mean so much to me, Nancy,' he said, cradling her in his arms. 'I know how badly you've been hurt and I know how difficult it's been for you to lose the fear.' She said nothing and he went on, 'It can't help that the rotter who put you through so much is still free and walking the streets of London.'

Nancy nestled in the crook of his arm. 'There's nothing we can do about Philip. He's far too clever to have incriminated himself. You have to forget him—I have.'

Leo rubbed his face against hers, then kissed her gently on the cheek. 'Why don't I believe you?'

'You must,' she insisted. 'It's true.' Only a white lie, she told herself, to save her husband further worry.

'So what have you been reading?' He loosened his embrace and picked up the catalogue she'd put to one side. 'Stanley Spencer at the Tate. It sounds interesting. You must go, once we get back from Cornwall.'

'I thought I would... Leo...' She decided to take the plunge. 'When we're back in London again, what am I to do?'

'Do?' He looked nonplussed.

'Yes. How am I to fill my days? I can't return to Abingers, can I?'

He hoisted himself onto one elbow and looked down at her, a puzzled expression on his face. 'You wouldn't want to, surely?'

If she thought about it objectively, he was right. She wouldn't. Not now. Initially, she had been thrilled to be offered a job at such an important auction house, but over the years disenchantment had grown. It hadn't taken long for her to realise the furthest she would ever progress in Fine Art was as a second assistant.

'I enjoyed it while I was working at Abingers,' she said a trifle defensively.

'But you're married now.' The puzzlement was in Leo's voice as well as his face. 'You've no need to work.'

'Some women do.'

'Some women have to, Nancy. You don't. And there is plenty to fill your days.'

'Like what?' she asked baldly.

'Well, this exhibition for a start,' he joked, his fingers flicking through the pages of the catalogue. 'And there will be plenty more of those. You could join a book group maybe, brush up your Italian, or do some voluntary work if you really want to get stuck in.'

None of it appealed in the slightest and Leo must have felt her indifference. 'How about starting to paint again? I know you gave up years ago, but wouldn't it be good to go back?'

Nancy didn't think so. When she'd first attended art school, she had been delighted to find a subject she excelled at. She might never master calculus, or be a star hockey player, but drawing, painting, even sculpting, was a different matter, and she had thrown herself into her studies with passion.

That was the problem. She no longer felt as passionate. Yet accepting that she would never make her living as an artist— the competition was just too great—she still needed a goal in life. Abingers had provided that, albeit one that in hindsight was impossible. But for a while, as she tried to work her way up the firm's career ladder, it had given her purpose.

Leo put his arms around her again and hugged her tightly. 'In no time, I'm sure you'll find your life filled with engagements. You'll be complaining how busy you are. So enjoy being free while you can—it might not last long.' He kissed the tip of her ear.

'Why not?' A small hope began to burn. Did Leo have a job in mind for her?

'Babies take up an inordinate amount of time, so I'm told.'

Babies! The word felled her. A family was something they had never spoken of. Nancy supposed most couples must discuss the possibility before they married, but she and Leo had wed in a bang, their marriage arranged in a few days. There had been no time to discuss anything beyond which dress she should wear at the chapel and how they were to obtain another train reservation to Venice at such short notice.

'Have I said the wrong thing?' he asked anxiously.

'No, no. Of course not. I hadn't thought…'

'There's been no time, has there? I understand. But we should be thinking about it. Before we know it, we may have a child on the way.'

'Yes,' she said faintly.

She had taken care to avoid such an outcome, assuming that Leo at forty-five would not want children. Most families, she knew, were complete before the husband was out of his twenties and Leo was older than her own father had been when she was born. Throughout childhood, she had felt the burden of having older parents. Would she want that for a child?

And how would this family work? Leo would often be travelling—he was in demand from individuals and galleries worldwide, and Archie would be travelling with him. She would be the one left at home, looking after the house, caring for children. She felt her heels dig a trench into the counterpane. That was not a life she wanted.

'Concetta is off to see her aunt this evening and I've asked her to leave a cold meal for us,' Leo said, swinging his legs off the bed. 'I hope that's okay.'

'Concetta has an aunt? How old must she be?'

'Around ninety, I think, and still going strong. She lives a little out of the way, in Santa Croce. The maid has been cooking all afternoon for her. But the cold meal?'

'Yes, fine,' Nancy said distractedly and plumped the pillow. 'I think I'd like to close my eyes now.'

'I'll leave you to rest.' He bent to give her a last kiss. 'Rest can only do you good. Dinner at seven?'

'Wonderful,' she breathed, trying to ward off unwanted thoughts.

*

Hours later she was still struggling to decide how best to deal with this new anxiety when Leo suggested an early night. Archie had left before dinner to spend the evening in one of the questionable bars he frequented and for once they were entirely alone in the palazzo. Nancy tried to appear pleased at the idea, but sounded less than convincing even to herself.

She was wriggling out of her underclothes when Leo came out of the adjoining bathroom, toothbrush in hand.

'You look beautiful.' He stood and watched her don her nightgown, a slip of silk purchased especially for the honeymoon.

She glanced sideways at her image in the gilded mirror. The garment flattered her slim curves, its luminous cream highlighting tanned limbs and the cloud of dark chestnut hair that fell to her shoulders. She had never looked better, she thought. If only she could feel as good.

Leo came over to her and encircled her in his arms. Then kissed her deeply. 'I'll be back. Don't run away!'

A few minutes later he'd closed the bathroom door and dimmed the two chandeliers that hung from the centre of the ceiling, leaving the room lit only by the gentle glow of a bedside lamp. He climbed into bed and for a moment they lay motionless, side by side. Then he turned to her, running his hands down the length of her body, caressing her slowly.

'I thought after our conversation this afternoon, we might make a start,' he said softly.

'A start?' She pretended not to understand.

'A baby, Nancy.'

When she said nothing, he asked anxiously, 'You do want a child? All women do, don't they?'

It was the way people thought. It was the way most women thought. Marriage and children was a girl's only true goal in life. That was made clear from an early age: the *Janet and John* books that taught them to read had Janet help Mother to cook, while John and Father did manly things with the car or the wheelbarrow. It was as though women were empty shells, hollow spaces, enduring a kind of non-existence until they became a wife and mother.

But it had never struck Nancy as a particularly fair or interesting destiny. Perhaps she had been single too long and found it impossible to envisage such a very different life. Whatever the reason, she balked at the idea. She needed to know Leo better, needed to have a handle on this marriage before she made such a huge commitment. But how to say that in a way he would understand?

'I suppose I do,' she answered, without any real belief. 'It's only that things have moved a little too fast and I'm still trying to catch up.'

His embrace tightened. 'It's been hectic, I know. And you're right, we should take things slowly. But if it happens, Nancy…'

'I'm sure I'll adjust,' she said as brightly as she could. 'But tonight, I'm still a little tired. How about you?'

He yawned. 'It's been a busy few weeks. I could sleep.'

And he could. He was asleep in minutes, his arms gradually loosening their hold. She turned slightly to burrow her face into the pillow, wishing she could sleep as peacefully. Bozzato's attack had taken a toll on her, dredging up memories she had constantly to suppress, but she couldn't tell Leo. If she confessed, he would want to know why she was outside the Moretto house, and inevitably the whole sorry story would be revealed.

In her heart, she almost wished for it, wished that she could tell him everything that had happened since the afternoon she had met Marta Moretto while eating an ice cream. But she couldn't do it, not without risking a coldness between them, one she knew would not easily disappear.

And if she were truthful, there were other reasons, weren't there, to keep quiet? She was still unsure of Leo. He was loving, kind, thoughtful, all those things, but there were times when she felt him withdraw into himself. Felt him place an invisible barrier between them. It might be a natural reticence, but equally it might be there were things he'd no wish to share with her.

Neither of them had been honest with the other and, because of that, she must endure a second uneasy day in Archie's company. Perhaps a few hours' drive would suffice, just long enough for her to talk intelligently about the countryside through which they'd pass, when she and Leo met tomorrow evening. If Archie's face were any indication, he was determined to drive the shortest distance possible. She closed her eyes, trying not to think of the difficult day ahead. There would be things to enjoy, she told herself severely. Beautiful landscapes, old towns, ancient churches… the convent of Madonna del Carmine. That was in the countryside, she remembered dreamily.

She sat bolt upright, the movement causing Leo to turn in his sleep. The murderous attack on her this morning, Mario Bozzato's bizarre claims, Angelica leaving the convent. There was a question there to which she'd never found a truly satisfactory answer. Why had Angelica left? The mystery of Marta's death had crystallised quite suddenly into one small question. Nancy could not imagine why she'd not thought about it before. Really thought about it. With barely a qualm, she'd accepted Angelica's assertion that she had left Madonna del Carmine to return home and look after a mother in failing health.

But realistically how sick would Marta have to be for her daughter to relinquish the vocation to which she had dedicated her life? For Angelica, leaving the convent would not simply be a case of moving house or taking a new job. It would be throwing away the life she had determined on for the past ten, twelve years. Assuming a new identity, becoming a completely different person, whose values would inevitably have to change, whose principles would inevitably be compromised. There had to be something bigger, greater, behind Angelica's decision than concern for a parent's health.

What would it take to make a strong woman cast aside a life she loved? Could it possibly be, as Mario said, that she had deserted the convent out of love for him? It sounded ridiculous but Bozzato had been insistent. *She chose me*, he'd said. She chose me, not God. And he'd been haunting the Moretto house, as Nancy knew to her cost. Had he been there simply to catch a glimpse of his goddess—or had he, in fact, been coming in and out of the palazzo as a welcome guest, now that Marta was no longer alive?

If Angelica had lied about her feelings for him, if the two of them had been acting out a charade, it put Mario back in the frame as a murderer. He'd been convinced that Marta was working against him, persuading her daughter against the marriage. Maybe Angelica had begun to have doubts. Marta had left the entire Moretto estate to the convent, and though Angelica would know the will could be challenged, it would be difficult for her to go against her mother's wishes. Might she have had second thoughts about marrying Mario without the money to ease their life together?

Bozzato could have decided on a drastic solution. He might have raided whatever savings he had and bought a ticket for *Madama Butterfly*, then as the cast took their final curtain call, he had struck. Mario Bozzato was a big man, a man used to physical labour, and he would be quite strong enough to heave a small woman over the barrier, even one not drugged.

Nancy laid back on her pillow, staring at the ceiling. It was nothing more than guesswork and she couldn't really believe in it. But how was she to discover why Angelica had acted as she had? She was running out of time, her suitcase packed and ready to go, unless... the car excursion tomorrow! The words danced behind her closed lids. If she could persuade Archie to drive her to the convent, it would be one last effort to help Marta, a last chance to solve the mystery of her death. A country drive was not obviously promising, but it was all that was left.

Leo had a meeting tomorrow with Signor Trevi. Earlier Nancy had felt unhappy she would spend the day without him, but now she reconsidered. Her husband's company would have spelt the end of her plan before it had even begun. His absence meant the freedom to throw her last card on the table.

Chapter Twenty-Nine

Maggiore had its offices next to a ramshackle garage and even from a distance the smell of diesel permeated the air. Ahead, she saw Archie almost at the office door and, clasping the errant hat tightly in her hand, she picked up speed. She had things to say to him before he went in.

She called out and somehow he must have heard her above the traffic because he stopped and turned slightly. 'I'll be a few minutes.' He sounded irritable.

'Archie—' she began.

'You'll have to wait,' he said. 'There'll be papers to sign and keys to collect. And I've no idea what kind of car they'll give me.'

'It doesn't matter as long as it works.' The vehicle they were to travel in was the least of her worries.

'Oh, and I doubt they'll have a chauffeur's cap for hire,' he said, his face set.

It was clear the journey was making Archie quarrelsome, but she ignored the provocation. 'One thing before you go … can you ask them for a map?'

He turned to face her fully, a frown creasing his forehead. 'Why do we need a map? The causeway leads to the mainland. We drive along the causeway and out into the countryside, through a few random villages and then back again.'

'Actually, I have a destination in mind.'

The frown turned to a glare. 'What now?'

'The convent of Madonna del Carmine. The one Marta left her money to.'

'Jesus,' he exclaimed, 'you never give up, do you?'

'I know. You can tell Him about it when we get there—Jesus, I mean.'

He gave a disgusted huff and pushed open the firm's door, leaving Nancy feeling light-headed with anticipation.

*

The car Leo had hired turned out to be an open-top Alfa Romeo, at least ten years old but classically elegant in deep blue with a red leather interior. The front seat, Nancy noticed, was designed to take three people, but Archie very deliberately opened the wide single door in such a way that she found herself herded into the rear seat. He was here to drive her, he was indicating. Nothing more. She could see he would need careful handling on this journey.

'Did you get the map?' she asked.

'No need.' He pressed the starter and the engine burst into life.

'Can you tell me why?' She kept her tone mild.

'The convent is on the road to Treviso, just south of a small place called Mogliano. Once we're on the Treviso road, it's a direct route.'

'That sounds nicely simple. And thank you for taking me.'

Archie made no reply and swung the car into the line of traffic making its way to the mainland over a causeway that ran parallel to the railway bridge, the two together ensuring that Venice was no longer an island.

In a short while they were out on the road and the city left behind, but through the window Nancy caught a glimpse of a forest of cranes and smokestacks, with clouds of filthy air beginning to drift towards them.

'Is that Mestre?' She remembered the horror with which Marta had mentioned the town.

'Porto Marghera. Mestre is next door. Marghera is the industrial zone, mainly chemicals.'

'It looks a wretched place.'

'It was more wretched after our bombers got to grips with it,' he said drily.

'I didn't think Venice was bombed in the war.'

'Venice wasn't. Marghera was. In the thirties there used to be sixty or so working factories. The place is gradually getting back on its feet, but it will take time.'

The mention of the war seemed to have eased the atmosphere. She saw Archie's shoulders visibly loosen and his hands on the large steering wheel relax. They were good hands. Nancy remembered how smooth they had been when they'd touched hers, then shut the image from her mind. But he was an excellent driver and she nestled back into the plush leather, knowing she would arrive safely.

They turned off the road that bypassed Mestre and Marghera and took the one signposted to Treviso. 'Is it far?' she dared to ask.

'Around twenty-five kilometres. We'll be there in half an hour, as long as I've been given the right directions.'

Nancy settled down to watch the landscape flow past. The road, snaking its way towards Treviso, travelled between wooded hills, their lower slopes terraced for vines, and through numerous small villages, each with their square-topped church and war memorial. In the far distance, the sight of the snow-capped Dolomites caught her eye. The mountains were rarely visible from Venice, beleaguered as it was by waves of humidity rising from the lagoon.

They had driven in silence for a good twenty minutes

and Nancy had begun to wonder if Archie had misheard the directions or, her suspicious mind prompted, whether he'd decided after all to drive at random, when he suddenly asked, 'Why are we going to this benighted place?'

'I'm hoping it isn't benighted,' she replied, relieved they were at least on their way. 'I've had a hunch—and don't groan.'

'Have I groaned?'

'No, but you're just about to. I want to know why Angelica abandoned her life at the convent. I don't believe she left to look after a sick mother and I'm still pretty sure she didn't give up her vocation for Mario.'

'And that's why we're going to say hello to the nuns? What happened to Dino as murderer in chief?'

'I don't know,' Nancy said a trifle unhappily. 'I've been thinking I may have got that wrong. Not that he's not a criminal. He is. But maybe not a killer.'

'You're as crazy as Mario. For days, you've been banging on about Dino forging pictures and killing to protect his reputation, and suddenly he has nothing to do with Marta's death.'

'I didn't say that. He might have. I just can't work it out at the moment.'

'No, and that's the problem. You can't find evidence for any of these little theories of yours. You were desperate to nail Di Maio for murder but you've failed, and instead of deciding to forget the whole damn business, you're scooting off in another direction. Now it's the nuns who'll provide the answer.'

'I just have this feeling.' Nancy sounded more feeble than she wished.

'Like the feeling you have that Marta Moretto was murdered when nobody else thinks so. Why don't you stick to having rattled Dino's cage and saved Renzo from a life of crime?'

'Marta *was* murdered and as long as I'm in Venice, I can't give up.'

'Thank God there's only a few hours left then. Tomorrow at nine o'clock we're on the train, and I won't be forced to cover for you any more.'

'I don't see you've had to cover for me today,' she said indignantly. 'We had to drive somewhere, so why not to the convent?'

'Possibly because your husband is an intelligent man and might just smell a rat if he knew where we're headed.'

'I hope not.' There was a small waver in her voice.

'So do I. I've had enough of being a stooge. I'm Leo's assistant not some partner in a crime-fighting duo.'

Archie had been particularly cutting today and she was finding it hard. But it was his way, Nancy realised, of emphasising the boundary that should exist between them.

'I'm very grateful for the help you've given me, Archie.' She tried to sound placatory. 'And once we're back in London, I promise to keep out of your way. I just have this one question I need answering. Then I'll be happy.'

'I doubt it. Anyway, I could probably give you the answer right now.'

'Why? What do you mean?' She leaned forward until she was almost speaking into his ear.

Archie stared straight ahead, his eyes never leaving the road. 'You want to find out why Angelica left the convent. For some unknown reason, the place is going to tell you everything you want to know. So... what if Marta visited the convent before she died? The woman must have visited at some point, she left the nuns her entire estate.'

'What if she did?'

'If we assume your crazy theory is right and Dino *was*

threatening Marta, the woman would have told her daughter what she suspected when she visited the convent, wouldn't she? Told Angelica how frightened she was for her safety. Wouldn't that be sufficient reason for the nun to hotfoot it back to the family home?'

'I suppose,' Nancy said unwillingly. 'But even if Marta visited, would she have had the chance to talk to Angelica? Aren't nuns supposed to be cloistered?'

'Search me. But if she did get to speak to her daughter and tell her the trouble she was in, a woman who loved her mother would return home to protect her.'

'She would have to love her deeply to give up such a strong vocation.'

'Who's to say she didn't? And in any case, it could be a temporary situation. She might have got permission to go home, sort things out, and then return to the convent.'

Annoyingly, Archie's idea was persuasive, though she wouldn't tell him so. He was overweening enough already. But he was right that if Angelica had known about Dino's wickedness before her mother died, it would better explain her decision to leave the convent.

'It would make sense, I suppose, of why Angelica so dislikes her brother.' Nancy was thinking aloud. 'If Luca stayed a close friend of the man she suspected of harming her mother, it couldn't have done much for sibling relations.'

'So Dino is your man. It's what you wanted.'

'What I wanted, what I still want, is the truth,' she retorted.

'You're as near to it as you're going to get. Shall I turn the car round?'

'No!'

Nancy still had to reach the convent. She couldn't explain why, but she had a visceral sense that everything depended on this visit. And there was something wrong with Archie's analysis. She sat and puzzled while he drove smoothly on.

'If Angelica left the convent because she knew her mother was in danger...' Nancy broke the silence. 'If Dino is our villain... and Angelica knew... then she has been in danger for weeks. Yet she's still alive. Her mother and brother are dead, but she's alive. What do you make of that?'

Archie made no answer, but turned the wheel abruptly to the left and slid the car between two narrow stone pillars. 'This is it!'

They were on a long, rutted track. Even in the splendid Alfa Romeo, they were jolted roughly from one side of the car to another, and the lane seemed to stretch for miles. The Madonna del Carmine, Nancy thought, could usefully spend some of the fortune it had inherited on a comfortable approach road.

Just when she thought that every bone in her body must be fractured, they rounded another bend and there it was—a large, sprawling building in honey-coloured stone, with a square bell tower soaring high above the front entrance. Tier upon tier of grey shutters were closed against the morning sun, lending the convent a face stripped of all expression. A facade that gave nothing away.

Archie brought the vehicle to a smooth halt outside the front entrance, making sure he manoeuvred into the solitary piece of shade. He climbed out of the car and began to walk round to her door, intending, she thought, to emphasise that he was here only as a hired chauffeur. But she pre-empted him, extricating herself from the car before he could reach her.

She had barely swung her feet to the ground when she realised he'd turned away and was speaking to someone.

'Enrico, you old dog. What are you doing here?'

Nancy looked over the top of the car in time to see a priest, black-robed and buttoned to the neck, throwing his arms around Archie. His matching cummerbund was stretched so tightly across a considerable girth that it risked bursting apart.

'What am I doing here, my friend?' the man boomed. 'I live here. Just over the way.' She followed his pointing finger to a small cottage tucked into the lea of the main building. 'But come, you must have a drink. And your lovely companion. It is too hot again, eh?' He passed a crumpled handkerchief over his wet forehead.

'But—' Nancy began, willing to forgo the drink in her eagerness to seek out the Mother Superior and question her.

'This is Mrs Tremayne.' Archie introduced her grudgingly. 'Enrico Conti.' He jerked his head towards Nancy to indicate he'd done his social duty.

'Ah, Professor Tremayne's wife.' The priest rolled towards her, smiling broadly. 'A good man. I am delighted to meet you, Mrs Tremayne, and delighted to welcome you to my home. Come, please.' Nancy had no option but to follow.

It was a very small cottage, but its stone walls were nearly a metre thick and the air was wonderfully cool. In the tiny entrance hall they were met by a woman who looked old enough to be the priest's mother. 'Giovanna,' he said to her, 'these are my friends—from London? No?'

'Venice,' Archie put in briefly.

Enrico spread his hands. 'Wherever, my friend. Put the water to boil, Giovanna. They will take tea with us—tea is best in this heat, eh?' He gave Archie a playful dig. 'And at this time of the day, too. Maybe later we open the whisky.'

When Giovanna had brought a tray loaded with cups, saucers and teapot and handed around the customary plate of small, hard biscuits, the housekeeper disappeared into the nether regions, though she could not have gone far, Nancy reckoned. The cottage was miniature in scale.

Archie leant back in his wicker chair, cup in hand.

'So what's new with you, Enrico? Are the winnings still mounting?'

'Not so much, I am afraid. These days I rarely get to Venice and here, you can see for yourself. We are rustics in a quiet countryside.'

'A boring countryside?'

'Tut, tut. The contemplative life is good for me. No excitement to disturb the heart.' He saw Nancy looking puzzled and said, 'Mrs Tremayne, your friend Archie is a demon poker player.'

'Not such a demon that he can beat you,' Archie said wryly.

'You gamble?' Nancy sounded more shocked than she'd wanted to, but the mention of poker playing and whisky was reshaping her image of the life she'd imagined for a Catholic priest.

'A little flutter here and there. Nothing serious, dear lady. But does Salvatore still run those games?' he asked Archie.

'Salvatore has other fish to fry.' His expression was solemn and the priest's eyebrows rose. 'In fact, he's up to no good,' Archie said baldly, but made no attempt to elaborate. Hoping to spare the priest bad news of a former friend, she imagined.

Enrico replaced his cup on the tray with great care. For a large man, his movements were unusually delicate. 'I am truly sorry to hear that.'

'I guess it's inevitable. Everyone is trying to make some kind of living and it's not easy these days. There's wealth in Venice if you know where to look—and rich pickings for the unscrupulous.'

'Not only in Venice, I fear.' The priest gave a long sigh and adjusted his cummerbund. 'Even in this backwater we have our problems, though it's difficult to believe. Burglary, theft—many from churches nearby.'

'That's bad,' Archie said. 'Are newcomers responsible or have the locals turned to stealing?'

'That I don't know, my friend. I like to think my parishioners are pearls beyond price, but ...' The priest shook his head sadly. 'In one way, you can understand, though not forgive. As you say, the country is still in the doldrums. Yes, there is new industry in Milan, in Turin, but here in the countryside and in the poorer parts of town, people are struggling and often hungry, and it is easier then to forget the ten commandments. The shadow of the war stretches far, does it not?'

There was a long silence, then Enrico appeared to recover his good humour and find his smile again. 'Mrs Tremayne, forgive me. We must not talk of such bad things. May I pour you another cup?'

'Not for me, thank you, but the tea was most refreshing.'

'Refreshing enough to walk around our ancient convent?'

'I hope so. I've heard how beautiful it is.' She forgave herself the small lie.

'The chapel is wonderful,' Enrico said. 'You must see the chapel certainly. Reverend Mother will be happy to welcome you, I know.'

This was good news and Nancy was relieved. She knew nothing of the nuns of Madonna del Carmine and had feared theirs might be an enclosed order.

'Father, will you introduce me to Reverend Mother?'

'But naturally.' He yanked up a chain and took a watch from his pocket. 'Sext is just finishing and the nuns will not pray again until Nones at three this afternoon. We should find Reverend Mother in her office. Drink up, Archie, and we will go.'

Chapter Thirty

Father Conti led them across the courtyard past the Alfa Romeo, sitting serene in shadow, to the convent's beautiful filigree iron door, and rang for admittance. As Nancy bent her head to peer through the ironwork, a single file of nuns came into view, walking in complete silence. She imagined they must have come from the chapel, from their midday prayers. As they drew opposite, one by one they scattered in different directions, still without exchanging a word. Except for a black wimple, their habits were entirely white, a short white cape over a white robe, seeming to be suited for nothing more vigorous than embroidery.

Yet on their way across the courtyard Enrico had mentioned that between set times of prayer the nuns worked extremely hard. Nancy had seen for herself the fields on either side of the track, cultivated with every kind of produce. She wondered how Angelica had enjoyed this back-breaking work.

An elderly nun answered the Father's summons, a cluster of keys jangling from her belt. She beamed at them as she opened the door, saying how happy the convent was to welcome Father Conti's friends. She would take them straightaway to the Reverend Mother, who had returned from the chapel and was now in her office.

They followed her along a cloister of honey-coloured stone. A series of majestic arches, the beautiful symmetry

273

of a sculpted white roof, the enclosed square of a garden filled with roses, had Nancy's soul sing. Even in September flowers were blooming and their sweet perfume followed the little party along worn flagstones to a carved wooden door standing sentinel at one end of the cloister.

Their guide gave a discreet knock and for a few minutes left them waiting outside while she consulted with Mother Superior. When she re-emerged, she was still smiling.

'Reverend Mother will be happy to receive you,' she said simply.

'I'll leave you in her capable hands then,' Enrico boomed. He seemed altogether too loud and too large for the restrained beauty of this place, but Nancy gave him a warm handshake and thanked him for his hospitality.

Reverend Mother rose from her desk as they walked through the door. She was an impressive figure, dressed entirely in black with only a white wimple to relieve the intensity, a mirror image of the nuns for whom she was responsible.

She motioned them to sit. The chair Nancy sank into was unexpectedly comfortable. In truth, she was surprised at how agreeably Mother Superior lived, her office exuding a degree of wealth. The fluted legs of the desk spoke baroque— not cheap Nancy noted—and there were painted chests, also baroque style, against two of the walls. In the middle of the room, two easy chairs faced each other across a small hand-woven rug. Otherwise the boarded floor was bare but polished to a high gloss.

'Thank you for visiting us, Mrs Tremayne, Mr Jago,' the nun began. 'We are always happy to welcome guests and honoured that you are interested in our convent. How much do you know about Madonna del Carmine?'

'Very little,' Nancy confessed.

Reverend Mother fixed them with a keen glance. 'The most important thing to understand is that the convent is a very old institution. It was established way back in the sixteenth century, though the building you see today is much altered. The original convent was designed to be a place of complete retreat. The nuns had little to do with the outside world. Their mission was to pray for it. Now we are a little different.'

She gave a small smile that Nancy sensed was hard for her. 'Nowadays we have fields to tend and produce to pick for market. Not only that, but livestock to care for, eggs to collect, honey to preserve. In effect, we are a small farm.'

'It sounds idyllic.' Nancy was uncomfortably aware of how vapid she sounded. But it was the first thing that had come to mind and, since Archie seemed determined not to speak, she felt pressured to contribute something to the conversation.

'I am unable to take you into most of the convent,' Reverend Mother went on. 'I hope you will understand that it is our home. But if you will come with me, I will be happy to show you our guest rooms. We are very proud of them. You may even wish to return at a later date and take advantage of the tranquillity they offer.'

She gestured for them to follow her out of the office and along a corridor that ran at right angles to the cloister. Nancy had no wish for a guided tour of the convent, but it seemed the only way she was likely to get her questions answered.

'Do you have many people coming on retreat?' she asked, matching the nun's brisk pace.

'Very many.'

'And how long do they generally stay?'

'It varies, Mrs Tremayne. For as long as they need—to find the spiritual peace that is otherwise missing from their lives.'

Nancy glanced across at Archie, who had pulled down the sides of his mouth. She guessed that spiritual peace did not feature too largely in his life.

There were a dozen guest rooms situated along a wide corridor with windows looking out on to the fields. Beyond that, Nancy thought, they had little to commend them. A stone-flagged floor and bare white walls, adorned with religious paintings too garish for her taste. And furniture restricted to a narrow single bed, a small wooden desk and hard chair, and a white hand basin that had been fitted into the far corner of each room.

'I believe Signora Moretto stayed with you,' Nancy found the courage to say, as they were leaving the final room.

Reverend Mother looked up sharply from locking the door behind her. 'You knew Signora Moretto? Such a great sadness for us when we heard of her death. Yes, she enjoyed a few days with us. But how do you know her?'

'Quite by chance. We got talking in a café one day. She was a lovely woman.'

'She was,' Reverend Mother said brusquely, her lips tightening.

'Marta told me her daughter was a nun here.' Nancy ploughed on, though she could see her host had no wish to talk of the Morettos. 'She spoke of the convent so warmly, it made me want to come myself.' It was a second lie, but in the circumstances Nancy excused herself. 'She seemed inspired to know her daughter was a nun — seeing Angelica here must have been a joy.'

'We do not encourage our nuns to have contact with their families. Marta Moretto visited for the same reason as many others — to find peace.' And now there was no mistaking Reverend Mother's annoyance.

Nancy saw Archie lift a hand as if to prevent her saying more, but then he let it fall. It made no difference. She wasn't going to stop now.

'I understand, of course, that families rarely visit. But since Signora Moretto was such a good friend to the convent' — she would make no specific mention of the legacy, but let the nun read into her words what she chose — 'allowing her to meet her daughter would be, well, a generous gesture, I suppose.'

'We do not imprison our nuns, Mrs Tremayne. And Sister Teresa,' the Mother Superior emphasised the name, 'would have been permitted to take a short walk with her mother when the signora visited.' She stared hard into Nancy's face. 'But allow me to show you our magnificent chapel.'

Nancy understood then that she would get no more. But Marta *had* visited *and* she had spoken to Angelica. It seemed very much that Archie's conclusion was correct: that Marta had confided her troubles to her daughter and Angelica had left the convent to protect her mother. She saw a smirk touch the corners of his mouth, as they walked back along the corridor in search of the chapel. Archie was enjoying being right.

The chapel was much as Nancy had expected: a flagged floor, upright wooden pews, a sculpted white ceiling and stark white walls. Cold, austere, uninviting. Until, that is, she walked down the narrow aisle and came face to face with an altar of solid gold. It was not a large altar, but its glow burnished the entire far end of the chapel, bringing statues and a dark-painted tryptych to life. And this glorious warmth did not stop with the altar. Above it, and seemingly hanging in the air, was an almost life-size golden crucifix. The *pièce de resistance*.

Mother Superior allowed them time to take in the magnificence of which she was justly proud. Archie soon sank onto a wooden pew, his interest in religious art limited, but Nancy stood for minutes absorbing the craftsmanship that had gone into making the altar and its accompanying crucifix. It was only when she heard the rustle of keys that she turned to say thank you to her host.

'It is the most exquisite altar,' she said.

'We think so.'

'And the crucifix. What date is it?'

'It is slightly younger than the altar. Eighteenth century, I believe.' Reverend Mother had unbent slightly, now that Nancy's questions were focussed on the place she loved.

The swish of a gown on the stone floor had them both turning. A nun was walking quickly towards them. She bowed to her superior. 'I am sorry to interrupt, Mother, but there is a telephone call for you. It appears to be important.'

Reverend Mother smiled graciously, relieved, Nancy thought, to be free of her troublesome guests.

'I'm afraid I must return to my office,' she said, 'but Sister Aurelia will escort you to the courtyard. Naturally you are welcome to look around our estate.'

'Thank you. You are most kind,' Nancy replied. 'But we must be getting back to Venice. We leave for London tomorrow.'

Mother's face expressed a pleased calm. She turned and walked swiftly out of the chapel, leaving Sister Aurelia to escort them back along the aisle.

'How many nuns live in the convent?' Nancy asked, trying to find a way to the question uppermost in her mind. Archie might be right about Angelica's reason for leaving, he probably was, but there was still a small part of Nancy that wouldn't let go, and Sister Aurelia might prove more forthcoming than her Mother Superior.

'Around fifty, Mrs Tremayne.'

'And do nuns ever leave?'

The Sister's face expressed shock. 'Leave?'

'Yes, leave. Can they walk out of the door if they wish?'

'The convent is not a gaol,' the nun said reprovingly. 'But nuns have a long time in which to make their decision. Many years to think whether they are suited to a life of devotion.'

'How many years?' She wondered how far along this road Angelica had travelled.

'They are first postulants for a year maybe, then novitiates for, say, another three, when nuns will take their first vows. But it is three, four, five years later before they will make final vows.'

'And those final vows—are they binding?'

'They are most serious.' Sister Aurelia's voice was grave. 'The nun has committed her life to God.'

'But if someone felt, for instance, that they no longer had a vocation?' Nancy was making it up as she went along.

'Then our Sister would go to Reverend Mother and talk to her. Reverend Mother would try to discover the problem, but if the nun still wished to leave, she must request a dispensation from the Holy See.'

'And is that easy?'

Sister Aurelia frowned deeply. 'It takes time.'

'And if she didn't have that time, could she walk out of the door?'

The woman looked scandalised. 'She would then live her life in sin—and die in sin,' she added crisply. 'Please, follow me.'

They were halfway along the aisle when Nancy saw a small side chapel she hadn't noticed before. Earlier she had walked right past, too entranced by the glory beckoning her to the main altar, but now she took a few steps through the archway and looked around. Archie had walked on.

The side chapel was unremarkable and, after a quick glance, she turned to go. Then something stopped her. On the bottom step of the modest altar was a gold statuette sitting atop a black pedestal of carved wood. Her gaze slid along the step. On the left side was a matching pedestal, but it was empty.

Nancy felt Sister Aurelia hovering behind. It was clear the nun was eager to usher her guests from the convent and was hoping this foray into the small chapel would be brief.

But Nancy knew that statuette. She swallowed hard. 'This is quite beautiful,' she said, marvelling again at the figure's luminosity and the skill with which every intricate detail of the saint's clothing and expression had been crafted.

'It is a statue of Santa Susanna,' the nun said. 'A saint very dear to our convent.'

'I see.' She pretended ignorance, though she remembered every word of that other conversation. She waved a hand at the empty pedestal. 'It looks as though there should be another to match.'

The Sister's face fell. 'You are right, Mrs Tremayne. We have lost the precious statue that was part of a pair. For centuries the convent has protected them.' Her voice cracked slightly. 'And then to lose them when we are guardians… it is so very sad. But over the last few years many places of devotion have suffered theft and our convent has not been immune. The depth of wickedness in this world is difficult to understand.'

'I am so sorry.' Nancy managed to utter the expected sentiment, though her head felt ready to burst. 'But do you have the remaining statue safe?' she gabbled.

'This is a replica. Made not of gold but of gold leaf. The original is under lock and key—we could not take the risk that it, too, would disappear. And next week the goldsmith will deliver a second replica and we shall have a pair once more. It will not be the same, but we must accept God's will and pray for the souls of those who would do Him harm. Now…'

Sister Aurelia extended her arm as though to shepherd Nancy away. 'If you have seen enough?'

'Yes, thank you,' she stumbled to say. 'You have been more than generous with your time.'

The Sister gave her a long look, as though she had divined the reason for Nancy's visit and could see into her heart. Then she folded her hands in her robe and bowed her head. 'May you go with God, Mrs Tremayne, and your troubles be as nothing.'

Nancy had the unpleasant feeling that her troubles might only just be starting, but somehow she followed Sister Aurelia out of the chapel and into the cloister. From there it was a short step to the wrought iron door and the courtyard beyond.

Archie was waiting for her by the car. He looked mystified, shaking his head slightly, when she weaved an almost drunken path towards him. 'What's the matter with you?' he asked, as she stumbled up to the car and collapsed against the bonnet. 'What's been going on back there?'

'The side chapel—the one I looked in.'

'Yes?'

'There was a statue there. Santa Susanna. Golden. Beautiful.' She was rambling. 'There should have been two, an identical pair, but one has been stolen.'

Archie gave a low whistle. 'It's what Enrico was saying— crime has reached this backwater. But why are you so wound up?'

'The statue—you don't understand. I know where the other one is. The one Sister Aurelia says has been stolen.'

Archie looked sceptical. 'Then you'd better go back and tell our formidable hostess where she can find it.'

'I can't.' Nancy's face was drained of colour. 'I can't,' she repeated. 'It's in the Moretto palazzo.'

Chapter Thirty-One

Archie looked dumbfounded. It was the first time Nancy had known him completely fazed. 'You saw the statue that's been stolen?'

'Yes. I'm telling you.' She straightened up and her voice was firm. 'I noticed it as I was leaving the Moretto house. It was such a beautiful piece that I went over for a closer look. Angelica said she was keeping the statue at the palazzo to take it for cleaning.'

'Do statues get cleaned?'

'Sometimes. But this one… I don't know. I imagine so. At the time, I didn't question it. I assumed she knew what she was talking about.'

Archie opened the car door and gestured to her to get in. 'We'd better leave or we'll be attracting attention we don't want.' He slid into the driver's seat, then half turned towards her. 'You're absolutely certain that the statue you saw matched the one in the chapel here?'

Nancy nodded. 'It was identical, even down to the story behind it. I learned about Santa Susanna from Angelica and a few minutes ago Sister Aurelia was telling me how much the convent venerated this particular saint.'

Archie made no reply but put the car in gear, turning the vehicle in a smooth curve to begin the bumpy ride back along the uneven track. The main road was in sight before he spoke. 'It has to be nonsense. What you're saying in effect is that Angelica Moretto stole the damn thing.' He sounded incredulous, as well he might.

'It *is* nonsense, I agree.' Nancy spoke quietly from the rear seat. She had herself under control now, though her head was still a maelstrom. 'Angelica can't have stolen it.' There was silence between them while Archie turned the car towards Venice, until Nancy burst out, 'But what other explanation is there?'

'A nun stealing a religious icon?'

Another long silence, then Archie said gloomily, 'I suppose there must be bent nuns. Why should they be exempt? And it would explain why she left the convent in a bang. At least, I'm presuming she did.'

'I wasn't able to ask about Angelica in particular. The nuns are very frosty about women renouncing the order. But it's clear from what Sister Aurelia said that after a nun has taken her final vows, it's difficult to leave. The woman has to jump through hoops before she's granted permission. And if she simply walks out, she becomes the worst kind of sinner for the rest of her life—and afterwards.'

'And the woman we're talking about is fanatically religious?'

'So Luisa suggested. And I felt it, too, even in the short time I spent with Angelica. That's why it doesn't make sense.'

Archie drummed his fingers on the steering wheel. 'Enrico might have helped. He must be pretty thick with the nuns—he'd be aware of any gossip in the convent. But he isn't at home. After he left us, he went off to be priestly and visit his parishioners.'

'So what do we do? Sorry,' she corrected herself, 'What do *I* do?'

'Nothing. There's nothing you can do and tomorrow we'll be gone.'

Nancy settled back into the comfortable red leather, but she was gripped by frustration. She was certain the missing statue was at the heart of the tragedy. The statue and the visit that Marta had made to the convent. But Archie was right. She had run out of time and there was nothing more she could do.

Her mind, though, stayed unquiet, and when they were once more passing Mestre and the distant smokestacks of Marghera, she said, 'If Angelica did steal, why did she do it? For money? But nuns can't possess property and, in any case, the Moretto family are wealthy, or have been. And if she stole money for a reason we don't know, wouldn't she have sold the statue?'

'That would be difficult.'

'Gold can be melted down and if she were prepared to take a lower price...'

How horrendous was that! Too horrendous for Angelica certainly. 'But if it wasn't for money,' Nancy went on, 'if Angelica stole it because she loved it and thought the convent owed her in some way, why leave it on open display for anyone to see?'

'Perhaps she didn't expect visitors.'

Nancy thought about this. 'I don't imagine they had many visitors, if any. It didn't seem a house you'd invite people to. But even so, her mother lived there with her—until a short while ago. Marta would have seen it.'

'So what if she had and recognised the work? She wouldn't have reported the theft. She would have protected her daughter. Anyway, Angelica could have hidden the object away and only brought it out after her mother's death.' There was a pause before he added, 'A death that was convenient, wouldn't you say?'

Nancy gasped. 'You're surely not suggesting that Angelica...'

'Just a thought. Marta's death was probably suicide, though no one will admit it—including you.'

'And Luca's?'

'Why not a mugging gone wrong?'

None of it rang true but Nancy's mind had frozen, unable to process the multitude of conflicting facts. She hadn't just run out of time, she'd run out of energy. And she still had to face Leo when they arrived home. Pretend she had enjoyed an innocent afternoon drifting through the Veneto countryside. How she was to do that, while she was in such turmoil, she had no idea.

She would have to play a part—she often did—and at least Archie could be relied on to say nothing of the convent. She watched him as he drove, hands firm on the wheel, eyes fixed on the road ahead. He seemed impervious to the constant stream of shocks that had come her way. But then he wasn't emotionally invested, as she was, in Marta's death.

Nancy was honest enough to recognise that her crusade, in part, had given her purpose, had helped her regain an identity, a voice. But it didn't explain why she cared so very much about Marta. Perhaps it was the vulnerability she'd sensed in an otherwise strong woman, perhaps a fellow feeling for someone who carried within her a deep sadness, yet was struggling to live a good life. Whatever it was, since their conversation on the Zattere, Nancy had not been able to forget her.

*

Archie delivered the car keys to the office at the Piazzale Roma and together they took the vaporetto to San Zaccaria. Neither of them spoke again of the missing statue, disembarking from the boat and walking the short distance to the palazzo in silence.

Leo greeted them at the door, a wide smile on his face. The meeting with Signor Trevi had evidently gone well. 'How was the trip? What did you see? Did you stop off anywhere?'

Nancy did her best to play the part she'd given herself, mentioning one or two of the places through which they'd passed, commenting on the bare fields, now harvested, the gentle hills and small villages. Her account was deliberately vague, but it didn't seem to matter. Leo appeared preoccupied.

They were still standing on the wide landing when Archie leapt up the stairs two at a time and went to pass them.

'Archie,' Leo called after him. 'I've packed most of my papers, but can you check I haven't left anything vital behind? And… if you have a spare minute, could you chivvy my suitcase into some kind of order? I've only just got back from the meeting and I've not had time.'

Nancy was surprised. It was unusual for Leo to ask for help with a personal chore, but when Archie had walked off down the long corridor to the small office at the back of the palazzo, Leo took her hand. 'I've asked Concetta to bring us tea as soon as you got back. Let's go into the salon.'

The maid was already laying out cups and saucers. There was something afoot, Nancy was sure. When Leo had poured the tea and handed her a cup, he sat down beside her, the sofa sagging to one side in its customary fashion.

'Nancy.' He cleared his throat.

'What is it? You're worrying me.'

'Sorry, it's not that serious, but I do have more apologies to make.' He took a long drink of tea. 'The meeting with Signor Trevi went well—it lasted hours, that's why I'm so delayed getting myself organised for tomorrow—but even so, there are still things we need to tie up.'

He took another sip of tea, and she waited patiently for him to go on. 'I wanted our last meal in Venice to be one we shared, Nancy, but Signor Trevi is staying in the city overnight before he takes the train back to Bologna and he's asked me to dine with him. I'd hoped Dino would have made the meeting today—or if not, taken the man out to dinner—that would have got me off the hook. But he called to say he was too busy. Apparently he's getting ready to sail tonight.'

A vision of the wooden crate came into Nancy's head. Was that where Dino was going? To Albania, to sell his fraudulent paintings? She had learned from a casual comment of Leo that the *Andiamo* had not left port since their trip to Burano; the crate she'd seen must still be on board. Dino and his captain would be keen to offload their criminal cargo and now, days after Archie's raid on the boathouse, and still no repercussions, they must have thought it safe to sail again.

'I know it's a wretched way to end our honeymoon, darling.' Leo reached out to clasp both her hands, interpreting her silence as disappointment. 'But Trevi is likely to contribute heavily to the art fund and I can't let the chance escape. You're welcome to join us, of course, although—'

'I'd be listening to several hours of business talk?'

'I'm afraid so. I think I've convinced him that his contribution will be worthwhile. Worth his while, that is— that his firm will get real advantage from it. Their name on all the publicity material, that sort of thing. But tonight I'm hoping to talk actual figures. If Signora Trevi were with him, it would be different, but she's still at home in Bologna.'

'Then I think it's best your dinner remains a men-only event.' Nancy took back her hands but smiled warmly at him. 'Have your last meal in Venice with Signor Trevi, but promise that your first in London will be with me.'

'I don't need to promise. You know it will.' He pulled her

close into his arms and nuzzled her neck. Then kissed her passionately on the lips. 'And you're a sweetheart,' he said, releasing his hold. 'Thank you for being so understanding — not many wives would be.'

Or so devious, Nancy said to herself. While Leo had been busy justifying his absence, inspiration had found her waiting and eager. Clear, bright, inspiration. If her husband were not here this evening…

*

She saw him off at seven o'clock sharp and went upstairs to finish her packing. But there were several garments she deliberately put to one side: that pair of grey slacks and a lightweight grey pullover. She would need to melt into the night — she mustn't be seen by anyone who knew her or Leo. Soft-soled shoes completed the ensemble, soft enough to creep downstairs without being heard by an over-curious assistant.

She had her hand on the outside door when she heard his voice from the top of the staircase.

'I wouldn't do that.'

Archie was leaning against the white plastered wall, arms folded, and shaking his head.

'How do you know what I'm doing?'

'It doesn't take too much brain power to work it out. As soon as Leo announced he was out for the evening, I knew you wouldn't be able to resist.'

'You can't stop me going.'

'True enough.' He shifted his position, so that from where she stood at the bottom of the stairs his figure loomed large. 'You can charge off like a deranged demon, gatecrash the palazzo and harangue Angelica Moretto, but do you think it's wise?'

'Wise or not, I'm going. And I've no intention of haranguing the woman. All I want is to know what happened—why Angelica left the convent so abruptly. Maybe even how her mother died. For two weeks, no nearly three, I've tried so hard to discover the truth. Now before I leave Venice I have a chance I didn't expect. And I'm going to take it.'

Archie began to walk purposefully down the stairs. 'Then I'm going with you.'

'No.' Nancy put up her hand to stop him. 'I'm going alone.'

'You don't need to worry. I won't follow you into the palazzo. All I'll do is stand guard outside.'

'What good will that do? In any case, I don't need a guard.'

'You never know when you might need an ex-soldier.'

He started down the stairs again. When he drew level with her, she turned to face him. His blue eyes were looking directly into hers and she almost weakened. 'I appreciate the offer, Archie, but I think an ex-soldier is the last person I'll need tonight. We'll just be two women talking together.'

Archie shrugged his shoulders, his face a sudden blank, and turned to go back.

'On your own head be it then!'

Chapter Thirty-Two

Walking to the vaporetto stop, Nancy felt a new hollowness. It was the thought that now she was truly on her own. Nevertheless, she was relieved that Archie had not been difficult and insisted he come with her. The meeting with Angelica would be, as she'd said, just two women talking, and that would be far easier without a third person in the room.

Archie was a curious combination, though. At one moment he behaved like so many other men, judging women on their looks, seeing them as objects to appreciate—or not—but at others, he seemed willing to treat them, to treat her, as an equal. When he'd turned back up the stairs a moment ago, she was sure he saw her not as a defenceless girl needing protection, but as a woman who knew her own mind.

Nancy wondered if that was his mother's influence. Morwenna Jago must be strong and confident. She was a woman who'd worked for years under harsh conditions in a tough industry and for little pay. A woman who deserved respect. And on occasions, Archie had shown *her* respect, Nancy thought, even if it had come grudgingly.

How different Morwenna's life had been from that of Leo's mother. Rachel Tremayne had enjoyed comfort and ease, but with an existence dictated by her husband. She had relinquished any professional ambition, to settle instead for painting pictures that would adorn the walls of Penleven. What had Leo said? That like so many women, his mother had not reached her potential. Had her son unconsciously imbibed the sense that women must always fall short, that dependence was their natural trait?

Leo would not have allowed her to walk out of the palazzo door tonight, for sure. Of course, he was her husband and had greater care for her. But over the weeks she had noticed that his desire for equality did not run deep. He was unhappy if she adopted an independent stance. He preferred to be the one making the decisions and expected her to go along with them. And for the most part she had.

He was not a controlling monster like Philip March. She found herself shaking her head to dislodge such a dreadful thought. Her husband was simply over-protective. And he had good cause, hadn't he? She wondered if a time would ever come when Leo would no longer feel the need to shield her, a time when she would escape her stalker's shadow and live the way she truly wanted.

Tomorrow they were to return to London where they would stay a few days while Leo fulfilled his most pressing engagements. Then on to Penleven for a week or so and back to London and more of Leo's engagements. His schedule was meticulously organised and it had become hers, too. Nancy wasn't averse to these plans—Leo had to earn a living and she knew she had a duty to visit his family home—but she'd had no say in them, and more importantly no say in how they would live when they were in London once more.

She had seen Leo's diary and it was packed, but where would she be while he was busy meeting potential contributors to the fund, or engaged for hours in valuing, or teaching eager students how to read a Renaissance painting? Doing a little shopping for herself? Not for the household, that was certain.

Mrs Brindley guarded her role as housekeeper jealously. A little light shopping then, a visit to the hairdresser, drifting through galleries, meeting women she hardly knew and calling them friends. It was not the future she wanted, but it was the one that Leo had assumed for her—until any children came. And she'd not yet found the courage to challenge it. The burden of gratitude still weighed heavily on her.

Suddenly conscious of her surroundings, she shivered. While she had been deep in thought, it seemed she had boarded a vaporetto and was on her way to the Zattere. At this time in the evening, the Giudecca Canal was quiet, the commercial traffic finished for the day and only a few small private boats and taxis passing by. She had taken an outside seat—a rare pleasure, they were always the most popular— but a damp mist had settled over the city, drifting in from the sea, and wrapping her in its tendrils. She wished she had worn a jacket.

The journey was swift, though, and a ten-minute walk along the Zattere brought her to *calle dei Morti*. She stood at the corner of the street, glancing with some apprehension across the road to the terrifying gap that yawned dark beneath a dim lamp. The fencing had been restored but it was still a fearful place, and she made sure to keep to the palazzo side of the *calle*, hugging the garden walls as she passed. At the Moretto gates, she looked around and took courage. The street was empty; there was no sign of Mario Bozzato.

Stiffening her shoulders, she pulled the bell. No one came. She pulled again and sensed the slight movement of a blind on the first floor. In a few minutes, the front door opened and what seemed in the muted light to be a dark column, appeared in the doorway. It was a woman, her dress flowing to her ankles and a curtain of hair to her shoulders.

Nancy was mystified. It was Angelica herself who walked

towards the gates. Where was the male servant who had admitted her previously?

'You!' The woman sounded surprised when she came closer. Nancy caught a glimpse of a beautiful face, but Angelica's expression was difficult to read.

'Come in, Mrs Tremayne.' She pressed a button and the gates swung open.

Something made Nancy unsure and she hovered in the gateway. 'Come in,' Angelica repeated, beckoning her to follow her up the path and into the house. The front door closed behind the two women with a sharp snap; neither of them had noticed the figure standing in the shadow of the garden wall.

Angelica's statuesque form led the way to the salon that Nancy remembered from her first visit. The room had seemed gloomy then—she remembered how she'd instinctively made for the window in an attempt to lighten the oppressiveness. Now it seemed a dark cavern of a space, lit not by electric but by several oil lamps that flickered restlessly in the slight draught passing through the room. The space appeared smaller, too. Was it the pools of darkness that lay beyond the lamplight, or was it solely her imagination? Whatever it was, Nancy felt the room closing in. The huge central sculpture seemed to have moved nearer, the scattered bowls and trinkets grown larger, and row upon row of paintings glowered more fiercely.

'May I offer you a drink?'

'A glass of water would be fine.' The room was unnerving her, something about it chimed wrongly, and Nancy felt hot and uncomfortable. Water might help.

'I can do better than that,' Angelica said. 'A cordial—the recipe is an old Moretto secret—but I promise you will like it.'

'Thank you. I'm sure I will.' Nancy's voice betrayed her nervousness.

Her hostess walked over to a side chest and poured two glasses of a claret-coloured liquid, handing one to her guest and sipping from her own glass before she sat down opposite.

Nancy took the chance to glance swiftly around. Something was missing. Even amid the overwhelming treasure, she could feel an absence. She looked again, trying to pierce through the gloom. In the far corner, the statuette of Saint Susanna was no longer there. She felt Angelica staring at her and looked quickly away, concentrating on the glass in her hand, but she was certain even from that brief glimpse that the statue had gone.

Something else was missing too. Noise. Not that it had been noisy on her first visit, but there had been a gentle buzz below stairs, the humdrum sounds of a small staff at work. Now there was silence. Nancy took a sip of her drink. It was sweet but palatable, and she drank a little more before she spoke.

'Have your servants deserted you?' she asked lightly.

'They must have a holiday, too, Mrs Tremayne. And really I am quite able to look after myself for a short while.'

Nancy nodded, seeming to agree, but that Angelica had allowed her entire staff to leave at the same time seemed curious.

'So,' the woman continued, 'why are you here? I confess I did not expect to have visitors tonight. The last time you came it was to warn me. Have you brought another warning with you?'

'No. I'm not sure. Perhaps.' Nancy hated that she sounded so uncertain, but she was struggling to know where to begin. 'I wanted to speak to you. Really to set my mind at rest. I hope you don't mind my calling unannounced.'

'Not at all. It is most diverting.'

It seemed an odd adjective to use, but Nancy pressed on.

'You see, Signorina Moretto, something very odd has been going on and I think you might have the answer. I hope you'll be able to help me... I think I may be able to help you, too.' At the moment Nancy couldn't quite see how, but she was extemporising wildly.

'I doubt that.' Angelica relaxed back into her chair. 'But you seem an altogether inquisitive young woman. I will answer your questions, whatever they are, though you may come to wish you'd not asked so many.' She leaned forward and put her glass down on the onyx table top. 'What does it matter, though? Tonight, one sinner more or less is insignificant.'

Nancy had no idea what the woman was talking about. She suspected that living so isolated, after the close communion of the convent, had begun to affect Angelica's mind.

'Go ahead,' her hostess urged. 'Ask away.'

She took a deep breath and launched into her tale. 'The statuette of Santa Susanna—I saw it. Today.'

'Really?' There was the slightest lift of an eyebrow.

'At the convent of Madonna del Carmine. The convent where you lived for years, where you took your final vows.'

She saw Angelica flinch, but carried on. 'The nuns said that once there were two identical statues, but one had been stolen this year. I saw that one when I visited here.'

'So?' There was a marked arrogance in the woman's voice. 'It's not here now.'

'No, it isn't. Santa Susanna belongs elsewhere—at Madonna del Carmine. And right now she is on her way there.'

'What good news. The convent will be delighted.' Nancy took another drink, then an even deeper breath. 'But why ever did you take it?' She couldn't bring herself to accuse Angelica directly of stealing. Some part of her kept hoping there might have been an arrangement whereby the nun had taken the statue for cleaning as she'd claimed, and perhaps only the Reverend Mother knew of it.

When she looked up, though, it was to see Angelica's face transformed into a rigid mask.

'You accuse *me* of stealing?'

Nancy shivered, feeling the ice pierce her warm skin. 'But the statuette was here. I saw it,' she stuttered. 'Who else could have taken it?'

'Think, Mrs Tremayne. Am I the only person who has lived here?'

Nancy was bewildered. A servant could not have been responsible. They would not have had the opportunity to steal.

'There has only been you and your mother?'

'Precisely.'

Nancy felt the breath punched out of her. Her mouth dropped open, her lips making the shape of an 'O'. 'You are saying… you are saying that Marta stole the statuette?'

Chapter Thirty-Three

'I'm not suggesting she put the statue in her handbag and walked out of the convent with it,' Angelica said drily. 'But it was certainly stolen on her orders.'

'That can't be.' Nancy's voice hardly sounded her own. This was something she could not believe. Would not believe. Her image of Marta would not allow it.

'Why not? Is it that you think my mother is an innocent? A saint herself? You have much to learn.' Angelica sat forward in her chair, fixing Nancy with a fierce glare. 'My mother was a sacrilegious woman, a monster who ordered the theft of some of the most beautiful icons in this region and sold them at a fraction of their value—to unbelievers—for her own personal gain.'

Nancy shook her head violently. 'She can't have done.' Her mind refused to accept what Marta's daughter was saying.

Angelica's top lip formed a sneer. 'You are stupid as well as too curious—but I cannot blame you entirely.' She gave a small shrug. 'Marta Moretto was known as a devout woman, a woman who took mass regularly, who was generous in her contributions to the Church. I, too, found it impossible to believe—until I saw the evidence with my own eyes.'

'How?' Nancy swallowed hard. She didn't want to know, but she had to.

'My mother visited Madonna del Carmine several times. I

did not see her on her last visit, but a few days afterwards, the chapel was violated and the statue stolen.'

'But that means nothing.' Hope flooded Nancy's heart. Angelica had no proof of her mother's wrongdoing after all. The woman was grasping at straws and perhaps had an ulterior motive in wanting to find Marta guilty.

'It means nothing, does it? Nothing to find the missing statue here in this palazzo, hidden deep in a cupboard in my mother's bedroom.' Angelica spat out the words, as though they bit her tongue to utter them.

'You must have gone looking.' Nancy was determined to defend the dead woman as long as she could. 'Why would you poke around in your mother's room?' All pretence of politeness had gone. They were two warriors crossing verbal swords.

Angelica's smile was almost lazy. 'Father Conti. Enrico Conti? You may have met him when you visited the convent. He talked to me of other thefts from other chapels. Thefts that went back several years. And I remembered the names of those chapels. Shall I tell you why, Mrs Tremayne?' Then without waiting for an answer, she said exultantly, 'Because they were all places my mother had visited, and I had her letters to prove it. She would actually write to me of how she visited this or that chapel and how wonderful each was. What amazing artifacts they housed—a golden candlestick, a filigree censer, and so on. There was a pattern emerging. Marta Moretto would visit and several days later there would be a theft—the candlesticks, the censer, would disappear.'

In an instant Nancy saw the answer to the question with which she'd come. 'That's why you left the convent so suddenly.'

'Ah, you are not so stupid. I left because I was convinced I had a mother who was the blackest of sinners. One who must be brought to justice. And who better to do it than a righteous nun?'

And a fanatic, Nancy said quietly to herself. Aloud she asked, 'Why would Marta have arranged such thefts? Moretto is a prestigious firm and your mother was greatly respected as a business woman.'

Angelica gave a delicate yawn. The conversation was evidently beginning to bore her. 'Money, of course. Isn't that always the case? However prestigious, the business was not doing well. My dear brother took it on himself to obtain a loan that Moretto could not repay. Marta could have sold the business, of course, but that would have meant losing face. She preferred to commit a mortal sin.'

Nancy felt her body slump, as though she had been winded by a physical blow. She wanted to shout, to protest that this could not be, but everything Angelica was saying possessed a horrible ring of truth. Only the details were left to discover.

'If your mother *was* a sinner, she was not alone. Do you know who else was involved?'

'The thief naturally.'

'Who was?'

'A man called Salvatore. I made my mother tell me. He is a small-time criminal who pretends respectability by working as the captain of Dino Di Maio's yacht.'

'I know him. And I know him for a criminal. But he is involved in forgery, surely not theft.'

'That, too? But you must be naive to think that such a man stops at only one crime.'

'And Di Maio himself?'

Angelica spread her hands. 'I have no idea. No doubt he is as crooked as my mother.'

If what this woman asserted were true—Nancy was still

grappling to absorb this new and dreadful information—it threw a wholly different light on her discoveries. There were two separate crimes, it seemed, with Salvatore the link between them. No wonder she had been so confused by pieces of a jigsaw that never seemed to fit. Salvatore working for Dino, delivering forged paintings. Salvatore working for Marta—she could hardly bear to say it even in her mind—stealing religious icons.

It was too enormous, too terrible to believe. 'When I met Marta,' she said in a last-ditch effort to defend the woman to whom she'd felt so close, 'she seemed to be hiding nothing. She was looking forward to the future, to doing great things, she said, for Venice and for the Moretto family.'

'Yes, she had plans,' Angelica said indifferently. '*Espiazione*. Atonement, I think is the word in English. But it was too late.'

'She left her entire estate to the convent,' Nancy protested, taking a large gulp of her drink. Even if the will hadn't stood, Marta's desire to endow the convent was an act of altruism.

'Too little, too late.' Angelica was implacable.

'Too late for what? I don't understand.' Nancy's head had begun to feel too heavy for her shoulders and her mind was blurred.

'My mother lived a wicked life and sins must be punished. There will be time enough in Purgatory for her to earn redemption. Purgatory is a place of suffering, Mrs Tremayne,' she explained, almost kindly. 'It is inhabited by the souls of sinners who must expiate their sins before they can achieve the purification necessary to enter the joy of heaven.'

This woman was her mother's arbiter and final judge. She was even dressed as a judge, her black robe flowing to the floor, and lacking only a white wig. Nancy brought herself up sharply. Why was she allowing her mind to wander into whimsy? And then came sudden enlightenment, a burst of horror.

'You killed her!'

'I liberated her soul.'

'You tipped her over the balcony.' Nancy's tongue seemed glued to her throat and she could hardly get the words out.

'It was not too difficult. I am a strong woman and my visit to her box was unexpected. But very welcome. I had turned down the offer of a seat to *Madama Butterfly*, but then, there I was, joining my mother for the last act. She was most happy to see me, happy to drink a glass with me.'

'You drugged her?' Nancy asked dully.

'There were tablets... ground down and mixed into strong cognac, pleasant enough. Marta always had a taste for cognac. By the time the final curtain call arrived, she needed support. Holding on to the balcony, holding on to me.'

Nancy slumped sideways in her seat. She felt dizzy and sick at heart. 'It's not Marta who is the monster,' she said in a voice barely above a whisper, 'it's you. To kill your own mother.'

'She ceased to be my mother when she took up arms against God.' In the dim light of the oil lamps, Nancy saw in the woman's eyes the heart of stone she carried. A fanatic's heart.

'And your brother? Did he take up arms, too?' She knew the answer already.

'Luca was weak. From childhood, he was weak, always doing exactly what Mamma told him. But he needed little persuasion—it suited him to thieve. Who knows, it may have been Luca who persuaded her into evil in the first place. He was the one who negotiated a loan so badly it put the business at risk. The one who had a vampire wife. A grasping woman. Money, money, money, was all she ever wanted. And all Luca craved. My mother at least repented in the end—I will do her that justice.'

Angelica rose majestically from her chair. 'She confessed it all, you know. She suffered such overwhelming guilt. But Luca was different. He was desperate to continue and they argued about it. I heard them, though they were not aware. He was frantic to carry on. He needed money to keep the creature he'd married by his side.'

'And you killed him, too?' Whether it was the dreadfulness of the revelations, or this ghastly room, or the sweetness of the drink, Nancy didn't know, but she had sunk into an unnatural calm.

'Of course. He deserved no pity.' Angelica gathered the empty glasses together and returned them to the side chest.

A strange curiosity took hold of Nancy, one she would ordinarily have suppressed. But tonight wasn't ordinary and the world she had entered when she'd walked through the Moretto front door was sickeningly perverse. 'He was a big man. How—?'

'A big man,' Angelica agreed cheerfully, 'but still my brother, and eager to kiss and make up. Why would he suspect a knife when I appeared out of the night and embraced him? But you are pale, Mrs Tremayne. Are you feeling unwell?'

'I feel…' Nancy tried to stand up, but was too unsteady and forced to fall back into her chair.

'You are a little confused, perhaps?'

'That drink,' she said slowly, enunciating every syllable. 'What was in it?'

'Don't worry. Nothing too poisonous. Nuns are accomplished herbalists, you know. It will wear off in a few hours, but I fear that will be a little late.'

'Late for what? What do you mean?' Fear gripped Nancy and she started up from her chair again, clinging to the arm to keep her upright. Angelica was beside her in a flash.

'I'm sorry, my dear. You chose the wrong night to visit. I told you, did I not, that you might regret your questions, and so it is. I cannot allow others to know the scandal that has been visited on my family. The Moretto name must remain pure. Our sins will die with us. With me and with you.'

Chapter Thirty-Four

Through the clouds befuddling her mind Nancy woke to her danger. She started towards the stairs, zigzagging a path to the salon doorway, but Angelica caught her easily.

'You are unsteady, my dear. Allow me to help you.' She took hold of Nancy's wrists.

The woman's grip was steel and, struggle as she might, Nancy could not free herself. Locked together, they stumbled to the door and for a moment, it seemed Angelica would release her hold. But it was not sufficient for Nancy to wriggle free, and in a second her captor had pulled a length of cord from the folds of her gown.

'I am afraid this will be necessary. An enterprising young woman like yourself will be looking to escape and I need you to stay with me.' She pulled Nancy's arms forward and wrapped the cord around her wrists, pulling it so tight that the girl gave a sharp intake of breath as the rope bit.

'Now you must move,' her gaoler commanded, pushing her towards the door. 'The drug is not so strong you cannot walk.'

'You are quite mad.' Nancy found her voice at last, though she slurred her words. 'Untie me or you will face trouble. I have someone waiting for me in the street.'

'I don't think so, Nancy. I am permitted to use your first name? In the circumstances, I feel I may. There is no one outside and we will not be leaving by the front door. Now, move!' She gave Nancy a sudden thrust that almost sent her to the ground. Somehow she managed to stay upright and walk out onto the landing.

'Down the stairs.' The voice behind her was inexorable.

'My husband…' Nancy started to say and then lost herself in a tangle of words that would not come.

'Quickly. You have interfered enough and you threaten my plans. I cannot allow that.'

Nancy was drowning in a jumble of disjointed thoughts— Leo, Archie, the palazzo, what plans and why had she been drugged?—but her poor bruised mind could find no focus as she half walked, half tumbled down the stairs to the ground floor.

'Keep going.'

There was another ungentle shove to her back, forcing her down a further flight of stairs and into an echoing space, empty except for an ancient ladder and several battered buckets. The rancid smell of stale water filled Nancy's nostrils. This was the basement Marta had spoken of, the one that flooded every year. But why had she been brought here? What was to happen to her?

Angelica was still behind her, still pushing her forward, now towards the double doors at one end of the cavern. Where would they lead? And then Nancy knew. The canal. Water. Drowning. She tensed her body, trying with all her strength to pull back.

'What is the matter, Nancy?' her gaoler taunted. 'Do you not like water? I promise it will be a very short ride.' So not drowning, but a boat. Imprisonment on a boat.

Angelica slid the double doors back. 'So easy.' She pulled her lips into what passed for a smile. 'I had the *portinaio* oil the doors before he left.'

A small speedboat bobbed at anchor, tied to a rotting wooden stake, and she gestured to it. 'The boat belonged to Luca. Years ago now. He thought he was so daring—a man about town—isn't that the phrase?' She gave a sigh. 'He was always stupid, but the boat will prove useful. Sufficient for my purpose.'

And what is that? Nancy's confused mind tried to fathom, but she was being ordered to step on to the boat and, when she hesitated, was pushed hard from behind so that she stumbled onto the deck, tripped on a coil of rope, and landed on her knees beneath the wheel.

'It really is best that you do as I ask,' her tormentor said. 'You will find it far more comfortable. Now, we must go.'

She kneed Nancy's prone figure aside and started the engine. A soft purr answered and the small craft began slowly to make its way along the canal that ran behind the *calle dei Morti*. With a struggle, Nancy forced herself upright and glanced frantically around, hoping to find help. It was hopeless. One or two rowing boats were moored at the rear of neighbouring houses, but there was no sign of their owners. Except for the quiet puttering of the boat driven at its lowest speed, the world was silent. And dark. Shadows floated fitfully across a fragment of moon and light from the street lamps did not reach the canal.

The waterway was widening slightly, Nancy noticed vaguely. But then her senses were slammed into full alert. The boat's throttle was suddenly opened and they shot forward. Into the lagoon. Nancy gazed in horror at the woman at the helm, a mad deity dropped from the clouds, with hair a wild tangle and her robe a billowing sail.

It seemed Angelica had forgotten her prisoner for the moment, and when she spoke, it was softly to herself. 'San Basilio is straight ahead. A pity that we will reach it so soon—

the water is wonderful tonight.'

Unnoticed, Nancy edged to the rear of the boat and managed awkwardly to clamber onto the flat rim that ran around its perimeter, clinging to the flimsy structure that supported the canvas sunroof. They were running parallel to the Zattere now and in a crazy moment she thought she might jump to freedom. Someone might be walking there in the darkness. Someone might see her plight.

But what was she thinking? She could not swim and her hands were tied tightly together. She would have no chance even of threshing the water to keep herself afloat until rescue came. And all the time the boat was gathering speed. The lights of San Basilio came into view, flashing gold across the waters of the lagoon.

For a moment, Angelica seemed to be steering towards the harbour and Nancy's spirits rose. Perhaps she was to be left there while this crazed woman carried out whatever plan she'd devised. But when they were some two hundred yards away, the boat swung back to run parallel to the dock. Two hundred yards from safety, but it might as well have been two hundred miles.

There was a figure running. Nancy could just make him out, a man waving his arms and shouting. Was he shouting at her? But what was he saying? The night air had helped to clear the fuzziness, but her head still felt the size of a pumpkin and she strained to make out the words. She half closed her eyes, peering into the gloom, trying to bring the figure into focus. It couldn't be! She staggered to her feet, desperately trying to see better. It was! Archie. Archie powering himself along the dock. The most tremendous feeling of relief flooded her body and she could feel her paralysed cheeks try to stretch into a smile.

But why was she smiling? Archie was yards away and she

was trapped on this speeding boat. She couldn't reach him and he couldn't reach her. Then the boat swung suddenly inland again at the same time as Angelica opened the throttle to its furthest reach. The boat's engine roared, an old vessel struggling to meet unfamiliar demands. And finally Nancy saw what the woman intended.

Ahead of them was a yacht, the only one to be lit, and moored separately from the other boats. She recognised its shape—the *Andiamo*—and it was about to sail. Leo had said that Dino was leaving tonight. The pictures, she remembered hazily, the forgeries. He was off to sell his contraband. On her right, the dock was nearer than ever and she could see Archie's figure clearly now. He was frantically trying to keep up, but falling further and further behind.

'Jump!' His cry came to her on the breeze.

She looked ahead, over Angelica's bent figure. The *Andiamo* was no longer at a distance but directly in their path. Surely, the woman would turn the wheel at the last moment, now she had thoroughly scared the yacht's occupants. But the speedboat kept going and the stretch of sea between them diminished by the second. They were both to die, she realised—and they would take Dino and Salvatore with them.

'Jump!' Archie's voice was a scream, but came to her now from far off.

Dying was certain, Nancy thought calmly, either by water or by fire, and drowning seemed preferable. She kicked off her shoes and clambered awkwardly back onto the rim of the boat, balancing uncertainly as she pulled herself upright. Then with a small prayer, her hands still bound tightly in front of her, she jumped vertically into the water.

In an instant the roar of the engine ceased. She was in a world of silence as the cold waters closed over her. Down, down, down, she plummeted, the breath knocked from her body by the force of her fall. Her eyes were closed, her limbs weightless and she floated dreamlike, without pain, without feeling.

But now there were hands on her waist, gripping, pulling, tugging. And she was brought, threshing and choking, to the surface. Archie had her in his arms, was turning her on her back, one hand beneath her chin to keep her mouth from the water. For a moment she heard the engine's roar once more, but then quite suddenly it stopped. Had she drowned again? No, her head was still above water and Archie was slowly and powerfully sculling his way back to the side of the jetty. There was a second of eerie quiet, then an enormous explosion somewhere beyond them. The sky above was lit as though it were day. Running feet. A gabble of voices.

They were against the side of the dock and men were climbing down the iron ladder and scooping her from the water as though she were no more than a feather. They lay her gently on the concrete and someone bent down to her prone body, his ear to her mouth. Nancy felt her head turned to one side and a gush of water drain from her mouth and nose. A knife was cutting through her bonds and someone was chafing her wrists to get the blood flowing.

Archie's face swam into vision. He was crouched low beside her, dripping pools of water. One of the men who had pulled them from the lagoon covered his shoulders with a blanket, another swaddled her in the same fashion. There were lights circling, blue lights, and shouting, somewhere to her right.

She was beyond exhausted. 'What's happening?' she whispered.

Archie crouched lower, speaking quietly into her ear. 'Don't worry. It's the police. They're reeling in Dino and Salvatore from their night swim.'

'They're alive?'

'Very much so. They had the presence of mind to jump, too.'

'But the *Andiamo*?'

'Shame about that. A beautiful yacht.'

'And Angelica Moretto?'

Archie shook his head.

Chapter Thirty-Five

'Why are the police here? Why are *you* here?' Nancy tried to sit up, but crumpled almost immediately.

'Take it easy.' Archie stayed crouched beside her. 'You've had a rough time.'

That was putting it mildly, she thought, but bewilderment meant she couldn't rest. 'I have to know. I don't understand—' she began.

'Then I'll tell you. I followed you to *calle dei Morti*.'

'You did what?' she spluttered, trying again to sit up, and this time succeeding.

'Are you about to tell me you wished I hadn't?' Archie sounded belligerent.

She shook her head, unable to answer. Instead, the tears began to fall. Hurriedly, she brushed them aside. She could not appear weak, not in front of Archie.

'Here.' He stood up and dug around in his pocket, then offered her a sodden handkerchief. 'Any use to you?'

That forced a limp smile from her. 'But what made you do it? The last I saw, you were on your way upstairs.'

Archie's smile was wry. 'I must have had a bad feeling about tonight. I thought I'd follow quietly, wait outside the Moretto place until you came out again, then leave you to make your way home. You'd never have known I was there.'

'So you saw me go in?'

'Yeah. And that was pretty odd. She opened the door to you. Angelica. No servants.'

'She'd given them a holiday, she said.'

'Or deliberately dismissed them?'

Nancy nodded slowly. 'She was going to make an end of herself tonight—I think that's what she'd planned—and then I blundered in there with my stupid questions. But if you were waiting outside the palazzo, how did you end up here?'

'You were gone far too long. I knew something was wrong and walked around to the rear of the houses. You can't walk along the canal but you can pretty much see its entire length from the back of the first house. There was a speedboat tied up at what I reckoned was the Moretto place and it looked as though it had been freshened up. Not a barnacle in sight. So what would Angelica Moretto want with a speedboat? While I stood watching, the doors opened and somebody was pushed out and onto the boat. I didn't wait any longer.'

'But how did you know she was heading for San Basilio?' Nancy's mind felt besieged. She was struggling to understand an evening that had become incomprehensible.

'I didn't. How could I? I had a crazy idea of finding a water taxi to follow wherever she went. But when she emerged from the canal, I could see she was heading for the harbour and keeping close to the shore. That's when I started trying to win the marathon. It was clear you were a prisoner and the woman was up to no good, but what she intended I hadn't a clue.'

'She was after Salvatore, I think. In her eyes, he had committed a terrible sin. He was the last guilty person she had to rid the world of. Her plan was to kill him and then kill herself.'

Archie gave a soft whistle. 'Two birds with one stone — or three birds. We mustn't forget Dino.'

'Angelica forgot him, but she had no compunction in killing him, too.'

'And you?'

'I'd had all my questions answered. I knew too much. And the Moretto name had to remain unsullied by scandal.' Nancy paused, then said with a break in her voice, 'If Angelica had known me at all, she would have realised I was the last person in Venice to spread vile stories about her mother.'

'I presume it was Angelica who was behind Marta's death?' It was a tentative question, as though he couldn't quite believe his own words.

Nancy wrapped her arms around her knees and curled in on herself. 'It's the most dreadful thing, Archie. She killed Luca, too.'

'Good Lord!' That had shocked him, though not for long. 'Was there a reason, or did she simply hate her family?' Archie was back to his flippant self.

Nancy couldn't tell him, couldn't bear to say the words out loud, but the look on his face demanded an explanation. And she knew he deserved one.

'Marta had organised thefts from churches, from convents,' she said in a tremulous voice. 'Your friend, Enrico, spoke of it. And Salvatore did the thieving for her.'

Archie's eyebrows twitched. 'Really? What an enterprising fellow he is. Forgeries one day, thieving the next, and a little luxury yachting in between.'

'The Moretto business was in trouble. Trade was slow, but then Luca took out a huge loan the firm couldn't repay.'

'Well, it will certainly be repaid by now — and with interest. The stuff that was stolen, even melted down, must have fetched a great deal of money.'

Nancy felt her throat constrict. 'She was sorry. Marta. She was a sad woman. I could see it in her face, hear it in her voice. And felt so guilty, I believe, that she had done such a dreadful thing. She called a halt to the thefts—she wanted to atone—but Luca disagreed.'

Archie nodded. 'Francesca,' he said.

'I think so. Not that it did him the slightest good. Even before he was killed, he'd lost his wife. He'd lost everything. Marta had already left her estate to the convent and he knew it would take months, years, of legal haggling to recoup the money. I'm sure Mother Superior knew of the thefts. Angelica must have told her before she left the convent. That's why the woman was so tight-lipped. But I know that if Marta had lived, she would have given everything she earned, everything she possessed, to the Church—it would be reparation, to make good the evil she'd done—but Angelica never gave her the chance.'

'Then ended up even more evil herself.'

'It's a truly dreadful story.' Nancy rocked herself back and forth, trying to find comfort in the rhythm. She could see pools of light in the distance, the flashing beams of police launches, and realised Archie had never explained their presence.

'Why are the police here? How did they know there would be trouble?'

'They're here because I phoned the Guardia earlier this evening. They're the ones who deal with fakes. When Leo mentioned that Di Maio was sailing tonight, I reckoned the journey was to offload his ill-gotten cargo. It was a great opportunity for the police to nab him, catch him in the act, as it were.'

She felt her forehead tighten at the thought that even now the police might be knocking at the palazzo door.

'Don't worry,' Archie said cheerfully. 'I gave them a

false name.'

'And the police believed you—without evidence?' She was astonished.

'They weren't keen on intervening, it's true. Dino is still an important man in these parts and I could easily have been a crank. But I told them there was a crate aboard the *Andiamo* that might prove interesting to them, but if they weren't bothered I was sure the art team of the Carabinieri—they deal with national heritage, that sort of thing—would be happy to investigate. That was spur enough. There's a nice little rivalry going on between them. The Guardia is exiled to offices in Mestre while the Carabinieri team is based at San Marco. The ducal palace, no less.'

'And that's enough to make them rivals?'

'Completely. Anyway, they obviously had a slack night and sent a couple of launches. The fireworks display came as a bonus.'

Nancy turned to face him. 'It's wonderful that Dino will be brought to justice. And Salvatore, too.'

'The police being here isn't so wonderful, though.'

'Why not? I can tell them everything I discovered.'

'First off, they'll want you to go to hospital to be checked. That was quite a jump to make at speed. You can break bones like that.'

'I know. That's why I jumped vertically.'

'Clever girl. How did you know to do it?'

'I've no idea. Some book I read,' she said vaguely.

'Okay, but even if they don't insist on you visiting the hospital, they'll expect you at their offices tomorrow to make a statement. How is that going to play with Leo?'

She bowed her head. 'He'll get to know anyway,' she said brokenly.

'Not necessarily. We could just about make it back to the

palazzo before him, if you think you can walk.'

'But the police—they won't allow us to leave.'

'If we go now, who's to stop us? They don't know our names, nor do the blokes who dragged us out of the water. At the moment, it's bedlam over there.' He pointed to a huddle of people and, amid the flashing lights, Nancy could see the men who had helped them. 'But if we hang around too long, we'll be the centre of attention.'

'The police will need us to help them make their case.' Her law-abiding soul balked at not seeing this through.

'They'll find enough evidence for themselves. The lagoon is afloat with bits of paintings, quite sufficient to nail the pair. And the police have ways of getting a confession. You can bet that Salvatore will squeal if he's promised a lighter sentence.'

'And Renzo?'

'Still on about him? He'll be in the Caribbean by the time the case gets to court. We should move, if you're willing to give it a go.'

Archie was right, she thought reluctantly. If their identities were unknown, if they could arrive home before Leo rolled in from his dinner with Signor Trevi, he need never know.

And there was Marta to consider, too. Always Marta. Angelica's death would almost certainly be pronounced a terrible accident. The poor woman had been under severe strain with her mother and brother dead, it would be said, had taken her brother's boat out for an evening ride and then lost control. And it would be for the best. There would be no mention of missing statues, no mention of Marta's crimes. She would continue to lie in her grave, her reputation unsullied, a pious lady and a revered patron of Venice.

Nancy tried to get to her feet, swaying dangerously, and Archie put his hand under her elbow to steady her. 'Are you sure you can walk?'

She nodded, but fatigue was getting the better of her.

'We must be quick. Let me help.'

He slid the blankets from both their shoulders and, taking her weight on his arm, hurried her towards the warehouses she'd noticed the fateful day they'd gone to Burano. Against a moon now fully emerged from its mantle of cloud, the buildings cast a dense black shadow. Passing from pool of darkness to pool of darkness, Archie guided her out of the dock area.

'The nearest stop is San Basilio,' he said. 'We'll make for that. You won't want to walk too far.' Nancy was grateful. She was without shoes and her legs were wobbling in a worrying fashion.

The vaporetto landing stage was better lit than the port area and for the first time she had a clear sight of Archie. Dismayed at what she saw, she looked down at herself, barefoot and ragged. The blankets had soaked up much of the water, but their clothes were stained and creased and clung to them awkwardly. She could feel her hair plastered to the sides of her head.

'Do you think the ferry will take us in this state?'

'Why not?'

'But we look so disreputable.'

'No worse than a couple of Saturday night revellers. Come on, the boat's here.'

The vaporetto's lights were a welcome sight and when Archie offered his arm to help her climb aboard, she reached out for his hand instead.

'Thank you for saving my life,' she said simply.

'Think of it as fair exchange.' He shepherded them forward into the closed cabin.

He was being generous. Dragging an unconscious man to the side of the lagoon with a boat hook hardly compared to

Archie's dive into deep waters to save a drowning woman. But she was too thankful to argue. And there was something deeper, too. Archie had been angry with her, resentful of her appearance in his life, but it hadn't stopped him sharing her troubles. Sharing her danger. She felt a closeness to him, a sense of amity, of belonging, though she knew it was a feeling she would be wise to bury.

They were fortunate the mist had gradually dissolved and the night become warm. By the time the boat reached San Zaccaria, they were both almost dry.

'How are you feeling now?' Archie asked, as they disembarked.

'Better. Able to walk in a straight line at least.' She was glad, though, that the walk to the palazzo was a short one.

The streets they passed through were narrow and mostly unlit, but it was a darkness broken by patches of light flooding from the several bars still open. People had spilled out onto the pavement, taking advantage of the improved weather. Glasses clinked, chatter floated on the air. All so normal, Nancy thought. As they made their way across the *campo,* strains of music reached them from the open door of the San Zaccaria church—musicians, a quartet perhaps, playing baroque music. She felt the notes flowing through her and, with them, a degree of calm.

'We should make it to the palazzo in time,' Archie said, as they rounded the last corner.

'I hope so.' She heard the trouble in her voice.

Archie must have heard it, too. 'You should have told Leo, you know,' he said, turning to her. 'Told him everything.'

'I couldn't. He expressly told me not to get involved.'

'But still… you were involved. And if you'd told him how you felt, he would have come good eventually.'

'I couldn't. I wasn't sure…' She faltered.

'Sure about what?'

They came to a halt and she breathed deeply. She was finding the walk difficult, even at a slower pace. 'I wasn't sure if Leo had any part in it,' she said awkwardly.

Archie shook his head. 'You said something like that before, but Leo! You have to be kidding.'

'He was odd about Marta,' Nancy protested. 'She mentioned how well she knew Leo, yet he said he'd had little to do with her. And he was quite cold about her death even though he went to her funeral.'

'He could have picked up gossip. He might have suspected something bad was going on and wanted to distance himself.'

'But there was his attitude to Dino as well. He refused to accept what I told him about the crate. He said Dino was his friend and I needed to forget it, then he went off with him to Rome and when they got back Leo didn't come home but went to the *casinò* and wouldn't really explain why…' It all came tumbling out, but then she paused. 'He'll be shocked when he hears about Dino, won't he? It's odd he made such a friend of the man—Leo is clever but he can't have had a clue about Dino's true character.'

'He's clever when dealing with pictures, not always so much with people.'

Nancy looked at him sharply. 'You mean me?'

'No, I don't mean you. But Leo is as straight as a die. How could you think badly of him?'

'I didn't want to, but I couldn't understand why he acted the way he did. It's different for you. You've known him for years.'

Archie pulled a face and she rushed to say, 'I know what you feel about my marriage, Archie. I can imagine what you're thinking.' Her voice shook a little.

'You've no idea what I'm thinking.' He took her hand in a firm clasp. 'But we'll keep this little adventure quiet?'

'A secret between us?' She felt warmth, relief, guilt.

'A secret,' Archie said, and they walked on together.

If you've enjoyed this novel, do please leave a review — a few lines is all it takes and is so helpful to authors and other readers.

And make sure you follow Nancy to the Caribbean where she finds more mischief than she bargains for, including her relationship with Archie.

Other Books by Merryn Allingham

A Tale of Two Sisters (2019)

House of Lies (2018)
House of Glass (2018)

The Buttonmaker's Daughter (2017)
The Secret of Summerhayes (2017)

The Girl from Cobb Street (2015)
The Nurse's War (2015)
Daisy's Long Road Home (2015)

Printed in Great Britain
by Amazon